La   FA
Lamplighter, L. Jagi

Prospero in hell

PROSPERO IN HELL

TOR BOOKS BY
L. JAGI LAMPLIGHTER

Prospero Lost
Prospero in Hell
Prospero Regained (forthcoming)

PROSPERO
IN HELL

L. Jagi Lamplighter

A TOM DOHERTY ASSOCIATES BOOK
NEW YORK

PROSPERO IN HELL

Copyright © 2010 by L. Jagi Lamplighter

Edited by James Frenkel

A Tor Book
Published by Tom Doherty Associates, LLC
175 Fifth Avenue
New York, NY 10010

www.tor-forge.com

Tor® is a registered trademark of Tom Doherty Associates, LLC.

ISBN 978-0-7653-1930-2

First Edition: August 2010

Printed in the United States of America

0 9 8 7 6 5 4 3 2 1

To Orville, Roland Wilbur,
Ping-Ping Eve, and the Elf King,
the best children in the universe

THE FAMILY PROSPERO

Eldest to youngest

THE DREAD MAGICIAN PROSPERO carries the *Staff of Eternity*
MIRANDA carries the *Staff of Winds*
MEPHISTOPHELES carries the *Staff of Summoning*
THEOPHRASTUS carries the *Staff of Devastation*
ERASMUS carries the *Staff of Decay*
CORNELIUS carries the *Staff of Persuasion*
TITUS carries the *Staff of Silence*
LOGISTILLA carries the *Staff of Transmogrification*
GREGOR carries the *Staff of Darkness*
ULYSSES carries the *Staff of Transportation*

CONTENTS

PROSPERO IN HELL

CHAPTER ONE

The Bird of Ice and Snow

The three of us hurtled through the night on the back of the winged horse. Miles of ice and pine flew by underfoot, glimmering in the moonlight. The Arctic night was bitterly cold, but even the biting chill could not dim the joy of flight, the crispness of the air, or the power of Pegasus's wing beats. How easy it would be to forget earthly life and dwell only in the sky!

Behind me, Mab shouted something, but his words were whipped away by the wind. Leaning over, I freed my flute from where I had secured it to the saddle and held it up for Mab to see. He nodded grumpily and inserted a pair of orange hunting earplugs with one hand, his other hand holding onto his fedora. Raising the four-foot length of polished pinewood to my lips, I played a quick trill.

The freezing northern winds grew gentler. Their constant roar muted; I could hear the steady flap of our steed's wings and the singing of my brother Mephistopheles, who sat before me. Mephisto had been keeping up a running narrative in song, ever since we left the North Pole. I thanked my Lady that the noise of the winds had previously protected me from his impromptu recital.

I secured my flute again, and Mab pulled out his earplugs. We were on our way home from the North Pole, heading for Mephisto's home in the wilds of North Canada. Our plane had gone down on the way to visit Father Christmas, so we were constrained to travel by one of Mephisto's many supernatural beast friends. Currently, we flew on Pegasus, the horse that once carried the Greek hero Bellerophon up the heights of Mount Olympus. Bellerophon was struck down with lightning for his impudence; I prayed that our journey would not meet a similar fate.

"There's a storm brewing, Ma'am. Snow's coming." Mab spoke with a heavy Bronx accent so that his "there" sounded like "dare." How an incarnated

Aerie One came to have a New York accent, I did not know, but a lot of things about Mab defied explanation. "Might not be good for us"—his voice grew heavy with sarcasm—"considering our mode of travel."

"Hey! You be polite, or Pegasus will hear you!" my crazy brother cried, interrupting his aria. "It's not his fault you crashed your stupid plane. Is it, Peggie?" He leaned over and stroked the winged horse's smooth neck.

"I'll take care of it," I interrupted before they could start sparring with each other. "Earplugs again."

Mab obliged, and I began to play again.

My flute sang with the voice of the cold wind. It was as if speech had been given to cloud, and night, and the chill of winter air. The song lightened my spirits. So glorious and enchanting was the melody that I nearly forgot my purpose and gave myself to the music and the night sky.

The winds I summoned dispersed the gathering clouds, and we flew on, unobstructed. Unhindered, Pegasus sped along, making good time. This cheered me. It was important we get back to civilization. A great deal of work awaited me at Prospero, Inc. Also, I had not yet finished carrying out the orders from my father's last letter, instructing me to warn my brothers and sister that the Three Shadowed Ones were after our staffs. On top of all this, I still had no idea what doom was supposed to befall my family on Twelfth Night. The demon had not been specific.

Whatever it was, only eleven days remained in which to stop it.

I strapped my beloved flute back into its holder. My wrist brushed against a firm bulge within the pocket of my white cashmere cloak. I smiled and reached inside to touch the slender leather volume: the *Book of the Sibyl*.

After five hundred years of searching, it was finally mine!

It saddened me that I had not had an opportunity to thank Astreus Stormwind properly. Just after he had handed the book to me, back at Father Christmas's mansion, an elvish servant had come running to inform us that Mephisto had been found facedown in the snow, as stiff as a board, the butt of some elvish prank. Luckily, a drop of Water of Life had revived him.

Then, while Lady Christmas fed my brother soup in her enormous kitchen with its rows of hanging copper pots, I went in search of Mab, whom I found hanging in a closet next to Father Christmas's many red and green robes, his trench coat caught on a hook so that he hung by his arms.

When I asked him what had happened, he just colored. "You . . . you'd rather not know, Ma'am. Just chalk it up to the folly of agreeing to eat dinner with elves."

By the time we came back to the main hall, the elven High Court had ridden out across the ice, except for Astreus, who had departed through the Uttermost Door, heading back into the Void to carry out whatever terrible task it was that the Elf Queen had bidden him to complete.

Before we were parted, Astreus told me how he found the original scroll in such sad condition that he could not take it away with him. Instead, he had copied it, in its entirety, in his own hand and carried it with him for over three hundred years.

Thinking of this helped drive back the biting cold. I recalled Astreus's laughing, his changing eyes, and, most of all, our marvelous flight the previous night, as we had soared through the midnight sky on the back of a giant black swan that had flown out of an unknown constellation. More than once, my thoughts returned to the taste of his lips—until I remembered our kiss had only been a dream.

What had motivated him to find the book for me? Had he been human, I might have hazarded an opinion. Human men undertake difficult quests on the behalf of maidens for predictable reasons. But, an elf? Who could begin to guess? They were prey to strange elvish impulses no mortal could comprehend.

"It's happening again, Ma'am," Mab said, overly loud. He had reinserted his earplugs. I played another rousing tune. Again, the clouds dispersed.

The moon set, and we rode for a time in darkness. Then, to our left, the fiery fingers of the rising dawn painted the sky with a rosy and golden hue, reminding me strikingly of the ever-dawn of Astreus's home of Hyperborea. Soon, the snow beneath us glowed with matching colors, so that the dark green spruces and firs seemed to sprout from an ocean of burning cherry and gold.

A snowflake blew cold against my face. I caught another on my tongue. Snowflakes!

"Something's not obeying me." I frowned and began to scan the skies.

"Good for them," Mab muttered behind me.

Mephisto cried, "Oh, yeah, Mr. Looks-into-Other-People's-Business-for-a-Living! Before you get all high and mighty about how my sister's flute jerks you around like a puppet, let me point out that *we're* the guys who are going to freeze our tushies off if the weather stops obeying the *Staff of Winds!*" Mephisto glanced over his shoulder at the flute. "Can it even do that?"

"The winds and Aerie Ones who have sworn upon the River Styx cannot fail to obey," I replied. "But we are somewhere above northern Canada.

There are spirits here no Prospero, Inc. agent has ever encountered; creatures we've never needed to bind because they seldom run into, much less trouble, human beings, creatures who had only ever been sighted by native peoples. Anything could be out there."

"Really!" A gleam came into my brother's eye. He stood up in his stirrups and peered into the night. The *Staff of Summoning,* still handcuffed to his right wrist, swung free as he gestured, nearly smacking me across the cheek. He rubbed his thumb and first two fingers together and made a *tta tta tta* noise and then shouted, "Here, beastie, beastie!"

"Shhh!" Mab reached around me and yanked on my brother's royal blue surcoat, which he wore over his parka, trying vainly to pull him back onto the saddle. "Put a lid on it, Harebrain."

"But I want to catch it!" Mephisto held up the six feet of intricately carved figurines, stacked atop one another like totems. The jeweled eyes of the many beasts and mythical creatures glittered in the moonlight. "For my staff!"

"Great," drawled Mab. "And what if it turns out to be one of the Three Shadowed Ones? I will remind you that our plane crashed because it was *torn apart by demons.*"

"Oh. Good point." Mephisto sat down again.

A tense moment followed. We peered into the distance, yet could see nothing but snow clouds before us and, elsewhere, morning sky. The winds remained quiet at my command, but the wall of white ahead loomed closer. I held my flute at the ready. Mephisto waited eagerly. Mab examined the sky, his hand gripping his trusty lead pipe.

A great alabaster bird, larger than a condor, flew out of the snowbank. Cawing angrily, it spread its jagged wings ahead of us. As the wings parted, a flurry of snow swirled toward us. Snowflakes brushed against my face like cool feathers; only as they began to melt against my skin did their intense cold reach me.

"A p-son-en!" Mephisto leapt up and balanced gracefully upon the shoulders of the flying horse. "I've always wanted one of those!" He threw his arms wide, his staff flailing. "Hi, I'm Mephistopheles Prospero. Don't you recognize me?"

"A what?" Mab called.

"P-son-en," Mephisto waved his arms welcomingly. "At least that's what the Abenaki tribe called these guys. Boy, he's far from home! I've only ever heard of them being seen in Algonquin territory, far east of here!"

Behind me, Mab put his face in his hand and shook his head.

"At least life with Mephisto is never dull." I smiled.

"No offense, Ma'am, but I could do with some dull about now," Mab muttered. "Two hours on a coat rack was more than enough excitement for me."

I asked him to explain, but he just shook his head and grunted. "You don't want to know, Ma'am. You don't want to know."

The p-son-en brought its wings together, as if it were clapping and then yanked them apart, screaming in fury. Shards of ice flew forth like flying daggers.

Everything happened at once. I raised my flute to call a wind to blow the icicles away from us, but as the cold wood touched my lips, I realized Mab had taken out his earplugs. If I gave the command now, the flute would compel Mab to obey it. He would be forced to leap from the horse and block the attack with his body. While the flute could control his will, it could not grant his fleshy body the power of flight. He would plummet like a stone.

True, he could depart his flesh in an emergency, but the fall would destroy his body. Without Father, I was not certain I could convince my sister Logistilla to make him another one—and, of us, only Logistilla and her *Staff of Transmogrification* had the necessary power and skill.

Lowering my instrument, I threw my arms up to protect my face, letting the incoming spears of ice bounce harmlessly off the shimmering emerald cloth of my enchanted tea dress. Mab swung his lead pipe and parried three sharpened icicles from the air. Puffing up his cheeks, he blew a gust of wind that knocked aside two more. Mephisto raised his staff but an ice shard struck his shoulder. He screamed in pain and pitched forward, arms windmilling. Before either Mab or I could grab him, he fell over the side of the horse, plummeting toward the pines far below.

Seeing his master plunging through the air, Pegasus neighed furiously. He dove, throwing me and Mab forward. As I sailed past the horse's neck, I grabbed onto the long white mane. Mab fared better, managing to grab onto the saddle.

The winged horse snagged Mephisto's pants with his teeth; the surcoat had blown over his head and was out of reach, which was lucky for Mephisto's neck. The *Staff of Summoning* dangled in its handcuff, safe and sound.

I was not so lucky. As the horse grabbed my brother and jerked upward, I was flung sideways, my feet swinging freely. My body gyrated wildly. Terror seized me as I felt the coarse hairs of the mane slipping between my cold-numbed fingers, which were also trying to hold my flute. My nose bumped hard against the horse's rib cage, and pungent horse sweat wet my forehead and cheek.

Far below, pines stood like decorated toothpicks, looking so small and dainty. Recalling Astreus's offer to drop me from a great height and thus speed my way to Heaven, I shuddered. Even the extra vitality I gained from the regular intake of Water of Life would not enable me to survive a fall of such a distance.

As I hung on for dear life, I closed my eyes and prayed to my Lady. A feeling of warmth and calm enveloped me, driving away both fear and cold. I was still dangling thousands of feet above the Arctic north, but I was no longer frightened.

Pegasus banked, and my legs swung dangerously toward his soft wings. I yanked them up, curling my knees to my chest to avoid damaging our flying steed. As Pegasus climbed upward, he, too, brought his legs toward his chest. There was a report like a gunshot as his hoof struck my shin.

I howled with pain. Horsehair slipped through my fingers. My hands clenched reflexively, to grip the mane tighter. My beloved flute, the *Staff of Winds,* slipped from my grip. Horrified, I watched it twirling end over end as it descended toward the sunrise-stained landscape below.

Mab grabbed my wrist and hauled me onto the horse's back. Then, he leaned over and watched the dwindling flute as it bobbed or dropped depending upon the wind current.

"Not sure what to do, Ma'am. On one hand, I'm delighted to see the last of the accursed instrument that controls the free will of my race. On the other hand, I'd hate to risk it falling into anyone else's hands, especially the hands of the three demons who are currently out there looking for it."

"Any suggestions?"

"I could leave my body, Ma'am, and go after it," he offered reluctantly. "Man, I hate doing that, especially after I just boasted to your brother, Mr. Theophrastus, how I almost never did it."

"No problem!" Mephisto called from where he dangled upside from the horse's mouth. "I'll get it!"

Grabbing the staff that hung from his wrist, he tapped it against his shoe. I began to imagine that a swirl of snow near him was fluttering like a bird. Then, a real swallow fluttered beside him. Mephisto yelled to it, and the swallow dived.

Only the flute was far too big for a swallow to do more than bump. Mephisto tapped his staff again, and I saw the jeweled eyes of the Peregrine falcon figurine glitter. Then, a falcon stooped, talons spread. As it approached the flute, it swerved suddenly to chase the swallow. Yelping, Mephisto tapped his staff twice in rapid succession. Both birds vanished like a dream.

"Great," said Mab. "Harebrain's no use, either. Any other bright ideas?"

"No, no! I got it!" Mephisto shouted back. "I just need something bigger."

He scrutinized his staff. A winged lion of whitest ash wood topped the long slender length. Below it, winged creatures carved from pale woods, such as beech and pine, made up the first two feet. The middle section of mundane creatures was carved from reddish woods, such as apple, cherry, and oak. Dangerous mythical beasts wrought from dark mahogany made up the lower third, and the very bottom was a tentacled monstrosity of ebony.

"Ah-ha!" He tapped the staff against the sole of his shoe.

The swirling wings that sprang so clearly to mind were larger and more powerful. Then, a gryphon screamed, slashing its lion tail. The mythical beast dived, rapidly closing the distance between itself and my precious flute. My heart leapt into my throat. Gryphons had razor-sharp beaks. Would he snap the flute in two when he caught it? If the flute broke, the terms of the servitude of the Aerie Ones who served my family—the eight winds, including Mab, and their many servants including sylphs, zephyrs, and other spirits of the air—would be at an end, freeing them to ravage the earth with tempests, hurricanes, and tornados.

The gryphon reached the flute and snatched it gracefully from the air with its eagle talons. Issuing its victory scream, it turned and began winging its way back up toward us. A second scream, lower in pitch, answered from above us.

The p-son-en burst out of a snowbank, its jagged wings releasing another volley of icy death.

I drew the war fan of Amatsumaru, the Japanese Smith God. Its moon-colored slats shone like a mirror, showing me a striking young woman with emerald eyes and hair so pale as to appear silver, her face framed by a white fur. In the moment it took me to recognize my own reflection, the spears of jagged ice bounced harmlessly against the far side of the fan. Behind me, I heard Mab's grunt of pain as one of the ice shards found its mark.

"Oh yeah! Mess with me?" Mephisto cried joyously, and I heard the tap of his staff against his shoe. "You'll rue the day you didn't join my team. I offer a dental plan and everything!"

The rain of icicles had stopped; I peered from behind my fan in time to get the distinct impression I could see a whirl of wingspan the length of two football fields. Then, a speckled bird that was longer than a house issued its war cry. The p-son-en turned and fled. The roc sped after it, talons splayed.

"Saved by the magnificent roc again!" Mab murmured respectfully. "I think we owe that bird a herd of buffalo or something."

The great bird snatched the smaller one from the air. We began to cheer. The p-son-en dissolved into ice and snow. It seeped through the huge claws. Reforming some feet beyond, it opened its wings toward the roc's unprotected breast. Mephisto tapped his staff, and the roc vanished, but not before we heard its screech of pain.

I patted the horse's sleek white neck. "Pegasus, see that mountaintop over there? Head for that." To Mephisto, I added, "Have the gryphon meet us there."

Pegasus dove toward the peak, Mephisto still dangling from his teeth. The p-son-en pursued, again raining razor-sharp icicles down upon us. Luckily, Pegasus could outrun the speeding icicles, but once or twice, Mab had to knock frozen shards aside with his lead pipe or blow them away from us with his Wind's breath.

As soon as we landed, I leapt from Pegasus's back and ran to my flute, courteously thanking the gryphon. Then, I called to my companions to duck. Raising my flute over my head, I swung it in a circle. Wind rushed into the holes, causing the instrument to whistle. The whistling grew louder and louder, and the air above me began to stir. Gusting eddies blew past my face. As I whirled it around more quickly, the speed of the winds increased. Within moments, I held a full-blown tornado by the twist of its tail.

It was like standing near a helicopter. The roaring winds sucked at everything. My hairpins ripped free. My silvery locks whipped wildly about my head, temporarily blinding me. Snow from the peak beneath us flew upward, filling the air. Mab's fedora flew from his head. He dived after it, snatching it just before it was absorbed into the cyclone. Still clutching it, he crashed, shoulder first, into the hard rock below, grunting painfully.

Flipping my flute forward, I released the twister directly into the path of the p-son-en. The bird of ice and snow opened its wings menacingly, only to have all its little snow daggers sucked up by the tornado. Freed of its restraints, the funnel of wind swept away toward the horizon, carrying our attacker with it.

"Wow! Did you see that p-son-en in action, Miranda?" my brother cried, leaping to his feet and gazing in admiration after the departing cyclone. "I've got to have one!"

MAB and Mephisto were both wounded, as were Pegasus and the roc. Before leaving the mountain peak, I had my brother summon up the magnificent bird, and lined the four of them up before me. I pulled out of my pocket a small pear-shaped crystal vial and swirled the pearly white liquid within. As I pulled out the stopper, a sweet refreshing fragrance spread through the frigid air. A single whiff brought to mind many joyous occasions.

"Water of Life, anyone?" I queried, smiling.

"Me! Oh, me!" Mephisto yelled, throwing his arm up as if he were in school and then wincing with pain as the motion tore his wounded shoulder.

Walking down the line, I used the dropper built into the top to put a single drop on the tongues of Mephisto, Pegasus, and the roc. Mab refused the drop on his tongue, pointing at where the ice shard had torn his arm.

"Better not partake, Ma'am. That stuff goes right to my head."

I let the pearly drop fall onto his wound and put one on Mephisto's shoulder for good measure. Water of Life did not heal instantly, but it strengthened the body and will. After a short rest, all four of them were well enough to depart. Mephisto sent away the gryphon and the roc, and he, Mab, and I climbed onto Pegasus again.

"HI, girls! I'm home!" Mephisto threw open a pair of bright red doors. "Uncover the will-o-wisps and stoke up the salamander. We have guests!"

We had reached Mephisto's place, which turned out to be an impressive mountain mansion located somewhere in the wilds of Canada's Northern Territories. Outside, the air was worse than frigid. As the doors opened, wonderful, welcoming warm air met our faces.

"Yeah, yeah, whatever . . . whoa!" Mab pushed forward and then halted abruptly. "Er . . . sorry. Didn't realize you girls were real. Thought

Harebrain was just pretending to have a life." Mab paused and peered. "Podarge! Is that you?"

"Of course, it's me! Who else might it be?" cawed an unpleasant voice. "Who are you?"

"It's Mab . . . er, I mean Caekias."

"Caekias! Is that you? You look a fright!"

"He doesn't look so frightening to me," came a sweet feminine voice. "He looks like a detective."

"That we can see Caekias at all is frightening," purred a third, huskier voice. Her voice became sharper; "Shut the door, by Bacchus! It's freezing out there!"

I stepped inside. Three women were gathered in the spacious foyer, from which arches led off in various directions. Near the main archway, a tall, powerfully built woman leaned against the railing of a curving staircase. She was dressed in panther skin with a snake for a belt, and carried a fennel stalk, twined with ivy, topped with a long, slender pinecone.

Closer to us, perched on a chandelier, was a creature that was half-woman and half-bird. She had wings for arms and powerful, cruel talons for feet. Her back and haunches were covered with feathers of gray and slate blue, but her ugly face and pendulous bosom were bare.

Below her and to the left, a round pool approximately six feet across had been set into the blue-and-green-tiled floor. A red-haired mermaid floated in the water, leaning against the rim, her pretty chin resting on her fist. Beneath the water, the scales of her multicolored tail glimmered like faceted jewels.

"Phisty!" The mermaid clapped her hands in delight as my brother strode into the large foyer. The harpy nodded grudgingly from the chandelier. The maenad gave him a jaunty two-fingered salute.

"You know these women, Mab?" I asked, entering.

"This is Podarge." Mab waved a hand at the harpy. "She's my . . . well, you'd call her my sister-in-law. She's the mother of Xanthos, and Pyrois, and those guys, the horses who pull the chariot of the sun—the ones your sister Logistilla was so steamed about having to hold."

"Pleased to meet you." As I stepped forward to shake Podarge's hand, an unpleasant odor assailed me. I withdrew across the foyer as soon as courtesy allowed.

"Xanthos and my other son, Balius, pulled Achilles's chariot, too," said the harpy with a flap of her great wings, "but did they get any credit for their hard work? No! It's all swift-footed Achilles this, and swift-footed Achilles that. What? Do they think he was running on his own two feet? Why do you think he was so swift, I ask you?"

"Er . . . right," murmured Mab.

Mephisto sauntered forward. Reaching up, he rubbed the harpy's head, tousling her hair, apparently unaffected by her stench. "Don't be such a grumpy-kin."

I grabbed the handle of my moon-silver fan, afraid she would rend him with her razor-sharp claws for his effrontery. Instead, she arched her neck, pleased.

"After all," he continued, "Homer mentions them, even says how they wept when Partrocles died."

Podarge shuddered with outrage. "And that's supposed to soothe a mother's wounded heart? Mentioned by Homer? Ooh! I'm swooning. Why didn't he call his poem 'Xanthos and Balius,' I ask you? Now, that would have been an intriguing work. Poets. Pah!" She spat, barely missing the mermaid, who whacked the water with her fish-tail to show her displeasure. "What do poets have to say about harpies, hm? 'Hatchet-faced'; 'loathsome'; 'ill-tempered.' Not a word about what wonderful mothers we are. Not a word about our feelings or our needs. No, it's just 'frightened this nosy king' or 'chased off by that pair of winged clowns.'"

"Careful," Mab growled. "Those winged clowns are my . . . well, you'd call 'em nephews." To me, he said, "She's talking about the Boreads: Calais and Zetes. They sailed with the Argonauts. Drove Pod, here, and her sisters away from King Phineus's table. Good boys, Calais and Zetes. They're filling in for Boreas, Caurus, and me as the heads of the Northerlies while we're working for you, Ma'am."

"Speaking of winds, how is Zephyrus?" asked the harpy. "Has he asked about me?"

"Not that I've heard, Madam." Under his breath, Mab muttered, "Never did quite see what Zeph saw in you birds."

The harpy had heard him. "Oh, and he's such a fine catch, himself, the jealous boy-chaser! Besides," she purred, brushing back her hair and preening, "I can be quite beautiful when I'm in my horse form." Then she let out a loud squawk and defecated. Her foul-smelling dung dropped to the floor and splattered across the blue and green tiles.

"Ew! Gross!" Mephisto pinched his nostrils shut. "What did I tell you about using the potty? Outside! Outside with you." He shooed the harpy out the door into the cold morning. "Agave, clean that up, will you?"

"Who me?" cried the maenad.

She struck the butt of her pinecone-topped thyrsos against the floor and glared at Mephisto, outraged. With each moment, she grew more terrible. Her hair spread about her like a mane. Mab and I drew closer together, and my hand found my fan again. The Water of Life that gave my family our immortality brought us more than human strength, but even so, I did not believe I could win a tussle with a maenad.

"Please?" my brother cooed, bringing his hands together. "Pretty please with cream cheese on top?"

"Cream cheese?" Agave cried, but her hair settled down again. She snorted impatiently and turned to the mermaid. "Morveren, be a sweetie and go fetch the yeti, would you? Tell him to bring a mop."

The red-haired mermaid dived down into the pool and, with a flip of her powerful tail, sped off through an underwater tunnel.

"That leaves you and me, Agave!" Mephisto sauntered over to where the maenad leaned against the stairs, and patted her fur-clad bottom. "Ready to shag? How about we sneak upstairs and go at it like greased weasels!"

"Ugh!" Mab winced. "There are ladies present!" He glanced at the towering maenad in her panther skin and muttered under his breath, "One lady, anyway."

"Not so fast, Staff Boy," the maenad replied in a low throaty voice. She tapped him on the nose with the long, slender pinecone atop her thyrsos. The snake wrapped about her waist like a belt raised its head and hissed menacingly. "We maenads are chaste, remember? We're saving ourselves for the Vine God's return."

My brother leaned over to stare into the serpent's eyes. "Hello, Soupy!" He stroked it under its pale scaly chin. "Remember me? Yes, of course you do. Soupy's such a good Snaky."

The serpent unwound from the waist of the maenad and circled about my brother's arm, hissing affectionately.

The maenad gave an exaggerated sigh. "Betrayed by my own guardian snake."

She stepped toward Mephisto who, despite being shorter than her, dipped her over his knee and smooched her.

"Woo hoo!" Mephisto pulled her upright and punched the air. "Come

on, Agie-poo." He hooked his arm through hers—the snake winding about
both of them—and headed off, not up the stairs but through the far left
archway. "Let's check on the others, and see if we can't scare up some dinner." Over his shoulder, he called, "Make yourself at home, Miranda! I'll
call you for supper."

꙳꙳꙳

The Marvelous Mansion of Mephistopheles Prospero

"Let's examine everything, Ma'am; leaving no pile of laundry unturned."
Mab stuck his head through one of the archways leaving the foyer. "I want
to see what else we can find out about your brother."

My hand clutched the slim leather volume, still wrapped in its smooth
green paper, that lay deep within the pocket of my white cashmere cloak.
"You go ahead. I'm going to find a warm place to sit and read my Christmas
present."

"It would be a whole lot more efficient for you to come with me, Ma'am,
being as Mephisto is your brother and all." Mab's voice sounded funny, as
if he had a bad cold. When he turned, I saw that he was pinching his nostrils
against the awful stink of the harpy dung. "You may recognize at a glance
something I won't be able to make head or tail of."

"We have plenty of time," I countered, inching toward the rightmost
arch, where I had glimpsed an armchair.

"I thought you were in an ungodly hurry to rush back. The Three Shadowed Ones could be offing your siblings as we speak," Mab countered.

"I appreciate your concern, but there's nothing we can do to speed things
up," I replied. "I sent an Aerie One to our offices in Vancouver with a message asking to have someone fly another Lear to Yellowknife. The Aerie One
has to fly there, and a pilot has to fly the plane back. This will take hours."

"Yellowknife?"

"As best as I can tell, we're in the Canadian Northern Territories, somewhere between Great Bear Lake and Great Slave Lake. Yellowknife should
be the nearest airport."

"As best as you can tell?" Mab scrunched up his cheek and scratched at
his eternal stubble.

"I've never been here before. I had no idea Mephisto had a house in

Canada," I said. "Heck, I didn't know he had a house at all. Which is probably for the best, because if I had known, I would have just sent him a note
telling him about Father's letter, and we never would have gone looking for
him."

"Good point. If we had not located the Harebrain, we would never
have found your brother, Mr. Theophrastus, or your sister." Mab nodded. He
added dubiously, "This Yellowknife airport. How are we going to get there?"

"We'll have to borrow Pegasus, but since we have hours, we should give
the beast a chance to rest first," I concluded happily. "So, I'm off to read.
Tootle-loo!"

"Whoa, Ma'am. Maybe we don't have to leave right away, but we only
have while your brother is otherwise occupied to investigate his house,"
Mab countered. "Can't whatever you're planning to read wait? You'll have
plenty of time to read on the flight back to Oregon."

The trip home seemed a long way off. For five hundred years, I had
searched for the *Book of the Sibyl*. Theoretically, another few hours should
not make much of a difference, but right now, with the little leather volume
burning a proverbial hole in my pocket, even these few seconds of delay
seemed an eternity.

This little book that Lord Astreus had copied for me in his own hand
held the secrets of the Order of the Sibyl, the only rank of my Lady's servants I had not yet achieved. Conceivably, this slender tome might hold all
the answers I so longed for. It was even possible that, by the time I finished
reading it, I would be a Sibyl!

And then . . . ah, then!

The rank of Handmaiden, my rank, came with the authority to travel to
the Well at the World's End—a journey of a year and a day—and bring
back the Water of Life that allowed my family to be effectively immortal.
The rank of Sibyl, however, came with six Gifts. The Gift of Absolving
Oaths would allow me to free my favorite brother, Theophrastus, from the
foolish vow he had taken to eschew the Water of Life, the vow that would
soon bring about his death through illness and old age.

The Gift of Visions would allow me to request information directly
from my Lady, perhaps offering answers to the many questions that plagued
my family. The Gift of Opening Locks . . . well, I did not know how powerful it was, but it was at least conceivable that, with my Lady's help, I could
unlock the very gates to hell itself, where my father was being held captive,
and force them to yield him up.

And then there was the Gift that would allow me to create Water of Life, so that I would never again have to take off a year and a day, abandoning all my other duties, in order to bring back only as much Water as I could carry.

Nor was it just that I wanted new honors and prerogatives. For five centuries, I had hungrily devoured every arcane manual and ancient tome that came my way, eager to discover more of the nature of my Lady and Her Divine Purpose. Long nights I had spent bent over musty pages, seeking the secrets that evaded me. After all this time, all this searching, I yearned to learn the answers to my questions.

I skirted around the pool. "I'm sure you'll do fine on your own."

"Okay, no skin off my back." Mab shrugged. "I'm just your head detective. If you're not interested in why Harebrain can turn into Big, Black, and Bat-Winged, I don't need to know, either."

I froze.

He had a point.

In a warehouse in Maryland, my brother had transformed into a sapphire-eyed bat-winged entity that looked sickeningly like a demon. It was our family's policy not to traffic with Hell. At least, it had been in years past—though now it was beginning to seem as if half the family had violated this creed. If a search of Mephisto's house could reveal clues as to whether he really was Mephistopheles, Prince of Hell, I owed it to Father to investigate.

An eight-foot-tall primate with thick, curly white fur came shuffling into the foyer carrying a mop and pail. When it saw us, it flinched back, hunching bashfully behind its great shoulder. Then, gathering its courage, it lunged at us, swinging its mop and baring its big yellow fangs.

"We better get a move on, Ma'am." Mab retreated cautiously toward the nearest arch. "We're making the help nervous."

MEPHISTO'S mansion was like no house I had ever seen. Rooms spilled one into the next in no discernible order. Some overflowed with chairs that faced no particular direction. Others were nearly empty except for piles of junk. Still others could have been chambers in a museum, with priceless statues and artifacts arranged in an eye-catching manner, each with its own brass plaque.

Nearly every room on the first floor had a pool. Underwater tunnels, similar to the passage Morveren had taken to fetch the yeti, led from one to another giving the mermaid the run of the house. There were other passages as well, doors that opened into narrow hallways, or crawl spaces that led from one room to the next. And everything, everywhere, was plastered with Post-It notes.

" 'Remember to water the asphodel,' " Mab read aloud. He looked left and right but saw no sign of a plant. Looking up, he paused, squinting at the ceiling. "Guess he wasn't kidding about uncovering the will-o-wisps. Do you think he really keeps a salamander in his furnace?"

I followed his gaze and saw that the illumination came from glass globes holding balls of brightly glowing flickers of light. "Very likely. How else would he heat this enormous place? He certainly could not afford to heat it with oil."

MAB performed several thaumaturgic experiments involving sextants, brown rice, peony seeds, rose petals and a slide rule. Eventually, however, he threw down his tools in disgust.

"It's no good, Ma'am." He shook his head glumly. "The place stinks so of magic, I can't tell anything. The inhabitants are magical. Half the objects are enchanted. Heck, the place has probably even got dimensional gateways similar to those in Prospero's Mansion, leading to only Setabos knows where." He gestured off toward the distance. "Maybe if I had access to some of the specially calibrated equipment from Mr. Prospero's study . . . but, as it is, this line of thaumaturgic investigation is useless. Might as well press on."

The next chamber might have been a drawing room, had it not been so crowded with statuary and stacked furniture. Mab paused and scratched at his eternal stubble. "Have you noticed all the wooden surfaces have been carved?"

Throughout the house, cabinets, doors, wainscoting, tabletops, and even chair legs bore signs of my brother's handiwork. Bas-reliefs of famous people, pastoral scenes of shepherdesses and their sheep, funny little faces that peered out from door lintels, carved doodles of ketchup bottles and Campbell's soup ads: every place we looked, another wooden surface had been transformed into three-dimensional art.

"Does any of this mean anything? Or is it just artistic babble?" he muttered, adding under his breath, "By Setebos and Titania, I wish I'd thought to bring a camera!"

"Some of both, I suspect," I replied. "Some of it probably has meaning—mnemonic images he still remembers from the period when he studied the

Ancient Art of Memory with our brother Cornelius. Some of it is probably just the product of his madness."

"You mean he just carves on things because he's cuckoo?"

"He likes to carve. Sometimes, he does it without thinking."

Mab scowled. "Like on the boat, when he tried to carve a figurine that would force me to let him summon me? Sure, he doesn't know what he's doing. Suuure."

Mab examined the fairyscape at length, writing copious notes. Then, he peered at a cluttered table stuffed in between two china cabinets. A golf bag embroidered with the letters T.A.P. leaned against one leg, tilted at an extravagant angle, as if it were about to tumble to its doom. The yellow note stuck to its tan leather read: NEVER STOP LOOKING!!!

"This mean anything to you, Ma'am?"

"No, though T.A.P. are our brother Titus's initials," I said. "He's the golf fanatic in the family. Perhaps that's his bag."

"So, why is it here? And what's this message mean? That Harebrain wants to beat his brother at golf? Is that why Mr. Titus disappeared? Your brother took him out to ax the golf competition?"

"I hardly think so," I chuckled.

"Snicker if you like, Ma'am," growled Mab as he stalked over to a red trunk. "But I say something's fishy about Mr. Titus's disappearance."

Mab turned back to the table and picked up a plastic pillbox that lay amid dozens of other knickknacks.

" 'Check on this once a week,' " Mab read the pink note on the plastic pillbox. After dutifully recording this message in his notebook, he opened the pillbox and peered inside. "Check on what? The thing is empty. And . . . oh, this is precious!"

He pointed at a faint blue Post-It that read: THIS IS A MNEMONIC. DO NOT MOVE. An arrow had been drawn next to the words. The place the arrow pointed to was empty.

"Pour sucker." Mab chuckled, shaking his head. He moved along, reading other messages as he copied them down.

This is a ring from the high wire of the Greatest Show on Earth! I gave
    Barnum my tiger.
Stirrup from the Steppe. Check monthly.
This is to remind me to catch the Thunderbird.

Wind this bandana in January, May, and September.
This is a hairbrush. I use it to brush my hair.

Mab ran a hand over his face. "Boy, Ma'am, your brother is a certified loony. We're not going to get anything out of this."

"You can say that again," I murmured, my fingers drumming impatiently against the cover of the *Book of the Sibyl*. As Mab's pencil still scratched away, recording my brother's babblings, I added, "Mab, there's no point in copying it all down."

"A detective is nothing if he is not meticulous, Ma'am. One never knows what's going to turn out to be important."

"Nothing here is important, Mab. It's just nonsense, babble!" I gestured briskly, knocking over a silver flute that had been leaning against the wall. I propped it up again and pushed the attached note back onto the mouthpiece. It read: BONEHEAD, MONTHLY.

Beneath the flute, a photograph lay on its face. Righting it, I discovered it was a silvery daguerreotype of my family, taken back in England before the days of proper photography. A pale green sticky note pasted to the glass read: THIS IS MY FAMILY, EVEN THE DORKY ONES.

The note made me smile. I looked at the picture and felt an unexpected fondness for my siblings. I could not help smirking at their muttonchop sideburns, which had been all the rage in that day. They made my brothers look so serious and so ridiculous at the same time.

Mab leaned over, peering at our faces. "I recognize most of them, Ma'am. You, Harebrain, the Perp . . . er, Mr. Ulysses—hard to miss him. He's the one wearing the domino mask around his eyes. That's Mr. Theophrastus when he was a young man, isn't it?" Mab tapped on the picture above Theo's face. "Even back then, he looked like a decent fellow."

"Yes. That's him," I said softly, blinking tears from my eyes.

"And Madam Logistilla," Mab continued, unaware of my sudden sentimentality. "I recognize her. She looks exactly the same as she did when we met her a couple of weeks ago. This big one must be Mr. Titus. Oh, and that's dead one, Mr. Gregor. Your father showed me a picture of him once. Who are the rest of these guys?"

"That's Cornelius." I pointed at one of the shorter figures. "This is actually a rare shot of Cornelius's face. Usually, he covers his unseeing eyes with a blindfold."

"So, that's Mr. Cornelius." Mab squinted at the picture and then picked up the blue and white bandana to which the note about winding in January was attached. He sniffed it carefully, frowning thoughtfully. "He's the one your sister thinks put the whammy on Mr. Theophrastus, right?"

"Right." I shivered, though the chamber was not particularly cold, and I was still wearing my cashmere cloak. "Logistilla claims she saw Cornelius use his staff, the *Staff of Persuasion,* to make Theo keep his vow to give up magic. Retiring from the family work was bad enough, but Theo had come to the bizarre conclusion that the Water of Life that keeps us young counts as magic."

"Which is why he stopped taking it and began aging." Mab patted his notebook. "I got that down."

I nodded glumly and thought about Logistilla's accusation. Ironically, the thought that someone had forced Theo to keep his vow cheered me. Then, his decline became someone else's fault, someone who might be capable of fixing the problem. I just did not want the responsible party to turn out to be a family member. I hated the idea that any member of our family would do such a thing to one another.

I glanced at the picture again. It was so nice to see us all together. What a team we used to make! Nothing could withstand us when we worked together.

How had it happened that we had grown so far apart? Why could we not always be the way we were in this portrait?

"And that fellow?" Mab pointed at my last brother, who smiled wryly through the long lank hair that fell over his eyes. He was the only one without sideburns.

"Oh. That . . ."—I could not keep the disgust from my voice—"is Erasmus."

Mab squatted down and examined him more closely. "The professor, right? He's the one you don't like. Got it."

" 'Don't like' is putting it mildly," I murmured. I glanced at my brother again and quickly looked away. Just seeing Erasmus's face again brought to mind a thousand offenses he had committed against me. I fought off the wave of loathing that assailed me.

"And that, of course, is Mr. Prospero." Mab pointed at the imposing figure of my father, with his gray flowing hair and beard. The print had captured the wise yet humorous gleam that lit his eyes.

I paused, struck by a sudden pain in my heart. Father! How I missed him. Until he retired three years ago, I had been his constant companion, helping him in everything he did. And now? If my Lady and our Ouija board séance were to be believed, he was a living prisoner in Hell, hardly a fate I would wish on an enemy, much less a loved one.

Behind me, Mab moved on. He prowled around on the far side of the cluttered chamber. Pausing be peered at an elaborate scene of maidens playing Ring Around the Rosy in a meadow near a pond that was surrounded by cattails.

Surreptitiously wiping my eyes, I joined him. The quality of the carving he was examining was exquisite. I trailed my finger along the curlicues of a complicated filigree.

Mab squinted at my hand, drew a handkerchief from his pocket, and ran it over the curves and narrow angles of the carving before us. Then he peered at his handkerchief and sniffed it.

"Weird. Everything's spotless. You'd think a house kept by your loony brother and his menagerie would be dusty, if not filthy. Oh, and this is a door."

"Huh?" I glanced around, confused.

Mab chuckled. "Look."

He tapped the carving three times, then pushed hard on the nose of a laughing girl in a kerchief and dirndl. The whole panel opened, swinging away from us to reveal a descending spiral staircase. The wonderful aromas of pastry and bubbling stew wafted up to meet us.

Mab and I glanced at each other. Mab grinned. We headed down. The passageway led into a wide kitchen with shiny copper pots hanging from a rack overhead. The maenad stood before the stove, sautéing vegetables and stirring a big boiling pot. Nearby, in yet another pool, the mermaid peeled potatoes. She was wearing earphones and humming to herself, her tail tapping the water to the beat.

"Welcome to our humble kitchen," she purred in her husky voice.

"Thought you and Harebrain were off . . ." Mab's voice trailed off, and his face became somewhat red.

The maenad snorted, rolling her eyes dramatically. "The master's all smoke and no fire. He was just trying to flatter me, so I'd agree to cook dinner for his guests."

"Probably wise that he abstains, considering what happened to your last son," Mab muttered. Realizing she had heard him, he flushed more deeply. "Er, sorry . . . Your Majesty."

The maenad gave him a withering look but restrained her comments to, "The master's out in the barn, seeing to the comfort of the wounded gryphon."

"Are you really that Agave?" I asked. "Queen Agave of Thebes?"

"Once of Thebes, long ago. Later of Illyria and of other places. Yes."

"But, weren't you . . . mortal?"

"I was born mortal. I lost my humanity when my son and I offended Bacchus." She scratched the slate tiles with the pinecone on top of her thyrsos, and a fountain of wine sprang up, filling the kitchen with the sweet scent of crushed grapes. Deftly sticking a bowl under the fountain, she caught some of the deep purple liquid and, measuring it out, poured two cups into the stew. The newly sprung fountain slowed to a dribble and then dried up, leaving a dark stain like old blood upon the floor. "Or maybe I lost it when I twisted off my son's head. Either way, I belong to the Vine God now."

"What about your immortal soul?" asked Mab.

"Don't know." The maenad tasted the stew from a long wooden spoon, washed it, and continued to stir. "We didn't know about such things back then. If you ask me, souls are a new invention."

"Humans have always had souls," Mab countered. "They can be good or evil, but they can't be lost, in the sense that you mean. Once a human, always a human, at least at some level. Not like me and the mermaid here."

"Hey, don't drag me into this," objected Morveren, who had removed her headphones. "I might have a soul. My father was a Cornishman named Matthew." She pouted thoughtfully, her girlish chin tilted upward, a finger twirling her red tresses. "What does a soul do for you, again?"

"It's the part of a human that allows him to remain who he is. Even if his situation changes, he can always find his way back to his original self," Mab said. "Unlike us supernatural creatures. If we change, our very natures transform. We have no essential self to fight off external influences."

A chill ran up my spine. Did Father know this? I thought of the stacks and stacks of naked Italian bodies, lying like corpses in the caverns beneath my sister Logistilla's house. If I was right, Father intended them for the Aerie Ones, so they would all have bodies like Mab's and could develop human judgment and feelings, as Mab had. But what would be the point if the Aerie Ones would automatically revert to their old ways the moment they returned to their original airy forms?

Surely, Mab's seeming humanity, his kindness, his gruff concern, was not just a side effect of his fleshy body?

Thinking of Father reminded me of another of his projects, his translation of Orpheus's poetry in an attempt to decipher the Eleusinian Mysteries.

I turned to Agave. "You're a maenad. Were you involved with the death of Orpheus?"

"I was there."

"Why did the maenads kill him?"

"Why did he have to die?" She picked up the pan and gave her wrist a twist. The sautéing vegetables flew into the air and came down again. "He was a prude. He spoke out against our rites, always preaching temperance and moderation and other hogwash. Besides, he knew secrets the gods did not want men to know."

"Like how to get reincarnated without losing one's memories?" I asked.

"Yes, like that." She gave me a sly, calculating look, and her hair began to rise up like a cat's.

Mab quickly changed the subject. "These Post-It notes everywhere, what are they for?"

"To remind the master of things he may have forgotten." Agave turned back to her cooking, her hair flattening.

"A bit of overkill, don't you think? He's goofy, I grant you, but his memory problems seem a bit exaggerated. Everyone talks about it, but I've seldom seen him actually forget something."

"That's because Miranda is here."

"Huh?" Mab peered at me suspiciously. "How so?"

"Just seeing members of his family reminds our master of all sorts of things. He's much worse when they're not around, especially when he gets into one of his morose moods. Sometimes, he can't remember a thing for days. Not even his name." Under her breath, she murmured, "He could use a bit of Orpheus's wisdom, if you asked me. One too many sips out of the Lethe."

"What was that?" Mab snapped.

"Nothing." She tossed the vegetables again.

Mab frowned thoughtfully but did not pursue the topic.

The mermaid tilted her head and sighed. "Phisty. He's so dreamy! I'm so glad he's home and has his staff back! I missed him!"

"Couldn't he just have come back to this house and visited you?" Mab asked.

Morveren shook her head. "We don't live here year round. We all have our own homes and haunts. We're only here now because the master called us all together for a big party—to celebrate finding us again!" She sighed again. "I'm so envious of Chimie for saving him and helping him get back the staff. I wish I could have saved the master!"

"Tush, tush," commented Queen Agave, as she slid chopped leeks from her cutting board into the stew. "We all have our purposes. No reason to covet someone else's role."

Glancing around the kitchen, Mab chuckled. "So, Harebrain was telling the truth. He really does have a maenad or harpy cook him breakfast."

"Harpy!" Queen Agave snorted. "That mean old bird has no hands. All she does is terrorize the poor *bwca* into doing the work for her. Harpy cooking breakfast indeed!" She paused, reaching for a cutting board marred with deep scratches. "Speaking of the *bwca* . . ."

Agave scratched her nails across the board. Creamy milk ran from the scratches. She caught the milk in a bowl, then scratched the board once more. This time golden honey dripped down the marred wood. She let a few drops fall into the bowl and swirled the milk around.

"Put this by the fireplace in the big empty room upstairs, would you?"

Mab took the bowl carefully and started up the stairs. On the second step, he paused.

"Eh . . . either of you ladies know anything about a big, black, bat-winged guy with sapphire eyes and claws?"

"Who, us?" Agave's expressive face was unnaturally blank. "No. I have never seen anything like that."

"Me, neither." The mermaid put on her headphones and began bopping to the music, the water rippling about her.

Mab turned and ascended the staircase without a comment. Once at the top and through the arch, he murmured, "She's lying."

"Obviously," I agreed.

He growled, scrunching up his face. I could tell that he would have punched his palm, except his hands were full with *bwca* milk. "Bet I could pummel the truth out of her!"

THE chamber with the great hearth contained only a few neat piles of gear and numerous pastel squares of paper. There was no pool, only a hardwood floor that creaked beneath our feet.

"*Bwca*, eh?" Mab put the bowl down beside the brick of the fireplace. "Welsh relative of the brownie. No wonder the place is spotless. Those fellows'll clean anything for a little honey-laced milk."

I slipped my hand into the pocket of my cashmere cloak, which I carried over one arm, my fingers seeking the supple leather of the little book. Several rooms back, I had spied a big comfortable chair, albeit one that was pushed up next to two smaller chairs. Still, it was beside a window with plenty of light. If I walked back there now, I might be able to read the entire book before dinner.

"Are we done?"

Mab shook his head. "If we're going to get to the bottom of what is up with the Harebrain, we've got to unravel the clues he's left all around us." He glanced at the mostly empty hall. "I'm convinced there's some method to this madness, and I intend to find it!"

"We're wasting our time, Mab," I snapped. "These messages are just notes my brother leaves to remind himself of things he's forgotten."

Mab stalked over to a pile of yellowed fencing gear leaning against the far side of the hearth. Following him, I saw jackets, helmets, two foils, and an epee. The note stuck to the wall above read: REMEMBER TO PRACTICE.

"Condemning evidence, that," I mused. "It's all clear now."

Mab gave me a long, level look. "You want me to work or not, Ma'am? It's your call."

I waved a hand. "Carry on."

Beyond, two cardboard boxes holding ribbons, wrapping paper, and a few children's toys stood to either side of an empty closet. Scraps of tape and brightly colored paper were scattered about the floor. The notes stuck to the wall above the two boxes read: FOR E.D. and FOR T.C.

"This must be recent. The *bwca* hasn't gotten to it yet." Mab leaned over and sniffed the scraps of paper and tape. Straightening, he pulled out his notebook and copied down the messages. "Apparently, your brother was sending someone Christmas presents."

Next to the closet sat a red trunk. Mab opened the lid and peered at the note attached to the inside.

"Creepy," he muttered, jerking back. I leaned closer. The note stuck to the open lid read: MEMENTOES OF DEAD FRIENDS.

"What is it?" I pushed the lid back farther and looked in.

The chest held hundreds of little wooden figurines with jeweled eyes, primarily animals. I reached in and lifted my hand: dogs, elephants, boars, birds, an alligator, and a cheetah spilled from my palm. They clinked, ringing like wood chimes, as they rained back upon their fellows, the multicolored gems of their eyes sparkling.

"These were part of his staff once," I guessed.

"From the *Staff of Summoning*?" asked Mab. "How so?"

"You've seen his staff, how it looks like a long narrow totem pole, with dozens of little figurines, one on top of another?"

"Like the one he tried to make of me back on the boat? The one we were just talking about?"

"Exactly." I nodded. "Each figurine represents a different creature Mephisto can summon, a creature he has befriended or made a compact with. Most of them are supernatural, like the gryphon, the maenad, and the harpy, but some are ordinary animals Mephisto has trained, like that swallow and the falcon.

"Only having a figurine in the *Staff of Summoning* does not make the creature immortal. Sooner or later, the mundane animals die, and Mephisto has to train new ones to take their places." I gestured at the trunk of discarded figurines. "Apparently, this is his graveyard for figurines of beasts that once belonged to his staff."

Mab leaned over and sniffed the contents of the trunk. I sniffed, too, but could only pick up a faint odor of lemon-scented floor wax.

Mab straightened and scowled. "Ma'am, the spell to summon a spirit is not for the fainthearted. But to summon a physical entity, like a bird or a mermaid, yanking it to you through time and space? That's one whopper of a spell! No ordinary magician could perform it. To pull it off, you need some kind of extraordinary magical authority. I'm not even sure the Lords of the Elven High Council could do it. How does the Harebrain manage it?"

"I don't know, Mab." I frowned. "In the old days, Father used to perform the actual spell for him—the part that made it so that when he tapped the figurine, the creature would be summoned. Father called upon the authority of the patron angel of the *Orbis Suleimani*."

"That would do it," Mab muttered. "Maybe your brother does it the same way."

I shook my head. "Mephisto was thrown out of the Circle of Solomon after he lost his sanity. He does not have the authority to call upon that angel."

"Perhaps . . ." Mab scowled. "Or perhaps, he's calling upon the authority of Prince Mephistopheles of H . . . whatever *H* stands for. And I tell you, Ma'am, there's only two places starting with *H* where the inhabitants have enough authority to cast the spell we're talkin' about, and I've never heard of a Prince of Heaven."

I remembered the rambling story Mephisto had told us about how he lost his staff. "Maybe that's what he uses Uriel for, when he's not having the seraphim act as his valet."

Mab shivered and pulled up the collar of his trench coat. "Either way, I don't like it, Ma'am. Even calling on angels is bad business for mortals."

"Enough, Mab." I glanced about the nearly empty chamber and saw Mab with his nose pressed against a seemingly blank section of wall. "There's nothing here."

"There's got to be, Ma'am! Harebrain's too harebrained to cover all his clues. There's got to be something."

"No, Mab. He's just a disorganized madman."

"Look, Ma'am. Here's another hidden door. If this one doesn't produce anything of worth, I'll call it a day."

THE hidden door opened into a chamber decorated in jungle décor. A foot below the ceiling, water pipes, wrapped in vines and palm fronds, crisscrossed the room. Heat radiated from them, making this room warmer than the surrounding house. Rubber trees had been painted onto the walls, and the furniture was upholstered in leopard and zebra skins.

The pool here was kidney shaped and tiled with a rain-forest fresco. Incorporated into the scheme were the mouths of the underwater tunnels leading into other parts of the house, which seemed to pop up under giant tree roots or have odd-looking animals peering out of them, as if they were dens.

"What's this room for?" Mab glanced around.

The windows were opaque with steam. Mab rubbed some of it away with his forearm, and we looked down upon a frozen lake. Pine trees bordered the shores and covered the surrounding hills. Beyond rose jagged snow-covered peaks, tall and majestic against the deep blue sky.

Nowhere were there any signs of mankind. A mammoth lumbered across the ice, however, and the chimera that had rescued us on St. Thomas's charged to and fro in a snow-covered paddock, chasing a large boar. In the next paddock, a cockatrice strutted. Beyond that, the reindeer Donner nuzzled Pegasus beside a sturdy red barn. On top of the barn, the magnificent roc roosted.

Seeing Donner reminded me of the reindeer barn where Mephisto had kept Pegasus while we sojourned at the North Pole. An elf had given me a brief tour of it while Mephisto readied the winged horse for our departure.

He had introduced me to all nine of the reindeer, each in his own stall with a brightly colored name plaque on his doors. One of the deer had eaten a slice of apple from my hand.

From the ceiling above us came a slithering and a flash of bronze and brown. Mab drew his lead pipe. I whipped out my moon-silver war fan and slid it silently open. Above, gazing down at us with beady black eyes, was a giant hamadryad. The thick coils of its long body looped repeatedly about the warm pipes. As its serpentine head peeked out from between two fronds, the back of its neck flattened, forming a wide hood.

"Trussst in me," the cobra sang, swaying hypnotically.

"Can it, Kaa." I closed my fan. "You'll get no supper here."

"Handmaiden Miranda. How sssplendid," The cobra curled around another heated pipe and fixed his beady eyes on Mab. A loop of his coils began lowering themselves just above Mab's head. "What'sss thisss? Can I eat it?"

"Certainly not, you overgrown pipe cleaner!" Mab huffed. His eyes focused on something beyond the serpent. "Hey . . . what's this?"

"Maybe, you should not go there . . ." the hamadryad began.

Mab ignored him. He pushed aside some silk vines and peered at a section of wall, tracing the bark of the rubber tree with his finger and tapping on the painted plaster in several places. Something clicked, and a narrow door swung open, revealing a closet filled with ponchos of every kind, color, and description: Mexican ponchos, Hopi Indian ponchos, multicolored knitted ponchos, a white velvet poncho with pom poms, bright yellow rain ponchos, and a poncho made out of soda-pop bottle caps. Each hung from a hanger marked with a description of the garment. After pushing through them, Mab brought out a golden hanger and held it up so I could read the message embroidered onto its cloth covering.

THIS HANGER IS FOR MY CHAMELEON CLOAK, GIVEN TO ME BY (SEE MURAL HALL). REMEMBER TO HIDE IT FROM MY FAMILY. A second note, stuck to the hanger reads: DON'T FORGET THE ELEPHANT'S TRUNK! Stuck atop this at an angle was a third note scrawled in angry red letters. THAT DOPEY THEO!

"The massster will be angry." Kaa withdrew up into the greenery and slithered away over the pipes, murmuring, "I wasssn't here. I had nothing to do with thisss, and I will deny everything if anyone sssaysss otherwissse."

Mab and I stared at each other glumly, the condemning hanger in Mab's hand. Water dripped. The window that we had wiped clean grew steamy again.

"Pretty much answers that question," Mab muttered finally. He put the golden hanger back and shut the secret door. "Now, we know your brother wasn't just babbling back at St. Thomas. That accursed Unicorn Hunter's cloak Mr. Theophrastus destroyed back in Vermont, the one we found at the thrift store? It really was the Harebrain's."

Despite the heat of the room, I felt chilled, as if I were again staked down to a stone bier during a thunderstorm while the Unicorn Hunters hid beneath their camouflage cloaks, waiting to ambush my Lady, when She came to rescue me.

"What's it mean?" I whispered hoarsely. "Why would he own such a thing?"

"It means I was right. The Harebrain's up to no good," Mab replied. Grabbing my arm, he backed us both rapidly toward the door. "Let's go, Ma'am. I just saw something bright fluttering near that flowering plant in the corner. Didn't Harebrain say something about a poisonous butterfly?"

"Nicssse ssseeing you," called the hamadryad as we retreated.

CHAPTER THREE

The Book of the Sibyl

"Whoa!" Mab cried, as he had stepped through the next archway. "By the West Wind! It's the War between Heaven and the Elves!"

A vast, elaborate bas-relief spread across the black marble walls of an enormous ballroom. As I came through the arch and down the two steps that separated the ballroom from the chamber with the great hearth, Mab pointed up at the nearest figure on my left.

"There's Metratron, Herald of the Big Guy! Jeepers! I can make out the individual constellations on all twelve pairs of his wings. This is some piece of work! Who carved this?"

"My brother Mephistopheles. I recognize his style." I surveyed the wall. "This must be the Mural Hall the note on the golden hanger referred to."

The sculpture began at the far left with the awesomely magnificent figure of the Metratron, Herald of God, towering above his angelic hosts. His halo, shaped like the spiral of the Milky Way galaxy, brushed the top border of the twenty-five-foot wall. Beneath him stretched the nine orders of angelic servants: Seraphim, Cherubim, Thrones, Dominions, Virtues, Powers, Principalities, Archangels, and Angels. My brother had portrayed each successive rank as shorter than its predecessor, so that while the Seraphim, with their nine pairs of wings, came to the shoulder of God's Herald, the single-winged Angels reached only to the height of his waist. Yet, these last were taller still than the faery knights on their elvish steeds who engaged the angelic hosts in battle.

A parchment Post-It, stuck to Metratron's wing, read: THIS IS A WALL I MADE TO REMIND ME OF STUFF. I CARVED IT FOR MY HOUSE IN ENGLAND LONG AGO AND HAD IT TRANSPORTED HERE TO CANADA ONE BLOCK AT A TIME BY OREADS. I PROMISED THE EARTH SPIRITS SOMETHING IN RETURN. DON'T REMEMBER WHAT, BUT I HOPE I KEPT MY WORD.

The bas-relief scrolled around the entire chamber. The War between Heaven and Faery was followed by a portrayal of the Faery Revel, the Ride of the Faeries on All Hallow's Eve, and the Faery Tithe to Hell. The River Lethe ran down the very center of the back wall, dividing the celestial and terrestrial from the infernal.

To the right of the river, Lilith, Queen of Air and Darkness and the original despoiler of mankind, sat enthroned, reigning over an Orgy of Her Servants, the *lilim,* the *ouphe,* and the evil *peri.* This debauchery was followed by the horrors of the Nine Circles of Hell. Fanged barghests pursued the shades of Limbo. Incubi and succubi tortured carnal sinners, while gruesome bat-winged fiends whipped the Wrathful and Sullen. The Lord of the Flies gloated over Tantalus and other gluttons, while the slothful slept beneath the outstretched wings of drowsy Belphegor. Abbadon, the Angel of the Bottomless Pit, fingered his dreadful Key, oblivious of the covetous wraiths of the envious who strived vainly to touch this treasure. Beyond these, Asmodeus and Lucifer sat enthroned, their infernal kingdoms separated by an awful curtain decorated with disembodied eyes.

Finally, on the far right, directly across from Metratron, towered another gigantic figure: Satan Entrapped in Ice, his three heads weeping rivers of pain, as hideous in his fall as he had once been beautiful in Heaven.

The final wall, above the door through which we had entered, was carved to represent storm clouds. At the very center, above the doors, the thunderheads had parted, torn by four jagged lightning bolts that radiated away from the break in the clouds. In the center, carved as if walking away through the opening in the storm, pausing to look back over her shoulder, was a dainty creature with four cloven hooves. A spiral horn rose from the center of her brow.

Mab took off his hat. " 'Tis the Mother of Us All!"

"My Lady." I curtseyed reverently. Mephisto had done Eurynome justice. Seeing the gentle yet unshakable expression in Her eyes, one could believe She was both the Lady of Spiral Wisdom and the Bearer of the Lightning Bolt.

Mab put his hat back on and made another round of the room, admiring the walls. "Boy! Mr. Mephistopheles knew how to carve!" He whistled. Then, pointing with great excitement at a small figure among the Faery Revel, he exclaimed, "Hey, I think I see one of my . . . well, you'd call it a cousin!"

Smiling, I walked the length of the room and came to stand before the back wall. From here, I had a clear view of both Maeve, the Elf Queen, and

Lilith, the Queen of Air and Darkness. Some bizarre whim had caused Mephisto to carve the two queens with identical faces.

" 'When the truth is known about the queen,' " I quoted softly.

"What's that?" asked Mab.

"Hmm? Something I heard recently. I can't remember where. Astreus said it, I think. No . . . Ferdinand, perhaps?" Mab just stared at me blankly. I gestured toward the wall. "I guess my brother was running low on beautiful faces. He gave both queens the same features."

"That jerk! How dare he besmirch our lady Maeve," Mab cried loyally, adding quickly, "Begging your pardon, Ma'am, I realize she wasn't very nice to you, but that is only to be expected. Humans should not truck with elves—no one should, for that matter," he muttered, perhaps recalling his unexplained night on the coat rack.

"It's an understandable error." I gestured toward the queens. "Various poets mistakenly refer to the Elf Queen by the title 'Queen of Air and Darkness.' My addle-brained brother might think they are the same person."

"Humans!" Mab gave a snort of disgust. "Can't tell elves from incubi!" Then, the humor died out of his eyes. "Weird thing is the Harebrain doesn't show that kind of discernment problem elsewhere." He gestured at the carvings depicting events in the Inferno. "I've never been Below, myself, but I used to have—well, you'd call 'em drinking buddies—who knew about such stuff. Your brother has lots of accurate details here in the way he's depicted particular imps and demons, uncomfortably accurate. And that curtain with the eyes strung up on it?"

"That's not in Dante!" I shivered.

"Exactly, and yet I've heard of it before. It's a fixture in Hell. But how did Harebrain find out about it?" He paused. "Pretty damning evidence, Ma'am, pardon the pun. The chameleon cloak—have they ever been worn by anybody other than Unicorn Hunters? Either way, they're as accursed as magical talismen come. The 'Mephistopheles, Prince of H . . .' quip he made before he vanished back at St. Thomas's, and now this. I think we can rule out the idea that the big, black, bat-winged body of his is a party favor."

"I think we knew that in the warehouse." My voice was low. "I just didn't want to believe it. Our family has always been so loyal to the Powers for Good! How long has this been going on?"

"For all we know, Ma'am, your brother may be Prince Mephistopheles, the same Mephistopheles who tempted Faust."

"I forgot to check when Kit wrote his play, was it 1608?"

Mab flipped through his notebook. "I looked it up. Here it is: Marlowe wrote in the late 1500s, but the first mention historically of the demon Mephistopheles is in the German legends of Faust that appeared in 1587. Of course, historical records are only so accurate, thanks to your friends the *Orbis Suleimani*."

"Not *my* friends," I murmured, adding, "Mephisto was still a member back then. Who knows what historical evidence he could have had altered or destroyed?"

"Or maybe that's when the demon Mephistopheles first appeared. Back on Logistilla's island, I asked questions about what everyone in your family was doing in 1589, when your Father moved back to Italy." Mab flipped through his notebook again and tapped his finger beside a particular note. "Here it is. Mephisto reported, and I quote: 'I was in Germany, learning a new trade.'"

"You think he was learning . . ."

". . . to steal men's souls? I wouldn't put it past him."

"But if so . . ." I gazed in consternation at the larger-than-life depictions of Hell looming about me.

"If so, what?"

"Why isn't he more evil?" I cried. "Why does he never seem to harm anyone? When he was in his big demon form all he did was save us. Could his goofiness all be an act?"

"Maybe, if the maenad was lying about him being more forgetful when you're not around. Though when she did lie—about not knowing about the bat-winged form—it was as obvious as a garden fence that had been visited by a Mack Truck, so maybe she's telling the truth." Mab shrugged. "Or maybe, he's forgotten he was supposed to be evil, ma'am, along with every-thing else. He neglected to stick up a Post-It reading: CORRUPT SIX SOULS WEEKLY. So, he doesn't."

"Could be . . ." I chuckled in spite of myself. Then, all laughter died. "If so, Mab, then I'm very glad we're leaving him here. I recently read an es-say of Father's on the effect of exposure to demons on the human soul. It was . . . horrifying! Each demon is associated with some sin or vice. Just be-ing in the vicinity of the demon increases one's susceptibility to its ruling sin. Father described it with the analogy: imagine our soul was made of iron filings and the demon was a magnet. Whenever the demon comes near, the whole mass of filings moves in that direction. If Mephisto is a demon . . ." My knees felt suddenly weak.

"Maybe the effect only happens if he's in his demon form," Mab suggested. "We only saw him that way for a few minutes."

"Maybe . . ." But I was thinking about Mephisto's way with women, and how I had let Ferdinand kiss me by the hearth in the Lesser Hall. Had I really wanted to kiss him? Or had I been swayed toward weakness by exposure to my brother, the fiend from the Pit?

Mab, meanwhile, scanned the third wall, his gaze pausing upon the face of each of the Seven Rulers of Hell, all of whom Mephisto had painstakingly depicted. "You never did find out who was behind the Unicorn Hunters, did you? Whoever gave Mephisto that cloak is depicted somewhere on this wall. His note said that he made it to remind him of things. And the note on the chameleon cloak hanger said GIVEN TO ME BY—SEE MURAL HALL. This has got to be the mural hall!"

"You think the secret enemy of Eurynome is here?" I spun and began searching the infernal bas-relief, but the Nine Circles of Hell revealed no secrets to me. Lilith was portrayed there, of course, my Lady's enemy of old. Could she have been behind it? As I turned slowly, examining the rest of the carvings for any hint or clue, however, my eyes fell upon a pale yellow Post-It on the floor beneath the carving of the River Lethe. I knelt and retrieved it. It read: THIS IS MY BEST FRIEND ASTREUS.

My heart thumped oddly in my chest. "Wh-where's this supposed to go, I wonder?"

Coming to join me, Mab paused before a figure kneeling just to the left of the river. "Hey, shouldn't he be drinking from a horse's hoof? I've always heard if you want to drink from the Styx or the Lethe, you have to use . . ." He stopped talking abruptly and leaned closer to the wall. "Well, I'll be . . . it's Lord Astreus."

I moved closer, the Post-It in hand. Mab was pointing just beyond the procession of the Tithing of the Elves, to the scene surrounding the River Lethe itself.

On one side of the river knelt a lone elf. He held an hourglass-shaped goblet near the bank, as if he prepared to scoop up the river's waters. On the other side of the river, a lone dark *peri* stood with a similar goblet upraised in merriment. The *peri* was vaguely reminiscent of our favorite incubus, Seir of the Shadows. The expressionless features of the stony-faced elvish knight were definitely those of Lord Astreus.

Mephisto had portrayed the angels and fairies so vividly. Why had he carved Astreus with no expression?

I bent closer, running my fingers over the smooth rock forming the handsome face. No, not stony-faced; the knight with the elf lord's face was grief-stricken.

I drew back, pondering. Grief was not an emotion elves normally experienced; sorrow yes, but not grief or regret. My brother Gregor believed this was because the elves knew if they allowed themselves to regret, they would be so consumed by their memories of Heaven, now lost to them, that grief would incapacitate them. Yet, Mephisto had masterfully portrayed grief as it might come upon an elf: the hollowness of expression, the glitter of unshed tears in the eye. Even as I wondered, I marveled at the mastery of his craftsmanship.

Had Mephisto portrayed this grief-torn elf with the face of the Lord of the Winds merely to remind himself of Astreus's features? Or was there some deeper significance to this scene? The repetition of the face of the queens suggested the first interpretation.

Mab drew a hand through his grizzled hair, muttering, "How . . . odd."

"What's that?"

"Ma'am, I haven't had a chance to tell you, but last night . . . I happened to overhear a conversation between Lord Astreus and your brother Mephisto. I . . . I hesitate to repeat it, because I've always been a great admirer of Lord Astreus. But, in light of what I see here . . ."

A strange cold sensation came over my limbs, but before Mab could say more, Mephisto burst into the room accompanied by a small circus.

DINNER was reminiscent of the Mad Hatter's tea party. Our company included two humans, an incarnated Aerie One, a maenad, a harpy, a yeti, a singing hamadryad who hung from the ceiling and swallowed his dinner whole, a centaur, a little leathery *bwca* still clad in his cleaning apron, and a mermaid who flipped about the pool at the center of the room, flashing her girlish bosom as she leapt from the water to catch tidbits Mephisto tossed to her.

Afterward, I was able to retreat to the library, a dark, quiet chamber on the second floor that bore a faint fragrance of apples. Curling up in a leather armchair just below a will-o-wisp globe, I pulled out the *Book of the Sibyl*.

My hand caressed the soft black leather. At last, and when I had nearly lost hope, the secrets of the Sibyl were finally mine! The answers I had been searching for all these years could be here, in this little volume. Compared to that, everything else faded into the background.

Giddy with anticipation, I drew out the little book. It was a short volume, only a handful of pages, but this was only to be expected, considering that it had originally been written on ancient scrolls. I opened the cover, breathing in its leathery scent. The vellum felt smooth and cool beneath my fingers. I spread the pages and read the entire thing:

I, Deiphobe of the Seven Hills, Sibyl of Eurynome, herein do record the secrets of my order:

The greatest secret in the Universe is no secret because it is known to all, though few pay attention. That secret is: Love. All the world was made for Love, and Love obliged Her creator by coming to dwell within the world; a gift to all created therein. Love rights all wrongs. Love banishes all fear. Whatever is impossible but good, is possible with Love.

Love is of the highest order of servants of the Alcreate, the Most High, the One Altogether Lovely. Her sisters are Truth and Spirit and her Handmaiden is Bitter Wisdom.

Love cannot be compelled. The other name of Wide Wandering Love is Free Will.

Sing out! Rejoice without ceasing; for unto us has been given such joy as the world cannot sunder.

Descent into Darkness
Wide Wandering Love looked down upon the inverted world of matter-and-darkness and knew pity. Departing the bower of the Alcreate, She descended into this darkness to bring the light of Love back to those who had strayed. She moves among the Shadowlands, but She is not of the Shadowlands. For She knows the true mystery of the ages—that sorrow is a sham, and death but a cheat.

The Purpose of Sibyls
Wide Wandering Love, being a primary emanation of the Alcreate, cannot perceive the murk of our low estate. Thus, the necessity for Sibyls. A Sibyl is one who dwells in these Shadowlands but whose mind so resembles Hers that the two may become as one. Only one who loves as She loves, who sees as She sees, whose heart is devoted to the will and purposes of the Most High, is worthy of the stature of Sibyl.

The Gifts of the Sibyl

Here follows an explanation of the six gifts granted to Sibyls:

Open Locks

What can bind Love? To open locks and free captives from their bonds, a Sibyl has but to touch her Holy Mark to the offending lock, and it will spring apart.

Cure Poison

Love is life. The Sibyl has but to glance at one who has been poisoned, and the strength of Her love will purify the sufferer, removing whatever is harmful.

Purify Water to Create Water of Life

Love brings forth abundance. The Sibyl has only to love the water, and the water will be made wholesome.

Command the Lightning

Where the Sibyl looks, love flows. Where a Sibyl loves, lightning from the heavens will follow.

Where the Sibyl disdains, Love is withdrawn. Without Love, life flees.

Only a fool would anger a Sibyl.

Seeing Visions

When two merge, one can see as the other. A Sibyl need only close her mortal eyes and open Eurynome's eyes to see as She sees.

Absolve Oaths

Free Will cannot be fettered. A Sibyl has but to draw attention from her Holy Mark to the offending oath, and the chains binding the spirit will part.

The Greatest Gift

To look into the eyes of another and see one's self: this is the greatest of gifts, the true Gift of the Sibyl.

Conclusion

Wide Wandering Love adores Mankind, but Mankind holds no special importance to Her; for She cares equally for all: Elves, Djinn, Spiritlings,

Angels, animals, trees, flowers, and even Demons and Dwellers in the Night. The very elements themselves rejoice in Her love, standing firm or fleeing as She requires. So great is Her compassion that She will not pause while even one of these remains in darkness. All will return to roost beneath the comforting wing of the Most High before She takes Her rest.

The Tithe of the Elves

Three times, I read through the *Book of the Sibyl,* meditating over every word. Once I understood the gist, I closed my eyes and prayed, asking my Lady for understanding and illumination. Then, I reread the book several times more, in light of my meditations revealed.

The *Book of the Sibyl* was everything I had hoped it would be. After five hundred years of searching, I now understood why the rank of Sibyl eluded me.

Sibylhood was the highest honor my Lady, the living embodiment of freedom, could bestow. As I had suspected in the chapel a week ago, no one who enslaved an entire race qualified as a representative for the living symbol of freedom, even if that race was enslaved for the good of mankind. Oh, how Mab was going to laugh when I told him.

But what choice did I have?

Had I learned this a hundred years ago, I could have broken my flute and depended upon Father, Gregor, and Theophrastus to hold the Aerie Ones in check if they began destroying mankind, to subdue them as they had the salamanders who caused the Great Fire in London and so many other supernatural menaces. But Gregor was dead, Father was in Hell, and Theophrastus was old, dying. If I freed the Aerie Ones now, who would prevent them from destroying mankind?

Had Astreus been at hand, I could have risked asking him for help. True, elves were not to be trusted, but he was the Lord of the Winds, the Aerie Ones' liege lord, who represented them on the High Council. He could bend them to his will, should he desire to do so. Considering how strongly he objected to their current state of servitude, perhaps he would have been willing to step in and keep them from having to be bound again. With Astreus away upon mysterious business in the Void, however, there would be no help from that quarter.

The secret of Sibylhood was mine, and I could make no use of it.

The sketch of Astreus's coat-of-arms, which he had handed me when he won our wager, slipped out from between the pages. It showed a shield divided in half on a diagonal with a picture of a cloudy sky, white clouds on blue, on the top, and a darker starry sky on the bottom. I smiled and pressed it to my cheek. The gratitude I felt toward Astreus for bringing me this book—for finding the disintegrating original, copying it in his own looping hand, and keeping it for me for over three hundred years—burst over me like floodwaters over a dam. Had he been present, I should have kissed him.

Strange. Twice in my life I had waited to meet a man and had met instead with disappointment, only to discover lately that both men had been kept from me by forces beyond their control.

I pictured how my life might have been had things been otherwise. Had Prince Ferdinand Di Napoli not disappeared in 1474, he and I would have wed. It was an easy thing to imagine the life we might have led together, a life of contemplation and joy, perhaps with children to fill my days. In time, we would have been king and queen of Naples, and our days would have expanded to include parties and politics. Then, within the natural span, we would have grown old and passed away, "our little lives rounded with a sleep."

Father might still have wed Isabella Medici, the marriage that produced Mephisto, Theo, and Erasmus. Without the Water of Life, however, he would have grown old and died long before engendering my other siblings.

The life I might have led had Astreus met me by the Avon in 1634 was far less certain. It is unlikely the elf lord would have figured into it prominently. I could hardly have married an elf, despite Mephisto's urgings. Nor would Astreus have offered for my hand, hawks not being known for marrying doves and all that. Yet, how might my life have been altered if he had given me the *Book of the Sibyl* then, back when my family was still whole? What wonders might have been open to us all, had I achieved Sibylhood during the reign of King Charles I?

A bitterness rose suddenly in my throat. What if Ferdinand—this new Ferdinand who had reappeared in my life—were telling the truth, and Father was responsible for his disappearance upon the eve of our marriage? Could Father have had a hand in Astreus's banishment as well? Two months ago, the idea would have seemed laughable, but, now . . .

I thought of Ferdinand standing beside my father's hearth nearly a week ago with the carved figurine of Astreus in his hand. The two men were so very different. Ferdinand was a warm Mediterranean breeze blown in from my childhood, while Astreus was more like the storm winds for which he was named—sometimes hot, sometimes cold, always unpredictable.

I had particularly enjoyed my long talk with Ferdinand. After all these centuries, what a novel pleasure it had been to have a confidant with whom I could relax who was not a member of my family. With the elf lord, the exact opposite was true. I had to be ever on guard and watch my every word. And yet, there was something captivating about the Lord of the Winds, as if some bond had been forged between us, the nature of which I did not understand.

There was no purpose to comparing them, of course. The elf had returned to the Void. I would not see him again. Ferdinand, on the other hand, I would see in less than a fortnight at my brother Erasmus's New Year's party. The thought made my heart beat faster. If I freed the Aerie Ones and successfully became a Sibyl, we could be marr—.

The library door creaked open.

"Ma'am?" Mab plopped himself down in another armchair. "Just wanted to go over a few things, if you have a moment?"

"Yes, of course." I hid the coat-of-arms sketch inside the back cover and closed the little black book.

"I've just been going over what we know." Mab flipped through his notebook. "We're still no closer on most of these questions than last time we talked, down in the Caribbean, Ma'am, but, here's the big ones we haven't touched on recently."

He handed the notebook to me. I read:

1. *What's up with Mephisto turning into a demon?*
2. *What's supposed to happen on Twelfth Night?*
3. *What was Mr. Prospero trying to do on September 23rd, when he freed the Three Shadowed Ones? And how do we rescue Mr. Prospero from Hell? (Note: Three Shadowed Ones are Baelor of the Baleful Eye—mind reader, Seir of the Shadows—teleporting incubus, and Osae the Red—shapechanger.)*
4. *Where did Mr. Prospero get his magic books and did he really turn the books into the magical staffs the Prospero Family now carry, like the demon Baelor of the Baleful Eye claims?*
5. *What's up with this Ferdinand Di Napoli guy showing up and*

       claiming Mr. Prospero dumped him alive in Hell five hundred
       years ago?
6. *Where's Mr. Gregor's dead body?*
7. *Where is Mr. Titus?*
8. *What's up with the voodoo dollhouse of Prospero's Mansion in the*
   library at Madam Logistilla's place in the Okefenokee Swamp?
9. *Does Mr. Prospero have Miss Miranda under a spell that makes*
   her obedient to him?

I read them over carefully, snorting at the last one, then closed the notebook and handed it back to him.

"The only question we're any closer to answering is number seven," I said. "Thanks to Father Christmas's scrying pool, we now know Titus's children are at Logistilla's estate in Georgia. When we get back to Oregon, I'm going to send an Aerie One to find out if Titus is living there—Logistilla hardly uses the place, she prefers her home on St. Dismas's—or if there are any clues in the house as to where he might be. I'd like to visit myself, and meet the children. They should not be in any immediate danger, however, as they do not have staffs. So, we had better find the others first."

"Can't you do it from here?" Mab gestured at my flute, scowling. "Send one of us, I mean."

"I could call up and send a local Aerie One, but I'd rather send someone I know and trust."

"Good point." Mab nodded. "Might be a good idea to post someone savvy enough to keep an eye on that dollhouse, too, while we're at it. Considering that Titus's children and freaky voodoo dollhouse are in the same mansion."

I shivered. "Hadn't thought of it quite that way. Let's send one of your people, someone who is schooled in the magical arts who can tell us whether there are spells on that thing and whether it would be safe to move it to a safer place.

"Here's a question you might want to add to your list," I added. " 'What is this curse on my family that the demon Baelor of the Baleful Eye mentioned?' "

Mab scribbled it down. "Oh, and I forgot, Number Eleven: 'How do we track down the teleporting perp?' Er, beg your pardon, Ma'am, I mean 'track down Mr. Ulysses.' "

"As to the rest of the questions, Ma'am, I've got some leads. My people are following up a couple of things as well, but . . ." Mab chewed on the back of his shiny pen. "Um . . . there's something else, Ma'am. Something I'm reluctant to talk about, but think you'd better know."

"Yes? What is that?"

"It's about Lord Astreus, Ma'am."

"Oh?"

A cold draft was blowing against the back of my neck. It had probably been there for some time, but, caught up in reading the *Book of the Sibyl*, I had not noticed. Now, I found myself shivering. I unfolded an afghan that had been thrown over the back of my chair and arranged it around my shoulders. A faint pleasant scent of lanolin clung to the creamy yarn.

"I thought you should know about the conversation I overheard, Ma'am. I came upon Lord Astreus at Santa's house. I was getting up my courage to say something to him, when your brother rounded a far corner. Lord Astreus greeted Mephisto and asked him how the years had been treating him. Mephisto answered in his usual dopey way, and they chatted for a few moments."

A growing icy sensation in my stomach warned me that I did not want to hear the rest of this, but curiosity held me captive. "About what?"

"Normal stuff, like the weather and the low décolletage of the elven ladies this season. That was your brother's contribution. Then—and this is the part I wanted to tell you about—Lord Astreus's voice dropped so low I had trouble making out his words, but he said something like: 'When last I saw you, circumstances were somewhat different, my friend. How did you manage to overcome your . . . affliction?' "

"Interesting!" I leaned forward, pulling the afghan closer. "What did Mephisto say?"

"Ma'am, your brother freaked!" Mab gestured emphatically with his pen. "His eyes fixed on the cup in Lord Astreus's hand, and he began whimpering, 'It's y-you. . . . You're the one who made me drink!' Then, he started screaming at the top of his lungs, 'No! No! Get away! I don't want to forget!' "

Dread gripped me like a vice. "What happened next?"

"Nothing." Mab shrugged. "Lord Astreus just walked away. His back was to me, so I couldn't gauge his reaction. As soon as he left, Mephisto reverted back to normal—if you can call anything that nut case does, normal. He acted as if nothing had happened; just poured himself a drink from a nearby samovar and went hummingly on his way. By Setebos, he's odd!

"Anyway," Mab continued, "at the time, I thought it was just the Hare-brain being his usual whacked-out self. But now, in light of that mural—I'm not so sure. . . ." Mab paused. "Do you remember the elves talking about a party in honor of Lord Astreus, for having excused them from the tithe?"

I nodded, recalling the terrible haunted look that had come over Astreus when I mentioned the incident.

"I . . ." Mab sighed. "I hate to speculate without facts, Ma'am, especially as Lord Astreus once did a great good for my people."

"Spit it out, Mab!" An odd hollowness hovered where my stomach used to be.

Mab was quiet for a long time. A loud thump came from some other part of the house, followed by a squawk and some bellowing. Eventually, the ruckus fell silent. When Mab finally did speak, his words spilled out in a rush. "Ma'am, I'm thinking Lord Astreus may have bought the elves their freedom that year by tithing your brother!"

"What?" I half-rose from my chair.

"It's just . . . the maenad made some comment about Mephisto having drunk too deeply of the Lethe. And that carving of his?" Mab gestured vaguely in the direction of the ballroom. "It showed Lord Astreus kneeling beside the Lethe, right at the end of the tithing procession, as if he was about to give the Water of Forgetfulness to the victim of the Tithe."

"But if Mephisto had been tithed, wouldn't he be in Hell?" I asked, agitated. "I mean tithed elves go bodily across the Styx . . . just like on Mephisto's wall mural, right? He would just have vanished, right?"

"Unless he made a deal with his demonic captors," Mab said grimly.

"You mean, like, he'll take a chameleon cloak and hunt the Unicorn, or seduce souls like Faust, carry out other dastardly crimes for them, if they let him go to the surface world?" I shivered. It felt like cold fingers walking up the inside of my back. "And they gave him a bat-winged body as part of the deal?"

I stood and began pacing about the library. "I wish we knew what normally happened to elves who are tithed. Do the demons eat them? That's what Gregor used to believe. He thought the demons consumed their essence and wore their skins like coats, so that they could slip out of Hell and pass among the elves, causing mayhem. He even theorized, at one point, that this was where the Unseelie Court came from, though he later abandoned that premise."

"Don't know, Ma'am. There are still a number of points that don't quite fit. If Mephisto was tithed, he must know what happens to tithed elves. So, why did he ask the High Council at the Christmas feast?"

"With Mephisto, who knows?" I shrugged. Outside the window, I could see the mammoth rubbing its shaggy side against a pine tree. "To rile them up? To hint that he knew? Perhaps, if he drank of the River Lethe, he does not know himself why he asks. Could be anything."

"If Astreus did tithe him, and this involved drinking water from the Lethe, it would definitely explain why your brother's such a rattle brain," Mab said. "It would also explain why, when he saw Lord Astreus with a cup in his hand, he freaked out and started shouting about not wanting to forget."

"Having drunk from the River Lethe would go far to explain my brother's condition," I said slowly. "Everyone in my family forgets things. It's part of living so long. Our minds weren't meant to stretch over five centuries. Except for Cornelius—who's made a study of memory—we all have days, years, even decades that have fallen into what Father calls the mists of time. Sometimes, things are forgotten entirely, other times our memory plays tricks on us. To this day, Theo and I cannot agree on who first introduced Leonardo da Vinci to our court in Milan. I swear it was Uncle Antonio, though Theo—who was also present—insists it was Uncle Ludovico. Mephisto, however, has brought this problem to a whole new level.

"He's not so bad nowadays," I continued, "but there have been periods where he didn't seem to remember anything—and if the maenad's telling the truth, he still has such spells, just not when family members are around."

"You think he was tithed?" Mab cringed, clearly hoping I would disagree.

"Mab, I would dismiss this theory out of hand," I replied slowly, "if it were not for one thing. You asked me once when Mephisto first showed signs of madness. The first time I saw Mephisto *sans* sanity was back in 1634, when he came to tell me that Astreus could not make our rendezvous. Mephisto and Astreus spent a good deal of time speaking together during that night in 1627 when we danced with the elves. And the first time I saw him without his sanity was exactly seven years later. The elves did not tell us why they were celebrating the first time we met them, but it could have been because the tithe was paid, and they were free for another seven years."

"You never mentioned a rendezvous with an elf!" Mab stated accusingly.

"That's because it never happened." I gave a dismissive wave.

"Humph!" he snorted. "I hate to say it, Ma'am, but that about clinches it. Instead of tithing an elf, Lord Astreus tithed your brother, then he told the elves that no tithe was needed that Sevenyear.

"Once tithed," Mab continued, "Mephisto must have made some kind of compact with the Powers of Hell that allowed him to become a demon. Except, since Mephisto is a human and not a pixy or a sprite—or whatever they usually tithe—he had a soul. This would keep him from permanently changing his nature, which might explain why he can change back and forth between demon and human."

"Maybe. . . ." I frowned. "In fact that had been my first thought when I saw his demon form . . . that he had made some infernal bargain to regain part of his sanity. But that would have had to have happened after 1634. If so, what about the references to the demon Mephistopheles from 1589? And Mephisto's 'new trade'?"

"Maybe the *Orbis Suleimani* backdated Mephistopheles for some reason. Faust's original demon might have had another name. Maybe Mephisto did it himself, to leave some kind of clue. Maybe I was just off base on that new trade thing."

"What I don't understand is: If Astreus betrayed Mephisto, why did my brother bother to come tell me Astreus could not make our rendezvous? How did he even find out Astreus was not coming? Why have a note that says: THIS IS MY BEST FRIEND ASTREUS. And what about this dire mission Astreus has undertaken for the queen? Is it related to the tithing of Mephisto?"

"Could be. I would not put much past Queen Maeve. She's a fine queen, but she's tricky—and she is the queen of the Unseelie Court, the seedier side of the supernatural world. Could be Astreus tithed Mephisto secretly, and the queen found out and is blackmailing him to accomplish some purpose of her own."

"But, why tithe my brother and then go way out of his way to get me the *Book of the Sibyl*?"

"The what?"

"The *Book of the Sibyl*, the one I've been seeking for so long."

"The *Book of the Sibyl*?" Mab frowned. "How's that figure in?"

I held up the little black volume. "Astreus gave it to me."

"You accepted a gift from an elf?" Mab exploded, the very picture of outrage.

"It was bestowed in the Mansion of Gifts," I replied crisply. "Were it not wholesome, Father Christmas would not have allowed it."

Father Christmas had more than allowed it, though I did not pause to explain this to Mab. He had actually arranged it. As we were preparing to leave, he had come into the reindeer barn, the ermine trim of his crimson robes brushing aside the straw, and asked me whether I had liked his gift, claiming it had been for the purpose of bestowing upon me the gift I had requested over a century earlier that he had fished Lord Astreus Stormwind from the Void. I thanked him profusely, but he just smiled and assured me that only a man who took great pleasure from a gift happily received would remain in his line of work. Reaching into his voluminous crimson sleeve, he drew out the coronet of silver and horn that Astreus had worn during the Christmas feast and handed it to me, saying, "You keep this for now. You may find it useful anon."

"When I asked what it was for, Father Christmas had merely smiled mysteriously and replied, 'When the time comes to use it, Child, you will know.'"

Mab, placated by Father Christmas's approval, took the black leather volume and examined it, sniffing carefully and flipping through its pages. I hid Astreus's coat-of-arms, which I had slid from the book as I handed it to him, in my sleeve.

"That's pretty spectacular, Ma'am. I'm glad for you. Know you've been looking for it for centuries. As to why Astreus brought it for you? That I don't know, Ma'am. Elves are capricious. Maybe he felt sorry for having deprived you of your brother. Maybe it was Mephisto's last wish, or something."

Mab's theory took all the charm out of the notion that Astreus had gone to so much trouble to bring me the book. The little book, which had been so dear to me, now seemed tainted, as if it had been paid for with my brother's blood.

"You may be right," I admitted wearily. I took the book back, replaced the coat-of-arms, and slipped the slim volume back into the packet of my cashmere cloak. "It would certainly explain the facts. If it is true, I'm glad that Astreus has spent the last three hundred years toiling on some unpleasant task, and I'm sorry I danced with him!"

Mab, who had admired his elven liege lord for many more centuries than I had been alive, did not share my fervor. Sticking his notebook into the pocket of his trench coat, he hunched his shoulders dejectedly and slouched from the room.

THE next morning, as we prepared to depart, Mab asked, "Before we leave, Harebrain, how did you find us?"

"Find thee?" Mephisto was standing in front of a floor-length mirror set into the sitting-room door, trying on the cavalier's hat Santa had given him for Christmas.

"How did you happen to arrive right as the Three Shadowed Jerks attacked our plane?"

"Ah, that," Mephisto replied, adjusting the hat.

He did not continue, but stood silently staring at his own reflection, his face contemplative. It was a handsome hat in a style Mephisto had often worn years ago, with a big indigo ostrich plume protruding at a jaunty angle. Seeing it on his head brought a pang of nostalgia for the company of the younger, saner Mephistopheles.

I looked at my brother. Was he secretly evil? Had he been tithed and made a deal with the Rulers of Hell to save his life? Or was I starting at shadows and seeing bogeymen where none were present? If he were working for the forces of Hell, why did he save us, first in the warehouse and then when the Three Shadowed Once destroyed our plane?

If Astreus tithed him, why had my brother portrayed the elf lord wracked by grief? None of it made any sense, and just thinking about it was making my head hurt.

Eventually, Mephisto gripped the hat by its wide black brim and, pulling it off, handed it to me. "You'd better keep this, Miranda. I'll only lose it."

"Er, thanks, Mephisto. Just what I always needed," I murmured dubiously.

"I'm not giving it to you. It's my hat," he replied frowning, as if he was concentrating very hard. "I just want you to keep it for me. Bring it along to Erasmus's New Year's Eve party, would you? Just in case I find a tux to match it. You did say you were going, didn't you?"

"Yes, I did." I thought of Ferdinand, and my cheeks grew warm. A giddy girlish sensation threatened to engulf me.

I stiffened. Was this natural or demon-Mephistopheles-induced madness? I frowned at my brother. "Were you going to answer Mab's question?"

"Huh? Oh, yeah." My brother shrugged and replied in his rapid casual manner. "How did I find you? I didn't. I was chasing them, the Three Shabby Ones. After they summoned Chimie back—and I snatched my staff out of their hands—I followed them around for a while, letting various friends have a chance at harassing them. They tried to teleport away, of course, but I'd snuck a few friends onto them: Soupy the Snake, and the poison butterfly, and guys like that. And . . . oh yeah, I just happened to be there when they were attacking you. They must have had a fell spirit watching your plane that alerted them when you were in the air. It probably had been following you ever since the Islands. Glad I was there, though! It would have been a shame if you'd crashed. That smooshed-to-red-paste look just wouldn't suit you, Miranda."

"Thank you, Mephisto," I said gratefully. Demon or not, he had saved me. Under the influence of hat-inspired nostalgia, I gave my crazy brother a hug.

Of Secrets and Revelations

A cold ride on Pegasus, a quick jaunt in a company jet, and we returned to Prospero's Mansion, in the foothills of Oregon's Cascade Mountains. Upon arriving home, I learned that Prospero, Inc. had just suffered a second disaster. An explosion had destroyed one of our warehouses in Michigan— luckily not the one in which Mab had stored the warded crate containing a gate to Hell his men had taken from the warehouse in Maryland. (It had been while fighting the creatures that emerged from this crate that we had first encountered Mephisto in his big bat-winged form.)

Following so soon after the loss of the truck carrying phoenix dust, less than two weeks earlier, even Mab admitted there might be some truth to the suspicions of foul play voiced by my familiar, Tybalt, Prince of Cats—and Mab hated to agree with anything "espoused by the furball." These suspicions grew stronger when the burnt remains of what might be a saboteur were found at the damaged building. Two of Mab's assistants were already on site examining the situation, but Mab did not trust them to do a thorough job. He headed off to Michigan himself, while I arranged for the replacement of the lost inventory. Luckily, this warehouse had stored only mundane goods.

ONCE that matter was in hand, I checked on the Great Hall, to see how the renovations were coming. *Oreads* and other spirits of the earth had repaired the damage Seir of the Shadows had done to the mansion when he attacked in early December. They had also restored about half of the statues of my siblings that had stood in the hall's alcoves. Alas, the rest of the statues were beyond repair. As I had feared, the joyous face of Theo's statue was among those that had been ruined.

Returning to the Lesser Hall, I sat down and read the *Book of the Sibyl* through several more times, contemplating each word carefully. Some of it was familiar to me, such as Eurynome's history, or made obvious sense, such as the description of how to open locks. Had I a Sibyl mark upon my forehead, it would be an easy enough matter to bend down and touch it to a lock I wished to open. Other descriptions, however, baffled me. Love the water? Where a Sibyl disdains, Life flees? What did these things mean? I frowned and rubbed my bare forehead where no Sibyl mark yet rested.

The matter of Astreus and Mephisto weighed heavily on my mind—so much so that I could not bring myself to start on the embroidery I had promised Astreus as the prize for his winning our wager over whether or not I would accept his gift. Using the excuse that there were more pressing issues, I put his heraldry aside and returned to the matter of the Three Shadowed Ones, the main threat to our family.

My family was clearly in danger. The demons had already attacked several times. I was beginning to wonder if warning my siblings, as Father had requested, was not going to be enough. In the old days, we would have banded together and done something to eliminate the threat. It was a shame that option was no longer open to us. We were so much more effective when we worked together.

Currently, I had no method to directly discover the demons' plans, but I felt that the key to all this lay in discovering what my father had been doing when he visited Gregor's grave last September. Poring over Father's most recent journals, I had examined his treatises—terrifying things that they were—and unraveled his poems, thanks to my familiar, Tybalt, Prince of Cats, who recognized them as translations of odes written by the ancient Greek hero, Orpheus, for the Eleusinian Mysteries.

The only avenue of inquiry I had not yet exhausted was Father's horticulture project. According to Tybalt, this project was located in the Wintergarden, here in Prospero's Mansion.

IN my father's house were many mansions, making for some very long hallways. Walking from one wing to another was out of the question, unless one had the time for a week's outing. So, to hasten my trip to the Wintergarden, I borrowed Father's magical Turkish throw rug.

The flying carpet floated down the hallway. Piloting it was Caurus, another of the three incarnated Northerlies. He sat cross-legged atop the flying rug, his merry blue eyes twinkling. Beneath a long scarf patterned with snow crystals, which trailed behind him in the breeze, Caurus wore a white and blue Icelandic sweater, seal-skin breeches, and long knitted socks. Over his shoulder, he had slung a pair of ice skates. A hornpipe protruded from his belt like a sword.

Caurus halted the carpet. I carefully climbed aboard and settled myself, my flute lying across my lap. The flying rug smelt musty, but a scent like a brisk snowy day blew about Caurus. I leaned close to him, breathing the fresher air and we took off, swooping rapidly through the long corridors, toward the spiral staircase that led to the underground passages.

Caurus was a good-natured fellow with straw-colored hair, a long narrow nose, and a pointed chin. He spoke with a Scandinavian accent. There was a pleasant, almost musical, rhythm to his speech.

"So," he said, leaping cheerfully into the latest gossip, "I hear you've been seen all round and about, Milady. As far north as North Pole and as far south as the West Indies."

"I've been visiting family."

"*Ja,* and I hear Mr. Mephistopheles retrieved his staff."

"Yes, that is so."

"Ah, I hear you saw our father."

"Your father?"

"As much as we Aerie Ones have parents, Dawn, with her rosy-colored fingers, is accorded our mother. Our father is held to be He Who Is Crowned with Stars."

It took me a moment to realize to whom he referred.

"Astreus Stormwind! I thought your father was a Titan?"

He gave me a cheerful grin. "Is it our fault you humans cannot tell elves from Titans?"

I gave no reply but thought: *No wonder Mab was dismayed by Astreus's betrayal!* Did Mab think of Astreus as his father?

Meanwhile, Caurus was saying, "I dreamt such a lovely dream last night, Milady. I dreamt I was free to come and go as I pleased. I could sleep or gust as the mood took me, and no man was my master, nor maid either. Wasn't that just a beautiful dream?"

I turned to glance back at Caurus. As his merry blue eyes met mine, I felt such sympathy for the Aerie Ones in their quest for freedom, as could hardly be put into words. Then, the moment passed. I felt more myself again.

I gripped the flying carpet and stared straight forward, shaken. Strange moments of sympathy, such as this, had been overtaking me ever since I watched an elderly woman cross an overpass in Chicago. When they first began, I feared I might be under some sort of supernatural attack. Now, a more sinister explanation occurred to me.

Perhaps, these experiences were not attacks, but a purely human phenomenon known as empathy, a phenomenon I had often heard tell of, but had seldom experienced for myself, having spent so much of my life in solitude and quiet contemplation of my Lady's will. While empathizing with others was not a bad thing in itself, I could think of no reason why I would suddenly start doing so now, unless Theo was right.

Could Father have cast some spell upon me, which was beginning to wear off in his absence?

"Yes. It is a beautiful dream," I replied softly, still haunted by the ghostly memory of that tremendous desire to be free that had possessed me when I met Caurus's gaze. "Someday it will be true, Caurus. Someday . . . but not today."

Caurus shrugged. "Dreams are what keep us going. We must have beautiful dreams, or we would wake up one day and realize we have nothing."

WE had come to the spiral staircase and now soared down, whipping about the tight turns. I held on to both the carpet and my flute, while praying my stomach would stay in my body, rather than continue on its present course and fly out of my mouth. Eventually, we reached the bottom and, after a heart-wrenchingly close encounter with the wall, zipped down the underground passage toward the Vault.

"Caurus," I asked presently, when my internal organs had settled back into their proper spots, "if I ask you something, will you keep it to yourself?"

Caurus laughed. "No, Milady, that is quite beyond my ability. It is the nature of winds to gossip and spread rumors. I could not keep myself from doing so if I wished to, which I do not."

"An honest answer," I replied, amused.

"I am accorded an honest fellow."

"I've heard you called a thief," I teased.

He laughed merrily. "Not my fault if people don't secure their things, and they get swept along as I blow through!"

I laughed, too. We had known each other a long time, Caurus and I, and something about his good humor always brought out my lighter side. Maybe it was because he had been my friend and companion when I was but a tiny child. Ariel had always been Father's personal servant, constantly at his beck and call, and the lesser sylphs, such as Gooseberry and Peaseblossom, were often about tasks of Father's devising. Caliban was my playmate, too, in those early days, but he was brutish and ignorant, and Mab did not come to work for us until over two hundred years later. Even then, I did not know him well until he incarnated into a body, which was during the first half of the 1940s.

Back in my childhood, Father had not yet bound Caurus. He was free to blow and gust where he willed; yet he came of his own accord to play with me: ruffling my hair, whispering me tales from foreign lands, and singing me lullabies as I drifted off to sleep. During the later years, after we left the island, I saw less of him. By then, Father had bound him, and he, too, had tasks to perform. Yet, when we did meet, he was always as kind and cheerful as ever. Even if a hundred years had passed since last he watched by my bedside, he never failed to sing me a lullaby before he departed.

"Caurus, as you are an honest fellow," I asked seriously, "answer me truly. If I were to set all you Aerie Ones free, could you keep your people from harming mankind?"

Caurus was silent for a long time. Finally, he replied, "No. I doubt I could. I understand now, about humans. Their bodies are so fragile, they tear so easily. But my people, my sylphs and Aerie Spirits, they do not understand this."

"If your people, all your sylphs and spirits and elementals, had a stint in a body such as you have had . . . would that help?" I recalled Mab's conversation with Mephisto's maenad. "Would you remember afterward?"

"*Ja,*" Caurus replied slowly. "We think differently outside these fleshy shells, but we do not forget. All those of us who have lived as men are changed—except Boreas, and even he is not as fierce as he once was. We are wiser in unexpected and uncanny ways."

Hearing Caurus's answer, I again admired my father's foresight in incarnating the troublesome Northerlies, but my veneration was tainted by an unpleasant feeling in the pit of my stomach. Whose side was my father on? What was he really up to?

I had been certain that none of us would ever traffic with dark powers—after all that we had seen! Apparently, I had been wrong about Mephisto. Could I have been wrong about Father, too? But Father was the one who set the standard for the rest of us. If he favored the infernal powers, why teach us to loathe them?

More than ever, I wished I knew what he had been doing when he accidentally released the Three Shadowed Ones. Was he attempting to revive Gregor? If so, where was Gregor's body?

TO reach the Wintergarden, we had to pass through the Vault. Father has since agreed this was a design flaw. His original idea had been to secure the doorway that led toward Fairyland with all the other magic talismans and guard them simultaneously. In theory, this was not a bad thought. In practice, however, it meant we had to open the Vault doors every time we needed to go to the Wintergarden.

Every time we opened the door of the Vault, we weakened its wards and made it more likely that something might break in. Just walking around in the Vault could disturb who-knows-how-many things that should be left dormant. It would have been better to put the gateway to Fairyland elsewhere and guard it separately.

Also, in retrospect, it would have been wiser to have the Vault as far from the entrance from Fairyland as possible, just in case something ever made it through the heavy door coming the other way. Father had compiled a list of improvements he hoped to add next time we rebuilt, including a supernatural "airlock," to make it easier to come and go and a separate facility for the gates to Fairyland, but for now, we were stuck with what we had.

It took us fifteen minutes of hard work to open the huge wrought-iron door. There were locks requiring keys, bolts to be slid, combination locks to be spun, and magical protections to be carefully removed. All of this had to be accomplished in the correct order. Worst of all, every second the door remained open, the magic gathered within the Vault lit up the supernatural world like a beacon, broadcasting to any and all spirits within thousands of miles that here lay a stockpile of eldritch power.

Remembering the lesson of the Great Hall, where Mab and I had the door open while we were inside, and this had allowed the incubus Seir of the Shadows to enter, I was determined not to make that mistake again. The moment we were within, we repeated the various steps to lock the door and secure the wards—this time with us inside. Hopefully, we had acted quickly enough.

Within, the Vault was organized into four wings or chambers, laid out like an *X,* with a rotunda at the center. Phoenix lamps crackled on the ceiling; each burning feather provided light to a section while scenting the otherwise stale air with its pleasant cinnamon odor. Of the five feathers, one had recently crumbled into ash and had not yet rejuvenated itself. This cast one arm of the *X* into darkness. Luckily, the dark chamber was not the one we needed.

When the great wrought-iron door was secured once again, I headed to the Treasure Chamber, which housed the doorway that led to Fairyland and to the far portions of Father's mansions. It stood toward the back, covered by a silk curtain. As I drew back the curtain, revealing a threshold plated in ivory, I heard the echo of Caurus's footsteps as he wandered off, exploring a different wing.

His voice floated back to me. "Oh *ja!* What a treasure trove! This sword is fascinating! It is supported by rainbows!"

"That would be *Kusanagi,*" I called back. "Do hurry, Caurus, we still have a while to go. There can be time shifts once we go through the Fey Threshold. I want to be back in time to meet Mab when he returns."

When he did not answer immediately, I went back to find him in the Weapons Chamber, surrounded on three sides by swords and other arcane weapons, each in its own glass case. He stood before a case containing an elegant katana wrapped in silk. Where a slim portion of the shining blade was visible near the hilt, a tiny rainbow arced beneath it. Caurus gazed at it in rapt adoration.

"It is beautiful! I love rainbows. What did you call it?"

"*Kusanagi, the Grasscutter.* It is one of the three hereditary treasures of Japan, given to the Japanese people by Amaterasu, their sun goddess and the ancestress of their emperors."

"*Ja!*" He stroked his pointed chin. "If it is so important to them, why is it here?"

"During the battle of Dannouru in 1185, the losers threw it into the sea rather than surrender it to the winners. Father had Mephisto's mermaid fish it out."

"You should rename it the *Bifrost Blade.* That would be more fitting for such a fine sword! And this one? Ugh!" Caurus had turned to peer into a smaller glass box containing a knife. A drain leading from the box to the floor below carried away the blood that oozed constantly from the corroded blade.

"That's the knife that stabbed Julius Caesar." I stepped up beside Caurus to see it more closely and then winced and drew back. The blade was unpleasant to the eye and exuded a menacing air.

Caurus halted before his hands touched the next case. A biting cold radiated from it, and its glass was misty with frost.

"This one is cold!"

"*Laevateinn.*" I spoke the name with a certain amount of reverence. I had seen what it could do.

"The Wounding Wand! Here?" Caurus whistled and swore in some language I did not know. "This is the sword the god Loki forged upon the gates of Niflheim? How did you come to own it?"

"In some tales, it is *Laevateinn* rather than *Twilight* that Surtur wields at Ragnarok. Father thought it best to take it out of circulation, just in case." I paused, shivered, and added, my voice low, "Erasmus used to fight with it."

Caurus goggled, amazed. "How could he, a mortal, pick it up without perishing?"

"With his Urim gauntlet."

"Oh. *Ja.*" Turning, his gaze fell on a tall spear with runes carved in its battered shaft. "By Thor! It's *Gungnir!*"

"Shouldn't you say, 'By Odin, it's *Gungnir*,'" I teased, but Caurus was too awestruck to notice. Reaching out tentatively, he touched the tip of a single finger to the rune-carved shaft and quickly yanked it away again.

"This is a mighty spear," he cried. "It cannot miss its mark, so long as the wielder names his target!"

My smile faltered, and I examined the spear more closely. "We didn't have *Gungnir* last time I was here. Where did it come from?"

I looked around the armory and saw many pieces I did not recognize. Some of them I knew from legend, such as *Gungnir* and the sword *Durandel,* but they had not been here last time I visited, back in the mid 1960s. Where had they come from? With Gregor dead, Theo retired, Mephisto mad, Cornelius blinded, and Titus seldom traveling, who was bringing Father new talismans?

I began prowling around the other chambers of the Vault. The second arm, the one that was currently dark, was known as the Elemental Chamber. Within it, barely visible in the dim light from the central rotunda, stood four pedestals. Three of them had large copper pots topped with lead that bore the mark of the Seal of Solomon. The fourth had been empty as long as I could remember. Each pedestal was surrounded by pentagrams and other arcane symbols of protection. Along the wall, a shelf held vials, rings, and lamps containing djinn, efretes, and genies bound either by Solomon or by my brother, Gregor. I peeked around a bit, but saw nothing that was obviously new.

Caurus, who had followed me in, saw the copper pots and took a careful step backward.

"The Kings of the Elements," he whispered softly, his eyes widening almost comically. "The kings trapped by Solomon!"

"Only three of them: Iblis, King of Flame; Makosh, Queen of the Earth; and Triton, King of Water."

"Where is our liege?"

The fourth king should have been Ophion, called the consort of Eurynome, though in truth, he was more like Her bodyguard.

"He should rest here." I gestured with my flute toward the empty pedestal. "But I don't know where Father actually put him. I've never even seen his jar. Perhaps Father fears that I might feel obliged to free him, out of loyalty to my Lady, and therefore hid him from me. I don't know."

We left the Elemental Chamber and continued clockwise. The Treasure Chamber contained a plethora of new pieces. In addition to objects I knew well—the mermaid's cap, the tarnhelm, a series of clay jars holding the innards of the great pharaoh Ozymandius, the Brisingamen necklace, and the Cauldron of Rebirth—there were a number I did not, including a mottled rock on a velvet pillow, a huge horn carved with Viking runes, a gleaming golden ring with a plaque that read, RHINE GOLD—that was what became of the dwarf king Alberich's treasure! I felt a moment of pity for his brother Mime, who had spent the last several decades clapped in irons for the alleged theft of it—a crown that shone with a pale, starry light, and a full-sized donkey of gold standing upon a golden circle of floor surrounded by an oval trench filled with a black liquid. Pinned to the side of the donkey was a sheet of gold with a message carved into it that read, DO NOT TOUCH!!!

Joining me, Caurus moved around the room, poking at things and sniffing them. He moved gingerly around the donkey, careful not to touch it, but he sniffed all of Ozymandius's organ jars and would have stuck his head in the Cauldron of Rebirth had I not shouted a warning. As I knelt to retrieve the key to the Fairyland door from its secret location, he squatted before a clay amphora painted with Orpheus and his lyre on one side and Hercules in his lion skin on the other. Beside it rested a ladle made of a horse's hoof and a narrow trough lined with overlapping scales of horse hoof.

"What is in here? Smells . . ." He leapt back, rubbing his nose. "Frightening!"

"Water from the Styx," I replied, chuckling. "Legend says it was brought back by Orpheus, though it was most likely Hercules who fetched it. Apparently, that jug has belonged to the *Orbis Suleimani* for a long time. It's nearly empty now. Shame there's no way to replace it. Styx water is so useful."

"What is it used for?" asked Caurus, still rubbing his long nose, which I suspected was mildly numb.

"Swearing oaths and making things invulnerable. That trough to the right? Logistilla ladles a bit of the Styx water into it. Then, she runs a thread through those notches at either end. That's how she made our invulnerable garments." I brushed my fingers across the satiny cloth of my emerald tea dress.

"Ah! Like Achilles." Caurus nodded. "He gained his invulnerability when his mother dipped him in the Styx. Only she forgot his ankle, poor tyke."

Chuckling, I pointed at the black moat around the golden donkey. "It also makes a superior ward. Neither the living nor the dead can cross it, just like the River Styx. Come on." I stood. "I want to glance in the last wing before we go."

The fourth wing, the Holy Chamber, was much as I recalled it. The breastplate of Moses's brother Aaron, with its decorations of shining Urim, hung on the wall. Beside it stood an entire suit of Urim, a glimmering metallic substance of gleaming silver-white. This armor, which once adorned a warrior angel, was missing the helmet, the breastplate, and the right gauntlet. The pressure of our footsteps upon the floor disturbed its stand, jiggling the Urim plates and causing them to ring like chimes.

On a table in the middle of the room rested a cart wheel made by the carpenter Joshua Ben Joseph, a tent made by the tentmaker Saul of Tarsus, and a net once used by Simon Bar-Jonah and his fellow fishers. The tent made by Saint Paul and the net that had once belonged to Saint Peter were ancient and delicate. Only the best efforts of science and magic had preserved them through the long years. The cart wheel made by Our Lord, however, was as sturdy and fresh as if the Savior had just finished planing it yesterday. It even smelled newly carved. There was something inspiring about its well-crafted simplicity. I always found it pleasant to gaze at it.

The last item on the table was a stand designed to hold the original Scepter of the Pope, made from a piece of the True Cross. The stand was there, but as I admired it I saw to my great dismay that the scepter was missing!

"Milady!" Caurus, who had bent down to examine the shimmering Urim greaves, leapt to his feet. "In the dark room! Something moves!"

I spun around. Within the darkened Elemental Chamber, I caught a glimpse of crimson eyes and a tiered opera cloak. Seir!

"You!" I cried. "What have you done with the Scepter of the Pope with its piece of the True Cross?"

Seir of the Shadows let out a peal of laughter. "Sweet Darling, I could no more carry away a scepter containing a piece of the True Cross than you could eat the sun! I know not whither it went."

The demon stepped forward from the shadows, revealing his inhumanly handsome features. His sharp horns now gleamed in the phoenix light. In his hand, he held a black staff cut with red runes, from which puffs of darkness billowed. I caught a whiff of brimstone.

"Grave robber!" I accused.

The incubus raised his hands, feigning innocence. "Dread Prospero opened the coffin. We merely took what was ours."

"Yours? How so? And where is my father? Is he . . ." I faltered.

"Dead?" he paused, red eyes glittering. "Alas for him, he is quite alive. He is held prisoner."

"Is he well?"

"He endures his torture bravely."

"Torture!"

"He could avoid all this unpleasantness, if he merely told us what we wish to know."

"Which is?"

Seir's scarlet eyes glittered. "Do you wish to tell us what your father will not, Darling? If you do, he can be set free from the Torturers who torment him." He drifted closer, emerging out of the darkness. "Shall we embrace and whisper secrets to each other while we share what pleasures we may? You need not fear me. I will be gentler than summer rain."

His sweet words and perfect face worked upon me like a narcotic. My mind swam and unpleasantly alluring images began crowding my thoughts. Desperately, I wished I had salt, or an athame, or water from the Styx, anything with which I might draw a ward between us, except Seir was one of those rare creatures who could cross the Styx. So, Styx water would not do.

A stab of fear numbed my limbs. I recalled Father's dissertation on the effect of demons on the human soul. Could exposure to Mephisto be weakening my defenses against the incubus? I did not recall feeling so vulnerable last time we met.

With a snort of amused annoyance, I recalled why. I dared not look away from the demon, even for an instant, so I prayed with my eyes open, calling upon my Lady for her protection. Like a cool autumn wind, Her answer blew the cobwebs of the demon's ensnarements from my mind, leaving me calm and alert.

My thoughts clear again, I turned my attention to defending the vault. Lightning symbols carved into the wall at various intervals marked places where Father had hidden electric batteries as part of the Vault defenses. I could draw from these nodes to cast lightning bolts with my flute. Lightning would harm the demon, but it would also damage a great many other things here, some of which were invaluable or would be dangerous if unleashed from their protective wardings.

Caurus stepped before me and raised his hornpipe, which was similar in nature to my flute, except it commanded only the winds and airy servants of the Northwest Wind.

The demon smiled indulgently and leaned upon my brother's staff. "Trouble us not, Little Spiritling, you have no power here. You are underground, locked away from the sky. No winds will answer your call."

Caurus eyed the walls of the Vault nervously, as if only now realizing that we were cut off from his element. I prayed he would not become claustrophobic. I had seen that happen to Aerie Ones. He held his ground, however, and said in a voice that was loud, if a bit shaky, "Keep your distance, messenger fiend. Milady has nothing to say to you!"

"Oh, but she does," the incubus said as he leaned against the threshold of the darkened Elemental Chamber. "Or at least, she has things she would hear me say to her." To me, he murmured in his syrup-sweet voice. "Send him away, that we might disport ourselves together. Or, if it would please you, he may join us. It matters not to me."

This time his blandishments had no effect upon me. Frowning sternly, I pointed two fingers at the nearest lightning symbol, then raised my flute to my lips.

"No! Wait!" Seir cried, alarmed. "I will answer your question!"

I hesitated, torn. At this moment, I had the advantage. If I waited, he might catch me unaware. On the other hand, I was mightily curious about what Hell wanted from my father. Curiosity won out. I lowered the flute.

"Tell me."

"What we seek from the Dread Magician Prospero is the secret of unbinding our more unfortunate brethren."

"Unbinding who?"

"Our fellows whom Prospero bound. We cannot free them, and he will not tell us how to accomplish it."

"What brethren of yours has Father bound? You mean someone in there?" I gestured toward the Elemental Chamber.

"How innocent you are." The incubus wet his black lips with a scarlet tongue. I raised the flute again. "Ah, yes. Well . . . perhaps, I should start at the beginning. . . .

"During King Solomon's reign, he lost his throne to the great devil Asmodeus for a space of three years, during which Asmodeus impersonated the wise king and performed many blasphemies in his name."

"Yes, I've heard that," I replied. "Asmodeus stole his ring, and Solomon had to get it back before he could reclaim his kingdom. Meanwhile, Asmodeus built temples to devils and false gods in Solomon's name."

"Exactly so." Seir smiled. "You are so wise, my Incomparable. What is known only to a few is this: After King Solomon regained his ring, he did not return immediately to his throne. Instead, he descended into Hell, claiming to be Asmodeus. Since it was known that Asmodeus was impersonating Solomon, this subterfuge succeeded, for we demons did not expect a mortal to walk willingly into the maw of the Inferno.

"Posing as the Great King Asmodeus, one of the Seven Rulers of Hell, Solomon called up all manner of wicked spirits and used his unaccursed ring to compel them to swear allegiance to him and to cease acting in accordance with their wicked nature. Once this was done, Solomon moved among the demons themselves, tricking nine of the greatest lords, those known for doing the most harm to mortal men, into his service.

"Solomon then smuggled these nine great demons out of Hell and bound them into nine scrolls. He put these scrolls into the keeping of a secret society created to watch and guard them, a living ward that he called his Circle."

"The *Orbis Suleimani*," I murmured. "The Circle of Solomon."

"We Infernal Ones eventually discovered the whereabouts of the missing lords. With our help, they nearly escaped, but the Circle of Solomon, the *Orbis Suleimani,* as you call them, discovered our attempt and bound the demon lords anew into great tomes.

"Solomon's heirs were vigilant, but where mortals are concerned, time is always on our side. We never grow bored or tire of our efforts to corrupt— just as I will never grow bored or tire of you, once you yield to my enticements. The very foundations of the Earth will shake from the fervor of our passion. Stars will collide and a new constellation will be born to celebrate the pleasure of our union."

"Shall I blow him to Kingdom Come? Not a pleasant place for demons, I hear," asked Caurus, holding his hornpipe just before his lips. Apparently, he felt there was something he could do down here, despite Seir's claims otherwise.

"If he doesn't get back to the point, be my guest," I replied grimly.

"We worked our influence upon Solomon's heirs," Seir continued, smiling graciously. "The *Orbis Suleimani* grew vain and corrupt. They began listening to the whispering of the tomes, to accept gifts the trapped demons offered, thus loosening the bonds binding the great lords of Hell.

"After centuries of waiting, our patience was rewarded. Two brothers came along who were ideal for our purposes. One was petty and power-hungry, the other obsessed with the pursuit of dangerous knowledge. The trapped Lords of Hell offered them gifts. Great King Paimon offered power over the minds of men, while King Vinae offered wisdom and secrets no mortal knew. When the brothers accepted, the demon lords began to describe the greater gifts that they could grant to the brothers, if the binding trapping the demons were released.

"All was in readiness. The day of release had been agreed upon and was approaching. The brothers were showered with gifts. Arcane secrets unknown to any other human were made known to them."

Seir paused here, his scarlet eyes glittering.

"What happened?" I asked.

"Treachery. One of the brothers betrayed us. He stole the tomes and fled."

My heart thumped oddly in my chest. An *Orbis Suleimani* member who stole great books of magic and fled? That sounded uncomfortably familiar. Unbidden, the memory rose of Uncle Antonio upon the battlefield in Milan, clad in his splendid armor, accusing Father of having stolen tomes of power from the *Orbis Suleimani*.

Could the pair of wicked brothers Seir spoke of have been Uncle Antonio and Father? If so, despite Father's equivocal comment to me about which one of the two of them—Antonio or himself—would be more likely to take what was not his, Father must have been the brother who fled with the books.

If so, what caused his change of heart? Why had he decided not to go through with freeing the demons?

I recalled warm nights upon the bluffs of Prospero's Island during which my father had spoken of his great love for my mother and how it had altered the course of his life. Could my mother's love have caused him to break faith with the demons? That was a lovely thought indeed, one that lived up to all my childhood ideals about my parents' marriage.

And what of these demon tomes? Were they the books of magic I remembered from my childhood?

Cold fingers of dread touched my spine. "These books . . . back on St. Thomas, you claimed Father transformed them into . . ." I looked at my flute.

"Into staffs," purred the incubus.

"Merciful Heavens!" I whispered in Italian.

"Exactly, Sweetest darling. Staffs such as the one you hold in your hand, which, unless I am mistaken, is the aforementioned Great King Vinae himself." Leaning toward the flute, Seir called. "Greetings, old friend, or should I say, old adversary? For what demon is friend to another, we who strive constantly against each other, seeking each to better his own position in our infernal home?"

"What a horrible way to live," Caurus murmured.

I stared at my flute, repulsed by the very instrument that, until this moment, had been so dear to me.

Could this be the secret Baelor had hinted at, the cause of my family's destruction? I recalled his inhuman voice: *I know . . . why Theophrastus's wrath leads him to embrace death, and Titus grows too slothful to maintain his vigil; why Logistilla is consumed by envy, while despair gnaws upon the innards of the once-proud sorcerer.*

Suddenly, I remembered our victory celebration at the *Hound and Eagle* after our successful raid on the Vatican when we stole the magic that had been collected by the popes of old. Fierce Titus, who carried the *Staff of Silence,* was unusually reticent that night, a quality that grew in him in ensuing years until sloth became his ruling vice. Good-natured Theo, whose staff caused devastation, provoked a bar fight. Was not wrath one of Theo's greatest vices, one he retired partially in hopes of overcoming? Mephisto, whose staff summons, found himself irresistible to ladies, a trait that has increased with each passing year. And Father had taken note of all this and frowned.

He knew! Father knew the price we paid for carrying these staffs! Father, who constantly emphasized how our family fought for Heaven and the preservation of Solomon's legacy; Father, who had written such graphic descriptions of the distortions that exposure to the presence of demons caused to the human soul!

But, if he knew, why did he give us the staffs? Why did he not tell us, warn us? Could it be he, too, had been corrupted by the staff he carried for so many years: the *Staff of Persuasion,* which can alter a man's mind? Could the demons finally have succeeded with him in his age, where they had failed in his youth?

If so, why did he now allow himself to be tortured, rather than revealing the method for releasing the demons, which presumably would have allowed the Three Shadowed Ones to free the demon trapped in Gregor's and Mephisto's staffs?

Of course, the incubus could be lying. . . . I stared at the four-foot length of demon-infested wood I had formerly called my beloved flute and shuddered as I wondered what ill effect its proximity had worked upon my soul.

"Milady! The Kings!"

In staring at my flute, I had taken my eyes off the incubus. My head snapped up in time to see Seir bring the butt of the *Staff of Darkness* down upon the brittle lead seal on the copper pot that held the King of Fire.

The Staff of Eternity

The ancient lead seal broke with a resounding crack. With a tremendous cry of exultation, the King of Fire rose from the copper jar that had been his prison for nigh unto three thousand years. His coal-black eyes hung in the midst of the mass of flames that made up his body. Heat radiated from him like water cascading over Victoria Falls.

"Iblis al-Shaitan am I, King of Flame! Lord of Djinn! Master of Salamanders! Prince of Efreeti! Look upon me and tremble!" he cried in a great voice.

Seir of the Shadows smiled. "Welcome, your majesty, tarry but a moment while I free your companions."

Iblis al-Shaitan's fiery body moved rapidly between Seir and the copper pot containing the Queen of Earth. The intense heat radiating from his body scorched the floor and wall near the djinn to a sooty black and filled the Vault with the smell of burnt paint. The incubus, however, did not seem disturbed. Perhaps he was used to fires hotter still.

"Cease! Their freedom does me no honor. If they are bound, and I am free, I will be the greater. Fire will rule Earth, Water, and Air." The coal-black eyes shifted amid the flames. "Where is Air?"

"I know not, Great Lord. The pot containing the King of the Air was not here when I arrived," Seir replied.

"Worship me!" boomed the King of Fire. "Why do you not bow down? Press your face to the floor!"

"Who? Me?" The incubus laughed. "I am no subject of yours, Fire-King. I am Seir, called 'of the Shadows,' a Mighty Prince of Hell. I myself govern twenty-six legions of spirits. I bow to none but the Seven Rulers of Iniquity themselves."

"Bah! The Great Seven." The flames of his body grew brighter until he glowed like a stoked furnace, and the air around him wavered from the heat. "I, Iblis al-Shaitan, am mightier than the Lords of Hell. Lucifer himself is but my servant. I was created by the Hand of Allah himself, from a pure and smokeless flame of fire! Into my keeping, he gave all vessels of crude clay who were not faithful to his Law."

"As you say." Seir nodded politely. As the King of Fire swept down upon him, he added quickly, "Perhaps you should concern yourself with them."

And he pointed at us.

CAURUS and I had not been idle while the supernatural entities quarreled. Caurus had grabbed the long shield and remaining gauntlet of shining Urim from the stand holding the angel's armor. Meanwhile, I knew I had to stop Seir before he broke open another seal, and the only means I had at my disposal was the lightning-throwing power of my demon-infested flute. I wanted to draw electricity for the blast from the node nearest to him, to minimize the damage, but as the Elemental Chamber was dark, it took time to figure out where the electrical nodes might be and to direct my flute—or the demon within it—to the correct spot.

As I was peering across the rotunda into the semi-darkness, trying to catch a glimpse of a lightning glyph as the Fire-King's body illuminated various sections of the wall, Caurus whispered, "Milady, what is your plan?"

"I want to dispense with Seir first," I whispered back. "Even if I don't manage to strike him, he will flee. Teleporters are like that." One had only to say 'boo' to Ulysses, and he would be halfway across the continent. "Seir might come back, but at least it should give us a few minutes to deal with the King of Flame."

"How do we do that?"

"I'm hoping something in the Weapons Chamber will stop him, if I can get over there."

"I will distract him!" Caurus swung his ice skates from his shoulder and tossed his scarf atop them, then slipped his right arm into the strap at the back of the long Urim shield. Glancing down at his knitted sweater and his large capable hand, he sighed. "I do hope this body does not get damaged beyond repair. I've gotten rather fond of it over the years."

"I as well, Caurus," I replied with sympathy. "I as well."

The King of Fire moved, and his flame lit a glyph. I pointed two fingers at the glyph and rapidly gestured toward the incubus. As I lifted the mouth-piece of the instrument to my lips, a wave of revulsion toward the demon within swept over me. I hesitated. It was at that moment that Seir had directed the Fire-King's attention toward us.

Pressing the demon-flute against my mouth, I blew a sharp trill. With a thunderous crack, a fork of blue electricity leapt from the wall, striking at the incubus, who vanished into the shadows like a dream.

"One down, one to go," I whispered, wiping the sweat from my forehead. Even where we were, a distance from the Fire-King, the air was becoming unpleasantly warm.

Iblis al-Shaitan poured out of the Elemental Chamber, swelling until the pure flame of his body filled the central rotunda, blackening the walls, which had begun to smoke. He glared down at us, his ebony eyes gleaming.

"Vile half-breed!" his words dripped with disdain. "Accursed *Nephilim*! Your very existence sullies Allah's kingdom!"

"I care little for your assessment of my nature, Fire-King," Caurus replied bravely, though I noted his limbs were trembling. Iblis was a far greater spirit than he, and winds were not particularly good at putting out fires. He lifted the invulnerable shield and stepped forward. "I am Caurus Skeiron Boreal, Lord of the Northwest Winds!"

The Flame-lord's eyes shifted to Caurus. He laughed contemptuously, "Little spirit, you are almost too small to concern me, save that every living thing should bow before me. Bow down now and worship me, and I will spare you."

"Every living thing?" Caurus laughed. "Been in that copper can a little too long, haven't you, Flame-Face! Begun to pickle?"

"Impudent fool!" roared the King of Fire.

Iblis al-Shaitan dived into the Holy Chamber, the towering holocaust of his body bearing down upon Caurus, who ducked behind his invulnerable shield. Fire curled around the edges of the shield. Caurus cried out in pain and I smelt the unpleasant odor of burning hair.

Determined that Caurus's bravery should not be in vain, I moved quickly away from the Holy Chamber, skirting around the intense heat of the Fire-King toward the armory. His burning body was eerie, for his flames were pure and silent. No smoke issued from them, neither did they crackle. Where the wall still smoldered from the heat of his passing, however, smoke billowed up, choking the rotunda with ash. I struggled not to cough.

A loud snapping-crackle behind me caused me to whirl about. The table in the Holy Chamber was aflame. To my horror, the tent made by Saint Paul and Saint Peter's net ignited. In a single instant, the fire consumed the two-thousand-year-old relics that had once belonged to the most holy men who ever trod the Earth. Helpless, I saw the tongues of fire began licking the Savior's wheel.

Unable to watch, I turned away and ran the rest of the distance to the Weapons Chamber. Behind me, to my great joy, I heard Caurus's voice.

"Look!" he shouted, amazed. "The God of the Bloody Cross is more powerful than the Lord of Djinn!"

"Arrgghhh!" The cry of Iblis al-Shaitan shook the room, followed by a burst of heat worse than any that had come before. Caurus screamed.

Glancing over my shoulder, I saw the Fire-King reeling back, clutching the simple cart wheel. No matter how much flame radiated, the wood remained untouched. As Iblis ranted and shouted, I saw Caurus, his sweater burned in places and his straw-colored hair singed black, slip away into the Treasure Chamber. My heart leapt into my mouth as I pictured all the precious fragile things in that wing, but there was nothing I could do. Plunging into the armory, I glimpsed Caurus crouching behind the golden donkey and heard him calling out taunts again.

Within the armory, I glanced rapidly from one case to another. Which of these legendary weapons could help me? *Dyrnwyn* could burst into flame, not a wise choice for fighting the King of Fire. *Durendel?* It could cut a man and his horse in half with a single blow but that would not stop a flame. Brutus's knife? Useful for killing friends, but hardly helpful here. *Kusanagi?* It was so sharp it cut water droplets in the air, forming rainbows, and it could cut grass, rare in a medieval sword, but I had never heard that it had supernatural powers beyond these. *Fragarach? Tyrfing? Nothung?* Fine swords all, but not what I needed now.

Gungnir? According to legend, Odin fought ice giants and fire giants. Tybalt claimed Odin, Jupiter, Zeus, and Alastor the Elf-king were all the same individual. Could the spear of the King of Gods and Elves stop the King of Fire?

I yanked *Gungnir* from its stand and hefted it. It was heavy and smelled of old ash. Behind me, Caurus screamed. As I turned to investigate, I smelled newly lit matches.

Seir?

Taking no chances, I threw the god's spear. I had no particular skill as a spearmaiden, but with this spear, skill was not required. I did not even need to know where the target was.

"*Gungnir!* Strike the incubus!"

Swift as a swallow, the rune-marked spear flew through the air and, swerving to find its target, struck the sable demon through the shoulder, pinning him to the wall.

Seir swore softly. Wincing, he pulled the shaft from his body.

I remembered a lesson long ago where Father had lectured me on the talisman of the Norse Gods. One of the gifts of *Gungnir*, if I recalled correctly, was that it would return to the hand of its wielder. The moment the spearhead was free of the incubus's shoulder, its tip dripping with bright red blood that matched Seir's eyes, I reached up, shouting:

"*Gungnir,* return to me!"

The great spear tore itself out of Seir's grasp and flew across the room to my hand. I threw it again, calling, "*Gungnir,* strike the incubus!"

Seir faded into shadow. The great spear hung in the air. Twice, the spear turned, speeding toward some corner where shadows gathered. Each time, Seir vanished before it could strike him. When the demon did not return again, the spear remained hanging in midair, humming with eldritch power as it awaited its prey.

Across the rotunda, in the Treasure Chamber, a scene of horror was transpiring. Caurus's ruse had worked, and the Lord of Djinn had brushed against the golden donkey of King Midas in its effort to reach Caurus. His outer flames were turning into gold. As quickly as he transformed, however, the heat of his body melted the gold, showering the molten metal across the precious talismans stored nearby.

The damage was horrifying! The silk curtain covering the Fey Threshold had burnt to ash, leaving the ivory doorway itself vulnerable. The tarnhelm and the Cauldron of Rebirth were splattered with molten gold, perhaps ruined. The heat had caused the mermaid cap, which Titus had suffered so to obtain, to shrivel away into nothing. The vessels continuing the organs of Pharaoh Ozymandius burst as I watched. His royal innards sprayed across the chamber. The amphora containing the precious water from the River Styx had spilled. Its priceless contents seeped over the floor.

The Halter of Clynoeiddyn, one of Mephisto's greatest treasures and an invaluable help in capturing magical beasts, was on fire, as was Erasmus's collection of swan and crane cloaks. The figurehead on Dagna's Harp sang a last swan song as it burned.

Tears filled my eyes. These precious things. All these beautiful precious things!

And Caurus? Where was Caurus?

Desperately, I ran back to the sword cases. There must be something here that could help me. As I looked here and there, however, nothing seemed promising. Even here in the Weapons Chamber, the air was now unpleasantly hot. Sweat ran down my face and down the back of my neck. In the distance, the Celtic harp's figurehead continued its aria. If I did not think of something quickly, this Vault would soon become my grave, for, right now, there was no way to open the door without letting the King of Fire loose upon the world.

It was possible that, even if he escaped, his previous oaths would still constrain him, but it was by no means certain. Should Iblis escape the oaths he swore to King Solomon, all fire, everywhere, would no longer be constrained to obey the laws of physics. Machines that relied upon combustion engines would not merely cease to work, they would turn on mankind. Gas mains would explode. Furnaces, dryers, and kitchen stoves would ignite, destroying the houses around them. Cars, trucks, and jets would burst into flame simultaneously.

Closing my eyes for an instant, I prayed to my Lady for guidance. Then, I spun in a circle. A refreshing coolness assailed me. Opening my eyes, I found myself standing before a long frosty case.

No! I was not going to wield that sword!

But what else could I do?

Quickly, I ran to the rotunda and peered around. On the floor of the Holy Chamber, the remaining Urim gauntlet lay where Caurus had dropped it when he fled. I sprinted across the hall and grabbed it.

With the angel's gauntlet on my left hand, I smashed the glass case that held *Laevateinn*. The *Wounding Wand* was an eerie, haunting weapon, as pale as bone. It had a cruel and curling hilt, and mist rose from the length of its fog-gray blade. Gingerly, I lifted it with my gauntleted left hand.

"*Kill. Slay,*" whispered a ghostly voice inside my head, its voice feather-soft. "*I and I alone can avenge the harm done your treasures. I will quench the King of Flames!*"

"Shut up!" I growled, terrified, and pelted toward the Treasure Chamber and its molten inferno.

THE heat at the entrance of the Treasure Chamber was unbearable and yet, despite the nigh-invulnerable gauntlet, the cold radiated by *Laevateinn* was biting and painful. There was no happy medium. Part of my body shivered and part burned.

"Eurynome!" I screamed as I charged into the Treasure Chamber and stabbed the King of Fire with the *Wounding Wand*.

The terribly cold sword struck the molten flames, and the Fire-King's body grew brighter. Terror seized me. What if that coolness I had felt had just been the cold of *Laevateinn*, and not a message from my Lady? What if the Wounding Ward could not help?

I need not have feared. Where the Wounding Wand struck the molten flames, a black smoke rose.

"Nooooo!" Iblis al-Shaitan screamed. "I smoke! My pureness has been sullied! Aiieeee!"

The Lord of Djinn's fire collapsed in upon itself, until he was no longer flame, but a solid body of dark smoke surrounded by billowing clouds of pale ash. Behind him, the pool of spilled Styx water was spreading. Despite the heat that singed my eyebrows and stifled my breath, the arm holding the sword was growing numb from cold. I drove the sword forward; the King of Fire withdrew until his trailing smoke touched the black liquid of the Styx.

"I freeze! I die! Vile abomination! What do you do to me?" the djinn cried.

"It is not him, but I!" I announced bravely. "I am Miranda Prospero, Handmaiden of Eurynome! Swear upon the Styx that you will go back into your copper pot and stay there until it is properly sealed!"

"Never! Aiiee!" His defiance turned to screams of agony as I pushed the sword deeper into his substance.

"Swear you will return to your pot and stay there for a year and a day!" That should give us enough time to figure out how to rebind him.

"Aiieei! I swear! I swear!"

As the Fire-King writhed, the cold feather-soft voice came again in my thoughts. *"With me in your hand, you have made the unconquerable Lord of Djin yield, but there are others who dare to defy you still: the Three Shadowed Ones, the wretched Caliban—should he still live, your brother Erasmus. You know the secret yearnings of your heart; together we can silence them, forever."*

Behind the Lord of Djinn, Caurus opened his mouth. A blast of Arctic wind caught up the smoke of Iblis al-Shaitan's body, and carried it out of the Treasure Chamber and back to the pedestal where the copper pot waited. A last low wail issued from the Elemental Chamber, as the King of Fire accepted his fate. Closer at hand, Caurus flopped over. His body lay burned and charred before the doorway to Fairyland.

The burning harp of Dagna uttered one last note and fell into ashes.

Quickly, I threw *Laevateinn* into the central rotunda, where it lay surrounded by mist. The floor beneath it cracked from its terrible cold. Grabbing the Urim shield that lay before Caurus's supine body, I ran to the Elemental Chamber and lay it across the mouth of the copper pot. I pinned the shield down with the Savior's wheel, which was still in pristine condition despite the Fire-King's best efforts.

As soon as this was done, I ran back to Caurus. His hair was half charred. Terrible burns marred his cheek and his shoulder. Kneeling beside him, I drew out my crystal vial and gave him a drop of the pearly liquid within. Its wondrous fragrance drove off the stench of burnt flesh and hair.

Yet, Caurus did not stir.

When the Water of Life failed to rouse him, terror gripped my heart like a giant's hand, squeezing. I shook him. I checked for breathing. There was none.

He could not be dead! Not Caurus! The Aerie Ones were immortal. Caurus was the Northwest Wind. He was a god! But Gooseberry had been an Aerie One, too, and the bullet that ended the life of his fleshy body had slain him. Was Caurus gone, too, burned to death?

Bowing my head over him, I wept.

My voice choked with sobs, I began to sing the lullaby Caurus had recited by my bedside so long ago.

Lucciola lucciola, gialla gialla
metti la briglia alla cavalla
che la vuole il figlio del re
lucciola lucciola vieni con me.

Firefly, firefly, yellow and bright,
Bridle the filly under your light,
The son of the king is ready to ride,
Firefly, firefly, come to my side.

AS I sang it the second time, in English, a voice joined me, reedy yet vibrant.

"Caurus!"

"Fear not, Milady," Caurus's inhuman voice—sounding much like the music of a hornpipe formed into words—spoke from the air over my shoulder. "I am well. My body is damaged, but will heal under your ministering. I merely came out of it to chase that scoundrel back into his pot!"

"Glad to hear it," I snapped brusquely, blushing. It was uncharacteristic of me to weep over a servant. To have been caught was unseemly.

Caurus's airy voice chuckled, "No need to be embarrassed, Milady. We all know you love us."

"I do?" I asked, astonished.

"Of course," he replied, "And we love you! Why else do you think we all work so hard?"

IN the end, I departed through the damaged Fey Threshold alone. While Iblis's oath theoretically kept him in the pot for the next year and a day, Caurus and I agreed that someone needed to stand watch until the pot could be properly sealed. Caurus returned to his body, and I gave him a second drop of Water of Life to speed his healing. He agreed to stand watch wearing the Urim gauntlet but refused to touch *Laevateinn* unless it was absolutely necessary.

I did not blame him. The sword terrified me as well. My right arm still tingled with numbness, and several times, I thought I heard its voice whispering to me, urging me to revenge. I left him standing guard with *Laevateinn,* stashed within the Urim sheath from the angel's armor, resting atop the empty fourth pedestal. The spear *Gungnir* hovered in the air nearby. It patroled the vault, still seeking its quarry, Seir of the Shadows.

LEAVING the Vault behind, I flew through the curving corridor that led to the Wintergarden. It took me a few tries to figure out how to pilot the carpet. I brushed the wall twice and nearly tumbled off once, but eventually, I got the hang of it.

I zoomed through the halls, banking and soaring. While underground corridors were hardly the sky, flying was still exhilarating. The gentle buoyant motion reminded of my recent trip through the night sky on the back of the giant black swan, which led to thoughts of Astreus. I pushed them away. The elf lord was too painful a subject, as gratitude warred in my heart with agony over his possible betrayal of my brother.

Emerging from the long dark halls, I flew into bright sunlight and took a breath of warm moist air. Beneath me stretched a lush garden. Overhead, an enormous latticework of iron and glass enclosed the entire area, creating a greenhouse, or, as we would have said during the reign of Queen Victoria, a wintergarden.

Outside, beyond the glass, lay the Faery Glade. Although it was winter outside the mansion, the gardens of the Faery Glade were in majestic bloom. Tiny winged beings, hardly larger than butterflies, danced upon the leaves, or stroked vibrant colors into the petals of the flowers. Every leaf glittered and shone with a brilliance no mortal gardens could achieve; though a few approached it, on early mornings, when sparkling with dew.

In the distance, beyond the gardens, stood the ivory curve of the gate though which lay Mommur, the seat of the elven court.

I tried to avoid entering the Faery Glade, for it was difficult to stay there any length of time and emerge unchanged. Long ago, when the Wintergarden and the grounds outside it were new to me, I fell asleep in the Glade once while reading a book. When I awoke, the little sprites had woven my hair into a faery knot, a lovely coiffure that was quite arresting to the eye. It graced my face and framed my throat and shoulders in soft silver.

I had thought the arrangement wonderfully simple, but I could never quite reproduce it. Since then, I have seldom dressed for a formal dinner or ball, including the recent festivities at Father Christmas's, without being haunted by the memory of that hairstyle, and how lovely it would have made me look. And this was just an arrangement of my hair! I shudder to think what life must be like for those who have eaten their food or drunk their wine.

The fight in the Vault had left me shaken and sore; merely entering the Wintergarden soothed my spirits. The air smelled lovely, an earthy fragrance full of spearmint and fennel. The Turkish carpet soared over the garden beds and brick paths which formed arched bridges where they crossed the quick-moving streams that flowed through the garden. Below grew thyme and tansy, St. John's wort and vervain, as well as rarer herbs whose virtues were known only to sages and mystics. Close by were healing herbs, such as rue and yarrow. A little distance away, pennyroyal and rosemary grew within a circle of brick pathway, along with another flower, a silvery-violet one, which I had not seen in some time.

Leaning from the carpet, I picked a bloom of it. It was moly, the flower the god Hermes gave to Odysseus to protect him from the shapechanging magic of the enchantress Circe. I buried my nose in its petals; its scent reminded me of barren mountaintops and olive trees.

Beyond the next rivulet grew the poisonous plants: deadly nightshade and hemlock, larkspur and foxglove, jimsonweed and its cousin, datura, the herb that figures into *The Thousand and One Arabian Nights*. To one side, away from other vegetation, a lone mandrake grew next to a large rock. The scent that hung in the air here was musky and mixed with the odor of wet dirt.

Somewhere amid these aromatic plants and deadly flowers was my father's horticulture project, the one missing piece in the jigsaw puzzle of his recent life. What this last piece would tell me, I did not know. Most likely, he had been growing appleberries or fairy-blossoms, or some other semimystical seed that would only sprout near the Faery Glade, something that bore no relation to the events on the night of the Equinox beside the grave of my dead brother.

And yet, I could not help feeling that this last piece would hold the key to the mystery of Father's purpose.

AS I knelt on the Turkish carpet, searching for some sign of a new plant or seedling, I caught a glimpse of a dark shape lurking among tall feathery ferns near the herb garden. Nervously, I noted that I was uncomfortably vulnerable. It was a long way back to the Vault, nor could I flee outside, for all around the Wintergarden lay the Faery Glade.

Not wanting to touch the demonic flute, I slid open the razor-sharp fighting fan of Amatsumaru; reflections of brightly colored petals shimmered in its moon-silver surface. Thus armed, I flew slowly toward the herb gardens, halting the carpet above the ferns. Was it Seir again? How had he gotten into this part of the house? It was extraordinarily lucky that I happened to be in the Vault when he arrived to free the Kings.

Or had Caurus and I let him in?

As I passed over the mint patch, my dark intruder rose from where he lay and stared proudly back at me with unblinking golden eyes. I relaxed, sighing. I had forgotten my familiar had his own ways of moving between Prospero's Mansion.

"You should be more observant, Handmaiden of Eurynome," said my familiar, Tybalt, Prince of Cats. "You circled twice before spotting me. What if I had been a goblin or an incubus?"

"You should be more cautious yourself, Your Highness," I replied folding the fan against my palm. "I might have cleaved you in half before I realized you were a friend."

"You? Strike me? I hardly think so." Tybalt gazed up disdainfully through the feathery ferns.

"Overconfidence killed the cat."

"Love of action brought him back," replied the black cat.

With a quick fluid motion, he leapt up through the ferns to land beside me on the carpet. He turned in a tight circle three times before settling against my leg.

"I thought it was satisfaction that brought him back," I opined.

"Depends upon which revenant cat you consult."

"Ah. Convenient meeting you here. I'm looking for Father's gardening project, the one you mentioned last time we spoke."

Tybalt washed. As I waited for his answer, the carpet floated forward, passing above the center of the garden. There, the waters of the many streams cascaded over short waterfalls to meet and mingle below in a single pool.

A low pedestal rose from the waters of the pool. On the pedestal, in a large porcelain pot, grew a single flower like a purple plume. The flower was the immortal amaranth, smaller and daintier than its mundane counterpart. In the earth from which the amaranth sprouted could be seen the gentle imprint of a deerlike hoof. As I watched, the amaranth began to tremble violently. Tybalt had crept up to the edge of the carpet and was batting at it.

"Tybalt! Those flowers only grow where Eurynome steps. They are sacred!" I snatched him up and put him on my lap.

Tybalt shrugged out of my grasp, saying, "You should not allow them to wiggle so temptingly if you do not wish them to attract attention."

"What do you suggest, that I tie them up so they cannot sway about?"

"Self-respecting passersby could then direct their attention at the dangling rope, and the flowers would be spared."

It never paid to argue with a cat.

"Father's gardening project, Tybalt?"

"Ah, yes. This way." He jumped down and began leading me through the Wintergarden.

At first, he walked casually along the brick walkways; however, he soon departed from the paths, to move amidst the greenery. He crouched and stalked, moving silently from plant to plant, almost disappearing altogether behind a rose bush or large feathery fern. He led me twice about the entire garden before coming to our final destination. I bore with him, saying nothing.

For Tybalt, there was no shorter path.

Finally, we arrived at a small area behind the linden trees, separated from the rest of the garden by an L-shaped partition of glass and iron that jutted from the outside wall. Within this private garden grew a young dogwood tree from which a branch had recently been cut. The wound had bled a rusty crusted substance that coated the bark and earth beneath it. The tree stank unpleasantly of old blood.

At the base of the trunk, something glittered amidst the roots. I wrapped my hair, which still smelled of smoke, across my nose to keep out the rotten stink and knelt to examine it. Half-buried in the dirt was a star sapphire as large as the pad of my thumb. Additional scrutiny revealed other gems, several of which were embedded into the sapling itself. Two, an amethyst and an emerald, bore the sign of a fish. I dropped the sapphire and straightened.

"What is it?" asked Tybalt. He leapt upon the sapphire and batted it about with his paw.

I pointed. "See the emerald with a fish carved into it?"

Tybalt sniffed the gems stuck into the bark. I wondered how he could smell anything other than the unpleasant rusty stink.

"It's an early Christian symbol," he replied eventually.

"Very good. These jewels once belonged to the popes of Rome. They used to decorate the Scepter of the Pope, the one made from a piece of the True Cross."

"Wasn't that one of the items your family 'liberated' from the Vatican?" Tybalt batted at the amethyst, but it would not come loose from the bark. "I thought the scepter was in the Vault. Why are its gems stuck in this tree?"

In my mind's eye, I saw eight young trees, each of a different species, growing in a circle on the island where I had spent my youth. They had not been there when I was a child, but when, many years after our escape, I returned to hunt my would-be rapist Caliban, I had come upon them. In among their roots, I had found curls of paper, the remains of Father's great tomes, I now guessed. At the time, I had not understood what I was seeing, but after hearing Seir's story . . .

I also recalled how Mab and I had come upon the alcove that housed my father's statue in the Great Hall and how, above it were the newly cut words: THE STAFF OF ETERNITY.

And, finally, I remembered a conversation with Theo, held decades ago near the banks of the Mississippi, during which he had said: "*Last time we spoke, Father declared if he could not convince me with words, he would have to demonstrate to me the foolishness of my position. But that was over a year ago, and I haven't heard from him since.*"

"This tree is the Scepter," I replied. "Father sprouted it—as once, long ago—he sprouted trees from his magic tomes to make our staffs."

"Oh? Why sprout it now?"

"What does one do with the True Cross?"

"Crucify people?" the cat suggested, rubbing his head against my leg.

I snorted. "What did my father do in September, immediately after coming here and cutting off a branch of this tree?"

"If the rumors are to be believed, he went to Elgin, Illinois, where the grave of your dead brother Gregor lies."

I squatted down and scratched him behind the jowls. As he purred. I reached out with my other hand and rubbed one of the heart-shaped dogwood leaves between my fingers. The leaf was smooth and cool.

"So. Now we know," I whispered.

"Know what?"

"What happened on the equinox."

"Which was?"

"Father used the *Staff of Eternity,* which he made by sprouting a piece of the True Cross, to open a gate to Hell—the gate through which came the Three Shadowed Ones and Ferdinand."

"But why open such a gate? Perhaps Dread Prospero enjoys being chased? If so, he need not have gone to such trouble. I could have chased him."

"Father did not go to be chased." I brushed off my skirt and stood. "He went to resurrect my brother Gregor."

CHAPTER SEVEN

The Eyrie of the Winds

I rode the flying carpet back through the long winding corridors that led from the Fairy Glade to the main house. Tybalt sat before me; his unblinking golden eyes kept careful watch over all we passed. We checked on Caurus as we came back through the Vault and assured him that as soon as Mab returned from his travels, we would send him to properly seal the jar.

When we finally arrived in the main wing, the Lesser Hall was frigid. My breath formed a misty vapor. Calling Ariel to inquire about the drop in temperature, I learned that during the few hours I spent in the Wintergarden, four days had passed in Oregon. The weather had taken a turn for the worse, but Ariel, being an airy spirit with no body, had not thought to turn up the heat. After fending off his customary inquiries as to when I would be freeing the Aerie Ones from their servitude to our family, I sent him to adjust the thermostat and to bring me some piping hot tea.

Tybalt leapt lightly from the flying carpet. I followed him, dismounting gracefully. Once back on solid ground, I wrapped myself in my white cashmere cloak, and lit a fire in the hearth, resting my enchanted flute across the mantelpiece. In doing so, I dislodged the little statuette of the elf lord Astreus from in its customary place upon the mantel. Its sapphire eyes glittered in the firelight as it fell. To my dismay, my heart leapt at the thought of him. I caught the figurine in midair and stood frowning at it.

So many questions plagued me. Had this elvish Lord of the Winds tithed my brother to Hell? Had Father sent my childhood love, Prince Ferdinand of Naples, into Hell as well, without even killing him first? I might be able to forgive my father, whom I admired for his many noble accomplishments, but not the elf lord. If he was responsible for my brother's madness, I vowed he would meet an even worse end than his current fate of being trapped in the Void on some endless errand for the Elf Queen!

Tybalt had settled onto a burgundy cushion and was washing his sleek, black, hind foot. "All this trouble you've been having—the Three Shadowed Ones chasing you and your siblings around like flustered mice—has it all been because your father wished to recover your dead brother? Why didn't Prospero ask Prince Mephistopheles to go to Hell and get Gregor for him?"

A shiver went through me, as if a troop of spiders traveled up and down my spine. Our suspicions were true. My brother was a demon.

"How did you know Mephisto was a Prince of Hell?" I asked slowly.

"Schrödinger told me."

"Schrödinger?" I asked, "When did you talk to Schrödinger?"

Schrödinger was Mephisto's familiar, although she had been called by another name in the centuries before quantum mechanics. Like me, Mephisto seldom practiced ritualized magic anymore. His familiar now acted as his secretary, reminding him of important tasks and appointments.

"Schrödinger doesn't have much to do these days. Sometimes she comes to see me," Tybalt replied.

"Doesn't have much to do . . . why? Mephisto is as confused as ever . . . was this during the period when he had lost his staff and couldn't call her?"

"She was hit by a car," Tybalt replied serenely. "Now, she's a ghost."

"Poor Schrödinger!"

When we had found Mephisto on the streets of Chicago, he had muttered something incoherent about a cat and a car. What had it been? *"A woman hit my cat with her car. She said she was sorry. Does that mean it's okay?"* It had never occurred to me he might be talking about his familiar!

"So my brother . . . really is a . . . Prince of Hell?"

"So Schrödinger claims," Tybalt washed.

"How long have you known?"

"A while."

"Why didn't you tell me?" I demanded.

The cat's golden eyes met mine guilelessly. "You never asked."

Gritting my teeth, I declared, "In the future, should you gain any information regarding my family and Powers of Hell, please consider yourself asked!"

"As you wish." Tybalt settled down and closed his eyes, a curl of sleek black fur upon the silken pillow.

"Very good." I paused. "Has there been any word from Mab?"

Tybalt opened one eye. "He has not yet returned from his last errand. What was it? Fetching the paper? Delivering parcels?" The black cat yawned.

"Why do you even bother keeping a company detective? Cats are ever so much better at finding things."

I was tempted to reply: *Because, unlike cats, Mab does what he's told,* but refrained. No good could come of my being drawn into the Mab-Tybalt rivalry.

"I sent him to investigate the latest incident of sabotage against Prospero, Inc."

"So, now he's calling it sabotage, too, is he?" Tybalt purred. "Do send by your 'company detective' with his formal apology when he returns. I promise only to tatter him a little."

I sighed. Apparently, cats had no compunction against saying "I told you so." Any rejoinder I might have made was interrupted when Ariel's fluting voice sang out, alarmed.

"Ill news, Mistress! Zephyrus and Notus have returned from their trip to the realm of the djinn, yet their news is not joyful. Angered that any lesser than the Dread Magician Prospero himself dared treat with them, the djinn showed their displeasure readily. They rended Zephyrus. Notus has conveyed him hither, hoping you, our Gracious Mistress, might spare a drop of your enchanted balm to heal his wounds, as you have done in days gone by when one of our race was in need."

"The djinn dared to attack one of mine, did they?" A smile that had nothing to do with mirth curled back my lips. "They will soon learn better! Great Prospero may be missing, Gregor may have perished, and Theophrastus the Demonslayer may be as good as dead, but Prospero, Inc. is not without its teeth!"

Rising, I headed for the eyrie. Over my shoulder, I called, "Ariel, send for Boreas!"

THE eyrie of the winds was located high in the house. A single window spanned the entire circumference of the round chamber, opening upon a landscape of clouds. Feathery cirrus, billowing cumulus, and gray-dark nimbus clouds rushed swiftly by, shifting and changing, yet ever resembling rolling mountains and gentle valleys. To the north, this rushing cloudscape parted, as the waters of a stream split about a protruding rock, around the base of an enormous black thunderhead that rose above the cloudy landscape to form a towering peak.

From the pearl-gray sky above, a huge whirling funnel of white cloud reached downward, its tip hovering just above the highest point of the majestic thunder peak. The two formed a black and white whirling hourglass, the only stable features in the otherwise ever-changing landscape. Of all the enchanted windows in Prospero's Mansion, I found this one the most eerie; this fleecy countryside was not in the waking world, but in the Land of Nod, where men wander while they sleep.

The eyrie itself had marble walls and columns. Marking the eight directions were towering throne of palest stone, each fashioned in the shape of the giant blossom most dear to the Wind whose seat it was. Ariel's beloved cowslip occupied the southeast, followed by a honeysuckle for Notus in the south, a foxglove for Afer, a snapdragon for Zephyrus in the west, a forsythia for Caurus, a crocus for Boreas in the north, and a rose for Eurus in the east. Between the crocus and the rose, Mab's daffodil had been pushed back against the wall, leaving deep scratch marks in the marble floor. In its place, a ring of chalk and salt surrounded a simple wooden cot.

Despite the eeriness of the view, or perhaps because of it, I loved this room. I could sit here gazing at the clouds of dreamland for hours. It always smelled fresh, as if newly washed by recent rain, and the place echoed with music. Today was no exception. Mournful, haunting Oriental tones swept through the chamber, accompanied by an irregular patter, much like rain on a tin roof.

So close to the realm of dreams was the eyrie that the Aerie Ones were visible to mortal eyes. They appeared as tall, overly thin, androgynous beings with long, slender fingers, billowing hair, and graceful feathered wings. A quartered livery, showing a face with puffed checks juxtaposed with a unicorn, adorned their flowing robes.

Zephyrus, usually so quick and lively, lay slumped across his snapdragon, his stormy eyes half closed, and his bagpipes abandoned on the floor beside him. Gathered about him were three of the Great Winds. Notus leaned over his wounded comrade, feeding him drops from his pot of honeysuckle nectar. His warm eyes of summer blue, usually so lucid and calm, were clouded with concern. The Southwest Wind, Afer, hovered in the cupola, gazing down with his rain-gray eyes; his pale yellow wings spread throughout the upper portion of the chamber. Eurus floated nearby playing his shakuhachi. His long unbound hair and his robes, both the color of sunrise blush, billowed in time with the Japanese flute.

The stairs came up in the center of the chamber, the trapdoor having been worked into the windrose design upon the floor. As I stepped from the stairwell and moved across the chamber toward Zephyrus, Ariel came through the trapdoor and closed it behind us. Here in the eyrie, he, too, was visible. He stood some nine feet tall, with enormous arched wings that curled around the columns. A wreath of cowslips crowned his narrow, intelligent face, from which pale blue-gray eyes, the color of early morning, regarded the wounded Zephyrus. A clarinet hung like a weapon from his belt. With Ariel's arrival, of the eight Great Winds, only the three incarnated Northerlies, Caurus, Boreas, and Mab, were missing.

I crossed to Zephyrus and lay my flute down beside the snapdragon. As I knelt beside him, my heart leapt into my throat. His long sinuous body was so badly torn that I could not distinguish his limbs from the shreds of his torso and wings. Golden ichor spurted from the long, raked, claw wounds. Where it struck the air, it hardened into chips of amber. They rained down against the stone floor, causing the *pitter-patter* I had heard. He moaned piteously, a sound reminiscent of the wind blowing among bowing willows.

Could even the Water of Life heal these wounds? Briefly, I closed my eyes and prayed to my Lady on Zephyrus's behalf.

A sense of peace came over me. Looking up again, I ran my fingers lightly over his airy body, speaking soft words of comfort. Slowly and painstakingly, he reached out long sinuous fingers and touched my face and hair. Gentle light taps, like insect's legs or the touch of a spider's web, explored my skin. I sang softly in his ear, soothing him.

"Be of good cheer, Zephyrus. Help is at hand," I promised gently. The forgotten elf figurine was still clenched in my left hand. I shoved it into the pocket of my cloak and drew out a tiny pear-shaped vial of cut crystal. Within glimmered a pearly liquid.

As I withdrew the stopper, the sweet scent filled the chamber eliciting a low chorus of *ah's* from the Aerie Ones. They watched as if spellbound as a single drop of the shimmering liquid fell upon Zephyrus's wounds.

Instantly, the long narrow rents ceased leaking their golden lifeblood and began knitting together; the Water of Life worked its balm far more quickly upon Aerie Ones than it did on bodies of flesh. Yet, after five minutes, only his shoulder and left arm had mended completely, and precious blood still flowed from the rents in his back and legs.

One drop of Water of Life was always enough to stave off death; his life was no longer in peril. However, if I left him as he was, his recovery might take weeks or even years. He might even remain permanently crippled.

I held up the half-empty vial, picturing the larger carafe in the chapel, which was also more than half empty, and began the complicated calculations to determine how long the remaining Water would last—given one drop per sibling per year, plus other necessary uses. Once it was gone, I could only obtain more by making the long arduous journey to the Well at the World's End. Now that Father had retired and turned the company over to me, it was getting harder and harder to spare the year and a day that the journey took.

From the snapdragon, Zephyrus's storm-colored eyes watched me, joyful and trusting. With a snort of self-contempt, I abandoned the calculations and pulled out the stopper again. Three more drops, for his back, legs, and right side, and Zephyrus's body knit itself back together.

Whole again, Zephyrus lifted his bagpipes and began a rousing march of gratitude. His airy companions raised their instruments and joyfully sang with him.

I sat with them, listening to their uplifting music and watching the ever-changing cloudscape. In days gone by, I would have picked up my enchanted flute and joined the celebration. Now, two things held me back.

First, traveling with Mab had made me more aware of how much the Aerie Ones resented the instrument. Second, for all my five-hundred-plus years, I had believed my flute's virtue to command wind and weather came from the fact that it had been carved from the pine in which the witch Sycorax had once trapped Ariel. Now that Seir had told me otherwise, I felt disinclined to play it.

The worst part of discovering that the power of my flute came from a demon was the shattering of my illusions. All my life I had loved this instrument, its four feet of pale polished pine, its sound, the way its music transported me beyond my mundane surroundings. In my naïveté, I had imagined that the flute somehow appreciated my affection and returned it. To discover my cherished instrument contained a creature of pure hatred bent upon my destruction broke my heart.

So I sat in silence, listening.

As their paean ended, Ariel spoke from where he sat regally upon his marble blossom throne. "Look upon our dwelling, Great Mistress, and have pity. Will not you forgive us the remaining three hundred and fifty years of our promised sentence of servitude and set us free to dwell in the sun-warmed cowslips of the fields, instead of blossoms of cold relentless stone?"

The other Aerie Ones lowered their instruments and turned their stately faces toward me, regarding me with eyes that reflected the varying moods of the sky.

Free the Aerie Ones? I considered again what I had learned from the

Book of the Sibyl. My Lady could hardly promote a slaver to the ranks of Her highest servants. After all, was She not the Living Embodiment of Free Will? It must have been my participation in the enslavement of the Aerie One race that had kept me from becoming a Sibyl all this time.

I envisioned the morrow, should I pick up the flute and snap it in two, freeing Ariel, Mab, and all their fellows. If my interpretation of the *Book of the Sibyl* was correct, it was all I needed to do to achieve my heart's desire. I saw myself as a Sibyl, with the ivory spiral mark of my Lady's favor upon my forehead. I pictured commanding the lightning, absolving bad oaths, and being able to make Water of Life at will—no more trips of a year and a day to the Well at the World's End.

If I were a Sibyl, rather than merely a Handmaiden, I would not need to remain a maiden to keep my Lady's patronage. The laughing elf lord and the dream-kiss we never actually shared danced before my eyes. Flushing, I dismissed him from my thoughts. As Astreus himself put it, elves would no more dally with mortal maids than hawks woo doves. After all these years, I would not be such a fool as to lose my heart to a creature incapable of reciprocating, especially when there was a much more promising candidate for my affections.

Five hundred years after we were so cruelly parted, Ferdinand and I would at last be free to marry. I saw us in my mind's eye, standing before the altar in the *Duomo* of Milan, the same altar where I had waited vainly for him so long ago. Hand in hand, we would pledge our vows, surrounded by the ornate marbled columns and gilded filigree of the magnificent gothic cathedral, which, even today, seven hundred years after it was built, remains the third largest church in the world.

After that? I could continue to run Prospero, Inc., while Ferdinand taught. He knew so many things of interest to modern scholars: history, Latin, Italian, sword fighting, even sailing. Perhaps, there would be children . . .

When I first discovered children, I expected soon to be a bride and a mother. I thought them the most precious things in the world. Later, when I realized there would be none for me, I thrust them from my mind. As a Sibyl, with Ferdinand as my husband, there would be nothing to stop us from having a whole parcel of little ones. With luck and my Lady's blessing, we could even raise them to treat one another more harmoniously than my siblings had. Perhaps he and I would even be blessed with perfect love such as Father had shared with my mother, before she had died giving birth to me.

A beautiful dream . . . yet, at what price?

Ariel spoke of pleasant zephyrs and cowslips. But what of Boreas? What of Afer? The storms they brought were no mild summer rains, but typhoons and tempests! Even mild-mannered Caurus had admitted that, were his followers not bound, he could not vouch for mankind's safety.

How long would it be before it began: hurricanes sweeping the sky of planes, tornados ripping roofs off schools and hospitals, tempests tossing trailers and flooding towns, cyclones knocking down skyscrapers, and twisters destroying power stations, plunging mankind into darkness?

True, the other sprits and elementals bound by Prospero, Inc. would still be obliged to carry out their contracts. Oil would be required to burn steadily, so engines would still run. The salamanders among our clients would be still required to keep their volcanoes from erupting, and those areas of ocean whose nymphs we had harnessed would still be constrained from flooding the land . . . so long as we kept our side of the bargain.

Without our airy servants, however, how could Prospero, Inc. continue to fulfill its contracts? Even if I were willing to allow mundane humans to work on our supernatural contracts, there would still be tasks only a magical creature could do. It would only be a matter of time before we failed to meet one of our delivery dates, and the *oreads* or the salamanders or the djinn or the *oni* rebelled.

Even if mankind could somehow survive the rebellion of the skies, I did not see how we could survive the desertion of the other spirits, the ones whose obedience to Prospero, Inc. contracts maintained the fragile set of conventions we called physics.

No. The price was too high. The Aerie Ones could not be allowed their freedom, nor I, my dreams of Sibylhood and marriage. Perhaps, one day, if the plan I believed Father to be hatching—to domesticate the Aerie Ones by giving them each a chance to live as a man in a fleshy body—succeeded, they could be released, and we might all achieve our hearts' desires. Until then, we would, all of us, have to remain at our current posts.

A cold wind blew across the back of my neck. The trapdoor had opened. On the top step, in the center of the chamber, stood a tall man with a black forked beard. A thigh-length coat of leather covered his immensely wide shoulders and upon his head sat a fur Cossack's hat. His face was rugged and fierce. His icy blue eyes crackled with an inner fire. He stood, arms crossed and booted feet spread apart, and surveyed the eyrie as if assessing its defensibility.

"Ah, Boreas," I smiled at him, thankful for the distraction. Unlike Mab and Caurus, Boreas's stint in a mortal body had done little to tame him. I suspected this was because, as our company enforcer, he had few dealings with human society.

"What is our mistress's wish?" he asked in his Russian accent, pronouncing "what" as "vot."

"The djinn have offended me. They wounded our herald, Zephyrus. Such effrontery cannot go unpunished."

Around me, the Aerie Ones murmured in approval.

"I understand," Boreas's voice was husky yet rich with wrathful glee. "It shall snow in the desert this day!"

He turned on his heels to leave. As he began descending the stairs, I called after him. "And Boreas, stay clear of the places where the mortals dwell."

Boreas paused and glanced back at me, a rebellious gleam in his icy eyes. By habit, my fingers opened to reach for my flute.

I stopped.

It was not just the demon in my flute that gave me pause. After all, I had been playing the *Staff of Winds* thus long. I would continue to play it whenever it was necessary to keep order, demon or no demon. No, what stopped me was the question, Was it necessary? For, in my mind, I heard again the voice of Caurus speaking from the air above my shoulder, as I had knelt beside his fire-damaged body.

"We know you love us, Milady . . . and we love you! Why else do you think we work so hard?"

If Mab hated the flute, Boreas, the North Wind, the most powerful of all airy spirits, could scarcely bear it much love. Now that he wore an earthly body, he, too, might develop abilities, such as Mab's detective skills, that the flute could not command. If I relied on brute force, the tyrant's tool, to rule the Aerie Ones, what recourse would I have once the flute was no longer an option?

I had to find a better way.

"Boreas, you would not stand by and allow an injury to one of your people to go unavenged, would you?" I asked.

"Never!" He gave a snort of indignant amusement.

"Good, but neither can I. The humans are my people. I must protect them. If they are harmed, I must avenge them. I cannot allow you to avenge your people unless you promise not to harm mine. They are not the ones who have offended us." I paused for a moment, meeting Boreas's gaze. "Is this not fair?"

Boreas's stare was as hard as Arctic ice, but I did not flinch.

"It is fair," he admitted grudgingly and began to turn away.

"Lady, are we to be set free?" Afer called curiously.

Boreas froze, his eyes burning, as he turned back to hear my answer. I paused, prayed to my Lady for inspiration, and spoke the words that came to me.

"I cannot free one of you without freeing all of you. Too many of your servants are wild and violent and would hurt my people, whom my duty requires me to defend. But if you eight, the Great Captains of the Wind, will swear an unbreakable vow upon the River Styx that you will keep your followers from doing undue harm to mankind, I will break my flute." And I lifted it up, horizontally, as if I intended to snap it in two.

In the hush that followed, my heart raced. Demon or no demon, the voice of my flute still called to me. Could I bear never to hear its song again?

Ariel's great wings fluttered in the air, each feather stirring its own eddy. He bowed his head. "From one oath to another? How is that free?"

"I must protect mankind," I repeated firmly.

Boreas stroked his forked beard. "Mistress, you ask the impossible. True, if we happen to be nearby when they misbehave, we can buffet them about, blowing them this way and hither, but beyond that, what hold has one wind upon another? No one can grasp the wind in his fingers. We cannot bribe each other. What would we offer? We cannot compel each other. How would we cause harm? You might as well ask us to blow the moon from the sky or to douse the flames of the sun."

"Very few things are impossible, Boreas, to those who are determined. When you can promise me that mankind's civilization will be safe, I will release you. Otherwise, you must wait until the appointed time. The matter is now in your hands."

Boreas glared defiantly. I gazed back, unperturbed. The other Aerie Ones, their musical instruments still in their hands, hovered about the chamber, watching us intently. Then, Boreas bowed his head, lowering his gaze.

"Fair enough, Mistress," he replied and, spinning about, his fur-trimmed leather coattails flying, he charged down the stairs and was gone.

TYBALT and I spent the rest of the day walking among the dark trees of the enclosed forest where my pet unicorns dwelt. We spoke little. After a time, Tybalt wandered off, enticed by some vole or shrew that had left its trail in the newly fallen snow. Snowfalls in December were somewhat rare this far down the slopes of the Cascades, yet it had already snowed twice this year. I hoped this was a pleasant happenstance and not a sign of yet another Priority Contract going awry.

Passing through the mansion, I continued down the long drive to the main road, I walked almost to the town; however, I had no desire to talk to people. When the snow-covered tower of the library and the white steeples of the two churches came into view, I turned and walked back the way I had come. Somewhere, car tires spun on snow.

As I breathed in the cold, piney air, my thoughts turned to my family. It had been surprisingly nice to see my siblings again, like putting on an old garment that was so difficult to don that one forgot how well it fit once one finally went through the effort. We had worked so well together when we were younger, before Father handed out our staffs. It often troubled me that those days were now lost to us.

Only for the first time it occurred to me that the future did not have to be like the past. We did not need to remain apart. Oh certainly, we might never work all together as we did in days gone by—for one thing, Gregor was dead—but I might be able to repair my relationship with some of them. Mephisto was certainly eager to be on friendly terms, and, despite her acerbic ways, I felt Logistilla had been pleased to see us. If I could find Titus and Ulysses, I suspected they would be happy to see me as well.

If I wanted any chance of gathering my remaining family in one place again, however, I first had to save Theo. If I did not act quickly, the brother I had always been closest to would die of old age. Of course, it was possible my previous attempt to interest him in life again had worked, and Theo had already left his farm and was off hunting Ferdinand. It was even possible he had taken a drop of Water of Life from the vial I left behind and was even now hale and whole, though he would still be an old man, unless he had sought Erasmus's help.

Possible, but unlikely.

If Logistilla were correct, Theo was now growing old, not because of any actual fear of Hell or hatred of magic, but because our brother Cornelius had used the *Staff of Persuasion* to enchant him, to force him to keep his foolish vow. My next step must be to confront Cornelius, to find out why he had done this terrible thing, and to make him undo it!

After that, I could follow up on some of my other suspicions concerning Cornelius's possible involvement in the disappearance of Father and perhaps even in the death of my brother Gregor, back in 1924.

Tomorrow, Cornelius would be attending the New Year's party thrown by our brother Erasmus. My brothers Titus and Ulysses, who I had not yet contacted, might put in an appearance as well. It would be a good opportunity to reestablish contact with them—and to pass on Father's message that the Three Shadowed Ones were pursuing our staffs.

Finally, I could discharge my obligation to warn my brothers and be free to turn my attention to saving Father!

I frowned, recalling the question Theo had posed to me: Why was I warning my brothers before I attempted to save Father? The answer, of course, was that Father had asked it of me, and so I had done so. Could Theo be right? Had my father used the *Staff of Persuasion* to enchant me? Was I incapable of disobeying him? Yet again, I dismissed the idea as foolishness: I would not give any credence to such a theory!

Of course, months ago, I would have sworn Father would never have attacked Ferdinand. Yet, if Ferdinand's story were true . . .

From behind me, I heard the crack of a stick.

I froze, listening. I was back amidst the trees of Prospero's Mansion, but not yet inside the stone wall that formed the circumference of the protective wards. Leaves rustled. Another stick cracked, then another. It was clearly footsteps.

Putting my hand into the pocket of my white cashmere cloak, my fingers closed around the moon-silver fan. I peered through the trees, but could see no one. Gazing back toward the house, I caught glimpses of the snow-sprinkled stone wall that girded the mansion. I gauged it at about a hundred and fifty yards away. If I ran, I could probably make it inside the wards before any intruder reached me.

On the other hand, the last time I had contemplated fleeing, the intruder had turned out to be my cat. Stepping behind a large gnarled oak, I peered in the direction of the noise and caught a ripple of gray between two beeches. The flapping movements resembled the leathery wing of an enormous bat. Memories of encounters with demons and the fates they visited upon their unfortunate victims flashed through my thoughts.

The flapping gray object revolved itself, and suddenly, my mind's eye adjusted to what I was seeing: a man, his shoulders hunched against the cold, dressed in a gray trench coat, with a fedora pulled close over a semi-shaven jaw.

"Mab!" I cried in delight, almost trembling with relief. He jerked, startled, then hurried toward me.

"Miranda!" His voice had grown harsh with cold and fatigue. He regarded me from beneath the brim of his hat.

"What are you doing in the woods? Why didn't you take the car?" I asked.

"You wouldn't believe it," he said, uttering a short laugh.

"I'll believe anything you tell me," I replied kindly. "You've proved yourself often enough."

Mab looked me over and chided. "You came out without your staff."

"It's safer in the house. Besides, I have my fan." I pulled out the weapon. It flashed in the sunlight, mirroring the snowy forest in its silvery slats. I slipped it back into my pocket.

Mab nodded and pulled his collar up against the biting cold. I noticed my teeth were chattering and said, "Come on. Let's go in."

"Just a minute," Mab replied. "There is something I should tell you."

"Yes?" A cold shiver traveled up my spine. Clutching my white cloak closer, I leaned against the great oak. "Go ahead."

Mab came closer, until he stood just beside me. His body blocked a little of the icy wind. I felt warmer.

"There is a side effect of living in these bodies Prospero didn't contemplate. After a time, even the most ethereal spirit starts developing appetites . . . fleshly appetites."

"What are you babbling about, Mab? And can't we discuss it inside?" I asked through chattering teeth.

"I don't think you understand," Mab said. Suddenly, he shifted his position so he stood before me. He leaned against the oak, one hand to either side of my shoulders, trapping me against the rough bark. "You are very lovely, Miranda, when seen through eyes grown accustomed to earthly flesh."

"Mab? You've gone mad! Get away!" and I shoved him.

He should have flown into the leaf-strewn snow. With the strength lent to me by the Water of Life, I should have been far stronger than any Aerie Spirit, even an incarnate one.

I could not even budge him.

Mab leaned forward, leering down at me. He pinned me against the sharp bark of the oak. Savagely reaching up to grab my hair, he dragged my head back. With his other hand, he pushed aside my cloak and began to slide his fingers along my thigh, lifting my skirt.

I screamed and threw my shoulders from side to side, trying to free myself, or at least grab the war fan. We struggled. The gray fedora got knocked to the snow. The eyes that leered from Mab's familiar face were reddish-orange, the same shade as the coat of an Irish Setter.

Osae the Red!

No wonder I could not budge him. Even Water of Life did not grant humans strength enough to wrestle shapechanging cacodemons!

"My Lady," I cried aloud, "aid me!"

"Yes," whispered the harsh throaty voice in my ear. "Pray to your mistress for the last time, Miranda. After today, She will acknowledge you no longer."

Terror gripped me. I fought back with all the strength I could muster, to no avail. No matter how much effort I put into twisting my shoulder away from his grip or raising my leg to knee him, he held me in place. A babe of one summer would have had more chance escaping a grown man than I had of throwing off my attacker.

A dark shadow separated itself from the trees and rushed toward my attacker. It bore down upon us like an avenging angel, crimson eyes blazing, sable capes flying against the snow-dusted trees. Before it reached us, however, an ear-splitting boom shook the oak at my back. Osae the Mab arched and screamed, his lips curled back in a snarl of agony, a splash of black ichor marring the shoulder of his trench coat.

Just as his body slumped, the racing apparition reached us. My emerald eyes met Seir's scarlet ones, and, for an instant, I thought he had come to rescue me. Then his pitch-black arms encircled the wounded cacodemon's waist, and both demons faded away like nightmares before the sun. I noticed the incubus's opera cape was still torn and matted with dried blood where the spear Gungnir had struck him. His perfect features contorted with pain as he lifted the heavy Osae.

The two Shadowed Ones were gone. Glancing about, I saw no sign of the third. I stepped away from the tree as steadily as I was able—my legs trembling uncontrollably—and peered in the direction from which the shot had come. Down the driveway, about a hundred feet away stood another Mab, the real Mab. Next to him, slowly lowering his rifle, was my brother Theophrastus.

CHAPTER EIGHT

The Ivory Door

"I can't believe you couldn't tell the difference between a demon and me!" grumbled Mab, as the three of us walked up the long driveway toward the mansion, snow crunching beneath our feet. "Would've been a big victory for the Three Shadowed Ones if the Prospero family lost the blessing of Eurynome. You're damn lucky we got here when we did, Ma'am."

"Watch your language, Spiritling! You are speaking to a lady," Theo said gruffly. He wore a bright red plaid hunting jacket and carried his Winchester over his shoulder. The smell of gun smoke still hung about him like a musk.

"I did notice you were acting oddly," I replied. My limbs still trembled, but I was pleased that my voice sounded calm to my ears. "Just hadn't occurred to me it might be the shapechanger."

"When dealing with Osae the Red, always think 'shapechanger'!" Theo shook his grizzled head. "That's what I found back in the 1620s when he was hunting me. I remember once stopping to free a half-starved cat that had gotten itself caught in a rabbit trap. The blasted cat tried to scratch my face off, then turned into a full-sized boar with beady red eyes. Are you sure you're not hurt?"

"You've asked me four times now, Theo." I smoothed back the strands of pale silver-blond hair that had escaped from their neat Grecian twist during my struggle with the demon. "I'm fine."

Theo walked a few steps in silence, then turned toward me. It was eerie to gaze at his face, with its deep lines and short-trimmed beard. He looked so old, and yet I could still see the handsome youthful Theo I remembered, lingering like a ghost behind the features of this aged stranger. My heart leapt every time I caught a glimpse of the young stalwart Theo.

"Like heck!" he swore. "Don't forget, Miranda, I've known you nearly your entire life. Your cool exterior doesn't fool me! Inside, you're seething. I've seen you arrange men's deaths because they treated you too forwardly, much less manhandled you and thrown you against a tree! You want us to throw everything else aside and devote all our energies to hunting down Osae the Red. Am I right?"

"I'm not angry, Theo," I replied, not meeting his eye.

Theo frowned at Mab. "If you will excuse us, I'd like to talk to my sister privately."

"Sure thing." Mab lowered the rim of his fedora. "I'll be inside . . . laying out the evidence bags."

Theo waited until Mab was out of earshot, before continuing. Crossing his arms, he began, "What's holding you back this time? Let me guess, it's because Father asked you to—"

I raised my finger and held it to his lips. He fell silent.

"I'm not angry." My voice sounded oddly faint. The distance up the driveway to the house seemed surprisingly long, as if the mansion were receding from us as we walked, and the forest seemed unnaturally silent. I started every time snow fell from the overburdened boughs.

Theo leaned toward me and peered at me closely, frowning. Then, he noticed my shoulders were trembling.

"Scared? You?" In his astonishment, Theo actually looked young again. "I don't believe it! But . . . why?"

I just shook my head mutely. Theo put his arm around me and pulled me roughly against his chest, hugging me. Following so closely upon the cacodemon's assault, Theo's embrace evoked a sense of rising panic, but the warmth of his body, the scratchiness of his coat against my cheek, and the familiar scents about him—gun oil, wood smoke, and a whiff of the same aftershave he had worn decades ago—broke through the cloud of fear, bringing comfort. I hugged him back, burying my face in the lapels of his hunting jacket. He patted my back.

When I could speak again, I blurted out. "Osae nearly got me! . . . If you hadn't shown up, Theo, that would have been it—for me, for all of us! And this is the third time in a month I've been attacked on my own property. Oh, and there are demons in our staffs! Father never told us!"

"You didn't know?"

I pulled back and searched his face. "You knew?"

"Certainly. Why did you think I was so adamant about giving up magic?"

"Why didn't you tell the rest of us?"

"Didn't know you didn't know. Though . . ."—Theo frowned—"now that I'm thinking about it, Father may have asked me not to mention it."

"Why?"

"He didn't explain. He merely said, 'It would be for the best.' "

"And you obeyed?" I asked.

"Of course, I . . ." He faltered, frowning.

"I obey Father for the same reason you do, Theo." I stared at where the confusion of our footprints marred the virgin snow. My voice was low. "Because he's our father."

Theo growled. "It's not the same."

I glanced back down the road toward where I had met the shapechanger, wondering what had become of the burning anger that normally would have been consuming me about now. Why was it was not rising to protect me from despair? Theo was right, I had demanded men be killed for far less than this, though Father always talked me out of it before anything came of my intent. I had even, as I recalled earlier, returned to the island of our exile to kill Caliban myself, after Father refused to slay him, so terrible was my anger at Father's misbegotten servant. I found no sign of him, though. Perhaps, left alone after Father and I departed, he had perished.

Only now, as I gazed into the bleak landscape where black tree trunks rose like prison bars against a sheet of unrelenting white, did I recall that I had only become angry at Caliban years later, after Ferdinand jilted me, after my stepmother treated me coldly, after I had grown stronger and more lonely. Back on the island, when he had seized me in his long hairy arms and dragged me down upon the loam, I had not felt anger. I had felt vulnerable and helpless, betrayed by one I had loved and trusted.

Arrogant mortal rakes, whose motive had been to slake their intemperate lusts, had earned my ire through the centuries, true, and I had wished to make an example of them. Osae's intentions, however, had been far more sinister. If Theo and Mab had not arrived, I would have been unmade, my position with my Lady revoked, Her wisdom lost to me. Without my Handmaiden status, I would no longer have access to the Well at the World's End. We would have had only as much immortal life left as Water remained in my diamond carafe and its few matching vials. By violating my virtue, Osae would have effectively slain my entire family.

Again, I trembled, and the thought that a creature as vile as Osae the Red could reduce me to this filled me with shame.

Yet, from some deeper level, like the still waters under a ruffled pond, the thought rose that my fear was the by-product of adrenaline and surprise. My spirits would soon buoy up again, and my legendary calm return. I clung to this thought, closing my eyes and drawing my awareness away from the tremors in my legs.

"My Lady," I prayed silently. "Comfort me."

Immediately, a sense of warmth settled over me, dispelling the haze of gloom. My heart swelled with gratitude, as I realized anew that my beloved brother Theo was here. He had left his farm. He had come out into the world. Maybe he would live after all!

I opened my eyes to find the day bright and picturesque, like a Christmas card, with Theo gazing at me, his dear face drawn with concern. When he saw my expression, his eyes crinkled with relief.

"Back, are you?" he asked with a grin.

"Yes." I glanced back down the road to where the demon had dared lay his hands upon a Handmaiden of the Unicorn. My hands balled into fists. "Now, I am angry!"

"Shall we hunt demon, then?" Theo gave a wolfish smile, showing his teeth. His eyes lit up with a life I had not seen in them in decades.

A spasm of coughing wracked his frame. The light died out of his eyes. He looked suddenly old.

"You will have to hunt with someone else, Sister," he said. "I cannot aid you."

"It can wait." I masked my disappointment. He had looked so strong and hale, I had begun hoping he had given up on dying and had made use of the vial of Water of Life I had left at his house. Now, I saw this was not the case. No matter, I told myself, so long as he still drew breath, I could keep trying!

Aloud, I said, "First, there is this matter of Caurus and the King of Fire."

THE three of us rocketed through the corridors of Prospero's Mansion atop the flying carpet. With Mab piloting, we traveled at speeds that made conversation impossible. I knelt in front, the breeze blowing in my face. Mab steered from the stern. Between us, Theo sat stiffly, gripping the sides of the rug with white knuckles, his rifle stretched across his lap.

Upon reaching the heavily warded doors of the Vault, we opened the numerous locks and took up the magical protections. Theo and Mab proceeded far more carefully than Caurus and I had, putting up new wards of salt and chalk before removing the protections on the great iron door itself.

Had Caurus and I done this, I suspected we would not have had to face Seir and the trouble he caused.

Eventually, the great door slowly swung open to reveal the central rotunda and the four wings. In the intervening few days, the fifth phoenix feather had rejuvenated and now glowed as brightly as its fellows. The feathers gave off a pleasant cinnamon scent that mingled with the less-pleasant burnt odor.

As we entered, a cheerful voice tinged with fatigue called out hopefully from the Elemental Chamber.

"Milady?" Caurus called. "Is that you? Please tell me Mab is with you! I can't stay awake much longer. I'm so tired, I'm hearing things. I keep dreaming this infernal sword is talking to me."

"I brought Mab," I called back. "And you're not dreaming. Don't listen to anything it says."

Theo stopped short. "Sword talking? Oh, no!" He threw up his hands as if to block an invisible attacker. "Surely you did not draw *Laevateinn!* The Wounding Wand is accursed! I'll have nothing to do with this! I've worked far too hard and suffered far too long to risk becoming contaminated by the dark arts at this late stage!"

"Then, get out of the way," Mab growled, exasperated. He pushed by Theo while pulling up his sleeves. "And leave the work to those of us who still care."

As Mab stalked forward into the Elemental Chamber, Theo remained where he was, frowning dubiously. I hesitated beside him an instant, then followed Mab.

Now that the Elemental Chamber was lit, the vials, rings, and old brass lamps piled upon the shelf that ran about the circumference of the room were clearly visible. Otherwise, the chamber was empty, except for Caurus and the four pedestals upon which sat the jars imprisoning the kings and queen of the elements. Ahead of me, Mab paused, taking in the two, untouched, lead-sealed copper jars, and the third jar, still capped by the breastplate of gleaming Urim and held in place by the finely fashioned cart wheel. The fourth pedestal held *Laevateinn.* When Mab reached it, he drew back in alarm, glaring at the sword, its hilt cruel and curling and pale as bone. Mist trickled out from the mouth of its ill-fitting Urim sheath.

Caurus, his Urim-clad left hand still hovering nervously between the wheel and the hilt of the sword, gave Mab and me a big welcoming smile. His long narrow nose and pointed chin were smudged with soot, and his singed straw-colored hair stuck out, much like hay. His once-long scarf now ended in a charred stub, his Icelandic sweater sported several large holes, and burn marks marred his sealskin breeches. Only the hornpipe protruding from his belt remained unscathed.

I was pleased to see the Water of Life had done its work. The terrible burn on his face was nearly healed.

"Milady!" Caurus cried gratefully. "And Mab! Bless the Stars!"

"So, what seems to be the problem?" Mab had his lead pipe in hand and was knocking it against his palm.

"Seir of the Shadows let the King of Fire out. He needs to be sealed in again," I explained.

Mab eyed the copper pot dubiously. "What's keeping him in there now?"

"He swore an oath." I recalled with pleasure the cleverness with which I had tricked the King of Djinn back into his jar. "He swore on the River Styx not to try to get out for a year and a day."

"Ah ha! . . . What was the exact wording of the oath?" asked Mab.

Caurus and I looked at each other.

"We were in the middle of a battle," I began.

"I wasn't even in my body," objected Caurus.

"You don't know the exact wording . . ." Mab asked in disbelief. "What do you remember? You did make him swear to go into the pot taking nothing, leaving nothing behind, and harming none, right? . . . You made him promise not to put any part of himself, even a flicker of flame, outside until after the pot was sealed, right? Please, tell me you . . . Dang!" Mab took off his hat and threw it against the marble floor, shaking his head with disgust. Picking up the hat again, he dusted it off and eyed the pot doubtfully.

"Not sure what to tell you, Ma'am. This might be a bigger case than I can handle. Might need to call in some professionals."

"Professionals?" I blinked, bemused by the idea that anyone could be more professional about such matters than Mab.

"You know, like those Orbie guys."

"You mean the *Orbis Suleimani?*"

"*Ja,* no! Surely there's a better way, Milady," Caurus cautioned. "The Circle of Solomon has no love for our kind! They're as likely to harm us as help us!"

"They won't hurt her." Mab stuck a finger at me. "Their leader is one of her brothers."

All this was too much for Theo, who came stomping into the room, still holding his Winchester.

"I am a professional," he growled, "and a member of the *Orbis Suleimani.*"

"Milord Prospero!" Caurus cried, delighted. "Are you a sight to cheer a weary spirit! How wonderful to see that the rumors of your death were false!" Then, suddenly, he drew back. "Wait! Alarm! This man bears not our Master's arcane aura! He is an imposter! Milady, run!" He lunged forward, his Urim-gauntleted hand reaching for the cruel pallid hilt of the Wounding Wand.

"Caurus, no! Stop!" I cried, but Mab was even quicker than I. He leapt forward and threw himself between Caurus and Theo, his arms outstretched.

Caurus froze. His gauntleted hand hovered just above the terrible sword, reluctant to touch it.

"This seeming, Milady! He is not your noble father!"

"He's not trying to look like Father, Caurus . . . that's my brother Theo."

Caurus tilted his head, amazed. "Lord Theophrastus?"

"The same," Theo replied gruffly. He was frowning at Mab's back, his brows arched in surprise. Mab lowered his arms and stepped away, clearing his throat.

Caurus peered at my brother. "You have changed, Milord. I had believed your family immune to the ravages of time."

"Only if we so choose," replied Theo. "You've changed as well. Last time we met, you were a disembodied voice in the air."

"Oh, *ja!*" Caurus waved his Urim gauntlet dismissively. "That was a while back. I've been in this body for some time now. Well, except for the day before yesterday." He looked at me blearily. "Or however long it's been. There's no clock in here."

Theo came farther into the chamber and squinted at the copper jars on their pedestals. "Where's the fourth one? The . . ."—he paused to examine the arcane symbols engraved into the side of each pot—"the King of Air? What was his name?"

"You mean our king?" Mab drawled. "The consort of Eurynome? He is known by the august and holy title: Ophion."

Theo frowned. "Miranda's Lady consort is called 'Snake'?"

"With whose help She created the stars!" bristled Mab.

Caurus leaned toward Mab, whispering loudly, "Tread carefully, Brother, the mortals heed a different account of Creation."

"I do not know where the fourth jar is," I jumped in. "In fact, I have never even seen a fourth jar. Maybe Father never had one. Did he ever mention it to you?"

Theo's brow furrowed. "I've never seen it myself, but Father mentioned more than once that, as Solomon's heirs, the *Orbis Suleimani* were the guardians of the four kings of the elements, whom Solomon bound into the service of mankind. Maybe the *Orbis Suleimani* still guards the fourth. I'll ask Cornelius."

I frowned, wondering if this was a good time to bring up Logistilla's suspicions about Cornelius and his staff, but my brother had turned away and was scowling at *Laevateinn*.

"Can't we get that thing out of here?"

"Nah. If I move it away, fire comes out of the pot."

"Great." Theo walked three times around the unsealed copper jar, examining it thoughtfully. He asked Mab for his notebook, wrote something down, and then handed the paper to Mab. "This is what I need," he announced curtly.

Mab peered at the paper and then back at my brother suspiciously. "I thought you said you weren't a magician?"

Theo scowled. "If you don't want my help, I'll go back upstairs where my immortal soul is not imperiled."

"Er, right . . . okay. Wait here. I'll find the stuff. Most of it should be down here. Mr. Prospero kept the place stocked for just this kind of emergency." Mab hunched his shoulders and stalked off toward the Treasure Chamber, muttering, "That's one of the things I've always admired about Mr. Prospero. He's always prepared."

Turning away, I smiled indulgently. Theo's pretense of not being a magician always amused me. For a fleeting instant, I regretted that Mephisto was not here to share the moment. Maybe Mephisto was not such a bad brother after all.

"Hold on. What's that?" Theo stepped over to the shelf along the wall and, shifting his gun to his left hand, reached out and picked up a gold ring bearing the Star of David that lay on a red velvet pillow. He laughed aloud. "Never mind, Mab! This is going to be a cinch! We've got Solomon's Seal! The ring he used to bind up the elemental kings the first time!"

"Er, Mr. Theo," Mab called from the next wing, his voice echoing through the Vault, "that's a fake."

"A what?"

"A fake. That ring's a counterfeit."

"It's not the real thing?" Theo looked disappointed. "Why is Father keeping it here?"

"The copy has some kind of magic in it. Mr. Prospero planned to examine it and find out what it does." Mab came back into the Elementals Chamber, his arms laden with candles, plumber's lead, carving tools, and other paraphernalia.

"Did he?"

"Don't know."

"Where's the real one?"

"Mr. Ulysses stole it," Mab replied. "He stole a bunch of stuff during his caper with the Warden device, then he returned everything . . . only, later, we discovered two of the items he brought back were fakes." He jerked his elbow at the ring as he put the things he had been carrying down on the shelf. "This was one of them."

"Dam . . ." Theo cut short his swear word, as the copper pot with the King of Fire in it trembled. It was never wise to call upon infernal powers around magical beings. He flushed, and I felt sorry for him. Here he was, so careful about not swearing, and the one time he slips up, something hears him. Little wonder he believed life to be a constant contest between the angelic and the demonic.

Mab, who had joined Theo by the false Seal of Solomon, stopped to examine the brass rings and stoppered vials. Picking up a ruby-colored vial, he peered into its swirling contents.

"Hey, I think I know this guy! It's my missing . . . well, you'd call it a cousin. Mind if I take him, Ma'am?" Mab started to put the vial into the pocket of his trench coat, but Theo glared at him. Looking chagrined, he put it back.

"Poor unlucky blighter," he muttered as he returned to stand by the pedestals.

Theo turned to Caurus. "You, Spiritling, can you wield the Wounding Wand?"

Caurus looked at *Laevateinn's* cruelly curling hilt, his face grown pale beneath the soot.

"If I must," he replied bravely.

"Good." Theo's eyes fell on me. "You! Out of here. Find a safe place. Maybe the Holy Chamber." He pointed across the central rotunda at the opposite wing. "I don't want you in the way when the flames shoot out."

I would have objected, but he was right, there was nothing I could do to help. The last thing Theo needed was a bystander to distract him at a crucial moment. I leaned close and kissed Theo on his scratchy cheek.

"Promise me you'll be careful!"

He touched his cheek and smiled obediently. "Yes, Big Sister."

I CHOSE the Treasure Chamber, which looked even worse than I expected. A layer of soot covered everything, except Midas's donkey, which was now coated with tiny golden specks. The items on the right side of the hall were coated with ash and flecks of splattered gold; those on the left were completely ruined. On the floor, a faint black film spread from the mouth of a broken amphora; it was the last remnants of our precious supply of water from the River Styx.

How was I going to run Prospero, Inc. without it?

The room smelled both pleasant and vile, as odors such as of charred cedar mingled with those such as of burnt hair. Mixed in was a trace of something putrid, perhaps the once-pickled organs of the pharaoh Ozymandius, whose canopic jars had exploded from the heat.

A wave of anger at the King of Fire swept over me, and I ruminated upon a suitable revenge. I was on the verge of returning to the Elemental Chamber to ask Theo and Mab if they could inflict some kind of punitive damage as they bound him, when I remembered that Seir of the Shadows was the true target of my wrath. If he had not broken the seal on the copper jar, the djinn king would never have escaped to plague us.

I wandered among the damaged treasures, searching for anything that might have survived the fury of the Fire King's blaze, discovering a bracelet here and a cloak pin there. The tarnhelm was still in one piece, but the helmet was damaged where it had been splattered with molten gold. Wondering if it were still working, I began to place it on my head, but thought better of it. Damaged magic items were chancy at best, and besides, the only mirror in this chamber was cracked and blackened. How would I be able to tell whether I had turned invisible?

Farther down the shelf, a glass slipper had survived the conflagration, but only burnt hulks remained where the red shoes had been. Probably for the best. I had argued for destroying them back when Gregor first took them off that poor dead girl's feet. Father, on the other hand, was frugal. He would never destroy anything that he might conceivably put to good use later. Though what good use Father imagined could be made of dancing oneself to death, he never shared with me.

Clinks and clatters of preparation sounded from the Elementals Chamber, along with a running commentary from Theo, as he muttered disparagingly about "lack of respect for an angel's shield" and "blasphemous treatment of Our Lord's handiwork." Good old Theo, he had not changed a bit.

Strangely, it occurred to me, being an old man suited Theo. He had always been the voice of caution and decency among the family. Now, he had the appearance to accompany his cautionary advice.

Among the wreckage, I found the remnants of the Halter of Clynoeiddyn. A memory sprang to mind of my brother Mephistopheles, long ago, back when he was sane, leaping atop the wild Pegasus and wrestling the shimmering halter over the head of the bucking winged horse, laughing all the while. This halter had come in handy, as well, when he caught the chimera and the cockatrice, and half a dozen other mythical creatures. Had Mephisto been unable to tame these fearsome monsters, Father would have had to send Theo to slay them. Instead, they remained alive today and at the beck and call of my brother's staff, which was a very good thing. Otherwise, Pegasus would not have been there last week to save us, when our plane went down on our way to the North Pole.

As the charred halter broke apart in my hands, my eyes filled with tears. What other noble beasts might now be doomed because Mephisto would never have the opportunity to tame them?

I sat down on the battered tarnhelm and wiped my eyes, blaming my sudden sentimentality on Osae the Red.

A splash of white caught my eye. Reaching out, I found myself holding the edge of what had once been a swan maiden's cloak. Its leather was cracked and twisted, but one corner had miraculously been spared. The downy feathers of pure white stood in stark contrast to all the blackened destruction. I lifted the corner of the cloak and rubbed the soft feathers against my cheek.

Whose cloak had this been? My brother Erasmus had collected such cloaks once. Unfortunately, each one had belonged to a particular maiden—a swan maiden or crane maiden—who could not return to her supernatural home without it. Sometimes, Erasmus killed the maidens. Once or twice, he brought her home and married her, though he never treated these fey women well. I remember him beating one, a swan maiden named Reginleif, with the handle of his whip after he caught her trying to feed slugs to their son. She had been fierce and proud once, and her captivity filled her with longing and shame. My heart had gone out to her.

I had felt so sorry for Reginleif that I went to the trouble of discovering where Erasmus kept her cloak and stole it. Before I could return it to her, however, Cromwell's Roundheads found her; the Puritans destroyed anything that smacked remotely of witchcraft, including young wives who laughed at funerals. A Roundhead soldier struck her over the head with a heavy golden crucifix and then put a dagger in her belly.

Titus held Reginleif as she died. I still remember coming upon them, a slender pale figure lying limply in the arms of my huge hulk of a brother. Reginleif saw the stolen cloak in my hands, and her dark eyes brimmed with tears of gratitude. She had reached out, but before her fingers could so much as brush a single feather, her spirit passed from her body, and she was no more.

I returned the cloak before Erasmus discovered it was missing, and Titus never breathed a word about the theft. Before I put it back, however, I could not resist the temptation to try it on.

The moment the garment clasped around my neck, the magic of the cloak transformed me into a swan, and for one glorious afternoon, I soared about the moors and over our loch, glorying in the freedom of the sky. I might have stayed a bird forever, so exhilarating was the experience; however, around evening, a Cavalier soldier pursuing the Roundheads took a shot at me, hoping to win himself a swan dinner. Quickly, I returned to the ground and, after a harrowing moment, during which I could not figure out how to unclasp the cloak, regained my proper shape.

Titus and Theo had wanted to chase down the soldiers and avenge Reginleif's death, but Erasmus could not be bothered.

"Don't worry," he had said with a laugh. "I can get another one."

As I pressed the few white feathers against my cheek, I wondered if this was the cloak that had once been Reginleif's.

From the other room came two ringing knocks, as if Mab had struck one of the copper jars with his lead pipe, followed by Mab's voice.

"Listen up! Know who's out here? Theophrastus the Demonslayer! That's right, you flame-headed lout! Bet even you have heard of him! So, you put so much as one flicker of flame outside the mouth of this pot, and the pain of trying to break an oath sworn on the River Styx will be a mere overture compared to the symphony of agony that we will visit upon you. You follow me? Good!" There came a pause. "Okay, Mr. Theo. Everything's ready."

A struggle followed. I heard shouts and swearing and, twice, cries of pain. Both times, I started to run toward the Elemental Chamber but stopped myself. Theo was right. Without my flute, unarmed, there was little I could do. My Japanese war fan, so useful against men and rhinos, would be useless against the Fire King. I resolved that if the screaming became prolonged, I would go. So long as my brother and the Aerie Ones remained in control, I would aid them more by remaining here.

Still, it was frustrating.

EVENTUALLY, I heard footsteps, and Caurus came to join me. He was covered with even more soot, yet the merry twinkle had returned to his blue eyes.

"Milady? Lord Theo has sealed away the King of Djinn, and I have locked the Wounding Wand back up in the Weapons Chamber."

"Thank you, Caurus! You did a difficult job here."

"Oh *ja*, Milady," he laughed shakily. "Winds aren't meant to be cooped up underground."

I nodded, struck suddenly by the hopelessness of the Aerie Ones' quest for freedom. As employees of Prospero, Inc., they saw firsthand how we dealt with spirits who mistreated human beings. Could they be so foolish as not to realize their longed-for liberty could never come unless they could demonstrate self-control?

"Caurus," I said slowly, "there is something you should know. I have promised the other Winds that if all eight of you should swear upon the Styx that you can keep your followers from harming mankind, I would let you go."

The lines of fatigue vanished from Caurus's face, and his blue eyes danced with a merry light. "A frail hope, Milady, but a little hope is better than none!" He bowed his head respectfully. "I thank you."

"You are welcome. I realize it's not much. Boreas explained how the lesser winds are hard to control, as there is nothing that you can offer them."

Caurus cocked his head. "Ah, but there is something all winds desire, Milady, and not just winds, but every spirit . . . all the supernatural beings and horrors we at Prospero, Inc. seek to tame. Something we want so much, we might do your bidding willingly could you provide it."

"And that is?"

"Water of Life."

"Really?"

"Oh *ja*. It is like nectar to us and like gold, too. It makes us strong and healthy, powerful and wise. Not only do we desire it for ourselves, but there are always lesser spirits we could cajole to do our bidding, were we able to offer them some." Caurus's blue eyes twinkled merrily. "If you could offer even a small store, say an ounce a decade? I would swear."

"Interesting . . ." I murmured thoughtfully.

An ounce a decade? That did not seem like much. Hope rose in my heart. Could freedom for the Aerie Ones become a reality?

Then I did the math, calculating how much Water would be needed to placate the Great Winds, some of whom I suspected would not be as reasonable as Caurus. Unless I could free up my schedule to make the year-and-a-day trip to the Well at the World's End three or four times a century, this plan would not work. Considering how busy I had been of late, it was not a very likely option.

Of course, if I were a Sibyl, I would be able to make Water of Life. This left me in a bind; if my recent conjectures were correct, so long as I kept the Aerie Ones bound, I would not be a Sibyl, but if I did not let them go, I would never have what I needed to free them.

Were I certain I would be made a Sibyl instantly upon releasing them, I would have been willing to try. However, it was not a sure thing.

As I considered all this, Caurus brought up another stumbling block. Frowning at the broken amphora on the floor, he pointed at the black stains. "But you have no more Styx water, Milady. How could we swear?"

"We can acquire more," I replied with false confidence. "Or we can hunt down the Three Shadowed Ones and take back the *Staff of Darkness* from Seir of the Shadows. You could swear on that."

"Oh *ja!* That would do it!"

As I spoke Seir's name, there came a soft hum. I turned.

A gleaming spear point rushed toward my head. Shouting, I dodged sideways into Caurus, and the two of us crashed down into the ash. Above, the spear hovered in midair, vibrating and trembling, like a massive vehicle on idle. Its battered ash shaft was carved with arcane runes. Not finding the incubus, its quarry, it began slowly circling the chamber. I breathed a sigh of relief and started to rise, but could not. My hair was caught on something.

"Milady! Don't move!"

I froze. To my left was the golden donkey. Out of the corner of my eye, I could see golden wires creeping through the air toward my head. A spasm of terror seized me. Escaped strands of my silvery hair, shaken free during my encounter with Osae, had fallen across the ward around Midas's donkey and were turning to gold. If the effect reached my head, I, too, would turn to gold.

I yanked my head away, only to be brought up short by pain. The golden hairs had apparently fused to the donkey. I could not move my head. To my left, I could see the gold growing closer.

Screaming, I reached up to tear out the offending hairs. Caurus knocked my hand away. Grabbing the hairs close to my head, he yanked them out and threw them back across the ward to lie at the donkey's feet. The pain caused my eyes to water.

Theo and Mab had come running when they heard my cry. Now they stood in the door, both singed and soot-covered, gazing at the hovering spear.

"Why is the spear *Gungnir* hanging in midair?" Theo stepped gingerly around Odin's spear and extended his hand, which I accepted.

"It's seeking its prey, Milord," Caurus rose lightly to his feet. "Lady Miranda set it after the incubus from the Three Shadowed Ones, and being a divine spear, it will continue to seek this prey until such a time as it shall strike it."

"Why don't we open the door and let it out?" I suggested. "Won't *Gungnir* then seek the incubus across the entire Earth?"

Mab shook his head. "Nah. Never wise to let *Gungnir* outside of the range of your voice."

"Otherwise," explained Theo, "after it stabs your enemy, it will remain in his corpse for his allies to pull out and send back at you."

"Ah . . . good point." I looked him over. His hair was singed, and his face smeared with soot. Otherwise, he looked all right. "How did it go?"

"Well enough." Theo shrugged. "Without either the Staff of Darkness or Styx water, we were not able to make him swear any new oaths. I just hope the old ones are still being enforced."

"I'll have my men keep a watch for instances of gas mains exploding, cars bursting into flame, or people spontaneously combusting." Mab stepped farther into the chamber and glanced around at the fire damage, scowling. "A rise in any activity of this sort would be an indicator that our binding isn't holding."

A glitter on my index finger caught my eye. My stomach gave an uncomfortable lurch. The outer skin of my finger was dusted with fine gold.

"Is this going to keep . . ."—I swallowed—"spreading?"

Visions of fingerless hands or stiff golden arms crowded my thoughts. My head felt light, and Mab's voice seemed to be coming from far away.

"Nah, not if it's no longer in contact with the donkey." Mab frowned and put his hands in his pocket. "Might have been wiser if you hadn't touched it, Ma'am."

"Right. Thanks, Mab. I'll remember that," I replied mildly.

"Milady, before you go," Caurus said suddenly, squinting at *Gungnir*. "The God's spear has reminded me—there is something you should see."

CAURUS led us back into the Elemental Chamber. Some seven feet above us, on the left-hand wall near the front of the hall, a small pale object about the size of a playing card had been set into the plaster. Examining it from where I stood, I saw a piece of ivory carved to resemble a small door, complete with fancy moldings and a doorknob. Mab and Theo joined us, and the four of us peered up at the miniature doorway set into the wall of the chamber.

"The spear kept circling, but it spent most of the time hovering beside that ivory rectangle." Caurus pointed up. "I could see it from where I was standing, but I dared not move away from the sword and the King of Fire's jar to investigate."

"That's strange," I murmured softly. "That was not here originally. Is this something Father added recently?"

"I wouldn't know, Ma'am. Mr. Prospero seldom let my kind in here," Mab replied. "Though I do know he put in some additional security measures after Mr. Ulysses's visit."

"Get the carpet," I said. "Let's take a closer look."

Getting all four of us onto the carpet was a tight squeeze, but we managed. Rising, we bobbed in front of the little rectangle of ivory. Carefully, I reached out to touch it.

"Better let me do that. You've touched enough things today, Ma'am." Mab moved the carpet forward so that the miniature door was beyond my reach. "Good employer, Miss Miranda, but with the self-preservational sense of a carrot," I heard him whisper to Theo, who failed to smother his chuckle. I would have shot my brother a reproachful glance, chiding him for encouraging insubordination among my ranks, but he was looking the other way.

As the carpet swayed gently, Mab reached out and touched the ivory door, tapping on it twice.

"Seems solid enough. Even has a doorknob. Wonder if . . ." Mab pulled on the tiny knob.

The little door swung open.

"Where does it lead?" I half rose off the carpet in my astonishment.

Mab opened the little door as wide as it could go. Through the open threshold, I caught a glimpse of a miniature corridor, much like the hallway outside the Vault, only the left wall was missing. Vaguely, in the distance beyond where this fourth wall should have been, I could make out a row of books. The books, unlike the tiny corridor, looked to be full size.

"What witchcraft is this?" growled Theo.

"Perhaps some well-appointed mouse wishes entrance to the Vault undetected?" Caurus offered jovially.

I did not reply but gazed at this enormous hole in our defenses. What use were all the spells and wards guarding this place, if there was an opening inside the defenses? Please, I prayed quietly to my Lady, let this be the last shock of this disorienting day. She gave no answer, which was not a good sign.

"Logistilla's dollhouse," Mab observed dryly.

"What!" several of us exclaimed.

"Remember Santa's scrying pool, Ma'am? That dollhouse we saw in the library where your brother Titus's children were playing? The one that had tiny ivory doors in it? Well, this looks to be one of those doors, and I recognize that globe over there. See, sitting next to the bookshelf to the left?"

"So, this room we are looking into is . . . ?" Theo began.

"Is inside a dollhouse that sits in the library of Logistilla's mansion in the Okefenokee Swamp," I replied frowning.

"But what does this mean?" asked Caurus.

"I don't know," I said, my eyes narrowing, "but below this spot, here in the Elemental Chambers is about where we first saw Sei—the incubus." I glanced quickly over my shoulder, but the hovering spear was nowhere to be seen.

Theo was still frowning at the little door. "Do you think the incubus came into the Vault through Logistilla's house?"

"That's about the smell of it," Mab replied grimly.

CHAPTER NINE

November 1, 1924

"It was sabotage all right!" Mab fumed the next morning. "Gads, but I hate having to admit I was wrong to a furball!"

He stood hunched over the teak table in the drawing room. A ray of early-morning sun glinted off a row of Ziploc baggies stretched out on the sheet of glass that covered the surface of the table. Beside the baggies sat a folded letter and a photocopy of a document written in a cramped script. Under the glass, the table held a large sheet of embossed metal formed and tinted to portray a three-dimensional topographical map of the world, circa 1692. A shelf set into the wall behind us held compasses, protractors, prisms, candles, plumb bobs, and other tools used for cartomancy.

To Mab's right, Theo sat, blinking sleepily and nursing a cup of coffee. I sat to his left, sipping tea laced with mulberry morath. A silver tray in the middle of the table held scones and Danishes. The scent of cinnamon and warm sugar brought back memories of Father Christmas's house. I smiled in reminiscence.

"Could we please draw the drapes?" Theo asked. "I am too old to be awake so early."

He sat with his hand shading his eyes. A bandage on his temple was the only visible evidence of his struggle with the King of Fire, but Marigold, the Aerie Spirit who helped bandage his burns, reported additional injuries on his forearm and chest.

I whistled a bar of Brahms's lullaby—with my personal house servants, I did not need to resort to the flute—and an Aerie One whisked the drapes shut. The drawing room was now illuminated by antique lamps set into the inner wall. If I closed my eyes and listened, I could hear the hiss of the gas.

"As I was saying . . ." Mab squinted in the comparative darkness. "I've got some news, and, well, you are not going to like it. It's bad, Ma'am, very bad."

"Go ahead, Mab," I replied.

"First things first. I examined the warehouse in Michigan from roof to cellar. There's no question that the damage was deliberate. I found shards of the explosive. There was also a body. The police had me go down to the morgue to see if I could identify it."

"One of our workers?"

Mab shook his head. Picking up the first of the Ziploc bags, he let the contents clatter to the table: a gold, six-pointed star, a ring with the imprint of an eye within a triangle, and a pin etched with an image of Blind Justice holding her balance scales. All three objects were smudged with soot.

"Cornelius!" Theo exclaimed. "These are his symbols. It must have been one of his people!"

I leaned forward, alarmed. Theo was right. Taken together, the two *Orbis Suleimani* symbols and the Blind Justice represented Cornelius. My stomach lurched painfully. So, I had been right! Cornelius was undermining the family. He had betrayed us all, just like Uncle Antonio before him!

"The same guy who used his magic staff to make you think you should grow old and die?" Mab asked.

"Who told you that?" Theo stood up. His coffee mug clanged against the tabletop.

"Is it true?" asked Mab.

Theo remained silent. Mab crossed his arms and waited patiently. I held very still, hoping; my tea cup forgotten at my lips. When Theo continued to glare at Mab, I repeated impatiently:

"Is it true?"

"Cornelius did use his staff on me—but only at my request."

"You asked him to enchant you!" I shouted.

"I . . . er."

"And you have the audacity to make accusations about me?"

"That's different." My brother crossed his arms. "If you had asked Father to enchant you, I wouldn't trouble myself. Or rather, I'd be troubled, but for a different reason."

"Well, I'm troubled for that different reason! Why, in the name of all that is holy, did you let him use his staff on you? You said you knew the staffs were actually demons! Wasn't the whole point of what you were doing to rid yourself of magic?"

Theo looked away, frowning, "I was sick of making resolutions and breaking them. I thought if I only had some help stiffening my resolve . . ."

Theo leaned over, coughing. Straightening again, he added stiffly, "In Cornelius's defense, he was against the idea from the start. Years later, he told me he did not activate his staff, he just let me look at it and make my promise."

"So he says," growled Mab.

Theo shrugged. "The whole thing was Ulysses's idea. He got tired of hearing me complain about the trouble I had keeping my vows, and suggested I ask Cornelius for help." He sat down again, reclaiming his coffee mug.

"The perp again, eh?" Mab nodded grimly, as if confirming some suspicion.

Was Cornelius not the villain Logistilla had made him out to be? Perhaps I had been entirely mistaken about him!

I felt both relieved and oddly deflated. It had been comforting to pin my fears about Theo upon a brother I disliked, to hope that there was some common cause between Father's disappearance and the death of Gregor.

I so wanted there to be an enemy. Someone who was responsible for our woes. Someone we could destroy, and then, maybe everything would get better again: Father would return; Theo would embrace life; Gregor would pop up from the dead; Erasmus would stop mistreating me; horses would learn to sing; and pigs would fly.

I did not blame myself for longing for something to blame for all my sorrows, but I should not have been so eager to find such a target among my own kin. Ashamed by this flaw in my family loyalty, I examined the Star of David, the eye in the triangle, and the pin again.

"Where did you get these, Mab?" I asked sharply.

"Off the body I found in the warehouse."

"The saboteur?" Suddenly, the ridiculousness of it struck me, and I burst into laughter. "We're supposed to believe Cornelius blew up a Prospero, Inc. warehouse? What will they try next? Planting evidence that the sun has been secretly coming up in the West?" I paused to wipe my eyes and laughed some more. "This was the Three Shadowed Ones, wasn't it? The idiots!"

Mab's eyes narrowed. He regarded me carefully. "You don't believe Cornelius was behind this?"

"Oh, I believed that Cornelius had enchanted Theo, and I was willing to accept that he might have been in league with the demons, but to believe my brother Cornelius would damage his own stock? Absolutely not! He's the sole other stockholder in Prospero, Inc. He'd eat his blindfold before he would deliberately reduce his own profits. The very thought is laughable."

"Then it was a good thing I went out to Michigan myself, Ma'am.

Because those posers who work for me would have told you Cornelius's man blew up the warehouse." Mab snorted in disgust. "I, on the other hand, thought to ask some pointed questions of the guy at the morgue. Eventually, I got him to reexamine the body. It had been dead for days before it reached the warehouse. Killed in some kind of crash would be my guess, probably an automobile crash."

Theo leaned forward. "Why would anyone wish Miranda to believe Cornelius was sabotaging the company? It makes no sense."

"I can only conjecture, Sir," Mab replied, "but, I do know something of the nature of demons. Demons are predictable folk; it's amazing any of you mortals ever fall for their tricks, as they use the same ones over and over. Sowing contention is one of their biggies. My guess is the Three Shadowed Ones' agenda includes setting you Prosperos at odds with one another. The more time your family spends spatting amongst yourselves, the less efficient you become. You should be suspicious of anything demons say to you."

I leaned back, suffused by a buoyant sense of gratitude and relief. All my suspicions about Cornelius beguiling Father, enchanting Theo, and orchestrating the death of Gregor were baseless. Of course, my brothers were not at one another's throats. We were a family. I may not like some of them but that did not mean they were traitors!

I had fallen prey to that most terrible of mental poisons—suspicion. Father's essay on the effects of demons upon the human soul came to mind again. Had the flute I so loved done this to me? Had I been paving the demon's way for years—setting myself up as demon bait—by grumbling against those members of my family of whom I disapproved?

I recalled the disappointment I had felt just now when I learned that Cornelius was innocent. Had I wanted to discover that he was disloyal so as to justify my antipathy? If so, perhaps I should consider the possibility that it was my attitude that was unjustified. Perhaps, even Erasmus deserved a second chance—though I found that hard to believe.

Silently, I vowed to remember that my suspicions had turned out to be false and to trust my family, even in the face of evidence to the contrary.

"Do you have any evidence the Three Shadowed Ones were behind this?" Theo asked.

"As a matter of fact, I do." Mab upended another Ziploc, scattering shards of red and gold crystal onto the table. He pushed one piece with his finger. "Remember I said I found pieces of their incendiary device? Shattered star spark globe. Same thing Seir used when he attacked here at the mansion. Not a weapon the *Orbis Suleimani* would have access to, Ma'am. Not unless they took one off a demon, anyway."

"But why frame Cornelius, whom I would never suspect of such a crime? Why not frame . . ."—I gestured randomly—"Erasmus, for instance?"

"They're demons, Sister Dear," Theo replied. "What do they know of what you will or will not believe? All they care about is sowing discord and mistrust."

"Bet they know you don't like Cornelius," Mab offered. "Probably thought it would make it easy for you to distrust him. Or maybe they just had one of Cornelius's men and used what was on hand."

"A car accident, you said?" There was a sinking sensation in the pit of my stomach. "Or a boat accident? Could that body have been Mr. Mustache?"

Mab raised his eyebrow. "That's what I like about working for you, Miss Miranda. You're sharp."

Listening to Mab talk, I suddenly felt like an imbecile. I should have realized Osae was not the real Mab the instance he addressed me as "Miranda." The real Mab never called me "Miranda." He always said "Miss Miranda" or "Ma'am."

Mab pulled out his cell phone and made a quick call. Folding it again, he declared, "Yep. Looks like you may be right, Ma'am. The body in the warehouse could well be that of the man who was piloting the boat that crashed behind us. His face was too damaged to identify him by, but the fellow at the morgue confirmed there was a Seal of Solomon tattoo on his arm. We know the Three Shadowed Ones were in the area at the time. Bet they fished the body out of the crash."

"Oh, no!" I clutched at the table, nearly spilling my cup of morath-laced tea.

"What?" Mab cried. "What is it, Ma'am?"

"Miranda? Are you all right?" cried Theo.

"I killed an innocent man!" I whispered.

"On purpose?" Theo asked, confused.

I shook my head. "We thought the man chasing us was one of the Three Shadowed Ones' agents, sent by a spirit who spoke during our information-gathering séance—the one we held at your suggestion. But, all this," I gestured impatiently at the ring and pins, "confirms that he was a member of the *Orbis Suleimani*. And if Cornelius is not in cahoots with the Three Shadowed Ones, then . . . !" My voice faltered. ". . . and I killed him."

"He chose to chase us in the dark, Ma'am." Mab replied steadily. "He could have turned his boat around."

"He must have been trying to warn us about something," I whispered, stricken.

Theo examined the symbols Mab had dumped on the table. "I am sorry, Miranda, but I can't help pointing out if you had not dabbled in magic, the man who owned these items would still be alive." He spoke bitterly. "I'm sure his widow will understand when you explain that she now has to raise her children alone because you mistook her husband for a ghoulish spirit."

"Theo. That's hardly sporting!" I cried.

I felt terrible about the death of Mr. Mustache, whose moniker now seemed oddly dear to me. If Theo continued to berate me, I feared I might weep. Being caught crying in front of an employee was more shame than I could bear, even if that employee was Mab. I closed my eyes and turned to my Lady for comfort.

Her warmth, like a breath of summer, settled over me. When I opened my eyes again, I still felt sad, but it was a calm gentle sadness, with no threat of waterworks.

Mab, meanwhile, was paging through his notebook. "Too bad we can't find Mr. Titus," he said, his finger resting on some note. "Maybe he could shed some light on what happened to his twin."

Theo and I looked at him blankly. Theo said, "Titus does not have a twin."

Mab frowned and flipped back and forth between two different pages in his notebook. "My mistake, Logistilla is Gregor's twin! She even called him 'Greggie-Poo.' How could I forget! Apparently, I wrote your brothers' names down on two different pages, listing two different relationships to each other." He looked up. "List them again for me, would you, in birth order?"

"I am the eldest," I replied. "After me comes Mephisto, Theo, and Erasmus, in that order. They were born in fifteenth-century Italy, after Father and I escaped from our island prison and returned to Milan. Their mother was a Medici. Next comes Cornelius and Titus, who were born four years apart."

"There was a child born between them, a girl, but she did not live past infanthood," Theo said sadly.

I nodded, recalling Father's tears at her death, one of the three occasions upon which I had seen him cry. How he loved his children! "Cornelius and

Titus were born in Scotland, in the 1550s, just before Queen Elizabeth the First rose to the throne of England."

"Then, the twins, Gregor and Logistilla," Theo offered. "They were born in Italy, in 1593."

"And finally, Ulysses," I said, "who was born in England, in 1823."

Mab whistled. "That's a long gap, 1593 to 1823. Any idea why Mr. Prospero waited so long?"

I shook my head.

Theo said, "Whatever the reason, Father had Ulysses on purpose. He mentioned to me that he had decided to have another child and asked if I would keep my eye out for a promising wife. It was I who introduced him to Priscilla, Ulysses's mother; she was the daughter of a good friend."

"Really!" I exclaimed, astonished. "I never knew that. I wonder why he didn't say anything to me?"

Theo shrugged and shook his head, indicating that the matter was of no interest to him, but his brow darkened, as if his suspicions against Father had been roused again.

"Ma'am, if you don't mind my asking," Mab said suddenly, closing his notebook, "what were you and Long-Nose doing in the Vault to begin with?"

Theo looked up. "Long-Nose?"

Mab gave a dismissive wave. "Caurus. Skeiron. Northwesty. Whatever you want to call him."

"We were on our way to the Wintergarden," I said. "I wanted to examine Father's horticultural project. I thought it might shed some light on the events leading to his disappearance."

"Did it?" asked Theo.

"Yes."

"What did ya find?" asked Mab, pulling out his notebook and his stubby pencil. Only this was a different stubby pencil from the last time, still blue, but of a darker shade. Apparently, he was saving the Space Pen he received from Father Christmas for a more perilous situation.

"Father sprouted a piece of the True Cross and made it into a new staff: the *Staff of Eternity*." I threw Mab a significant glance. He immediately flipped through his notebook to a list of questions he maintained and began scribbling under the heading: WHAT IS THE STAFF OF ETERNITY. I continued, "When Father disappeared last September, he was in Elgin, Illinois, beside our dead brother's recently opened grave." I paused again, until Mab stopped scribbling and looked up. "He was trying to resurrect Gregor!"

Theo nearly shot out of his seat. He had to grab his coffee mug to keep his coffee from spilling.

Mab merely shook his head disparagingly. "Ma'am, it just goes to show. Mortals should not meddle in arcane matters. He should have consulted me before trying such a harebrained scheme. I could have told him no good would come of it."

"Father thought he could bring Gregor back from the dead?" Theo seemed genuinely shocked.

"He had been investigating the Eleusinian Mysteries, which according to Tybalt, involves getting the goddess Demeter to adopt you, so that Persephone, the wife of Hades, will consider you family and sneak you out of the Land of the Dead without wiping your memory when it comes your time to be reborn." I met Theo's gaze squarely. "Apparently, he was trying to save you."

"Me?"

"As best as I can tell, he wanted to show you the futility of your stance. After all, if he could bring back Gregor, he could bring you back, too."

"Would not have done him any good," Theo replied stiffly. "I would have returned to wherever he called me up from."

"Oh, yeah?" Mab scratched his permanent six-o'clock shadow. "How?"

"Suicide's a sin!" I reminded him, perhaps more harshly than was warranted. "No matter how you happened to come to be among the living."

Theo was silent. He sipped his coffee absentmindedly. I began to wonder if he remembered we were here. Finally, he put down his now-empty mug and spoke to Mab.

"This news of yours regarding the warehouse was not so dire—except for the fate of the poor man who was killed. If you knew already Cornelius wasn't behind the explosion, why did you give us that doom-and-gloom 'you're not going to like it' speech?"

"Oh . . . that wasn't the bad part." The animation drained from his face. Mab picked up the folded letter and the photocopies. "This is the bad part."

Before Mab could continue, we were interrupted, as a silver tray bearing fresh coffee floated through the door. The aroma of deep-roast permeated the drawing room. When the tray reached us, a coffeepot rose into the air and poured a stream of steaming liquid into Theo's mug. Theo jerked back in his chair, moving away from the scalding liquid.

I turned to Mab, eager for him to continue, but Theo spoke first.

"Ariel, is that you? Stay a moment. I'd like to ask you a question."

Ariel's fluting voice replied from midair. "As you wish, Sir."

"What was Miranda like when she was a girl? Was she well behaved?"

"Theo! Please do not bother Ariel with your conjectures!" I could see where this was leading. Next, Theo would ask whether Ariel could remember a point before which I was a little hellion and after which I suddenly became docile. Then, he would spout accusations about Father and enchantment again. "There is absolutely no evidence that Father has me under a spell!"

Theo leaned toward me and spoke in a low voice, "Is that so? What about back in 1666, when you would not step outside the house for eight months because Father told you to mind the house until he returned?"

I frowned, recalling the year in question, the year Cornelius gave up looking for a cure for his blindness, the year Father gave us our staffs. Minding the house while Father was away had seemed perfectly reasonable at the time. I had to admit, though, stated the way Theo put it, it did sound odd.

Ariel answered, "I am a creature of the air. I flit. I fly. I race the very lightning bolt. Of the behavior of men, I know naught. Upon what basis could I judge whether the mistress behaved as other human children do or nay?"

Theo grunted, and I bit into a Danish to hide my smile. Good old Ariel. I turned back to Mab, my sense of uneasiness growing.

"Is there naught else?" asked Ariel. When Theo shook his head, Ariel said, "Mistress, before I depart, there is that which has been promised me but not delivered. Rumor's tongue brings more talk of Prospero's death. Will not you relent your harsh stance and set us free to wind our way about the myriad of worlds, eldest child of your father?"

Before I could answer, Theo rounded angrily upon the spot from which Ariel's voice issued. "Spirit, you overstep yourself! I will not hear such evil spoken of my father!"

"Master Theophrastus, I knew you not at first glance, because you had taken upon yourself a countenance like unto your father's—that of an aged mortal. Surely, this means that Dread Prospero uses his no longer? If he has perished—" Ariel began.

Theo cut him off. "There will be no talk of ill to Prospero in this house."

There was a pause. Then Ariel's fluting voice replied, "As you wish, Young Master."

"Hmph!" Theo muttered as he sat down. "You should keep a tighter rein on those spirits, Miranda. One would almost think Ariel believes he might sway you with his protestations."

"No, of course not, why would he think that?" Mab replied sourly, glowering at my brother. "A reasonable argument has never swayed Miss Miranda before."

"You, too, Spiritling!" Theo spoke as he might have in years past to some infantryman under his command who dared to give orders to his fellow soldiers. "My sister grants you too many liberties. You forget your place."

"That is enough!" I snapped. Both men looked toward me, startled. Mab was still glowering, but Theo's face showed only surprise. "Mab is an employee of Prospero, Inc., Theo. He has the same rights and perquisites as all other employees, mortal or otherwise, including the right to his own opinion. What would be the use of a company gumshoe who wasn't allowed to speak candidly?"

"Thank you, Ma'am," Mab said, mollified. "I was about to tell you to figure this matter out for yourself, but as you have come to my defense, I will proceed. As for you, Mr. Theophrastus. I think you're a fine fellow for the most part, but it's a shame you're such a bigot. So, sit down and buckle your seat belts, because you aren't going to like the ride."

Mab took a deep breath. "Here goes. . . . You may remember, Ma'am, while I was checking out what happened to your father, I got into a conversation with the local sheriff who promised to send me a copy of some microfiche reports from the time of Mr. Gregor's death. Well, I stopped at the post office on my way back from the airport and found this in the mailbox. Miss Miranda . . . I'm afraid your brother Gregor was murdered."

"Gregor? Murdered?" I cried, surprised. Theo and I exchanged glances. This was news to him, too. "But . . . I thought he was struck down by a stray bullet, during a shoot-out with whiskey runners."

"I don't know where you got that idea, Ma'am, but nothing like that happened. He was murdered . . . and it gets worse."

Theo and I stared at him.

"What could be worse than murder?" asked Theo.

Mab looked pained. "Look, why don't I read this to you?"

"Please," I said weakly. I had been enjoying the sweet creamy filling of my cheese Danish. As Mab began to read, I discovered I was no longer hungry, and put the rest aside.

Mab read:

Regarding the murder of the watch factory worker Gregory Prosper: 'On the first of November, Nineteen Hundred and Twenty Four, the watch factory worker, Gregory Prosper, was shot point blank in the chest by a stranger.

Gregory Prosper, a Pennsylvania man, had been living in our town of Elgin for about three years. He was a rough-spoken but well-mannered man, never known to be involved in brawling or bootlegging. He was law abiding, attended church on Sunday, and served on the yearly Fourth of July committee.

On the day of his death, Mr. Prosper was walking with Mr. Smythe and Mr. Wickerson near the well by the post office when a stranger approached the group. According to eyewitnesses, Mr. Prosper waved, greeting the stranger in a familiar manner. The stranger reportedly said, "Sorry about this, old chap. Must tie up a few loose ends." Next, he pulled out a revolver and shot Mr. Prosper twice at point-blank range, once in the chest and once in the head.

"Darnation!" whispered Theo.

"If only we had known!" I cried. "Avenging Gregor was just the cause we needed to draw us back together back then. Even Ulysses would have fought off his wanderlust long enough to avenge his favorite brother."

Mab continued reading.

Before Mr. Smythe or Mr. Wickerson could react, the stranger leaned forward and took from Mr. Prosper's fallen body the gold and black knife with the ruby pommel, which Mr. Prosper was known to carry. Misters Smythe and Wickerson gave chase, but the stranger escaped before he could be apprehended.

"That's the same knife Mephisto had on the boat!" I interrupted. "The one he found at Logistilla's place."

"I remember that knife," said Theo. "Titus made the blade and Mephisto made the hilt. How could Logistilla have a knife that Gregor's murderer stole?"

"Ma'am, Mr. Theophrastus . . . there's more," Mab said gravely.

"Go on, Mab," I replied softly.

Mab read, " 'Misters Smythe and Wickerson described the stranger as a wealthy gentleman, well dressed and distinctive in appearance.' "

A cold shiver traveled down my spine. My head felt oddly light. Mab's words seemed to be coming from far away.

" 'According to Misters Smythe and Wickerson, the stranger had a mustache. In addition to his revolver, he carried a tall walking stick, almost as high as his head, with a single star-sapphire set into the top of it. Except for his spats, which were of purest white, the fellow was dressed entirely in gray . . . and, strangest of all, he wore a domino mask which covered his eyes.' "

A low moan issued from Theo's throat. "No! It can't be."

"Sorry, Sir, but I never forget a perpetrator. And I recognize this perp, Ma'am. Mr. Ulysses shot Mr. Gregor."

CHAPTER TEN

Erasmus

Later that day, we crunched our way across the snow-covered sidewalks of Boston, bemused by the locals, who apparently crossed the busy streets any time they wished, without concern for traffic laws. Beside me, Mab snapped his cell phone closed and stuffed it into his trench-coat pocket.

"That was the guy from the graveyard," he informed Theo and me. "They found your brother Gregor's coffin, Ma'am."

"That's a relief!"

"Not really." Mab paused, then blurted out, "It was empty."

"Empty!" Theo's face had taken on an unnatural pallor. I began fearing for his health. "Where is Gregor's body?"

"We don't know," Mab replied. "His body may have fallen into the gate your father opened."

"Could Father's spell have worked? Could Gregor be alive? Either on Earth, or in Hell?" Theo insisted.

Mab and I looked at each other.

"I suppose he could," Mab replied. "I never thought to follow up that other fellow who came out of the grave. I assumed it was your sister's old boyfriend, that Ferdinand guy."

"Could you go follow it up now, Mab?" I asked. Theo's pallor worried me. He was still Catholic enough to find the disappearance of his brother's body tremendously alarming. I hoped the notion that someone was pursuing the subject would help soothe him. "It could be important."

"Sure," Mab stuck his hands in his trench-coat pockets. "You're probably better off without me underfoot during your family reunion anyway. I'll head down to the library, get the laptop out, and make some inquiries. If necessary, I'll fly to Illinois."

"Thank you, Mab," said Theo. "You are a decent fellow."

"You're welcome," Mab tipped his hat to Theo. "Always nice to be appreciated."

MY brother Erasmus lived in a large Victorian mansion with bright curly trim like a gingerbread house. When we knocked on the front door, a smartly dressed parlor maid let us in and took our coats. She led us to a drawing room, where we were instructed to wait while she informed Professor Prospero that guests had arrived. Before she could do so, however, Theo asked to use the facilities. While she was showing him the way, I slipped out the far side and headed up the stairs in search of my brother.

I found him in the library, leaning languidly against a table, reciting poetry to a gathering of pretty young women, presumably students. He wore a dark green turtleneck and black slacks, and looked much as I remembered him: handsome and clever, with dark hair falling over mocking green eyes and a narrow chin. In his hand, he held an old leather-bound volume, from which he was reading a work by Marvell. The young women stared at him with rapt attention, absorbing his every word.

One of the students noticed me, and Erasmus raised his head and glanced toward the door, smiling charmingly—a smile that died stillborn the moment he recognized me.

"That's all for today, ladies." He shut the leather volume with a snap. "Family business intrudes."

The young women rose and departed reluctantly amidst a wave of mingling perfumes. Some smiled at me as they left. Others were hostile, perhaps fearing I might be some rival for my brother's affections, which made me speculate, unpleasantly, as to the nature of his relationship with his female students.

Stepping into the library, I pushed aside a sliding ladder and allowed the young women to pass. The room was long and narrow with wall-to-wall books, save for where the windows looked out on broad snowy lawns leading to the frozen Charles River. The air was warm and smelled of books and leather and spiced chai. Several young women had left mugs resting on or near their seats.

"Miranda!" My brother rose. "You've crawled out of your moldering heap. What an unpleasant surprise."

In the rush to come here, I had forgotten how disagreeable Erasmus was. Until he had opened his mouth, I had actually been glad to see him. Now, however, all the old grievances came rushing back. A blinding rage swept over me. Clenching my fists, I turned my back on my brother and examined his library, as I struggled to regain my composure.

Portraits painted by Erasmus were placed here and there about the library. I recognized Queen Elizabeth, Sir Walter Raleigh, King Charles II, and the portrait commemorating the first time Father sat for Parliament. In fact, all of the art was Erasmus's, except for a tapestry, which hung between two of the windows, that I recognized as Logistilla's work. It showed a green-clad angel with five sets of seagull wings and five halos of storm and spray. Ignoring Erasmus and his smirk, I crossed the room and reached toward the tapestry, my fingers not quite brushing the cloth.

"Muriel Sophia," I breathed, recalling the day she had come to me, so long ago.

Erasmus started. "Don't speak that name aloud! Where did you hear it? Only the Inner Circle are cleared to know it. Who betrayed us to you?"

"She told me," I replied simply, gazing up at the angel. By "Inner Circle" and "us," I assumed he meant the *Orbis Suleimani*.

Erasmus snorted. "As if such as she would come to the likes of you! You read the name in one of Father's books, didn't you? *Tsk tsk*. Father would be so ashamed, his sterling Miranda reduced to a common snoop."

"Enough of this." I was becoming annoyed in spite of my resolution not to allow Erasmus to disturb me. "I've come regarding the matters I spoke of in my letter."

"Your letter?" Erasmus asked. "Oh yes, the one I threw on the fire without reading. I do so tire of your eternal whining."

"You . . . you threw it . . ." I sputtered. "But Erasmus! Our lives are at stake!"

"Our lives?" My brother clicked his fingers. "Oh, that's right! I did hear something about you being all a dither over some message meant for me."

"Meant for you?" I sat down in one of the large overstuffed chairs his overly eager students had recently occupied. The seat was still warm. "How do you mean?"

"Something about a message glimpsed in phoenix-light? Phoenix-script is the method Father and I normally use to communicate," Erasmus leaned forward as he spoke and gazed mockingly through the strands of his dark hair. "That means the message was meant for me."

I drew back, more shaken than I wanted to admit. Had Father's mysterious letter not been addressed to me? No, I now recalled that the greeting had merely read: "My Child." All this time—during which I had been putting aside urgent work in order to carry out Father's wish that my siblings be warned of the dangers to their staffs from the Three Shadowed Ones—had I been dutifully carrying out an order not even intended for me? Perhaps Theo was right, and I *was* under a spell!

And how disconcerting to discover Father and Erasmus had a means of communicating of which I had been unaware. Why had Father not shared this secret with me?

"Did you receive the message, too?" I asked Erasmus.

He nodded, still smiling.

Chagrin turned to anger. "Then, why didn't *you* warn *me*? You knew where I was. Why didn't you warn Mephisto or Theo?"

"Father is always firing off dramatic messages, Dear Sister, you know that," Erasmus replied. He flipped open the book of poetry and glanced down at it, no longer bothering to look my way. "I wouldn't worry your frosty little head about it."

Outside the window, students were building a snowman on the lawn. I watched them work as I contemplated this latest revelation. Erasmus was usually one of the sharper members of the family, but he had made a grave error if he had read Father's message and ignored it. I could not help feeling the tiniest smidgeon of smugness.

"Where do you believe Father is now?" I asked.

"Off gallivanting somewhere, enjoying his retirement," Erasmus replied airily. "Really, Miranda, for someone of your advanced years, you are shockingly gullible."

"Father is in Hell!" Theo stood in the library door, huffing from the exertion of the stairs. The parlor maid peeked meekly from behind him.

"Wonders upon wonders! You pried the Old Man off his farm!" Erasmus crowed, a grin of delight spreading across his face.

"Watch your tongue, Young Whippersnapper! I've always been older than you," Theo stalked into the room, leaving the maid hovering timidly in the hallway. My brothers met and embraced. Both were smiling.

"That will be all, Lucinda," Erasmus murmured. The maid bowed her head and hurried away. "Brother Theo, Sister Miranda, to wha . . ." His voice suddenly rose oddly. "Where did you say Father was?"

"Father is in Hell, Erasmus," I said. "He tried to resurrect Gregor and got sucked down through the gate he created. While this gate was open, several things escaped, including our old enemies, the Three Shadowed Ones. Now they are hunting down the family and trying to steal our staffs."

"High Holy Heaven!" Erasmus paused, thunderstruck. "Are you certain?"

"Yes."

"Is Father alive?"

"Yes."

"Well . . . we'd better rescue him!" Erasmus replied. Despite his spirited rejoinder, he seemed stunned.

"There's more, Erasmus," Theo said.

"It gets worse?" he asked sadly.

"Yes, in fact, that's just the beginning," Theo replied.

"Ah, life. It always hits you just when it seems to be at its rosiest. Happiness never lasts. All is fleeting." He had retreated again behind his mask of studied indifference. Leaning against the great oak desk again, he quoted from William Dunbar's "Lament for the Makers."

Death comes unto all estates,
Princes, prelates, and potentates,
Both rich and poor of all degree:
Timor mortis conturbat me

Hearing Erasmus's recitation brought back a memory that was not truthfully mine, yet I had heard tell of it so often that I could recall the scene as vividly as if I had witnessed it myself. My brothers seldom took their magic to human wars, preferring to save sorcery and enchantment for battles against the supernatural. Upon occasion, however, something would snap, and one of them would turn the dire power of his enchanted staff against men.

The Battle of Vimeiro, the first battle of the Peninsular Wars against Napoleon, was led by the general who would later, upon being made a duke, be known as Wellington. It was a hot humid August day on the hillsides of Portugal. The British right flank was proceeding in an orderly fashion, but the left flank was in imminent danger of losing the hill and, more importantly, the six precious cannons positioned upon it. There was always a shortage of guns and gunners during the wars against Napoleon, and it did not help that our brother Titus was among the gunners manning the ninepounder.

Erasmus and Theophrastus marched that day with the 43rd Foot, a rifle regiment known as the Royal Green Jackets that was part of the force defending the hill. Mephisto and Gregor were in the distance, on horseback with the 20th Light Dragoons. Theo, who was an excellent shot, often joined the riflemen, but I do not know why Erasmus had joined the infantry rather than the cavalry for this campaign. Perhaps the name, the "Royal Green Jackets," appealed to his aesthetic sense. He had undertaken other dangerous duties for equally frivolous reasons.

The French grenadiers swept up the hill, pushing the Royal Green Jackets before them. Suddenly, the forward edge of the living blue wave vanished in a cloud of dust. A warm puff of breeze blew the dust away, leaving a circle of dead grass, in the midst of which stood my brother Erasmus.

He wore his dark green jacket, and his lank black hair hung before his eyes. His upraised right hand was covered in a gauntlet of shimmering silver-white. Within this Urim-gauntleted hand, he held aloft the *Staff of Decay,* which spun and hummed in his grasp, rotating too quickly for the human eye to see, so that it appeared as a long gray blur.

Erasmus stood motionless, heedless of the deafening cracks of firing muskets and the choking smell of gunpowder and blood. A slight mocking smile played about his lips, which moved, though no words could be heard above the din.

Without any change in his mocking expression, he advanced down the hill, waving the gray blur of his terrible staff before him. He came forward steadily, a relentless, irresistible force. The blue-coated grenadiers who stood their ground grew older before the eyes of their comrades, aging ten years, then forty, then sixty. Their flesh shriveled upon their limbs, until they were as gaunt and dry as mummies. Then they had flesh no more. Their dried horrified eyes looked out from bare skulls, until even their bones dissolved into dust and were blown away by the Mediterranean breeze.

Some tried to fire their weapons, but the wood of the muskets crumbled in their age-spotted hands, the metal parts falling to the ground in pieces. Terrified, the grenadiers began drawing back. Those who had encountered Erasmus's scourge without perishing stumbled with the tiny halting steps of the aged or crawled, dragging their weakened, dilapidated bodies.

As terror spread and weapons were discarded, an unnatural pall fell over the hill. In the sudden stillness, Erasmus's words could be heard ringing out across the silent battlefield.

He takes the knights into the field
Enarmed under helm and shield;

Victor he is at all melee:
Timor mortis conturbat me

He takes the champion in the stour,
The captain closed in the tower,
The lady in bower full of beauty:
Timor mortis conturbat me

From behind the retreating grenadiers, a brave French soldier broke through the ranks and charged up the hill, shouting in his native tongue, "English devil! I will send you back to Hell!" Still outside the range of Erasmus's devastating effect, he fired his pistol directly at my brother's face. Titus, who watched from his position beside the guns at the top of the hill, told me his heart stopped, for he was certain that bullet carried Erasmus's death.

Erasmus's smile never faltered. He never even looked up. He merely waved his arm, and the bullet dissolved into dust. Another step forward, another stanza, and another pass of the staff, and the brave Frenchman gaped in horror as his pistol rusted away and his outstretched arm withered to nothingness, moments before he followed them to oblivion.

Throughout all this, Erasmus's recitation never faltered:

He spares no lord for his puissance,
Nor clerk for his intelligence;
His awful stroke may no man flee:
Timor mortis conturbat me

The British lost seven hundred twenty men at Vimeiro. The French lost over two thousand, including several hundred soldiers who gave themselves up, preferring to become captives rather than face old age or worse. They fled in droves, allowing the British to capture thirteen of the twenty-three French cannons. The *Orbis Suleimani* have cleaned up the official records, of course, omitting any mention of my brother. Those few unfortunate souls that tottered away from their direct encounter with the *Staff of Decay* met their death soon after upon the blades of *Orbis Suleimani* assassins. Soon, no evidence of Erasmus's involvement remained.

As I listened to Erasmus recite the same poem now, I pictured how he must have appeared to the French grenadiers who lost their lives to his magic at Vimeiro, and I shivered: not a pleasant man, my brother Erasmus.

When Erasmus finally fell silent, Theo asked gruffly, "Very well and good, but what about Father?"

Erasmus rose and smiled his ironic, mocking smile. "I am a poor host, am I not? You probably have not even been offered refreshments. So there is worse news to come, is there? Why don't you both come with me, and I will have Lucinda bring us drinks while we wait for Cornelius. Misery loves company. Why not share the wealth with him as well?"

"Is he here?" I asked.

"He arrived yesterday."

AFTER sending his maid for refreshments, Erasmus led us to a drawing room on the ground floor. African masks of woven, dyed straw and brightly painted clay hung upon the walls, along with a full Lakota Indian headdress and an Aztec fan of bright red and blue parrot feathers. In keeping with Erasmus's sense of humor, amidst these primitive masks and fans, there hung a dainty lady's hat adorned with the blue-gray feathers of the extinct passenger pigeon.

Lucinda brought us mango juice and slices of quince poached in a cardamom syrup, not what I would have served guests on the thirty-first of December, but perhaps young coeds who came to hear poetry expected exotic desserts. The drinks were served in tall fluted cups of cranberry glass—a favorite of Erasmus's because it gets its deep red color from adding trace amounts of gold, his favorite metal, to the molten glass. Cranberry glass is beautiful, but through it, the yellow-orange juice looked like blood.

I sipped my mango nectar and stared across the snowy lawns. In the distance, skaters risked their lives upon the frozen waters of the Charles River. Somewhere beyond lay the city of Boston. It had been a long time since I had been to Boston, longer still since I had visited any of the cities of my childhood.

What was Milan like today? How had it weathered the encroachment of this modern world? Would I find it hostile and altered, like coming upon a stranger where a loved one should have been? Or, had it improved with age, the changes muting its faults and preserving its virtues?

My family fell into the second category—with a few exceptions, such as Ulysses. While time had taken its toll, the passing centuries had also brought a maturity to my brothers they had lacked in earlier eras. A month ago, I would have thought it impossible that we would ever again join willingly together to accomplish something—even something as grim as confronting Ulysses over the death of our brother Gregor. While my youngest brother's treachery still shocked me, he was centuries younger than the rest of us and had not lived through the many experiences that had forged us into family. Sitting in Erasmus's drawing room, the sunlight falling through the tall windows and onto my face, I felt, to my surprise, unexpectedly charitable toward my younger siblings. Perhaps I had been too hard on them.

There was a knock, and the door opened to admit a dark-haired boy in purple and gold livery, leading a man by the hand. The man was dressed in a somber suit. A length of royal purple silk had been wrapped about his head, covering his eyes; in his free hand, he carried a blind man's cane topped with a large sphere of amber: my brother Cornelius and the *Staff of Persuasion*.

He tilted his head and asked in his gentle voice, "Brother, I hear you have guests? Are they anyone I know?"

"Someone you knew once," Theo replied gruffly.

"Father . . . no, Theo!" Cornelius's face split into a smile. "What a pleasant surprise! And who is this with you? Is that your lovely wife whose sweet scent I smell?"

"My wife is dead," Theo said bluntly, and I recalled the photographs of an unknown woman that had graced his living room. With a pang of anguish, I realized this woman had lived, been loved by Theo, and died without my ever even having met her. Yet, Cornelius spoke as if he knew her.

The boy led Cornelius to a chair and helped him to sit. There was something familiar about the child, with his dark eyes and thick black hair. I could have sworn I had seen him before.

"Have a mango juice," Erasmus offered graciously, handing a ruby-colored glass to Cornelius and a second to the boy, who took it tentatively and retreated to stand by the window.

"Hello, Cornelius, it's been a long time," I said quietly.

"Miranda! Even more surprises! When you did not make the last Centennial Ball, or should I say, the Millennium Ball, I feared you, too, had become a recluse," he said, his voice gentle and soft. "We had quite a turnout. All the Plantdanu attended, the younger Greek gods—what's left of them—and the Eight Fortunate Ones of China. Even the Archmage came down from the Himalayas. But of our elder sister, we heard nary a peep."

"I had intended to come; unfortunately, business interfered," I replied, recalling a hectic weekend spent chasing wayward sprites who were spreading rumors among the supernatural community that the turn of the Millennium would absolve all oaths and covenants.

I glanced around the room, my gaze resting upon my siblings' faces: Erasmus, Cornelius, and Theo, all in the same room. What a joy it was to have so many of us together, and, by tonight, there would be still more of us. It was almost like old times.

"What brings you two here today? Erasmus's party?" asked Cornelius.

"Not that either of them were invited," murmured Erasmus.

"We came because Father's in trouble," I said, "because the Three Shadowed Ones claim some kind of doom will fall upon our family by Twelfth Night—which is only six days away now—and because we have some disturbing news about Gregor's death."

"Gregor's death?" Cornelius's voice rose in surprise. "I thought that matter had been long forgotten."

"Not by me," muttered Theo.

"Not by Father, either," I said. "Apparently, it's been troubling him terribly. He did not retire because he was weary of working. He retired so that he could spend all his time trying to find a way to save Gregor. The matter culminated this September, when Father went to Gregor's grave and attempted to resurrect him."

"Trafficking in black magic?" Cornelius asked, amazed. "Father?"

"He used his new staff, which he made by sprouting a piece of the True Cross," I replied. "I suspect Father thinks this makes it white magic. Either way, he failed. He was captured and is now a prisoner in Hell. His attempt let the Three Shadowed Ones free and led to the letter I sent you."

"Father, is he . . ." Cornelius's voice wavered. "Is he dead?"

"He's alive, as best we have been able to find out, but that's not what we came about," I finished, glancing at Theo.

"Read them the journal entry," Theo said gruffly.

So, I did.

WHEN I finished, Cornelius sat stock still, his nose and chin pale as milk beneath the royal purple silk of his blindfold. Erasmus, however, began to laugh, a low chuckling sort of laugh that grated on the nerves and reminded me of numerous unpleasant incidents from the past.

"An amusing forgery. What of it?" he asked mockingly.

I examined the copies in my hands. "You think someone deliberately created this document to fool us?"

"Oh, I think 'someone' deliberately invented it, yes . . . but it won't work, Sweet Sister. So, you might as well come clean and tell us for what perverse reason you wish to turn us against Ulysses, hmm?" Erasmus purred.

His implication was so absurd that a moment went by before it sank in.

"You are accusing me of forging this document and sneaking it into the records of the Elgin, Illinois, police department?" I asked, astonished. "Why? To what purpose?"

"I have only your word as to where the document is from," he replied smugly. "How am I to know there is really such a journal at all?"

Once someone does not believe your word, it becomes impossible to hold a conversation with them. Erasmus knew this. He must also have known I would never lie, and yet still, he made such accusations. In the past I would have ranted at him. After everything I had endured recently, however, I did not see the point.

Instead, I said tiredly, "You've gone mad, Erasmus. You are madder than Mephisto."

"See here, Erasmus," Theo interrupted. "I was there when Miranda learned this information. She did not invent it. It came in a letter from Illinois."

"I'm sure it did," answered Erasmus smoothly. "And if I attempted to check its authenticity, I have a good idea what I would find: newly minted, antique-looking sheets recently rushed into place by eager airy servants . . . isn't that so, Sister Dear?"

"How could she have set up such a letter just for my sake when she had no notion I would be visiting?" barked Theo.

"How can I tell what tricks our sister plays or why? Her malicious machinations are a cipher to me. I know not nor care how she weaves her tangled skein, but I'll not be taken in by her schemes. Run along now, Miranda, we've seen through your little trick."

"Miranda's right, you have gone mad," Theo growled, crossing his arms and sinking back in his chair.

Cornelius, who had been sitting motionless, listening to the exchange, now spoke. "I hesitate to participate in family disputes, but I fear in this case I must take Erasmus's side. I know Ulysses. I have listened to the music of his heart. He could not do this thing of which you accuse him. He is a thief, yes, but not a murderer. He loved Gregor. Perhaps, he might have it in him to kill a brother in the heat of rage, but a cool, calculated murder such as this describes?

"No. Miranda," he continued, "I do not know what dark powers have possessed your heart that you feel you must turn us one against the other, but I beg you to reconsider. We have only each other against the ravages of time. We cannot afford treachery."

"You can hear the goodness in Ulysses, who is not here, but you can't hear the honesty in my voice?" I asked, amazed.

Cornelius hesitated. Finally, he said, "I do not detect any falsehood in your voice, Miranda. However, as your nature is different from our own, I may be incorrectly interpreting what I hear."

"Different?" I asked, astonished. "Different in what way? Because I am a female? You seem to be making a great effort not to admit that you know I'm telling the truth. Why?"

"There's no point in continuing your ploy, Miranda," Erasmus replied snidely. "We know all about your mother. We haven't confronted you about it before this because we did not want to embarrass Father. But, as he is not here . . ."

"What's this about Miranda's mother?" asked Theo, confused.

"You know *what* about my mother?" I echoed, a cold feeling in the pit of my stomach.

The thought of discovering that some horror had been inflicted upon my mother . . . After so many recent earthshaking revelations, it seemed utterly unbearable. I had always believed her to have died in childbirth. Please, I prayed desperately, do not let me learn Father also did her some harm, as he had apparently done Ferdinand. I could not bear to learn the sainted Lady Portia had been stowed away in Hell, where she suffered alive and tormented.

On the other hand, this could be yet another ploy of Erasmus's. He had always been jealous of Father's love for my mother. His mother, Isabella Medici, had been Father's worst mistake in choosing a wife: politically, a savvy move, but privately, a disaster. I recalled the night she died, an embittered old woman of eighty-seven. After the necessary arrangements had been made, Father had slipped aside and opened a bottle of rare enchanted wine, with which he and I had gratefully toasted his freedom and the return of his sanity.

Erasmus grinned his oily smile. "Do not pretend ignorance, Sweet Sister. I am speaking of the identity of your true mother, and of your real nature—the great secret you have been hiding from us all these years. You may think you have been deceiving—"

He was interrupted by the urgent voice of Mephisto, who came bursting through the drawing-room door crying: "Erasmus, wait! She doesn't know!"

Erasmus's subtle features froze. He snapped, "What do you mean . . . she doesn't know? Hasn't she been deceiving us?"

"I don't know what, Mephisto?" I asked with equal vehemence.

Mephisto looked around at the gathered crowd, his mouth forming a silent "o" when he saw Cornelius and Theo. He was dressed in a dark blue parka and a pair of jeans and might have fit into any modern setting, were it not that the six-foot length of his staff, its carved wooden figures stacked together like a totem pole, was handcuffed to his right wrist. I noticed a newly carved image of a jagged-winged bird had been added near the top.

The pleasure of having five of us in one place was lost amid the nauseating fear that gnawed at my innards.

"Ah . . . nothing." Mephisto looked up at the ceiling and pursed his lips as if pretending to whistle. "Um, maybe this is not the best time to talk about this, Erasmus. Why don't we all have a cup of hot chocolate and forget the whole thing? We must have bags of stuff to talk about. Cornelius! Theo! It's been so long!" He spread out his arms in welcome, smiling cheerfully.

"On the contrary, I discern this may be the best time for this conversation," said Cornelius. "Miranda has made some harsh accusations against one of the family. We must hear the truth, so that we can properly evaluate her accusations."

"I didn't do it!" cried Mephisto, throwing up his hands. His staff flew wildly, pivoting about his wrist, nearly striking Theo, who ducked.

"No one has accused you of anything, Mephisto," I said tiredly.

"You mean someone's in trouble, and it's not me? Oh, well, I guess that's all right." He sighed with relief and threw himself into the nearest armchair. "Okay, I'm settled. Tell me all about it!"

Erasmus crossed over to Mephisto and leaned very close to him, his foot resting on Mephisto's chair.

"What did you mean by 'Miranda doesn't know'?" he asked in a voice whose softness bordered on menacing.

Mephisto drew back and squeaked. "She doesn't know. I never told her; neither did Father. She doesn't know. What's so hard to understand about that?"

"You mean . . . she hasn't been lying to us all these years?"

"No, how could she? I told only you."

Erasmus turned and glared at me, his dark eyes speculative. "Hmm. How disconcerting."

"Enough! What is it no one has told me?" I asked, harshly this time. "What happened to my mother?"

"Nothing," squeaked Mephisto, "except . . . she wasn't your mother."

Erasmus came cruelly to the point. "Your mother was the witch Sycorax, whom Father summoned by magic. He merely told you it was Lady Portia to protect his reputation."

This was the most ridiculous accusation Erasmus had made yet. I snorted with contempt. "Nonsense!"

"It's true," whispered Mephisto softly. "Father told me himself."

I clung to my chair, hoping to stop the feeling of vertigo.

"He . . . he did?"

"Well . . . sort of. Once we were talking about the summoning spell, the one used to make my staff? He told me the first time he used the spell, what he had summoned came back nine months later and gave him Baby Miranda. Basically, he and the thing he summoned . . . well, you know . . ."

"After Mephisto told me this I searched Father's journals," Erasmus continued gleefully. "The first mention of this spell is when he summons the witch Sycorax. Nine months later, he clearly states that she brought him a child, which he refers to as 'the fruit of that first summoning.'"

"You mean, I am . . . Caliban's sister?" I asked horrified. My own brother had tried to rape me? Did that make the crime less heinous, or more so? More so, I concluded grimly, though this news gave me new insight into why Father had refused to kill the horrible creature. Perhaps he had promised his hideous lover that he would protect both her progeny.

"Oh, there's more," Erasmus continued with relish. "There are numerous references to 'Sycorax's Unruly Child.' Apparently, you kept troubling the 'A.T.,' by which I believe Father meant his Aerie Spirits—the journals are in Greek. Then, when you were about five, there is a definite reference to you by name, in which Father wrote, and I quote." He recited a brief passage in the original Greek, but we were an educated lot. The meaning was plain to us all:

"'*May 4th. Today, I consecrated little Miranda to the Creatrix Eurynome. It is my hope that Her divine influence will curb the natural tendencies of my daughter and make the child more like unto human kind.*' Seems you were not always the perfect daughter you pretend to be now," Erasmus finished smugly.

"I knew it!" Theo muttered angrily, "I knew Father had Miranda under a spell!"

"If Erasmus's discoveries are true, it may be best for us all that he did," replied Cornelius. Turning to me, he asked, "You truly knew nothing of this?"

"Nothing!" I responded faintly. "I'm not sure I believe it still. It's . . ."

"The journal in which I found the reference resides in my library." Erasmus gestured upward.

I drew back, hugging my glass to me. Had Father truly said such spiteful things about me? It could not be! I recalled so clearly our many chats about my mother, Father sitting beside me on the bluff that overlooked the northwest coast of our small isle. His keen blue eyes shone with love as he spoke of her.

Could he have been speaking of *the foul witch Sycorax, who with age and envy was grown into a hoop*? No. She could not possibly be the woman who had inspired such greatness in him. Erasmus and Mephisto's story made no sense.

And yet, I recalled the King of Fire glaring at me, his eyes ablaze with fiery menace, as he sneered, "Vile half-breed! Accursed Nephilim!" A Nephilim was, if I recalled correctly, a term used for the half-human, half-supernatural monstrosities that roamed the earth before Noah's Flood. I had thought Iblis referred to Caurus—an Aerie One in a fleshy body.

Only, I recalled with sudden alarm, the King of Djinn did not turn to address Caurus until after he had spoken his half-breed insult. When he originally spoke the words, he had been staring directly at me.

Could it be the woman of whom Father had spoken of so tenderly was not my mother? I struggled to keep the pain this notion caused me from showing on my face.

"Enough about past sorrows." Mephisto cheerfully threw out his arms. "Let's get to the present sorrows. What's this family tragedy everyone's yammering about?"

Erasmus handed Mephisto the letter. Mephisto read it silently, making faces as he went. As he approached the end, he cried out: "O dastardly Ulysses! What a monstrous thing to do!" He was quiet for a long time, tears in his eyes. Finally, struggling to put on a brave face, he declared tremulously, "What a bonehead! I hope he plans to pay up on the money Gregor owed me!"

"Erasmus believes Miranda invented this document," Cornelius said softly.

"Miranda? Why would she care what Ulysses or Gregor did? What a dopey thing to think, Erasmus," Mephisto replied, dismissing the idea out of hand.

I felt a flood of affection for my hapless brother. Suddenly, I was very glad I had not abandoned him on the streets of Chicago.

Behind me, Theo began to laugh. It was a harsh wheezing sound at first, but it developed into a deep throaty laughter that reminded me of Father. The laughter led to a bout of coughing.

When Theo could breathe again, he said, "What a sad world you must live in, Brother Erasmus, believing the worst of a guileless creature like Miranda." He shook his grizzled head and put down his untouched glass of mango juice. "Come, Cornelius. Let us get ourselves a cup of something hot, as our good brother Mephistopheles suggested. There perhaps, we can ponder today's revelations and decide what, if anything, to do about them."

"A goodly plan, Brother Theophrastus," said Cornelius, rising and putting out his hand for the young boy beside him.

As the young boy left his post by the window and came forward to take my brother's arm, I was again struck by how familiar his features were. He felt my eyes upon him and gave me a cheerful smile. As he did, I realized that I had seen him before: in Father Christmas's scrying pool.

He had been playing in the street with several other children, and one of the masons we had seen repairing the Lincoln Monument called him home. I knew now that those masons were *Orbis Suleimani* who worked for Cornelius. The mason had clearly borne a resemblance to the boy and seemed to be his father. Could it be his position as Cornelius's guide that led the Scrying Pool of Naughty and Nice to show him to me as if he were part of our family?

As I smiled at the boy, I was reminded of the many years I spent serving my father. A wave of sympathy for this child, who would probably rather be out sledding, washed over me. For an instant, I felt as if it were I who dutifully led the blind Cornelius out the door.

I had begun to rise. Now, I dropped back into my chair and sat, shaken.

It had happened again, this strange empathy with a stranger. But what did it mean?

Theo exited the room, still chuckling and coughing, He was followed by Cornelius and his young guide, and a moment later, by an eager Mephisto. This left Erasmus and me alone, amidst masks and feathers.

CHAPTER ELEVEN

The Chamber of Gold

"Erasmus, why do you hate me so?" I asked.

"Surely, you know," Erasmus replied, his mocking dark eyes smiling at me from beneath his straight black hair.

"Humor me," I said tiredly. "Why?"

"Oh, I think not," he replied, leaning back in his chair and sipping his mango juice. "I know better than to sharpen my enemy's weapons."

I sighed. "May I see Father's journal, the one you quoted from?"

"Certainly not! You might sully it."

My eyes narrowed. "You made all this up, didn't you? There is no journal!"

"There's a journal, all right!" Erasmus replied. When I continued to look skeptical, he said, "Oh, very well! But you must promise to wash your hands first."

Rising, he led me back toward the library.

A MAID had opened one of the library windows, and a cold breeze had blown away the aroma of perfume and chai, leaving the room chilly and smelling of snow. An enormously fat cat covered with black and white splotches lay curled in Erasmus's chair by the desk. I had to look twice before I recognized him as Redesmere, Erasmus's familiar and the dire enemy of Tybalt. I paused briefly to give him a pat. Erasmus glared at me, but I remained undaunted. After all, his glare was nothing compared to the stare my own familiar would have given me if he had caught me at it.

Redesmere opened one golden eye, contentedly observed my homage with the *nobles oblige* of true royalty, and closed it again.

At the far end of the chamber, Erasmus pulled out a key to open a door set between two bookshelves. Shelves were set into this door as well. To unlock it, he had to reach down a narrow gap between two books.

It opened into a short corridor, also lined with bookshelves. At the back was another locked door. The key to this door, when he pulled it out, glittered yellow in the dim light of the overhead bulb.

As he opened this second door, he flipped on the light, illuminating a chamber ablaze with gold. I raised my hand to shade my eyes and peered through my fingers. Beyond, everything sparkled and flashed. A golden chandelier hung from a gilded ceiling, shining its light upon a windowless hexagonal library. Delicate chairs of finely wrought gold stood around a table with a mirrored surface and burnished crackle legs upon which sat a chess set of onyx and gold. Upon the table sat pens, ink wells, and paper organizers, all of them of the gleaming yellow metal.

The books, older and rarer than those in the main library, rested upon heavy bookshelves of solid gold. I recalled the effort he had gone to gathering the ore and learning to smith it—and two occasions upon which an entire floor had collapsed under their tremendous weight. The wooden ladder that slid along the bookshelves, allowing access to upper shelves, was gilded, and the small stepping stools shone like little rectangular suns. Even the white marble of the floor contained aurulent flecks.

In my youth, we would have called wealth like this "a king's ransom." Nowadays, men count wealth in terms of how many aircraft carriers or bombers it will build. Amidst the fourteen karat bookshelves, the dazzling table, and the rest, there was more than enough to ransom a king, but I doubted all of this would be enough to buy even a single aircraft carrier.

"Impressive," I murmured, blinking.

"Ah, gold . . ." he smiled lazily. "The most beautiful substance in the world, like sunlight trapped in solid form. Doesn't age, rust, or rot."

I had forgotten about Erasmus's love of gold. It was not the wealth of it that drew him, as it might Cornelius or Ulysses, but its immunity to the ravages of time, and thus to his *Staff of Decay*.

"Odd choice to house a library of fragile old books," I mused aloud.

"I thought the contrast fitting," he replied airily.

Walking to one of the six walls, he slid out a long flat drawer upon which lay a very old tome. The leather of the cover was brittle and cracked, and flakes of parchment lay about the ragged edge of the pages. Yet, despite its great age, I recognized it, recalling the thousands of times my child self had come upon Father writing in that very book.

Yet, how old it had become. How fragile! Seeing it now, I could almost forgive Erasmus for not wanting to let me touch it.

My brother opened the book with great care, turning almost immediately to the page containing the quote he had mentioned. The musty odor of decaying parchment assailed my nostrils. I sneezed.

To my dismay, the passage was just as he had recited it. Farther down the page were additional unpleasant descriptions of Sycorax's unruly child.

"What makes you think this passage here refers to me, rather than Caliban?" I pointed at the page. "Here, Father uses the masculine form of 'child.'"

"It is common to use the masculine for 'child' in Greek, regardless of the gender of the offspring," Erasmus replied. Smirking, he pointed. "Just there, he describes the child as a force for destruction even though it is 'no higher than his thigh.' Caliban, who was already living on the island with his mother when Father arrived, would have been larger than that. Wasn't he already half grown when Father arrived?"

I clenched my fists and glared down at the journal. I disliked talk of Caliban. The mere thought of him still filled me with an old rage. Caliban . . . my brother?

As I stared dull-eyed at the passage, a strand of my pale silver hair, escaped from its clip, floated beside my cheek. I caught it and frowned, trying to figure out how to poke it back into my coiffure. Erasmus misinterpreted my dismay.

"You looked so much lovelier when your hair was vibrant and black, Dear Sister." My brother's smirk widened. "But then, we all know how vanity is a sin! So, perhaps you should thank me."

My sharp retort was halted by a thought. Father's essay on the horrors of contact with demons claimed that each demon had a vice and any mortal who remained too long in its company would become vulnerable to that vice. What vice was associated with the demon in Erasmus's staff? Did this bitterness that ate at him, causing him to constantly attack me, originate from the demon in the *Staff of Decay*?

"Did you know our staffs have demons in them?" I asked bluntly.

"Of course," he replied blithely. "Didn't you? No? Daddy didn't see fit to tell you, eh? Probably thought little Miss Perfect would have a hissy fit. How did you find out?"

I turned back to Father's journal and continued reading, ignoring his barb. There was no point in bickering for bickering's sake. Were I to answer, my brother would either accuse me of consorting with demons or mock me for believing an incubus; never mind that Erasmus himself had just attested to the truth of Seir's words. Coming to the bottom of the page, I reached out to turn it.

"Ah, ah, ah! No touchy." My brother stepped between me and the book. "You did not stop and wash your hands."

"Very well, you turn the pages." I crossed my arms.

"Now see here, I am hardly . . ." Erasmus trailed off, frowning thoughtfully at the top of my head. "Wait here!" He pointed at the spot where I was standing. "Touch nothing until I return!"

He departed, locking me into the golden room so I could not flee with his precious books and riches.

I considered yanking out the nearest book on principle, reasoning that since Erasmus had left without obtaining my agreement, I was not obliged to obey his wishes. As my eyes trailed over the shelves, however, my sympathy for him increased.

I stood amid a rare-book collector's paradise. A brief glance revealed three-hundred-year-old volumes of Shakespeare and Bacon, original works by Leibniz and Spinoza, disintegrating editions of Descartes, and a hand-illuminated Harvey, probably filled with notes written by Erasmus during his time as a student of that great father of modern medicine.

In among these ancient worthies were titles of a more arcane or esoteric nature, some of which I had been seeking for centuries! *The Secret of Secrets* by Duban the Sage, *Iconography from the High House of Dreaming, Habitats of Water Nymphs, The Journeys of Randolph Carter, Oneironaut, The Theonomicon, Seven Nights In Elfland: an Eye-Witness Account,* and *Four Hundred and Seventeen Alchemical Salts,* this last, apparently, by Erasmus himself.

To my astonishment, I even found books I had thought lost or that should not exist at all: *Euclid's Book Four, Aristotle's Dialogues, Andromeda* and *Helena* by Euripides. Where had he gotten these? *Revelations of Hali, The Whole Art of Detection, The Architecture of Small Country Houses* by John Drinkwater? I had believed these last three volumes merely imaginary!

I stared goggle-eyed at this bibliographic feast, my mouth watering. Ever since childhood, back on Prospero's Island, books had been among my favorite companions. Of late, I had been concentrating on Father's journals and seeking hints regarding the secrets of the Sibyl, but there had been a time when I had read nearly every volume available to the known world. That was impossible now, of course, due to the recent increase in the number of books published, but it had been possible in my youth.

As I came to the next shelf, my heart nearly stopped. The entire bookshelf, from top to bottom, held black leather volumes bound with a strip of yellow cloth along the spine. I recognized those books. They were Father's *Libri Arcani,* the journals into which he entered the results of his magical experiments. When Father retired, he gave me his personal diaries, black leather volumes bound with a strip of red, into which he noted his daily thoughts and contemplations. When none of the ancient yellow-striped volumes were among the collection, I thought they had been lost. Yet, here they were, pristine and whole, in Erasmus's library. I moved my hands across them, my fingers hovering a hair's width above the spine, then leaned in to breathe deeply of their musty leather.

As I came around to my starting point, I noticed the spine of the Spinoza was charred. Seeing the blackened binding evoked a memory. I recalled Erasmus kneeling on the grass, surrounded by scattered books, weeping bitterly. The rest of us stood around him, watching tongues of flame flickering in the windows of our great Scottish mansion. The books lying on the grass were the armfuls he had brought out on his first two trips. He had tried to run back into the flames yet again, but my other brothers had stopped him; Theo and Titus restraining him physically.

It was a tense few hours for all of us, for our staffs were still inside, and we did not know if they would survive the conflagration. It was worst for Erasmus, however, who lost most of the library he had been gathering for over two hundred years, some volumes of which were the last-known existing copy of a particular work. This loss pained me as well, but less so, partially because, while I loved reading as much or more than my brother, I was not a collector, and partially because the books I loved most were in my chapel and, consequently, not in danger from the fire.

When the blaze finally died away, and we were able to return to the blackened hulk of our home, only a few volumes of Erasmus's ten-thousand-book library had survived. This copy of Spinoza's *Ethics* had been one of them.

I dropped into one of the delicate filigreed chairs and absentmindedly slid the queen's bishop's pawn forward, imitating an opening I had tried the last time I had played Erasmus. In our youth, I often beat my brother, I who had spent so much time playing Father in my youth. But Erasmus stuck to the game and I did not, and so he had become the master, even besting the supernatural competition at some of the Centennial Balls. Only the subtle elf lord Fincunir was his better.

Shakespeare had presented me as playing chess with Ferdinand—most likely because chess was one of the few activities that a young man and woman could perform alone without her virtue being considered compromised. In the play, my namesake worried about whether Ferdinand would play me false, before claiming that she would not mind even if he wrangled kingdoms from her. The scene was entirely of Shakespeare's invention; I had beaten Ferdinand soundly on the few occasions that we had played.

And yet, I wished I had not recalled this, for the notion of Ferdinand playing me false caused a sudden chill. I released the chess piece and glanced back at the burnt copy of Spinoza upon the shelves.

Perhaps Father and I were not the only ones who would be dismayed by the loss of the ancient tomes that had been damaged during Seir of the Shadows's first attack in the Great Hall of Prospero's Mansion. Any sympathy I might have felt for my bibliophile brother faded, however, as I considered how he would react if I told him of this recent tragedy. I could picture him sneering triumphantly, as he contrived some way to imply that the attack on Prospero's Mansion was my fault. Whatever else one might say about Erasmus, he was tremendously good at sneering.

The memory of my brother weeping gave way to a recollection of the time he auctioned off his shares of Prospero, Inc. Once, all ten of us, Father and we children, had owned shares of the company. After Gregor died, and Theo had abandoned us, Father gave control of Gregor's shares to Cornelius and Theo's to me. Over the next quarter century, the others bailed out as well. Since, under our charter, they received a stipend whether they owed stock or not, they felt they would prefer not to be bothered the annoyance of attending stockholders' meetings and running the company. Titus and Logistilla gave their shares to Cornelius. Mephisto and Ulysses gave theirs to me. Father—who was already preparing for his retirement, though he did not officially retire until three years ago—decided I would succeed him as C.E.O. and signed over his shares to me. This left only Cornelius, Erasmus, and me as shareholders.

One frosty day in February of 1975, Erasmus announced he, too, had decided to bow out of Prospero, Inc., and he wished to auction off his shares to the highest bidder. If I won, I would have a clear majority, sixty percent to Cornelius's forty. If Cornelius won, we would be tied fifty-fifty. Since the idea of a deadlocked board, with no tie-breaker available, seemed daunting, I was willing to do anything reasonable to win Erasmus's shares.

What Erasmus asked in return for choosing me was beyond the pale of reason! He wanted a full carafe of the Water of Life. I offered him a little vial of Water, but that was not enough; only a full carafe would do.

I did not have enough Water left to fill a carafe. To meet his requirement, I would have to take the journey of a year and a day to the Well at the World's End. I argued with Erasmus for three days, explaining how this was a very bad time for me to take a year off. Normally, I prepared for these journeys decades in advance—and that was before I became the C.E.O of Prospero, Inc.—but he was adamant.

Resolved to win the auction and protect the company, I took the journey. A year and a day later, I returned with a full carafe, which I took directly to Erasmus. He met me on the steps of his palatial mansion, near Philadelphia, and announced with a smirk that I was too late. He had gotten tired of waiting, he declared with a casual wave of his hand, and had given his shares to Cornelius.

I objected that I could not possibly have arrived any sooner and pointed out how he knew this would be the case when he asked me to go. Erasmus just shrugged and replied that he had never intended to give me his shares. He had held the auction for the purpose of irritating me.

When I arrived back at my office the next day, I learned that, while I was gone, a contractual dispute between the Aerie Ones and the Eastern undines had led to the worst typhoon in a century. Their dispute had been over a simple matter. Had I been present, or even had proper time to prepare before I departed, I could easily have solved the dispute; however, I had taken my flute with me. Without it, even Father could do nothing. A hundred thousand Chinese died because I had left my post, because Erasmus found it entertaining to irritate me.

As I stood there, fuming at the memory, I heard his footsteps in the hallway. He unlocked the door and came striding back into the hexagonal chamber, singing merrily. On his right hand, he wore a gauntlet of shining silver-white, the mate of the gauntlet Caurus used to wield the *Wounding Wand*. In the gauntlet's grip, he carried a five-foot tube of a transparent material. Enclosed within it was a square staff with alternating sides of black and white. Erasmus tapped the clear exterior against the carpet once and then held it up. Within it, the square black and white staff began to rotate, whirling and humming as it gained speed, until it appeared as if Erasmus grasped a single gray blur.

I took two steps back.

"Fear not, my cowardly sibling. You are not my target today," my brother announced lightly. "Have you destroyed anything while I was gone, hmm?" He glanced over the shelves. "No? What a lucky accident for us. Slipping up, are you, Sister?" Then, holding his staff aloft, he strode to the back of the library, singing to himself cheerfully.

I waited wary.

Stopping before Father's journal, Erasmus raised the *Staff of Decay* and brought its whirring length down upon the ancient book.

"No!" I cried, leaping forward. I would have thrown myself forward to save the precious journal, except I knew Erasmus would have been only too happy to wither me along with it, happier, most likely. He did not harm books easily. "Don't destroy Father's journal on my account!" I cried. "Please! I'll—"

"Destroy a book? Do you take me for a madman?" Erasmus asked, running his staff back and forth across the ancient pages. "On second thought, Mephisto is a madman, and even he has the sense not to destroy books."

I watched his progress, my eyes glued to the crumbling parchment of Father's journal, as if the force of my gaze alone could preserve the pages. The staff's hum decreased in pitch, and the air about the tome grew warm and bluish. Before my eyes, the parchment brightened, and the binding grew more supple. Soon, the journal looked as it had in my youth: hale and strong, and filled with endless wisdom.

"You'll . . . what?" Erasmus asked mockingly, as the whirr of the staff died away. "What could you possibly offer me? Or was that supposed to be a threat?"

"May I examine Father's journal now?" I crossed my arms.

"With that scowl? A little gratitude might be in order, don't you think, Sister? Another person might even say: 'Thank you,' but not you. That's the one thing I like about you, Miranda, you're reliable: selfish to the end!"

I drummed my fingers on my forearm and waited. I was grateful—if grateful is the proper word to describe what one feels when someone goes out of his way to help substantiate a claim against one's character—but any attempt to express gratitude would be lost in the general storm of malice. Erasmus was a master at interpreting virtuous impulses as vices, and I refused to be drawn into yet another of his pointless games. Mankind could not afford it.

"Be my guest." He waved expansively at the book, bringing the whirring *Staff of Decay* dangerously close to my head. I jumped back, startled. He gave a short cruel laugh. "Don't want to be a child again, eh? Can't say I blame you. As you are about to learn from Father's journal, the first time around was unpleasant enough!"

He shook the staff, and the whirling center section slowed until the two distinct colors of white and black could be discerned again. "I shall leave you in peace. Spend as much time investigating your misbegotten childhood as you desire. Yank the bell pull when you want to be let out. Tootle-loo!"

He strode out of the chamber, humming, and locked the door behind him.

SURROUNDED by the burnished gleam of the sun's metal, I explored Father's journal, flipping here and there, examining Father's sketches, and reading his descriptions of our life on the island. There was much about "Sycorax's Child" troubling his beloved "A.T." and numerous complaints about Caliban, but little mention of me by name. The longer I read, the more my heart constricted. Had Father not loved me at all?

When it came to other matters, Father was a meticulous chronicler. With great love and care, he described the flora of our island prison-home, including detailed sketches of palm leaves and orchid blooms. As I read, the mists of memory that hide our childhoods from us thinned, and I could again hear the cry of the storm petrels and smell the brine of the sea.

Turning a page, I came upon a sketch of little me, standing amid the orchids, charming and sweet. Underneath, in Italian, Father had written: LITTLE MIRANDA, THE JOY OF MY LIFE.

Happy tears welled up over my lashes.

As I wiped my face with the back of my hand, I realized, with sinking heart, that this picture had been drawn when I was six; well after my fifth birthday, when I had been consecrated to Eurynome. Perhaps Erasmus was right. Perhaps I had been a hellion, and only after the Unicorn tamed me did I become the joy of Father's heart.

On the other hand, if it were my service to Eurynome that brought about the change in my youthful character, that hardly counted as the enchantment Theo so feared, any more than one would bewail the loss of wildness in a child who had later been schooled in good manners by nuns. If Father had cast some additional spell upon me to make me pliable, I found no mention of it in his journal.

I would disregard Theo's theory entirely, if it were not for one disturbing matter. These bizarre moments of sympathy, such as the one that had formed between Cornelius's young charge and myself, were growing more frequent. In the last two weeks, similar incidents had occurred between me and others: Caurus on the flying carpet; an elf maid in Lady Christmas's kitchen; a nameless young woman in a plum coat on the steps of the Lincoln Memorial in Washington, D.C.; Mephisto in Vermont; and an old lady tottering across an overpass in Chicago. Never before in my over five hundred years of life had I experienced anything like this.

What were these strange experiences? Magic? A spell? A perfectly normal occurrence? If they were perfectly normal, why had they not happened before? Why had they begun almost immediately after I learned of Father's disappearance?

Had Father cast some spell over me long ago, cutting me off from the normal range of human emotions so that I remained always calm, reserved, and biddable? If so, what else might I expect as this spell wore off? Fits of passion? Bouts of rage? Was my whole notion of myself a sham?

As I paced about the library contemplating these questions, I longed to have someone to discuss it with, but there was no one. I could not talk to Mab. One did not discuss the state of one's mind with subordinates. My brothers? Obviously not Erasmus! And Cornelius, and Mephisto were out of the question as well.

Theo? Years ago, I would have gone to him first, but now? He seemed old and pained, and even crankier than in his youth. He would worry needlessly, which would do me no good. What I needed was a sympathetic ear, someone who would not jump to conclusions.

Ferdinand Di Napoli.

I glanced at the golden clock standing upon the mirrored table. In roughly six hours, Ferdinand would be arriving for Erasmus's New Year's party. The last time we spoke, before the hearth at Prospero's Mansion, he had proved himself a careful and diligent listener, willing to consider matters objectively and offer sound advice. Perhaps we could sit together in the main chamber of the library, side by side in the deep green overstuffed armchairs, with him smiling thoughtfully as he listened, looking into my eyes, leaning toward me, his eyes aglow . . .

Stopping before I could finish that thought, I sat down, wishing I could leave the hexagonal room and breathe in the outside air. It was stifling here, heavy with the odor of old and musty books. I began to wonder what I would do if I pulled the rope and no one answered. At least I would not be obliged to soil myself. On one of the bottom shelves, Erasmus had squirreled away a solid gold chamber pot.

I returned to the sliding drawer upon which lay Father's journal. As I continued flipping through the volume, reading snippets here and there, the words "my brother Antonio" caught my eye. I peered closer, striving to make out Father's looping hand. Roughly translated, he had written:

Already the trap is set. I have learned the necessary spells and taught my spirit-servants their part. All that remains is for M. to arrange matters so that my brother Antonio and his ally in the household of the King of Naples take a journey by sea. This last, M. informs me, may take some years, but this may be for the best, as that way all my plans may come at once to fruition.

"M."? Who could that be? Not me—I would have been too young, nor had I ever been in a position to make arrangements for the household of the King of Naples. Mab, perhaps? No, Father had not captured him yet, and, besides, back then he was called Cockias.

Reading further, I found another reference to "M." Here Father wrote: "Lead on, M., My Fair Queen, and I shall follow, even to the ends of the earth."

My Fair Queen? What queen could possibly have been helping Father in his plot to regain his proper position while we were on the island? I had known he had airy servants helping him, but an ally? By the sound of it, M. was a supernatural ally, not merely a human companion. Someone who was in a position to influence Antonio, and who was powerful enough to inform Father that he must wait years, which no subordinate would have dared do. Who would have been in a position to aid him thus, and why had Father never mentioned such a person?

For a moment, I entertained the idea that "M." might stand for "Monocerus," but dismissed it. If Father had been in such direct contact with Eurynome, he would not have approached me as an intercessor when he had questions for Her, which he did regularly over the years. Besides, I cannot imagine the Unicorn troubling herself with the petty dealings of human princes.

I continued paging through the journal, baffled by the puzzle of Father's mysterious ally. As I neared the end of the journal, I skimmed the pages to see if this M. put in an appearance during the events recorded in *The Tempest*, but found no mention of her.

On the very last page, I came upon a sketch of the ship that had taken us home to Milan. In Father's drawing, I stood upon the deck, a lovely maid of fifteen, laughing, my hands upon one of the lines. Behind me, his arms about me as he guided my hands, Father had drawn a young man, hardly more than a youth, with thick dark brows and a large jutting chin. He was handsome in a rugged boyish way, but not breathtakingly so. I frowned, trying to recall who this youth might be. One of the boat hands, perhaps? Odd that Father had sketched him with me instead of Ferdinand.

Finding nothing further of interest, I closed the journal and reached for the pull rope. To my relief, Erasmus only kept me waiting for ten minutes before he released me.

THE New Year's festivities were held in the grand ballroom of Erasmus's Victorian mansion. Soft strains of Strauss, issuing from the string quartet seated on the balcony, underscored the hum of the partygoers below. Long tables held ice sculptures, fountains of champagne, and delicacies from many nations of the world. The scent of richly spiced meats caused my mouth to water.

At the far end of the hall towered a huge grandfather clock. Earlier that afternoon, the clock had been synchronized with the digital clock in Times Square. Tonight, the celebrants would watch this clock's second hand as they counted down to the New Year.

The guests arrived in droves: society women in pearl-trimmed evening gowns, professors in their ceremonial robes, local potentates in fancy tuxes, and students made boisterous and rowdy by their awe at the company they kept. Moving unnoticed among them were a dozen *Orbis Suleimani* agents. These dapper Italianate gentlemen mingled among the other visitors, all the while keeping an eye out for the slightest sign of trouble, supernatural or otherwise.

There was no sign yet of Ferdinand.

As I mingled with the guests, I noticed many of those present were from charities to which my brother donated money or time. Much as I disliked Erasmus, I felt compelled to acknowledge that, when it came to his devotion to mankind, he shined far above the rest of us. My brother was a philanthropist in the best sense. He cared about improving the everyday lives of ordinary people. Most of all, he cared about extending those lives. Most of my siblings never gave a second thought to the fact that we could not share our immortality with the rest of mankind, but it bothered Erasmus a great deal.

Unable to extend the lives of men through magic, he had turned to science, applying his keen intellect to the problem. He had taken up the study of medicine back in the early seventeenth century, shortly after the births of the twins, and had never given it up. A great many medical improvements in the last hundred and fifty years had been discovered or financed by him.

Erasmus helped implement the concept of military medic units. He was one of the first supporters of Clara Barton's Red Cross. He had founded and maintained hundreds of hospitals: some in civilized places such as London and Boston, and some in distant and nigh-inaccessible places, such as the interior of Africa or Nepal. He even used to volunteer, in the days before anesthetics, as a guinea pig for untried procedures, figuring that between the Water and his staff, he had a better chance of surviving than an ordinary volunteer. For all that I hated him, I had to grudgingly admire this good he did for others.

As I came down the sweeping staircase, my sister arrived in high style. She was decked out in a tight-fitting gown from the flapper period that rippled sensually as she walked. To the untrained eye, it might resemble a mix of satin and watered silk, but real cloth would never have flowed so naturally. The garment was woven from night's air and the reflection of moonlight on black water.

Behind her, held by a dainty golden chain, was the eight-foot grizzly bear that had approached me on the beach in front of Logistilla's house when we visited her island retreat a couple of weeks ago. The bear towered above the other guests, who quickly cleared a path for the creature. It moved slowly and sluggishly, however, as if unaware of its great strength, its head obediently bowed to Logistilla's whims.

I myself wore a Worth original of violet damask bordered with silver fox. The pointed waist of the bodice directed the eye toward the beaded irises cascading down the length of the skirt. Short puffed sleeves of dotted mousseline de soie under a ruffle of beaded satin framed a square décolleté. A pair of matching gloves covered my arms to the elbows. It was a lovely creation.

Despite its loveliness, I had been loath to wear it. So long as our enemies were at large, I felt safer in my enchanted tea dress. However, Erasmus had personally chosen the Worth ball gown for me earlier in the afternoon, taking it from a collection he kept in the mansion and graciously restoring it, through the gift of his staff, to its pristine Victorian glory. In the interest of family unity, I decided not to spurn his single gesture of kindness. Besides, while the enchantments on my tea dress caused its emerald satin to remain ever clean and presentable, I had been wearing it nearly continuously with all my recent traveling. Ferdinand had yet to see me in anything else.

It was pleasant to don a different garment for a change. The Worth gown had a beautiful line and fit my figure nicely. If only I could have remembered how to manage that flattering faery hair knot, it would be a perfect ensemble. I hoped Ferdinand would find it pleasing.

The motion of the crowds soon brought Logistilla and me together. She complimented my gown, and I hers. I wanted to ask her how she had come to possess Gregor's knife. After much debate, however, it had been decided that none of us would question Logistilla until after Ulysses had appeared. Since the presence of the knife could mean that she and Ulysses had conspired to murder Gregor together, we did not wish to give her the opportunity to warn Ulysses of our suspicions.

"Quite a gathering this year," my sister offered, when the exchange of compliments waned. "I see all the usual white-haired professors and wide-eyed coeds are present. Who is here from the family?"

"Myself, Theo, Cornelius, and Mephisto," I said, "and of course, Erasmus."

"Theo? The old codger bestirred himself to come and hobnob with the rest of us? Well, that's a surprise! Is Titus here yet?"

"If so, I haven't seen him," I replied.

For some reason, this made Logistilla laugh. "When you do, tell him to look me up. We have some matters to discuss. By the way, do you recall I mentioned being attacked by a shadowy figure? Well, it has happened twice more; the second time was just this afternoon, here in Boston! The bear chased him off, but I suspect it was one of those fellows you and your man were carrying on about back at my island. The Three Shakoes was it?"

"Shadowed Ones," I replied perfunctorily.

"Ah, of course." Glancing down, she eyed the silver fox on my gown distastefully, her mouth forming a disapproving moue. She pointed a long tapered finger at the fur trim. "Really, Miranda, no one wears dead animal anymore. How do you manage to always be so horribly out of fashion? Did Erasmus pick that gown? Probably his way of warning his guests to beware the heartless, pitiless monster that is his eldest sister. Clever boy. Well, I'm off to the punch bowl. Do you think Erasmus would mind terribly if I let the bear get drunk?"

I watched her sail off in the direction of the punch bowl with the great ginger beast in tow, led by its dainty gold chain. The poor creature glanced back at me with deep, soulful eyes. I felt sorry for the man it had once been and looked away.

ANOTHER turn around the party and I found myself nervously glancing over my shoulder. I told myself not to worry, that apprehending Ulysses would go smoothly, but, in my heart, I knew it was not Ulysses's imminent arrival that caused these internal butterflies.

Would Ferdinand's meeting with my family go well? Erasmus and Cornelius would approve of him, I decided, particularly if I could arrange for him to meet Erasmus before my brother learned who he was—which meant restraining Mephisto from making a scene at his arrival. As for Logistilla, I prayed she would not embarrass herself. She had a way of turning herself into an idiot whenever a good-looking man was present.

Theo, however, was another matter.

Theo's appearance at my house in Oregon, rifle in hand, suggested that he intended to keep his vow to defend my honor. How I was going to explain to Theo that Ferdinand was now a friend, and yet keep my brother from going back to his farm and giving up on life, I had no idea.

But I felt Theo would like Ferdinand, if they met under the right circumstance. They both were such decent men.

I laughed out loud. What was I, a schoolgirl? Here I was, over five hundred years old, worrying about whether or not my brothers would approve of my beau.

But I did care what they thought, I realized with some astonishment. I loved my family—annoying as they could be—and I cared about their opinions, even Erasmus's. Much as I also hated him, I knew his judgment was good—in any area not involving me.

It slowly dawned on me that, all this time, I begrudged my siblings going their own way because I missed their company. Why had I not realized it? I had been so busy resenting them and criticizing them, I had not stopped to consider why their absence bothered me so. Oh, sure, Prospero, Inc. was harder to run without them, but, in truth, that was the least of it.

I missed them. True, sometimes they were hard to get along with. In my heart, however, I knew we belonged all together. Each one of us was like a portion of a whole. And something felt empty when any one of us was gone, like ghost pains in a missing limb.

I had always felt it, I realized now, but my heart had been so cold. I had been so cut off from the rest of humanity, that I had not even noticed. I had not recognized my pain for what it was—love.

ERASMUS kept his house cool, but the press of bodies had raised the temperature, until, even in my short-sleeved gown, I found myself uncomfortably warm. In the corner farthest from the entrance, a maid had opened one of the tall windows. I crossed the room to stand beside it, enjoying the play of cool breeze across the bare skin of my arms.

Outside, all was dark and as silent as falling snow. As I leaned closer, breathing in the crisp night air, a pale young man stepped out of the darkness. He paused on the casement, his cloak of black feathers swirling about him like the folding wings of a swan. His features were familiar; yet, for a moment, I could not place them.

"Fiachra!" I exclaimed, when the mists of time parted long enough for me to dredge up his name.

The pale youth leapt lightly to the ballroom floor and bowed over my hand, pressing it between his own. His skin was cool and smooth, like porcelain. His hair was midnight-black, and as he leaned toward me, I caught a whiff that reminded me of moonlight and faraway alpine flowers.

"Aunt Miranda."

"It has been a long time," I smiled.

"As mortals measure it, perhaps. Where I dwell, in Tir Nan Og, time is meaningless. What need have the Forever Young of clocks and hourglasses?" His voice was beautiful, like song, but one could not hear it long and still take it for human.

"Sounds heavenly," I said dreamily, his voice and feathered cloak evoking memories of my recent flight amidst the stars. Recalling that flight brought other memories upon which I dared not dwell, such as the pure melodies of the Music of the Spheres I so longed to hear again, or the laughing gleam in Astreus's eyes as he knelt among the black plumage, watching me gape at the living constellations. I banished those memories quickly, embarrassed that, with Ferdinand so close, my thoughts would betray me and linger on the forbidden elf.

" 'Tis a land of peace and wonder, true; yet only the naïve confuse our fair realm with paradise. Those Who Know never entirely forget the shadow of Tithe and Hell." He gazed at me, and a black lake reflecting purple mountains beneath a starry sky swam in his swanlike eyes. I stared fascinated.

"What brings you here?" I asked.

"My father has bound me by a vow that, once annually, I would step foot within his house. I fulfill my obligation by attending this, his celebration honoring the death and rebirth of the year," he replied gravely.

"Interesting. What was his purpose in having you swear such an oath?"

"He feared I would forget him entirely if I stay away too long; and so I might, for who in the Land of the Young spares a thought for those without, unless bound and bidden to do so? And yet, when my foot touches this floor and I again breathe the scents of the mortal world, all my affection for my father rushes back to me."

"How funny we should meet. I was just thinking of you," I said, struck by how little he had changed in three centuries, rather like someone else I knew. I glanced briefly over my shoulder, searching the crowd, but caught no glimpse of the face for which I sought.

"How so?" he asked, and I flinched, searching for an answer that did not include Roundheads with bloody crosses or the smell of burnt swan-cloak.

"Do you remember the time your mother tried to feed you slugs?" I tried. A faint flicker of a smile visited his pale face.

"And Father was furious. Yes, I have heard the tale."

"Is he a good father, my brother Erasmus?" I asked curiously.

Fiachra cocked his head like a bird and regarded me with his starry stare. "Good? To whom would I compare him? He is the only father I have."

"Ah . . . of course. Well. Good to see you again, Fiachra Swan-Lord, son of Reginleif, the Swan Maiden."

He bowed over my hand again. "And you as well, Lady Miranda, Hand-maiden of the Unicorn."

I MADE a circuit of the room again, but saw neither Ulysses nor Ferdinand. A pretty maid, dressed in the same livery our servants had worn back in the seventeenth century, served punch from a large bowl of cranberry crystal. I accepted a glass and went to stand beside an ice sculpture shaped like a swan. The air was slightly cooler there. As I sipped the drink, which tasted of mulberries and sherry, I pondered Fiachra's claim that merely a whiff of the mortal world was enough to bring back his recollections of his life with his father.

Memory worked like that in my experience as well. The smell of mulberries still brought back to me pleasant fall afternoons spent preparing those berries to make morath, and a particularly sorrowful encounter with an old friend. The gleam of the chandelier reflected off Logistilla's enchanted gown recalled a hundred balls in a dozen different ballrooms over a span of years longer than the life of the United States of America. The sketch Father had drawn of us on the ship that sailed us triumphantly back to Milan brought back memories of creaking riggings and salty wind and laughter as Ferdinand and I became tangled in the ropes and fell to the ground together in a wickedly forbidden heap.

The red punch glass slipped through my fingers and bounced against the polished floor, its bright content spilling slowly across the wood.

I could remember the scene as if it were yesterday: the swaying of the ship, the smell of his skin, the pressure of his hands as he taught me to pull in the lines, the scratching of Father's charcoal against the parchment of his journal as he sketched us together, Ferdinand and I.

But if the youth in Father's picture, with his Italian brow and rugged jutting chin, was Ferdinand . . . who was the ungodly handsome Adonis I had invited to meet me here tonight?

CHAPTER TWELVE

A New Year's Night Dream

Like the shock of an icy wave bursting through a dam, I remembered.

It had been a cold January day in 1774, during the reign of Mad King George. Logistilla and I shared an open-topped carriage, hurrying through snow-flurries in hopes of making curtain-up at King's Theatre, where Shakespeare's *Tempest* was to be performed as a ballet for the first time. We were late because we had stopped by my sister's favorite horse dealer. High-steppers were just coming into fashion, and Logistilla insisted on having a pair to breed with her Arabians. So, precious minutes had been wasted haggling over Hackneys and Norfolk Trotters.

Just as we rounded the corner into Haymarket, a jarvey driving an open car like Jehu son of Nimshi—or, as one might say today, a cabbie driving an open carriage like a daredevil—came careening around a bend and collided with our carriage, entangling wheels. My sister, our maidservants, and I all spilled out into the snow.

As we sat upon the road, brushing slush from our ruffles and muffs, an astonishingly handsome young man appeared out of the falling snow, smiling like something from a dream as he asked if we were whole. I assured him no harm had been done, but Logistilla gave him a tongue-lashing, ranting on about how he might have killed us or, worse, broken our necks and left us paralyzed for life, and how would he explain that to God upon his Judgment Day?

Chagrined, the gracious Adonis had helped us to rise and climb back into our vehicle, which our driver and the jarvey had now set right. As he departed, leaping back onto the hired cab, with Logistilla still shouting abuse at him, he gave me a conspiratorial wink.

Imagine my surprise, when we arrived at King's Theatre to discover our handsome Adonis dancing the part of Ferdinand.

I saw every performance of that ballet. Watching the warmth and grace of that young man as he danced, evoked such vivid memories of my lost love that, for a time, I forgot the modern day and lived again the wonder and enchantment of my childhood.

Looking back, I suspected it was during this period that Shakespeare's version became commingled in my memory with the original events; just as the face of that graceful dancer settled into my memory, replacing the features of the real Ferdinand. I glanced nervously around Erasmus's ballroom, now dreading to catch a glimpse of the same face I had, only moments before, longed to see.

How had the imposter—the man whom I met at the Lincoln Memorial and later let into my house—known to impersonate the false image?

The answer, when it came to me, made my skin crawl: Baelor of the Baleful Eye. The mind-reading demon must have riffled through my thoughts, like some mental Peeping Tom, stealing the image of my lost love. What else had he taken? Time tables of phoenix ash-bearing trucks? Locations of Prospero, Inc. warehouses? I shuddered, contemplating other damaging information he might have pilfered from me.

Baelor himself could not be the modern Ferdinand; however, as he could not speak without a victim to possess, much less carry on hours of intimate and witty conversation. So, who then? Osae the Red was a shapechanger, true; yet he was hardly more than a brute. He could not even impersonate Mab without his bestial passions getting the best of him. I doubted he could pull off a character as subtle as Modern Ferdinand. That left . . . With a low moan, I hid my face in my hands.

To have been suckered by an incubus! And at my age!

Me. The daughter of the mighty Prospero. The Handmaiden of Eurynome. For over five hundred and fifty years I had avoided the depredations of rakes and incubi, only to be hoodwinked the moment my father stepped out of the picture! If nothing else suggested I had been under some kind of an enchantment that was now wearing off, this did!

Hope kindled in my breast when I recalled the Aerie Ones had also recognized Ferdinand, but it died just as quickly as I remembered that Ariel had not recognized our visitor until after I called him by name. Ferdinand's unexpected enthusiasm over his reunion with my airy servants was also explained. Seir, who did not realize how little Ferdinand had known of Ariel and his kin, had overacted.

I reviewed the possible candidates again and came, regretfully, to the same conclusion. Of the Three Shadowed Ones, only the incubus could have pulled off a subterfuge of such finesse. The Ferdinand I had met—and kissed—must have been Seir of the Shadows. I rubbed my lips hard against my palms, as if I could cleanse away the demon's touch.

No wonder the Ouija board had hesitated when I asked if Ferdinand were a shapechanger. The Three Shadowed Ones must have instructed the spirits responding to answer literally. No, he was not a shapechanger by nature, he was an incubus. I should have asked whether he was a demon!

Even my Lady had tried to warn me. She had protected me from Seir when he appeared as Ferdinand in my dream. I had not heeded Her warning, because I had banked on the fact that Seir of the Shadows could not alter his shape in the waking world.

So, how had he changed his shape?

Logistilla's staff! What else could be causing her staff to flash unexpectedly except the Three Shadowed Ones, who had already demonstrated they could manipulate our staffs? Baelor must have fed the image of the false Ferdinand he had stolen from my mind to the *Staff of Transmogrification* and caused it to alter Seir's appearance.

More shameful still: It was not that I had confessed family secrets to the enemy that troubled me most, but the realization that I would be denied the chance to voice my worries to Ferdinand's sympathetic ear.

Oh, how far I had fallen!

My face burned as hotly as if I stood beside a roaring hearth. I turned and fled, seeking solitude.

Only there was no solitude to be sought. Merry partygoers chatted in every nook and corner, and the library room and the many sitting rooms were occupied by guests involved in quiet conversations or romantic tête-à-têtes. So I wandered like a ghost among the throngs of glittering guests, seeking solace in anonymity.

I walked amidst the velvets and silks, a silver-blond vision in lavender with cheeks afire. I wove this way and that, dodging clumps of merrymakers and the eager helpful faces of concerned strangers. Eventually, the sea of faces blurred, and I forgot, for a time, that I was not really alone.

The one comfort, to which I clung, was the knowledge that no one but my servants knew of Ferdinand's nighttime visit to Prospero's Mansion. Ariel would never betray me; no one else need ever know the true depth of my foolishness.

As if ice giants breathed upon my grave, a terrible chill seized me. I had invited Ferdinand here, tonight! I had informed Seir of the Shadows and his cohorts of the time and place of my brother's New Year's party. They had even made use of Logistilla's staff since she arrived here in Boston. The Three Shadowed Ones knew the family was gathering here.

They were coming!

WITH a heavy heart, I sought out Erasmus. I hoped to find him alone or in private conversation, but the fates were not kind to me tonight. My brother stood at the center of a large crowd, regaling them with witticisms and colorful stories. He cut quite a dashing figure in his deep green velvet suit, a garment I had last seen him wear upon the floor of Almacks in the age of the Prince Regent. The ladies present must have agreed with my assessment, for quite a number stood about vying for his attention. They eyed me coolly as I came up beside him and touched his shoulder.

"Erasmus, I must speak with you!"

My brother turned, picked up my hand, as if it were some slimy insect, removed it from his shoulder, and dropped it. His guests, who had no idea I was his sister, watched in amusement.

"Why? So you can whisper poisonous rumors about other family members?" he asked softly.

"Erasmus, this is serious," I whispered back.

"How serious, Dear Sister? Serious enough to interrupt my lovely guests? Shame on you! Just because you have chosen to be an old dried-up prune doesn't mean others must follow your example." He raised his voice as he spoke this last line, and the ladies in the crowd gave a titter of excitement mixed with shock. From their expressions, I gathered they were not used to rudeness from Professor Prospero. I, however, was in no mood to banter.

"The Three Shadowed Ones are coming!"

"Oh, ho? And what makes you think so? A horoscope? Tea leaves? Another fiery letter?"

Anger welled up in me. What was the point of choosing my words carefully, if my listener would deliberately misconstrue them? Better to get my point across simply and clearly.

"Because I invited them."

The look on Erasmus's face was priceless.

"CLEVER of you, Miranda, to invite the minions of Hell to our yearly family gathering," drawled Logistilla, waving her glass toward me. Droplets of champagne splattered across my face. "Get rid of us all, in one fell swoop. Your only mistake was to put in an appearance yourself."

We stood in Erasmus's billiards room, the velvet tables stretched out before us in the semidarkness. My brother had not bothered to turn on the lights, so the only illumination came from the hallway and from the reflection of the ballroom windows on the snow outside. My brothers stood about me in a ring, listening intently. Logistilla had moved to one side, where she sipped from her fluted glass and stared out at the chiaroscuro patterns on the snow. I did not know where in this old Victorian house one might stash a bear, but she must have found a spot, because she had not brought the great grizzly to our family gathering.

"Run this by us again," Erasmus spoke with an exaggerated calm. "Why exactly did you betray your family to our enemies?"

"Because I mistook Seir for someone I knew," I responded, my voice tight.

Theo crossed his arms. "And you told him about our party because . . . ?"

"I wanted to get my brothers' opinion of him," I answered.

"Well, you may have our opinion," Erasmus replied icily. "Your judgment stinks!"

"Who are we talking about here?" cried Mephisto. "Not Ferdy?"

I nodded solemnly.

"That dirty rat!" Turning to the others, Mephisto chimed, spreading his arms. "Guess what? I found out something Miranda hadn't told us. She neglected to mention Prince Ferdinand chucked her at the altar. Imagine knowing someone as long as we've known each other and neglecting to mention you'd been jilted by the fiancé whom you claimed to have finessed?"

"Oh, I knew she was lying about that," purred Erasmus. "That's one reason I'm sure she's lying about so many other things."

"How could you have known?" I asked, shocked.

"Uncle Antonio told me."

"Oh!"

Erasmus continued, smirking, "Do you recall how I found Uncle Antonio on the battlefield before he died? As he lay in the mud, gasping out his last breath, he confessed to Prince Ferdinand's murder. Apparently, he feared that if the prince married you, the two of you would conceive an heir, and he, Antonio, would be out of the running for future King of Naples. He murdered Ferdinand and tried to take his place in the affections of his father, the king. Apparently, it worked for a while, though eventually he and the king had a falling out."

I stared numbly at Erasmus, wondering why the room had begun to spin. "You knew? All this time? You knew what happened to Ferdinand, and you've never told me?"

"Were you interested, Sister? Funny, you never mentioned the subject. I figured if you ever told me the truth, I would tell you what I knew. Otherwise, why enlighten you?"

"*Santa Maria, madre de Dios* . . ." I whispered, reverting to the language of my childhood.

My love had died, died long ago . . . murdered by my uncle. The same wicked uncle Father had forgiven for his previously crimes against us, crimes that had resulted in Father and my infant self being exiled to the Island. The grief of it blended with the grief of my current humiliation, and my heart ached as if Ferdinand had died anew.

From beside me came a deep hoarse growl. "Explain to me, in plain English—exactly who is actually an incubus?" asked Theo.

"Prince Ferdinand Di Napoli is Seir of the Shadows," I replied, tensing for the coming onslaught.

"And you invited him here?" Theo cried, outraged. "What happened to 'O Brother, he insulted my honor'?"

"I . . . we thought we should hear his side of the story," I stammered.

"Then, we all went for Italian food, and he tried to kiss Miranda. It was romantic! Those inkies sure know how to woo women," Mephisto chimed in happily.

"Don't tell me the ice princess fell for an incubus's tricks?" purred Erasmus.

Mephisto shook his head loyally. "Nope, she was as cold as stone."

"That, at least, is to her credit," admitted Erasmus, and Theo looked slightly mollified. My cheeks burning, I left it at that. No one need know about my second meeting with the fake Ferdinand at the mansion.

Cornelius had sat down on one of the stools and was leaning against the nearest pool table, resting his head on his hands. Without looking up, he spoke up in his customary calm voice. "All this family history is no doubt fascinating, but do we not have a more pressing matter to discuss, Brothers and Sisters?"

"Let him come." Theo hunched his shoulders and his lined face broke into a harsh grin. "I've got a few questions for him."

"What if he brings his friends?" asked Cornelius. "Will it be safe for the guests? Should we cancel the festivity?"

"We must cancel." Erasmus tipped his head back and looked at the ceiling. "This party is a Boston tradition. There are hundreds of people present. If we let them stay and our uninvited guests harmed even a single one, I would never forgive myself. Ah, what a shame, and we haven't even served the salmon mousse yet." He turned on me suddenly. "You did this on purpose, didn't you? To ruin my evening?"

This was too much.

"Oh yes, Erasmus," I fumed. "I sent engraved invitations to the Three Shadowed Ones asking them to come by and collect our staffs, as we are going to be all gathered together in one place. This was after I cut off Father's head and framed Ulysses for Gregor's murder, which I secretly committed myself. Tomorrow, I plan to destroy the Earth with my fellows, the other wicked children of Sycorax, but not until I've irritated Theo into having a heart attack. Can't leave any stone unturned. Satisfied?"

"Glad to hear you're willing to admit some of your sins," Erasmus replied, as cool as ever. "It's a start. A few more outbursts like that, and maybe we'll get the truth out of you."

I pressed my fingers against my temples, which were beginning to ache. "You are incorrigible, Erasmus."

"So," asked Logistilla, who was looking at me oddly. Too late, I remembered I was not supposed to mention the Ulysses matter. "The plan is to send the guests home and then pig out on Erasmus's food until our nemeses arrive? And then what? Defend this rickety old place as best we can?"

"That's about the face of it," replied Erasmus.

"Oh, goody!" Mephisto cheered. "A fight!"

I STOOD on the narrow flat center of Erasmus's roof, leaning against the small railing that surrounded it, and gazed out over the steep sloping sides, through the darkness and across the pale snow-covered fields below. The air, while chilled, was surprisingly balmy for a snowy Boston night. The silhouette of the single gargoyle, hunched above the main entrance on the far side of the roof, was my only companion.

After our talk, Erasmus dismissed his guests with some story of a sudden breakout of an infectious disease. Meanwhile, Theo, Mephisto, and Cornelius posted themselves in various strategic positions to guard against the approach of the Three Shadowed Ones. Even Logistilla was given a guard post, to her great consternation. Only I, whom Erasmus refused to trust, was at loose ends.

Not wishing to encounter any of my relatives, I had gathered my cashmere cloak and, after a brief chat with the local Aerie Ones, gone directly to the roof. Now, standing in the chill of the night, I contemplated all I had recently learned.

It was as if someone had shredded the tapestry of my life.

A scant month ago, my days had been pleasant and unruffled, my life following the same smooth course it had continued along for centuries. I was the cherished daughter of a noble man and his long-departed true love. As C.E.O. of Prospero, Inc., I worked diligently to maintain the company my father had created and to uphold its purposes and principles: protecting mankind from the ravages and depredations of the supernatural world. True, one of my brothers was dead, another was mad, and a third had broken with the family to follow a path toward his own destruction, but I knew my family would never do one another any true harm, never betray one another. The only sour note in the melody of my life had been that I had not been making progress in my effort to rise to the rank of Sibyl.

Then came the fateful day in early December, less than a month ago, when I held Father's journal up to the Phoenix lamp and received his cryptic message, a message that had apparently been intended for Erasmus.

And now?

I stood at the railing, staring into the darkness, feeling as if I stood at the edge of a precipice, gazing down into the utter blackness below. It was as if the brink were still before me, giving me an illusion of safety, but I could feel my feet slipping. If I could not regain my balance, my descent into the chasm below would be certain . . . and there was nothing I could grab to slow my fall.

Erasmus's accusations echoed in my thoughts. *Sycorax.* Her name alone evoked revulsion. Goose bumps rippled along my arms. How she had terrified my child self! I recalled running across a field, chasing my ball. I must have been about eight. As I entered a glade of orchids, a sudden shadow eclipsed the sky. Hovering over me was a vulture of an old woman whose body was as bent as a question mark. She smelled of brine and rotting flesh as she scowled down at me, breathing putrid breath. Reaching out for me with crooked bony fingers, she muttered in a singsong voice: "Pretty child, lovely child. Tasty, I wager, to fill an old witch's hunger."

At that moment, Father appeared, amidst a thunderclap, and chased her off with his staff. That was the last time I saw her, for she died soon after.

Only now, as I looked back, did I realize that she must have smelled so terrible because she was deathly ill.

Could that horrible harridan be my mother? Could Father have lied to me all these years, merely pretending I was the daughter of his beloved Lady Portia, the kind and loving soul who had provided the guiding star of Father's life, transforming him from a petty duke into a noble enchanter? I would have sworn not, but then I would have sworn Father would never have sent my first love bodily into Hell . . .

But he had not!

Uncle Antonio had killed Ferdinand. Father was innocent! Relief buoyed me, and the brink receded, only to draw suddenly near again as I considered the false Ferdinand. Despite the night's chill, I could feel the burning in my cheeks. Incubi seduce schoolgirls out of convents, not worldly enchantresses, such as myself.

Yet, when, during our conversation by the fire, he had spoken of suffering centuries of torment for the innocent love of a chaste maiden, I had been completely taken in. It was as if some façade had been ripped away, revealing the true torment of his soul. I had believed him entirely. What acting skill Seir possessed, to fool someone as experienced as I! Even now, when I recalled it, I felt impressed by his sincerity. His protestations had seemed as sincere as my father's description of his great love for Lady Portia. . . .

Had that been a lie, too?

My knees gave way, and I sank to the rooftop, resting my forehead on the cold metal of the railing. After Erasmus's revelation, I had feared I might not be the child of Father and his great love. Now, a worse possibility occurred to me. This great love of Father's, to which I compared all others and found them wanting . . . might that, too, be a deception? A tale woven from faerie dust to entertain a troublesome girl-child?

If so, perhaps I had been taken in by Seir because my standard for sincerity was a sham.

If my own judgment was suspect, then only the grace of my Lady had kept me from doom all these years. If I were to lose her guidance, I would be utterly lost, a babe in the woods. No wonder Theo thought me a guileless thing.

Shivering under my cloak, I remembered Osae the Mab's attempt at rape and knew fear.

TIME stood still as icy terror gripped my heart. The night closed in around me, frigid and menacing. Finally, I gathered my cloak tightly around my shoulders and retreated toward the stairs. Perhaps due to the disturbed state of my thoughts, the presence of only one gargoyle on Erasmus's roof suddenly struck me as ominous. Were not gargoyles usually posted in pairs? Cautiously, I began inching my way back toward the door behind which lay safety and the warmth of the house.

Silent as an owl, the gargoyle's many-horned head swiveled toward me. Sapphire eyes gleamed against the pitch-blackness of the silhouette.

I screamed.

"Good evening, Fair Sister," said a familiar deep voice.

"Mephistopheles?" I gulped hopefully. "What are you doing here?"

The sapphire eyes vanished as the demon returned his gaze to the road below. "I await my enemies, the Three Shadowed Ones."

Clutching my cloak tightly, I briskly walked the length of the roof and stood beside my brother, the Prince of Hell. Glimpses of obsidian black skin were visible through the rents in what had been my brother's fine tuxedo. The *Staff of Summoning* lay beside him, still cuffed to his wrist.

"Any sign of them?" I asked cautiously.

"I smell no infernal scent." He sniffed, then abruptly continued, "Sister, this news you brought sits not well with me."

"How so?" I asked, my voice rising unnaturally. Silly mad Mephisto had believed my innocence. Was his demonic alter ego about to side with Erasmus?

"Ulysses's behavior stinks of Hell's touch," he said grimly. "The *Staff of Transportation* can go anywhere it has been. Where has it been? And, most pressingly, can it bring our foolhardy brother to locations from which he cannot escape—not without selling some essential he might otherwise prefer to keep?"

"Such as his soul?" I asked, shivering involuntarily.

"Such as," agreed the demon. "And yet, the buying of souls is over-rated."

"How so?"

Mephistopheles fixed his gleaming eyes upon me, bathing my face and hands in an eerie blue glow.

"Demons may ask a man to give up his soul. No matter what the man agrees to, however, the denizens of Hell cannot compel him to keep the bargain. Men are not the keepers of their souls. Souls belong to God in Heaven. The Demons have no means of collecting their collateral, unless the person who does the selling follows up on the sale by leading a wicked life.

"If a man who promised his soul to the Devil were then to lead a *virtuous* life, the Devil would gain nothing. No. When demons make bargains, they must continue to work to ensure their clients live up to them. They do this by coercing them into committing wicked acts—such as killing one's favorite brother."

I started to ask another question, but Mephistopheles cut me off.

"They come! I must return to my lack-witted self lest worse fates befall me. See to your safety, Sister. I go." Spreading his wings, he leapt from the roof and vanished into the night.

CHAPTER THIRTEEN

Auld Lang Syne

I leapt down the stairs two at a time, pausing only to grab my flute. When I reached the last stair above the balcony, I halted. Creeping silently to the rail, so that those below would not notice me, I looked down upon the ballroom.

My siblings were bunched together in the middle of the floor, clutching their staffs, except for Theo, who was empty-handed. Behind them were a dozen *Orbis Suleimani* security guards. These dapper agents had their hands over their heads and their backs pressed against the wall, a pile of guns at their feet. Nearby, Logistilla's bear stood on its hind feet with its paws extended, like a grizzly exhibit in a museum. Had I not seen it moving but an hour ago, I would have taken it for stuffed.

In the center of the ballroom, an exceptionally tall man in a scarlet turban stood on one of the long tables. Trays of food and broken pieces of an ice swan lay strewn across the floor beneath the stranger, where he had apparently kicked them off the table. Even up on the balcony, I could smell the spilled duck pâté.

The stranger had a .45 trained on Theo's head.

My heart in my throat, I examined the gunman more closely. He wore long arcane robes embroidered with dark cabalistic symbols. His vaguely Arabic features were unnaturally placid, with one eye huge and swollen, and the other small and squinty. I recognized his face immediately. I had seen him huddled in a doorway in Chicago the day I first met the false Ferdinand. What was he doing here?

As I studied him, my skin began to crawl. I felt as if I had turned over a sturdy log and found the bottom rotted and writhing with maggots. It was not that his deformed eye unnerved me. Rather, his expression was wrong, as if a colony of ants, or spiders, had hollowed out a human corpse and were trying to move the face to express emotions they could not comprehend.

Repelled, I jerked backward and stepped quickly into the upper hallway, shivering with distaste. Nothing this abhorrent could be a mere lackey! This was Baelor of the Baleful Eye without his Egyptian death mask. So, I had been right. The enemy had read my mind and ripped from it intimate secrets about the workings of Prospero, Inc. and my personal idea of Ferdinand's appearance. The stranger on the side of the street whose eyes I had glanced into back in Chicago had been the demon mind reader!

I contemplated the scene below, my mind racing. Most of us had the stamina to survive a gunshot wound or two, assuming we were not killed instantly. The Water of Life made us hardy. I feared for Theo, however, as I doubted he had the strength to endure a serious blow of any kind. So, how best to protect him?

Neither Logistilla's nor Cornelius's staffs could stop bullets. Cornelius might be able to convince a weak-willed human not to shoot, but that was not likely to help us here. Erasmus's staff could age a bullet in midair, but only if it was fully warmed up, and this took time. Currently, it lay dormant and still, a wand of black and white. That meant the matter of our defense was in my hands.

Normally, this would not trouble me. I was used to having to rescue my younger siblings. However, a stuffy ballroom was hardly ideal terrain for me. With only one window open, and that one merely cracked, there was not much air to command. On top of which, there was the fact that Erasmus was very touchy about his belongings. If I were to call up a whirlwind, for instance, and it damaged his house, I would never hear the end of it; never mind that it saved his brother's life. While this would not stop me, of course, it did dampen my enthusiasm.

I was not entirely unprepared. During my chat with the local Aerie Ones on my way to the roof, I had issued them instructions. A single toot was the signal for them to form a protective cushion of air that was thick enough to deflect a bullet. Such a wall was not a natural occurrence, which made it difficult for the Aerie Ones to maintain. They would only keep it up as long as I kept playing. If the music stopped, the protective barrier would fail. Also, I could only produce it in one place, which meant I could not protect both my siblings and myself.

My current view, from where I stood in the upper hallway peering around the corner onto the balcony, allowed me to see the table where the demon stood but not my siblings. As I contemplated what to do, a large ruddy bear with beady gray eyes lumbered across the ballroom. Below,

Logistilla snickered. Apparently, Osae the Red's version of a grizzly did not impress her.

The reddish grizzly shivered and shrank, becoming Osae the Red dressed in a gray suit. His red hair stuck out in wild spikes crusted with human blood. Stepping up beside the table, he glanced about the ballroom and asked in his raspy voice, "Where is Seir?"

To my eternal shame, my heart began to race at the incubus's name. Truly, the incubus had brought about my total humiliation. I glanced at the portion of the ballroom visible from my position but could see no evidence of Seir . . . or Ferdinand.

Baelor shrugged, his huge horrible eye never moving from its target.

Osae leered toward my siblings. "Theophrastus the Demonslayer! After all this time. Three hundred years, we spent trapped in the depths of Hell, thanks to you. Finally, your day of reckoning is at hand."

There came a clatter from near the front door. Creeping forward a bit, I could see that Mephisto, dressed in the shreds of his once finely tailored tux, had pushed his way inside and was struggling to draw an antique sword from its scabbard. As he did so, he lost his balance and crashed backward into a coat rack, his staff, still cuffed to his wrist, flailing upward as he fell. Coats rained down upon him. The Cavalier's hat Father Christmas had given him, which I had only this afternoon returned to him, fell off the rack and flopped over his face. It was a pitiful sight.

Osae the Red laughed. "What can a madman with a rusted sword hope to achieve against the might of the Three Shadowed Ones?"

A floorboard creaked behind me. Mab came up beside me, his fedora low over his face, his expression grim. He gave me a quick nod, crouched down, and crept across the balcony on his stomach, straining for a better view. I hissed softly. When Mab turned, I held up the flute and tapped my ear. Mab quickly inserted his earplugs.

Theo jerked suddenly into my line of sight. His face had gone slack, and his body rigid. His mouth opened, and a deep, jarringly inhuman voice issued from his lips. Baelor of the Baleful Eye had taken control of my brother!

"Pathetic flesh worms. Surrender now, and I shall allow my own servants to whip you and rape your women, rather than deliver you to the Torturers of the Tower of Pain—where far worse fates await you."

"Nice options," muttered Mab.

Theo's face contorted in sudden anger. He was not able to speak himself, but he shook his head fiercely. Nevertheless, the inhuman voice continued to issue from his throat.

"Ah, Theophrastus, once called Demonslayer. My old adversary. Turned your back on the occult to save your soul, did you? Yet, so long as you keep the STAFF OF DEVASTATION, *you are guilty of the sin of thievery. Return it to us and rid yourself of this burden."*

"Never!" Theo growled defiantly, momentarily winning control of his vocal cords. Then, his body jerked again, and his face went blank.

"And when you die of the wretched mortal illness, who will guard your staff then?"

When Theo did not respond, the inhuman voice, speaking from his tortured windpipe rasped out: *"What of the rest of you? Will you allow the Demonslayer to speak for you? Or will you chose the wiser path?"*

"We stand united," Erasmus replied airily.

"Pity," replied the terrible voice. *"Prepare yourselves, Spawn of the Dread Prospero, to join your father in Hell!"*

It was about to begin. Closing my eyes, I prayed to my Lady for instructions. Her response was immediate: *Act now!*

I blew softly, so that the sound of it was barely audible to my ear. Even at this low volume, the flute's lilting voice lifted my spirits, stirring hope and confidence. I noted this with trepidation, hoping it were not some false, unholy emotion, the work of the demon imprisoned inside the instrument.

The crack of the gunfire shook the chandelier. My heart in my throat, I peered over the banister, still playing. Below, I saw the faint shimmering where the cushion of air was still taking shape and the brown fur of Logistilla's bear. The big brute had leapt in front of Theo! The bullet intended for my brother's brain buried itself in the fatty flesh of the bear's left flank.

The creature roared with pain but did not falter. It charged forward, its huge claws extended toward Baelor's distorted face. Unruffled, the demon gestured. Osae transformed into a bear again and lumbered forward to tackle it.

The two beasts fought, ripping at one another's flesh and gripping each other in bone-crushing hugs. Logistilla's was larger and seemed to be the better fighter; however, Osae the Bear had a distinct advantage, as he was not suffering from a gun wound.

From here, at the railing, I could see my siblings again. While the bears fought, pearly green light from the top of Logistilla's staff illuminated Baelor's face. His features began to melt and change. Logistilla gave a triumphant laugh. Her laughter died abruptly, however, when her staff went dark, and his features stabilized, returning to their former cast.

"How dare you!" Logistilla cried, shaking her staff. "I did not issue that command!"

Around Baelor, the shards of scattered ice sculpture melted into puddles and evaporated in puffs of steam. The duck pâté became tiny piles of dust on a tarnished silver tray. Black rot ate away at the ballroom floor, and the air reddened as the very light began to age. On the table, Baelor's turban and robes rotted to rags. The flesh of his face began to wither.

"That's the way, Erasmus!" Logistilla cheered. "Get him!"

As Erasmus advanced, dodging the brawling bears, the gray blur of the *Staff of Decay* humming in his Urim gauntlet, the demon's face grew more emaciated. His deformed eyes withered in their sockets, becoming first prunelike, then raisinlike. What had been his flesh cracked and began raining down upon the table. Beneath, where his face had been, glittered a golden death mask, such as the pharaohs wore as they slept within their tombs. The rotten rags of his garments ripped and swirled, until they hugged his body like a mummy's wrappings, and a horrible, nauseating imitation of laughter that made my hair stand on end issued from Theo's throat.

"The Lords of Hell trapped in your staffs—Great Marquis Oriax and Great Duke Vepar—hear my voice in their minds and recall their true loyalties. Your staves will not avail you against me."

The hum of the *Staff of Decay* fell silent. Erasmus cursed and leapt backward to avoid being crushed by the wrestling bears. Ever fastidious, Erasmus stopped to wave his staff once more to restore the blackened ballroom floor to its pristine polished state, before retreating behind the shimmer of my now fully formed wall of air. The staff hummed again as he did this; apparently the demon within did not object to ballroom restoration.

An enormous crash shook the hall, taking both Baelor and Erasmus by surprise. The fighting bears had collided with the great grandfather clock and sent it spinning to its doom. Splinters, glass, and tiny gold springs scattered across the floor. Stepping on the debris, Osae the Bear cut the pad of his foot and fell.

"So much for marking the New Year," murmured Erasmus. "Ah, well. *'Timor mortis conturbat me.'"*

Osae the Bear remained where he had fallen, blinking his great bear eyes in confusion, until Baelor fixed his horrible eye on Cornelius's staff.

Theo's voice rasped: *"Of all the staves Prospero wrought, the great Marquis*

Paimon, who dwells within the STAFF OF PERSUASION, *is most accessible to me, for he and I hail from the same Infernal House."*

Again, Theo's vocal chords issued a rasping mockery of laughter not proper for a human voice. Baelor now addressed the demon in Cornelius's staff directly.

"Paimon, my old adversary, how pleasing to see you trapped. How paradoxical that you, who were once so great, now must depend upon me, who was once your lowly servitor. I bask in the irony. Even when you are restored to your high estate, the knowledge will always goad you, like an eternal thorn in your side, that you were once reduced to this."

Freed from Cornelius's spell, Osae the Bear now leapt up and rushed the other bear, his bulk altering to that of a rhinoceros as he charged. Logistilla's bear was thrown some distance, sliding across the floor into the champagne fountain, which tumbled forward, showering his thick fur with bubbly and glass. He twitched, but did not rise. Logistilla's hands flew to her mouth, and she screamed.

Baelor spoke again.

"Even before Prospero opened the gate for us, Paimon heeded Hell. Through him, we have influenced those around you for centuries, imprudent Cornelius, feeding upon their greed, their malice, their fear. At our Great One's command, Paimon woke and worked the entirety of his will upon your brother Theophrastus, when that one stared into the staff's heart and made his rash vow. Oh, the beauty of that! How satisfying to watch Theophrastus the Demonslayer—whom none of us could touch—destroy himself. A pity for him that he has learned of this, his folly, too late."

And he fired at Theo's head.

The bullet shot through the air, struck my airy shield, and ricocheted sideways, hitting one of the great arched windows.

I had saved him. I had saved Theo!

My glee was short-lived, as the meaning of Baelor's late words began to sink in. The demons woke up Cornelius's staff? They used it to enchant Theo? They made him keep his vow to give up magic—to give up the Water of Life—against his will?

Theo's desire to give up magic, so as to get into Heaven, was an *attack from Hell?* How ironic. Ironic and horrible.

This terrible revelation had one tiny silver lining. Finally, there was an enemy; someone responsible for the harm done to my brother. Someone we, as a family, could gather to smite!

We just needed to discover the identity of Baelor's "Great One."

As everyone else looked toward the broken window, crashed in a shower of tinkling glass, Baelor's blank golden mask faced the air wall and then turned up toward the flute and me. As his gaze fell upon me, I was struck with a wave of pure hatred. I leapt back around the corner, still playing.

From below, Theo's inhumanly harsh voice called, *"Great King Vinae, turn your wrath against your captors."*

King Vinae. That was the name Seir had used to address the demon within my flute. Alarmed, I realized that, to quote Job, the thing which I had greatly feared had come upon me. The flute, upon which I had lavished so much of my life's love and affection, was about to betray me. Could it command the Aerie Ones to rend us? Or would its betrayal be more direct? A picture sprang to mind of jagged spikes jutting from the instrument and piercing my mouth and hands.

Terrified, I nearly threw it from me, but the calm steady presence of my Lady stayed my hand. Heart hammering, I commended my soul to Eurynome and continued to play, though whether it did any good, whether the airy shield still held, I could not see.

Below, a startled hiss escaped Theo's tortured throat. *"What is this? Ophion? Serpent of the Winds, how came you here?"*

Ophion? The King of Air? The Great Serpent of the Wind who had danced with Eurynome in the Void to bring order out of Chaos? Was he here? I searched the ballroom, moving my head carefully as I played, but saw no great wind, or any sign of a newcomer.

To whom was Baelor speaking?

A picture came to my mind of an empty pedestal. Ophion had not been in the Elemental Chamber with the other kings. I had assumed that Father had squirreled him away somewhere, but what if I were wrong?

Seir! I had assumed he appeared in the chamber after we did, taking advantage of the hole we made in the wards. But if he had come in the little ivory door, there was no saying how long he might have been there. Could Seir have spirited away Ophion before Caurus and I arrived? If so, how could we possibly face the King of the Air and survive without the full cooperation of my flute?

From below, the harsh, inhuman voice continued: *"Serpent of the Winds! Why do you defy me? Surely you cannot desire to help your captors! How came you to be trapped here, and where is Great Vinae? No matter. Exert yourself, King of the Air! Seize control of the* STAFF OF WINDS!*"*

Slowly, my eyes dropped to the four feet of polished pine I held between my fingers. It could not be, and yet . . .

As is the way with Handmaidens, I knew suddenly: the Serpent of the Winds was here, imprisoned within my flute. For over five hundred years, my Lady's consort had been my constant companion, bound in this piece of pine. No wonder I was not yet a Sibyl! Why had she never asked me to set him free?

A sharp burst of joy dispelled my confusion. My beloved flute! It was not—it never had been—a demon!

Silence brought me back to myself. In my amazement, I had ceased playing. Horrified, I resumed immediately, but the damage had been done. As I ran to the rail, flute at my lips, I saw an opening in the shimmering wall of air. Baelor saw it, too. He raised his gun, taking aim.

EVERYTHING happened in a blink of an eye, though, to me, time appeared to move very slowly. As Baelor raised his arm, a figure leapt silently into the air at the far side of the table. This lithe acrobat flew across the table, somersaulting in midair as he approached the demon. A rippling greatcoat flowed about his body, and one hand held tight to a black cavalier's hat with a great blue plume.

Gliding smoothly past the chandelier, he landed on the long table with catlike grace. From under his greatcoat, he drew a saber. In one fluid motion, he lunged and sliced the demon's gun hand from its wrist, just as the demon was pulling the trigger.

The gun fired high. As the hand flew away from Baelor's body, trailing a stream of black ichor, the swordsman continued forward. The tip of his sword slid through the tiny eye slit in the golden mask and pierced the spot where the great Baleful Eye had been, before Erasmus rotted his human face. The demon let out a piercing scream.

"Aroint thee, Fiend, and return to the fiery pit from whence thou came!" cried the swordsman in an Elizabethan English accent, and he drove the point of his weapon through the demon's skull.

"By Setabos and Titania!" Mab cried softly, loosening one earplug. "Who in tarnation is that?"

The swordsman stood up, and I saw his face. My heart leapt. From below, I heard Logistilla's giggle of surprised delight.

"The Greatest Swordsman in all Christendom!" I laughed, leaning over the balcony rail and waving my flute back and forth triumphantly. "My brother Mephistopheles."

"That's the Harebrain?" Mab gasped. He peered down at the studied calm of the swordsman's face. "Guess you're right. The features are the same, but the expression's different. He looks . . . focused."

"That's the real Mephisto . . . the sane one."

Mab pushed his earplug back into his ear, muttering: "Must be the hat!"

THE instant Baelor's hand was parted from his body, Erasmus's men grabbed their weapons. As my brother Mephisto leapt lightly from the table, tossing aside his feathered hat, they fired at the mummified demon. The report of the guns was like a symphony played in thunder. The floor where Mab and I stood trembled. I grabbed the lintel of the door, afraid that the balcony might collapse.

Baelor's body fell backward, twisting and flopping. Osae the Rhinoceros had been charging Logistilla's bear, who was slowly climbing back to his feet. Upon seeing Baelor's fate, the rhino turned and fled. He charged the wide windows, crashing through the glass and thundering onto the snowy lawn, where he transformed into some flying beast and escaped into the night.

Below, Mephisto was sitting on the long dining table, gazing about in a confused haze. Theo grabbed him and shouted something in his ear. I could not hear his words over the thunder of the guns, but I could see Mephisto mouthing the words "Bully Boy" as he gestured with his staff. Moments later, I began to imagine what it would look like if a large dark-haired man stood near my brothers. Then, I was not just imagining him, he was there: an enormous fellow with wide shoulders like a blacksmith, dressed in an inexpensive suit jacket, a clean white shirt, and a pair of new blue jeans. He looked about in undisguised surprise.

Mephisto shouted something into the ear of his "Bully Boy," and the huge man ran up the staircase, taking the stairs three at a time. He soon reappeared with the old battered trunk I had used for a seat back in Theo's living room. Hurrying down, he dropped the trunk at Theo's feet. With some difficulty, Theo bent down and opened it with a key he wore on a ribbon around his neck.

Inside the cedar-lined trunk lay all Theo's discarded treasures: his Toledo steel sword, his breastplate of shining Urim, his enchanted goggles, and, lying upon a pillow of crimson velvet, the *Staff of Devastation*. No wonder my brother had cringed when I chose that trunk as my seat back at his farm in Vermont. I remembered how he had started toward his house more than once when trying to decide how to dispose of the body of Osae the Bear. He must have been debating whether or not to fetch his staff.

The *Staff of Devastation* was a gleaming length of white metal in two parts. Kneeling before the trunk, Theo screwed the parts together, and then twisted the wide ring that circled the top of the upper portion. The metallic length began to hum with a noise like a dynamo. Resting it upon his shoulder, as one might a rifle, he pointed the nozzle at the jerking body of the mind-reading demon.

"Wait!" screamed Erasmus. "For God's sake! Not in the house!"

At Erasmus's orders, several of his men ran forward and dragged Baelor's body out through the window Osae had broken. Theo followed, striding grimly behind him, his staff humming upon his shoulder. He put on his enchanted goggles, which looked like something out of a 1940s comic book, and tapped the right corner, adjusting them. Each time he touched the control, the lenses changed color. I recognized some of the settings: gold for spirit sight; blue for eagle vision; silver for night vision. Others, I did not know.

Erasmus's men put the body down in the snow, some fifty feet from the house, and scattered like antelopes before a lion. Stepping out through the pieces of broken window, Theo set his feet, took aim, and fired.

The resulting explosion lit the night with the brilliance of a small sun. For a time, it was too bright to even glance that way. Its light illuminated the fields to the river. In the distance, I caught a glimpse of the steeples of Boston. Then, the explosion died away, leaving a crater of burnt earth and fused glass, bare of grass or snow.

"There," Theo said with grim satisfaction. His voice sounded hoarse and scratchy, but at least it was his own again. He twisted the top ring, and his staff fell quiet. "He won't be bothering us again any time soon."

"Wow!" whispered Mab, blinking his eyes from the brightness. "That was . . . wow!"

Mab and I came down the stairs and joined Erasmus, Cornelius, Logistilla, Mephisto, and Mephisto's Bully Boy, where they gathered by the broken window. We stood silently, surrounded by *Orbis Suleimani* agents, staring at the smooth crater where the demon had just been. A few of the agents began cautiously moving forward, guns drawn, to examine the crater and to confirm that no sign of the demon remained. Meanwhile, Logistilla began to fuss over

Theo, who pushed her away, declaring in a hoarse croak that he was fine and did not need coddling.

Watching them, I recalled a youthful Theo exhibiting the same bothered expression as a younger Logistilla fussed over his war wounds after each campaign. I smiled, relieved that serving as the demon's voice piece seemed to have done my brother no lasting harm.

Heavy footsteps drew my attention, and I saw, to my great delight, Logistilla's brave bear. The great beast came lumbering up behind us, limping and wet.

"Ah, Titus!" murmured Cornelius, as the pondering footsteps came to a rest beside him. "You've come to join us at last! I had been worried about you, old friend."

Erasmus and I both laughed at his expense, our one moment of camaraderie in this tense, hectic day.

"Your legendary hearing has betrayed you, Brother," Erasmus stated goodnaturedly. "You have mistaken a beast for a brother."

Cornelius reached out a hand and felt the blood-matted fur of the bear. He frowned. His soft voice gained a dangerous edge.

"Logistilla?" he asked. "What have you done?"

"Whatever do you mean?" Logistilla asked with a shrill little laugh.

"Turn him back," said Cornelius.

"Cornelius," I began, "that isn't Titus. That is Logistilla's bear . . . one of her clients."

"Turn him back," ordered Cornelius again, ignoring me.

"I don't know what you are talking about," Logistilla insisted.

Cornelius raised his staff. The amber stone gleamed. His voice grew sterner. "Turn him back!" he commanded.

Logistilla's eyes became unfocused, and she obediently tapped her staff upon the floor.

Pearly green light bathed the bear. It began to change, fur shrinking away, flesh growing pink. Moments later, my enormous brother Titus stood among us. His brown hair was sweat-soaked and lank. His naked flesh was blood-splattered and rent by ugly claw marks. A bullet wound gaped in his left thigh.

"Titus," I whispered, grief-stricken, recalling how the bear had tried to reach me on Logistilla's beach. "I'm so sorry . . . I d-didn't know."

Despite his injuries, Titus stood tall and smiling. His gaze met mine; his deep brown eyes held no condemnation. I reached into the pocket of my coat for the tiny crystal vial containing the Water of Life and stepped toward him.

A brilliant flash of pure white light illuminated the center of the ballroom. The light curled about itself, forming bones, organs, skin, and garments, in that order. Then, the light was gone, and in the center of the floor stood an impeccably dressed young man in an exquisite dove-gray tuxedo, complete with spats. A matching dove-gray domino mask covered the upper portion of his face revealing only a pencil mustache and a narrow chin. In one hand, he held a richly carved mahogany staff topped with a gleaming star sapphire. Seeing the empty ballroom, the young man pulled a handsome silver pocket watch from his vest and examined the time.

"Where is everyone?" asked my brother Ulysses. "Have I missed the party?"

CHAPTER FOURTEEN

Ulysses

"On the contrary, the party is just beginning." Erasmus smiled through his raven-dark hair as he grabbed Ulysses's arm. "Unfortunately, it is beginning someplace else, and you have just been elected Chief of Travel Arrangements. Come, Brothers and Sisters. Everyone grab on!"

Erasmus gave a few last-minute instructions to his men, while the rest of us crowded together, holding hands. Mab and Mephisto's Bully Boy crowded in with us. The Bully Boy, whom Mephisto called Calvin, demonstrated he was made of something other than just brawn when he had the perspicacity to put down Theo's trunk long enough to take the great coat from Mephisto's shoulders and drape it over the shivering, bloodied, and naked Titus. Meanwhile, Mephisto retrieved his hat.

"Where do you want to go?" asked Ulysses, clearly puzzled by the absence of partygoers and the bizarre behavior of his siblings. He glanced around, his gaze falling on Titus. "Titus, old chap, that's a new look for black tie."

"Quite true," Titus replied wryly in his Scottish burr. His voice was gruff from disuse, and his speech sounded more like a bear's growl than his normal baritone.

"Uh . . . I hate to interrupt this touching reunion," grunted Mab, "but, in case the rest of you did not notice, we've just been attacked by *denizens of Hell*. Maybe we should take this opportunity to leave the premises . . . just in case they happen to come back with reinforcements."

"Do you mean demons?" Ulysses glanced nervously about. "Which demons?"

"They've left for the moment." Theo's voice was barely more than a hoarse whisper. "As it will probably take them time to organize without Baelor, who is back in Hell, I reckon we have at least, oh, ten minutes before they return." From his tone, I thought he might be exaggerating but it was best to err on the side of safety.

"You've been attacked by demons?" Ulysses asked, glancing about furtively. "Uh—look, I really don't care to tangle with demons. Gives me the willies, if you must know the truth. Can't you lot get a ride from someone else?"

"Certainly not." Erasmus tightened his grip on Ulysses's arm. "Now, where should we go? Preferably to some place that Miranda has not yet compromised."

"Father's mansion in Oregon?" suggested Theo.

"Too dangerous," said Mab. "The demons have been there three times."

"Oh, good going, Miranda!" Erasmus quipped, continuing before I could defend myself. "How about Logistilla's place in the Okeefenokee?"

"Absolutely not!" replied Logistilla. "The children are there."

An argument started as Erasmus, Cornelius, and Logistilla hotly argued about where to go, while Mab and Theo contributed dire warnings about the dangers of not leaving immediately. Mephisto joined in by shouting out places he would like to visit, such as the Eiffel Tower and the South Pole. Meanwhile, Ulysses was growing more and more apprehensive, and Titus was beginning to sway on his feet.

Disgusted, I reached through the crowd, touched the cool wood of Ulysses's staff, and commanded, "Home."

Ulysses's face went chalk white. He tried to voice an objection, but the *Staff of Transportation,* which had been Father's for so long, knew my voice and touch. The ballroom dissolved into light and silence.

MOMENTS later, color and noise rushed back into our environment. We stood on a slate veranda breathing warm and salty air, perfumed with the scent of exotic flowers. Above, a seabird was silhouetted against the faint glow of the predawn sky, its cry piercing the night. Closer at hand, lush tropical foliage completely surrounded the veranda. Orchids flowered everywhere: red sophronitieses, yellow dendrobiums, orange featherlike cattleyeas, purple and white phalaenopses grew among the rocks or hung from the tree trunks, so that we seemed to be entirely surrounded by brilliant blooms. In among them flickered tiny lights, dancing and darting like a thousand fireflies. They were not fireflies, but tiny feylings, distant cousins of my Aerie Ones.

"Happy New Year, everyone," I smiled as I glanced toward where the pre-morning glow had dyed the eastern sky a peachy gold.

"No! Don't go ther . . . huh?" sputtered Ulysses, his alarm fading as he beheld our lush twinkling surroundings. "W-where arc wc?"

My other siblings were equally puzzled, except for Mephisto who was tying his shoe. The voice that answered, though congenial, was not one I recognized.

"Of course! We're on Prospero's Island!"

I swung about to find Mephisto's Bully Boy gazing with pleasant familiarity at the cypress trees and white star-shaped Aerancoids. He noticed my glance and nodded, his smile both pleased and abashed.

"Hello, Miss Miranda. It's nice to see you again." He thrust out his great hand toward me. I shook it, puzzled, trying to place where I might have met him before.

"Who on Earth is this big hulk of a fellow?" Logistilla exclaimed with interest, pushing forward so as to examine him better.

Illuminated by the faint early morning light and the green glow from the globe on the top of Logistilla's staff, Calvin looked like a construction worker who had groomed himself for a New Year's party, except that he was enormous, taller and broader even than Titus. He had thick black hair, large cheerful features, and a strong chin that reminded me vaguely of Gregor's. His arms were unusually long, and thick black hair poked out from under his wrist cuffs.

"Oh, that's just my Bully Boy. Miranda met him before, but it was a long time ago, so she probably doesn't remember. His name is Calvin. You can call him Calvin Klein if you like. That's not his name, but he does wear jeans, so I'm sure he won't mind," Mephisto said hurriedly. Taking my arm, he announced, "So, this is Daddy's place! Come on, Miranda, give us the grand tour."

BEHIND us rose a wall of flowering vines. Walking over to it, I pushed aside the greenery to reveal a thick oak door set into a stone wall. At my touch, the door swung open. Beyond, a staircase led upward into darkness. As I stepped forward, a sudden breeze rushed down the staircase and circled me, tugging at my hair and gown, causing my skirts to rise and billow.

"Mistress, you've come home," soft feminine voices spoke out of the breeze. "The master departed and has not returned."

"Hello, Pinbell and Apple Blossom and Columbine." I delighted in the feathery touch of these old friends upon my face. Continuing up the stairs, I said, "I know, Father is missing. We are seeing to that. Please make ready the music room for my brothers and myself."

"And where am I supposed to go?" snapped my sister. "Perhaps you'd prefer if I stood outside? Maybe you have some horses you'd like held?"

"For my brothers and my sister," I said, sighing.

Behind me, Erasmus said, "No horses here, Dear Sister. You'll have to content yourself with holding the door for the rest of us."

I did not catch Logistilla's response, but moments later Erasmus's mocking laughter echoed up through the stone walls of the stairway. Ahead of him and just behind me, I could hear Mab pestering Mephisto as the two of them mounted the now pitch dark staircase.

"Don't give me any of your jaw! I saw you attack that demon," Mab hissed. "Why are you still carrying that hat? Put it on your head!"

"Shhh," Mephisto whispered back loudly. "No. And, you can't make me! It's an icky hat! It looks stupid."

"Actually, it's rather a sporting hat," offered Ulysses, from behind them.

"You stay out of this!" Mephisto insisted.

"If you're taking about that Cavalier's chapeau you were wearing earlier this evening, it's exactly the kind we used to wear," said Theo, wheezing from the exertion of the climb. "Makes you look like your old self, Mephisto. You even acted like your old self when you took out Baelor."

"That's the problem," Mephisto hissed under his breath.

"What's that, Harebrain?" asked Mab.

"Harebrain?" Erasmus's laugh was followed by a sudden, "Hold on. Who's that speaking?"

"Beware!" cried Cornelius. "That last voice was not a human one!"

"Geesh! And what else is new?" Mab asked grumpily. "Or did you mean Mr. Erasmus? Technically, he talked last."

I chuckled. "Fear not, Cornelius. It's just one of your employees. Mab's an Aerie One."

Cornelius replied, "I beg to differ, Sister, but I distinctly hear the wet breath of flesh when he speaks."

"He's an Aerie One in a body," snapped Logistilla. "I should know. I made the body myself."

"An Aerie One in a body? So, it works! How extraordinary!" breathed

Erasmus. "I've been hearing about this project for years, but somehow I've never gotten to actually see one with my own eyes."

"I guess you sold your stock in the company too soon," I replied briskly. "Otherwise, you would have seen many."

"Perhaps I did," Erasmus replied, speaking, for once, without rancor. "How extraordinary!"

It was difficult not to be amused at Mab's expense. For all my dislike of Erasmus, his enthusiasm was refreshing. I would have expected his reaction to be more negative. On the other hand, Erasmus had always been ruled by insatiable curiosity. Sometimes, it served him well; it led him to become one of the first alchemists to abandon that art for scientific inquiry. Other times—well, he had more lives than a cat!

UPON reaching the top of the stairs, I emerged into a long stone hallway. The smell of dank mildew assailed me. I covered my nose with my hand. In my youth, this hall had been a cheerful, warm place lined with rich tapestries. The tapestries still hung here, but what was left of them was moldering and moth-eaten. Apparently, Father had not gotten around to renovating this hallway since his return to the island a few years back, when he retired from Prospero, Inc.—so as to be able to spend his full time pursuing the matter of how to save Gregor. I surveyed the dim corridor with a lump in my throat and hoped very much that we would find the rest of the house in better repair.

To my relief, the music room was in pristine condition. Many of the antiques were still as I remembered them: harps, flutes, lyres, and trumpets of gleaming brass hung against the basalt walls. Others had been replaced by shiny modern instruments, among the new pieces: a saxophone, a trombone, and a guitar. Of the larger instruments, the harpsichord stood just where it had in my youth, but a grand piano, a newer invention, now stood across the chamber from it, taking up much of the far corner.

The music room contained only two wooden armchairs and a Roman-styled couch. As we trooped in, the airy servants gathered chairs from other wings of the mansion. Overstuffed armchairs, stools, and recliners floated over our heads, zipping left and right in order not to collide with a family member or one another. Some of the chairs and stools were over five hundred years old. The armchairs and recliners had been added when Father returned here three years ago, of course. No such devices had existed in my youth!

The chamber opened, literally, onto a deep, forested ravine, visible only from the mansion or the heights of the island's highest hill. No glass separated the chamber from the ravine beyond it, though a cushion of air pushed back anyone who approached the brink too closely. Beyond the barrier, a sheer wall of water fell from somewhere above, crashing over the rocks of the cliff toward the gorge, far below. The water flowed past the roof, which was made of quartz, smoky and clear in patches, causing dappled light to play across the chamber's dark interior as the rays of the rising sun fell upon the water and the quartz. Along the outer wall, the passing breeze whistled across flutelike openings in the black basalt. The resulting music, much like the voices of a hundred oboes, clarinets, and flutes, varied with the velocity and direction of the wind.

Though the morning sun was rising, its rays had not yet fallen upon the depths of the gorge, so glints of feyling light still twinkled among the deep green of the foliage. Theo, Mephisto, and Calvin gazed admiringly at this vista, while Ulysses wandered about the music room examining the instruments and commenting, with much enthusiasm, upon how much they might be worth to a collector. Nobody, however, was as affected as Cornelius, who stood thunderstruck, his face contorted in mystified wonder, as he listened to the mingling sound of the roaring waterfall and the fluting of the walls.

"An Aerie One in a body," repeated Erasmus, as we waited for the chairs to be arranged. "Let me see!" He took one look at Mab and burst out laughing. "He looks like Humphrey Bogart!"

"Not exactly like Bogart; I made a few changes," objected a flustered Logistilla.

"Fleshly Aerie Ones," Erasmus exclaimed again with evident delight. He circled around Mab, peering closely and poking here and there. "How utterly extraordinary! What a brilliant idea of Father's!"

"Brilliant idea? This abomination?" Cornelius asked sharply without turning away from the wind flute and the falls. "Or have you forgotten that we seek to lessen the amount of magic befuddling Mankind?"

"Remember the great project," Erasmus said softly, as if he hoped only Cornelius would hear.

"How could I forget . . ." Cornelius replied, frowning.

"How could you, of all people, not know about the fleshly Aerie Ones, Cornelius?" Logistilla asked. "Considering how you spend all your free time."

"It is one thing to prepare for abominations, Sister, and another thing to meet one in the flesh," Cornelius replied stiffly.

Addressing his attention to Mab again, Erasmus asked, "And you can live as a man and dress like one and everything?"

"Sure," Mab growled, "just like anyone else. I eat, I drink, I drive, I vote . . ."

"You vote?" Theo asked surprised.

"Of course. I'm an American, aren't I?"

"Quite astonishing," Erasmus exclaimed with great delight.

"I've never quite adjusted to the custom of letting the proles vote," Ulysses commented. "Bound to lead to bread and circuses, or some other sort of trouble."

" 'Adjusted?' " I asked. "The rank and file in America were voting fifty years before you born."

Ulysses shrugged. "Can I help that? Wish they'd kept their practices to themselves instead of importing them across the Great Puddle. The kingdom's quite the worse for it, I dare say. All this socialistic claptrap."

"But I thought you were a socialist," said Erasmus.

"Saw the error of my ways," Ulysses replied blithely. "If every man's wealth is equal to his neighbors', what is left worth stealing?"

Erasmus chuckled, and Cornelius murmured under his breath. "I thank God that Ulysses finally came to his senses."

I nodded in agreement, only belatedly realizing that my gesture was lost on my blind brother. It was nice to see Ulysses put some of his more outlandish beliefs behind him, but I was not certain I approved of the morality of his reasoning.

"I'm hungry!" Mephisto interrupted, waving with his hat. The feather brushed across Cornelius's nose, causing him to sneeze. "Do we have to just stand around goggling at the bodyguard? Or can we get something to eat?"

"Miranda, you travel with a bodyguard?" Erasmus asked, looking even more amused. He poked Mab again.

Mab slapped his hand out of the way. "Despite what your cotton-headed brother says, I am not a bodyguard, Professor Prospero. I happen to be Prospero, Inc.'s foremost detective. At the moment, my tireless investigating has turned up some very pertinent information, the details of which, no doubt, will fascinate you all. So, if you people will stop poking at me as if I were some kind of blue-ribbon pig, we can get down to the real meat of the matter."

There was something extraordinarily pleasant about listening to my brothers banter together, about having so many of us together in one room.

It evoked a feeling of coming home, even more than these familiar old walls. Though it was strangely disorienting to recall that most of my family had never been here, having been born long after our return to Milan. Still, I liked seeing them here, as if we had all come back to where we were meant to be.

Finally, we were doing something all together again.

"My apologies," Erasmus replied cheerfully, giving Mab's shoulder one last poke. "I was overcome."

"By what?" drawled Mab, rubbing his shoulder. "No, don't tell me. I don't want to know."

"I'd like to sit down now," Titus said, his voice sounding patient but strained. Then, his eyes rolled up in his head, and he fainted, his great bulk falling slowly toward the floor.

FATHER'S Aerie Ones caught Titus before he struck the flagstones. They floated him to the couch, where Erasmus and I tended to him. I placed a single pearly drop of the Water of Life on his tongue, then let Erasmus, who had studied medicine many times through the ages, remove the bullet and bind his wounds. The servants brought a robe of Father's that barely fit over Titus's great biceps. Logistilla hovered like a worried mother hen, clucking and cooing over Titus's unconscious body. However, she made no effort to help.

Rising from where he knelt beside the peacefully sleeping Titus, Erasmus crossed to where Cornelius stood, stupefied by the symphony of water and wind. He had to repeat whatever he said three times before Cornelius shook himself free of his trance enough to nod brusquely. Cornelius stood a while longer, then finally turned to make his way across the room, his white cane tapping before him.

Stopping beside Ulysses, Cornelius made some comment I could not hear and gestured toward the umbrella stand beside the door. The amber gem atop his cane sparkled in the light of the three oil lamps hanging amidst the instruments. Beside me, Mab stirred, sniffed, and began eyeing Cornelius suspiciously. Ulysses immediately walked over to the door, placed his staff in the umbrella stand, and returned to the center of the room. Then, he sat down in an overstuffed armchair recently deposited by the Aerie Ones.

Jerking his head, Ulysses glanced around with a start, commenting, "I say! Why did I put my staff over there?"

Cornelius, still standing nearby, leaned over Ulysses, the amber gem on the top of his white cane still twinkling. I was close enough to hear his words, despite the loudness of the winds and the falls.

"We have a few questions to ask you," he said kindly. "You'll cooperate, won't you, Brother?"

"Certainly, old chap. Wouldn't think of doing otherwise," Ulysses said vaguely.

"What are you doing?" Logistilla cried, brandishing her wand. The green globe glowed dangerously. "Stop that at once! I thought we agreed never to use our staffs on each other!"

"You're one to talk," Erasmus murmured, throwing a glance Titus-ward, though his efforts were wasted, as she could not hear his soft words over the roar of the falls.

Logistilla said, "I warn you, leave Ulysses alone, or you'll spend the next year as a dog!"

Erasmus raised his own staff, which began to spin, the stark black and white lengths blurring into gray. His mocking grin widened. He raised his voice. "Care to tango, do you, Sister? Oh, do try me! By the time we're done, I might be a dog, but you'll be an old hag."

"You're both despicable," hissed Logistilla. "It's a wonder the rest of us put up with you."

"The rest of you?" asked Erasmus. "I assume you mean yourself and Miranda?" This caused Logistilla to turn and glare at me.

I threw up my hands, indicating that I had nothing to do with this. Normally, my sympathies would have been with Logistilla. Using our staffs upon each other set a bad precedent. Under the circumstances, however, I grudgingly found myself in Erasmus's camp. Our suspicions against Ulysses were severe enough to warrant more serious treatment. Besides, after Titus the Bear, Logistilla was hardly in a position to object.

Theo, who was still standing with his back to the rest of us, gazing out at the ravine below, grumbled, "Maybe we should all put our staffs aside. They do have *demons* in them, after all. Look what just happened, for Heaven's sakes! What if Baelor had instructed our staffs to turn against us? Then, where would we have been?"

Erasmus leaned back and pressed the tips of his fingers together. "Why didn't he, I wonder?"

"Begging your pardon, people," Mab said, raising his voice to be heard over both the noise of the waterfall and the bickering family members, "but I have a piece of news you may want to hear. It concerns your dead brother

Gregor . . . or, more particularly, it concerns your might-not-be-so-dead brother Gregor."

That got everyone's attention.

"Whoa now!" cried Ulysses, coming to himself again and glancing about wildly. "How so?"

"Hold your horses," Mab said dryly. "I'll explain."

"That was a slight against me, wasn't it?" Logistilla snorted. "Hold your horses indeed!"

Mab ignored Logistilla and dived directly into his material. "Down at the Boston city library I found this." He held up a copy of a newspaper article with a URL at the top. In one corner was a black-and-white photograph of a tall, stocky man seated on what appeared to be the stage of a talk show.

"God's Head! It's Gregor!" Logistilla gasped.

Erasmus, Theo, Mephisto, and Ulysses all rose and leaned forward to get a better view. Cornelius did not rise, but asked eagerly, "What are you seeing? Brothers? Sisters? Describe it to me."

"A photograph of Gregor seated on the set of a talking heads show. Looks like a recent photo," Erasmus replied, peering closely.

Mab pulled the article back and began reading aloud. The music of wind and thunder of the falls made it difficult for us to hear him. I walked over and pushed a lever that closed the flues. The music of the winds fell silent, to Cornelius's dismay. With a gesture, I instructed the Aerie Ones to increase the solidity of the permanent barrier of air blocking the opening. The sound of the waterfall fell to a dim distant roar.

Mab read the headline first, MAN FOUND WANDERING IN GRAVEYARD, CLAIMS TO HAVE DIED IN 1924, before continuing:

Chicago, IL. Eli Thompson has been making news recently with his unlikely claim that he died in 1924, shot by a man who had provided him with a new face. According to his claims, Mr. Thompson had been a small-time criminal in Pennsylvania in the teens. In 1921, the police were closing in on him when a stranger offered him a chance at a new life, a chance Mr. Thompson accepted. The stranger, calling himself Ulysses after the then-popular James Joyce book, altered Mr. Thompson's shape by some unknown process until his face and body were those of a completely different person. Three years later, the stranger returned and shot Mr. Thompson point-blank in the chest. This is the last thing Mr. Thompson claims to remember, until he woke up this September beside the gravestone of Gregor Prosper, the man whose identity Mr. Thompson had adopted.

We all sat on the edges of our seats, hanging on every word. Our chairs were arranged in a rough circle, so we could see one another's faces. Erasmus and I sat stony-faced, our wooden armchairs positioned to either side of the couch upon which Titus slept. To Erasmus's left, Theo rocked angrily in a rocking chair. Cornelius, brow furrowed, reclined beside Logistilla, who sat ramrod straight, looking downright frightened. Beside them, Mephisto and Calvin shared a cream-colored love seat. Calvin—who was looking more and more familiar to me, though I could not place him—sat comfortably, but Mephisto listened so actively, leaning forward to hear better, that he slipped off the love seat and ended up sitting cross-legged on the cold stone floor.

Beyond the love seat, Ulysses chewed nervously on his nails. He was still seated in the plush green armchair to which Cornelius's staff had directed him. Mab had bypassed the second armchair and was reading the article from the piano bench, just outside the circle.

When Mab paused, Ulysses broke in, objecting. "I am not named after the Joyce character! I'm named after the bloke from *The Odyssey.* Joyce wrote well after I was born. Doesn't anyone read the classics nowadays?"

Cornelius's cell phone emitted a series of beeps as he flipped it open and dialed. A moment later, he sighed and pocketed the phone.

"Out of range," he said mildly. "This man must be stopped. Shapechange and men rising from the dead . . . these things should not be spoken of. The *Orbis Suleimani* will have to perform a clean-up operation. Very clumsily done, Ulysses."

"What makes you think it was me?" My youngest brother's voice squeaked as he spoke.

"What indeed? Other than that you just admitted it, with your comment about Joyce," said Erasmus. Pulling the letter from Elgin from his pocket, he read aloud the passage from the sheriff's journal that described the murderer.

"I say . . . you don't think that bloke with the gun was me? Just because we both wear gray? Many people wear gray," insisted Ulysses, hastily removing his domino mask and stuffing it behind his back.

Without the mask, his blue-gray eyes seemed larger and darker. The skin about his eyes and nose, where the mask had rested, was several shades paler than the rest of his face. The look reminded me of Theo, whose face, over the centuries, had often borne a pale, reverse-raccoon imprint from where his goggles had protected the skin around his eyes from the deep tan he acquired from repeatedly firing the *Staff of Devastation*. Ulysses had admired Theo tremendously in his youth. I wondered if Theo's goggles had been the original inspiration for Ulysses's ubiquitous domino mask.

"We would like an explanation," said Cornelius. His cane twitched in his fingers, but the gem remained dark.

"Certainly, I can explain," Ulysses said huffily. His eyes flicked from face to face, taking in our hostile expressions. He raised his hands and crossed them nonchalantly behind his head. "You see, it's like this . . ."

A whirling whine issued from the large sapphire ring on Ulysses' right hand. A dart shot out of the center of the ring trailing a slender silk line, flew across the music chamber, and embedded itself in the wood of his staff in the umbrella stand beside the door. The mechanism in the ring immediately retracted the silk, and the staff flew across through the air, landing in Ulysses' outstretched hand. White light was already beginning to swirl along the length of the wood.

Erasmus leapt forward and lunged at Ulysses, but he was too late. Ulysses was gone.

The Cat and the Hat

"Imbeciles! You let him get away," screeched Logistilla. "You should have been using your staff to control him, Cornelius!"

"Of all the hypocritical . . ." Erasmus snorted with laughter.

Mab had risen to his feet and now moved about Ulysses's chair, taking readings on a brass instrument and tossing rice into the air. As he bent down to squint at the trajectory of the falling rice, Erasmus, grinning like a boy, rose from his seat and came forward to watch what Mab was doing.

"Amazing! I've known that supernatural travel creates fractional drift anomalies for several centuries now, but I never thought of using it to detect gates. How exceedingly clever!" exclaimed Erasmus.

"Could you please back up?" growled Mab. "You're disturbing the evidence,"

"Oh . . . right." Erasmus took a small step back.

"It troubles me that you encourage this abomination, Erasmus," Cornelius commented. "Even if the great project requires such a thing, it does not mean that we should fraternize with it."

"Lighten up, Cornelius," Erasmus's eyes were still fixed on Mab and his efforts. "Not everything is a dire attack on the sovereignty of humanity. Too bad you can't watch him work. Even you might learn something."

"Perhaps you should direct your attention back to the matter at hand," Cornelius replied.

"And do what? Moan and bewail Ulysses's escape?" asked Erasmus. "I'm waiting to see if Daddy's company detective can figure out where he went."

"I'd do a better job if you weren't breathing down my neck," murmured Mab.

Sighing, Cornelius inclined his head toward Theo. "Brother, did you notice something inexplicable about this matter?"

"Inexplicable?" Theo asked.

The slightest smile tugged at the corners of Cornelius's lips as he said mildly, "How did Ulysses manage to change the shape of this Mr. Thompson using the *Staff of Transportation?*"

All eyes turned toward Logistilla.

"Why is everyone looking at me?" she demanded.

"Not everybody," objected Mephisto. "Cornelius isn't looking at anyone."

"Who else could have made Mr. Thompson look like Gregor?" Cornelius asked placidly.

"Yeah, and how come you had Gregor's knife?" demanded Mephisto. "It was supposed to be buried with him or with . . ." He frowned and glanced at the article. "Mr. Thompson. Or maybe that was his staff . . . I forget."

"I have no idea what you are talking about," Logistilla began haughtily.

Titus's hulk loomed up behind Logistilla's chair. He had risen from the couch without our noticing. Now, his massive hands encircled Logistilla's pale porcelain throat. He tightened his grip, and Logistilla gasped for air, her eyes bulging in their sockets.

Titus's voice was still gruff from disuse. His Scottish accent was stronger than was his normal wont. "Woman, me slightest exertion will crush yer windpipe. With as much effort as it takes ye to peel an orange, I can part ye ribs and hold ye cold heart up to the morning sun. All I need do is flex me fingers, and ye will die. Do you know what is stopping me?"

"N-no!" mouthed Logistilla.

The rest of us waited, astonished at this outburst from placid Titus. Seeing Cornelius's confusion, Mephisto cried out with great excitement, "Titus is strangling Logistilla. Her eyes are popping out, and her face is turning purple. It's great! Too bad you're missing it!"

Ignoring him, Titus continued. He was calmer now and his accent less pronounced. "It is because I am a man who values self-restraint. By sheer effort of will, I can resist the desire to do you harm. However, if you push me any further, even my legendary self-control might break." He paused and took a breath. "I recommend you answer our good brother's questions as rapidly and truthfully as you are able—before the true horror of what you have taken from me sinks in, and I change my mind."

Titus spread his hands and stepped back. Logistilla gasped for air and rubbed her neck indignantly.

"Gregor's not dead," she wheezed.

"Not dead!" the rest of us replied in chorus.

"Then where is he?" growled Theo.

Logistilla sat tight-lipped, refusing to answer. Erasmus and Cornelius both raised their staffs menacingly. When she still refused, Titus stepped forward again, his big hulking bulk looming just behind her chair. As his hands came toward her throat, Logistilla relented.

"He's on Mars," she pouted.

"Mars!"

Mab still crouched beside Ulysses's chair, flipped open his note book. "Ulysses worked for NASA in the seventies. He may have had access to one of the Mars landers."

I said, "All he would have had to do was touch it once with his staff, and he could have teleported to Mars when it arrived."

"Whatever for?" exploded Theo. "Why is Gregor hiding on Mars? Why is he pretending to be dead?"

Logistilla squirmed uncomfortably. "Gregor's not hiding, he's . . ."

"He's what?" asked Erasmus coolly. "A prisoner, perhaps?"

"Prisoner is such a harsh word," Logistilla replied, pouting again.

"What word would you prefer?" Erasmus asked sweetly.

"Ulysses got himself into some trouble. To get out alive, he was forced to make some . . . unwise promises. One of them involved Gregor no longer being 'a living man upon the Earth.' He thought it better to have Gregor a 'prisoner' than himself dead, or worse," said Logistilla.

"Why didn't Ulysses tell us?" Theo cried in anguish. "Gregor and I could have taken out whoever was compelling him."

"That is probably why his oath was worded so as to forbid him from telling you," Logistilla replied acidly.

"How come you know?" asked Mab suspiciously, looking up, a compass in his hand.

"I? I . . . rather found out through my own source." Logistilla evaded our glances.

"And how come you didn't tell Theo and the others?" Mab continued, whipping out his notebook and his stubby pencil.

"I had . . . problems of my own."

"This line of questioning is not to the point," Cornelius's soft voice interrupted. "The point is: How are we going to rescue Brother Gregor?"

"There are only two possibilities," I said. "A mundane spaceship, or the *Staff of Transportation*. Either we hire NASA or another program like it, or we find Ulysses."

Cornelius said, "Building a ship to go to Mars might take years, and there would be no guarantee the vehicle would fly as designed. No, it will have to be the *Staff of Transportation*."

"For that, we need Ulysses," Logistilla said primly.

"Having Ulysses would clear up a number of things," mused Erasmus.

"I know," Mephisto piped up from where he sat on the floor. "We summon him!"

"Come again?" asked Cornelius.

"The staff trees," continued Mephisto. "We go to the staff tree grove and use the original tree from which the *Staff of Transportation* came to summon it back to us . . . using the same spell I use to get new friends for my staff, the one Daddy used to summon Miranda's mother. We summon Ulysses and make him take us. If he lets go of his staff while we are summoning it, we'll get the staff without Ulysses, which might be even better!"

"I'd love to be a bug on the wall the first time Ulysses has to hail a cab to get home," Logistilla chuckled throatily.

"What grove?" Erasmus asked dubiously.

"Mephisto means the grove where Father planted his old books—the books which grew into the trees he fashioned into our staffs," I explained, pleased that there was finally something I knew that Erasmus didn't. "Mephisto, how do you know about the Grove of Books?"

"Saw it when Daddy brought me here to tam . . ." He paused, glancing at Calvin, perhaps hoping his Bully Boy would prompt his memory, then gave an elaborate shrug. "Well, for some old reason. You know how my memory is." He tapped his temple cheerfully. "So, should I go summon him up?"

"Whoa! Whoa!" said Mab, abruptly coming to his feet. "I know the spell you're talking about, and it's no namby-pamby spell for humans to be mucking around with—especially if you're going to cast it to summon one of the high lords of Hell, which we now all know to be in the staffs. We're talking a class one, disturbs-the-ethersphere, incantation here. The kind Archmages use when they want to destroy a whole civilization. You cast that spell here, and you'll have every last lamnia, leanan-sidhe, and edimou of the outoukkou in a thousand leagues breathing down your neck in no time."

"Quiet, Spiritling, your contribution was not requested," Cornelius said sharply. "Can you manage this spell, Mephisto?"

"Yeah, sure!" Mephisto announced cheerfully. "Easy as pie."

"Let's do it then," said Erasmus, rising to his feet. "What do we need?"

"Darkness would help," Mab muttered.

"Silence!" Cornelius commanded.

This was too much.

"Cornelius," I said crisply, "in the future, you will refrain from ordering my people around."

"I will remind you, Sister, he is a Prospero, Inc. employee. That means he works for us both—" Cornelius began.

Mab cut him off. "It's okay, Ma'am. If your know-it-all brother thinks he can do without my help, more power to him. But, if the two remaining Three Shadowed Ones show up and make off with his staff, don't blame me."

Cornelius was so shocked by Mab's impertinence he could think of nothing to say. I, too, said nothing because everything that came to mind was inflammatory, and I felt this was hardly the time to begin an argument. The tension was broken by Erasmus's laughter.

"And he's sarcastic to boot! Are you sure you can't be persuaded to part with him, Sister Dear?" he asked.

"Positive," I replied severely.

"Anyone have a better plan?" asked Cornelius. When no one answered, he said, "Very well. Normally, I abhor unnecessary uses of sorcery, but I agree that this is in a good cause. What do we need to do, Mephisto?"

"Best done at night," said Theo. I was pleased to hear that his voice was recovering. He no longer sounded so hoarse. "Sunlight interferes with magic."

I saw Mab smiling to himself as he sat back on the piano bench.

"Very well, then. Tonight at nightfall at this Grove of Books," said Erasmus.

Titus had lowered himself heavily into the empty green armchair and closed his eyes. Now he opened them and said, "Woman! Gregor can't have been on Mars since the twenties. Where was he?"

Logistilla hesitated for a long time, worrying the black cloth of her silky dress between her fingers. At last, she admitted in a small voice, "He was . . . a leopard."

"You mean, one of your leopards?" asked Theo, his voice dangerously low.

"Well, it was better that than let the demon kill Ulysses," she replied.

"Bah!" spat Titus. "Your own twin."

"Better than having him dead," Logistilla spat back. "Or, than losing Ulysses. Besides, life among my menagerie's not so bad. I don't know what you are talking about: 'realize what you had lost.' It was only two years. Nothing in comparison to your long life."

Titus rose unsteadily to his feet and glared down at Logistilla.

"Two years to me is as nothing, it is as dust in the desert. But, two years in the lives of my children . . . that is something of inestimable value that can never be reclaimed. The eldest one has passed from the idyllic days of childhood into being a youth without me there to guide him. I was not there to offer them wisdom or love. I was not even there to mislead them through well-meaning incompetence. Worse, you unnatural witch, you were not there, either." Grimacing in disgust, he turned his back on her and sat down again. Crossing his arms, he growled, "I don't know what it is with the women in our family. No natural womanly affections. Miranda at least has an excuse: her abstinence buys us immortality. But, you! You have no excuse."

Taken aback, I asked, "Pardon me, but I'm missing something here. How does Logistilla's not raising your children make her an unwomanly witch?"

"They're my children, too," Logistilla objected hotly. "And I believe I make a fine mother. I've visited them on every birthday they've had, and at Easter, and during all their holidays. Well, I've missed a few, but I was there for most of them. The rest of the time, they are busy. They attend a very prestigious boarding school. I chose it myself."

Silence fell throughout the music room.

"Your children, too?" Theo asked puzzled. "Are these children adopted?"

"Ewww!" cried Mephisto. "Titus! How could you?"

"Didn't realize we could *do* that," murmured Erasmus, amused. "What of you, Theo? Care to take a stab at marrying your darling Miranda?"

Theo crossed his arms and glared at Erasmus, but beneath his gray beard were the telltale signs of a deep blush.

"Logistilla is only my half-sister," Titus explained evenly, without a trace of guilt or embarrassment. "We were born more than thirty-five years apart. We did not even grow up in the same country. There are not many immortal women to choose from, you know, unless you care to wed soulless swan maidens and selkie like Erasmus, and we've all seen how that's turned out. I am tired of having wives dying out from under me. Besides, I thought if I married Logistilla, our mutual children might meet even Miranda's definition of family."

"Mine!" I exclaimed, startled. "What do I have to do with it?"

"You control the Water of Life," Titus explained. "I am also tired of watching my children age, wither, and die. I want them to live. Like us."

"Me?" I exclaimed. "Father's the one who decided who got the Water and who did not. I merely carried out his instructions."

At this, Theo frowned, and Erasmus threw me a look of such malice that anything I might have added died unspoken.

"Father's then," Titus continued placidly. "I thought children of two members of the family would clearly fall under the fullest definition of family. . . . Wonder how the boys are."

"They were fine as of a week ago," Mab drawled. "We saw 'em in Santa's scrying pool, the one he uses to 'know if you've been bad or good.' "

"I am pleased to hear it," said Titus, and his battered face broke into a warm fatherly smile. "It has been a long time. I believe I will leave you all and go to them."

He started to rise. He looked so determined, despite his wounds, and so pleased at the thought of seeing his sons again, that I was hesitant to break the truth to him.

"How?" I asked.

"What do you mean?" Titus hesitated.

"Ulysses brought us here," I said. "There is no other way off the island."

"You could ride Pegasus!" suggested Mephisto.

Titus turned. His expression was one of sad amusement. "Within the last hour, I was shot by a gun, mauled by a bear, and nearly gored by a rhino. Even though the bullet has now been removed and I have been fortified with Water, I doubt I am fit enough to endure a several-thousand-mile ride on the back of a winged horse."

"How are the rest of us going to get off this island?" asked Cornelius.

"I'll send an Aerie One to the mainland," I said. "They can contact Prospero, Inc. and have a ship or a Lear sent."

"Don't bother," replied Erasmus airily. "We can all stay around to confront Ulysses tonight and welcome Gregor back, and then Ulysses can take us each home . . . or we can take ourselves home with his staff, depending upon how Ulysses's meeting with Gregor turns out. Somehow, I expect our Martian brother is not going to be too pleased with good old Ulysses."

"Very well. I'll wait. After two years, what is a few more hours?" said Titus, sitting back down in the armchair. He promptly fell asleep and began snoring.

* * *

AS soon as we split up, Mab hurried over to me, clutching his notebook.

"I'd like to make my report, Ma'am. On the subject of the disappearance of Mr. Ulysses. Then, I suggest we go question the Harebrain."

"And exactly what did you find out about our good Ulysses's escape?" asked Erasmus, leaving Cornelius and Titus by the window and coming to lean against the back of my chair. His dark eyes watched me, mocking and arrogant; a wicked smile played across his thin lips.

I raised an eyebrow. "Don't you owe me an apology, Erasmus?"

"For what?"

"For having accused me of forging the document about Ulysses."

Erasmus considered, then shook his head. "You may have been innocent in this case, Sweet Sister, but I'm sure you have done some other vile thing I have not yet discovered. So, in keeping with the law of conservation of apologies, I'll let my accusations stand."

What was it that made men refuse to apologize to me? My brother was nearly as obstinate as a certain elf I knew.

I sighed. "Do you work at being obnoxious, Erasmus? Or are you naturally that way?"

"It comes naturally to me," Erasmus replied, smiling, "as it does to you."

"Do you mind?" asked Mab, gesturing toward his notebook.

Erasmus was smiling broadly now. "Oh, don't mind me. Go ahead with your detecting."

Mephisto clapped Erasmus on the shoulder and announced, "He's just jealous because he's behind Theo and me in the 'marry a sister' queue. You do prefer me to Erasmus, don't you?" he finished hopefully.

"I see this is going to be a long day," Mab observed dryly, shaking his head.

"Go ahead, Mab. What did you find?" I repeated, ignoring my brothers.

"Well, it's like this, Ma'am. Best as I can tell from the evidence, Mr. Ulysses had a miniature grapple-gun device in his ring. He used it to snag his staff. The staff carried him to some place on this world, probably a secret hideout he had set up for just such purposes. Staff was probably preset to transport to said spot if stabbed with the dart from the grapple. My readings suggest this hideout is somewhere in the Himalayas, but you just don't get the kind of accuracy on in-world hops that you can get on interdimensional jumps. Sorry about that."

Erasmus asked, "Are you telling me that our brother Ulysses managed to hit a stick about an inch wide from across a room with a dart he shot out of a ring on a finger that was behind his head?"

"Yeah," said Mab. "I know I got that part right, I saw it with my own eyes."

"Incredible," Erasmus exclaimed. "I couldn't do that, could you? I don't have that kind of aim."

"Mr. Ulysses is a perp, Sir. Thieving is all he does. Apparently, it's all he's ever done, for more than a hundred years. I'd recommend you feel proud of yourself if you can't pull off a stunt like that, Professor Prospero. It means you haven't wasted your time on immoral frivolities."

"Oh, I have most certainly wasted my time on immoral frivolities, just not the same immoral frivolities as Ulysses—and you may call me Erasmus," said my brother, flopping down on the Roman couch and folding his arms behind his head.

"Ah . . . right, Mr. Erasmus, then," Mab said. He screwed up his face and scratched at his eternal stubble. "That about covers Mr. Ulysses, Ma'am. It's time we had a talk with the Hatless Wonder, here." He glanced down at Erasmus. "A private talk, I'm thinking, Ma'am."

"Oh, don't let my presence interfere," Erasmus began cheerfully.

"We won't," I said, rising and grabbing Mephisto by one arm. Mab grabbed the other, and we practically dragged him toward an inner door that led to Father's instrument repair shop.

"Bye-bye," called Mephisto to a bemused Erasmus as we shoved him into the repair shop. Behind us, I could hear Erasmus chuckling.

WE made our way into the repair shop and pushed Mephisto up onto the workbench, where he sat amidst lathes, scraps of wood, piano strings, and sharping bars while Mab and I found three usable chairs. The small room smelled of wood oil and damp stone. As I helped Mephisto down onto a three-legged stool, Mab knelt and sniffed the sawdust by the foot of the workbench, grunting noncommittally.

Joining us, Mab said, "Okay, put on the blasted hat, or we'll hold you down and shove it on that empty head of yours."

"If my head is empty, where do I keep the rabbit brain you keep talking about, hmm?"

"Rabbits have far more brains than you do, punk. Now put on the hat!"

"No." Mephisto shook his head stubbornly and threw the hat down onto the wood chips.

I took a different tack. "Have it your way. I'll go get Erasmus and Titus.

I'm sure they'll be happy to hear all about your Mephistopheles, Prince of Hell, routine. Or perhaps, I should get Cornelius and his staff?"

"Shhhh!" Mephisto held his finger up to his lips and looked furtively about. "Quiet about the Rince-pay of Ell-hay! What if someone hears you? How did you find out about that, anyway?" He peered at me suspiciously.

"You showed us," I stated.

"Oh," he blinked, then shrugged. "Guess I had my reasons. Okay, give me the hat."

Mab picked up and brushed off the hat. He peered inside, pointing to a band of overlapping pieces of some kind of horn, which wrapped around the inside of the hat. "Horse hoof," he muttered. "Wonder what that's for?"

Mephisto looked at it thoughtfully and then tapped his staff on the ground.

I began to imagine the straw and wood shavings were a cat, a white cat with brindle spots. After a moment, I could imagine it very clearly, as if the cat were really here. Only, unlike the way Mephisto's staff usually worked, no cat appeared. Or at least, my eyes could not see it. Yet, every time I glanced at the spot beside Mephisto's stool, I received a distinct impression of such a cat.

A soft high-pitched voice spoke out of the air. "My name is Schrödinger. I am your familiar. You are Mephistopheles Prospero, son of the great magician Lucretius Prospero, once Duke of Milan. You are his eldest son and heir. You have asked me to remind you of this because you have damaged your memory in order to escape a great curse. You brought this curse upon yourself through the use of demonic powers you cleverly obtained. You must keep the existence of these powers a secret from your brothers, lest they kill you. You cannot see me because I have been struck by a car and am now a ghost. Nonetheless, I am present and can answer your questions and do your bidding."

"By Setebos and Titania!" muttered Mab. "Poor thing."

"Ah! Someone else is present!" I imagined the cat's green eyes glancing from Mab to me, straining as if it had trouble seeing into our realm. "How . . . unfortunate. I apologize for any secrets I have unintentionally spilled."

"Schrödinger, Santa gave me a hat that restores my memory. Miranda wants me to put it on and tell her things. Should I do it?" Mephisto asked.

The ghostly cat spoke. "Do not don the hat. If you recall the particulars of the situation that led you to your current condition, a dire fate will befall you. Leave the room. If your sister will promise not to repeat what she learns, I will answer her questions. You may tell her that Tybalt vouches for her."

"I promise," I said, amused that Schrödinger was willing to trust me based on the good word of my familiar.

"I don't like this," Mab began. "It's bad luck to consort with ghosts. I think we should get Harebrain to . . ." but Mephisto was already jumping down from his stool.

"Oh, goody, I'm off the hook," he declared, dropping the hat into my lap. The feathers brushed my face, tickling my nose. "Here, Miranda, you'd better keep this. I might need it some time." Then, he went charging back into the music room shouting, "Yoo hoo! Who's up for a game of Scrabble? Titus? Wake up, you sleepyhead. Your snoring is disturbing the dead. I know! I just saw a ghost stirring in the little room over there."

THE door swung shut, blocking out the rest of Mephisto's inane banter. I turned to the cat, or more accurately, I turned toward where the cat was not, but where I continued to believe that it sat licking its paw.

"What happened to Mephisto?" I asked.

"Mortals are not so different from cats," Schrödinger began. "When we want something, we hunt it down. When you want something, you hunt it down. In this way, we are alike. Cats are wise enough not to hunt down beasts too large for them to catch. Your brother, I fear, does not share this wisdom."

"How so?" I asked.

"The Faery Queen danced before him, and he was fool enough to consider himself her equal. He called upon his secret art to summon her and bind her, but she proved too subtle for him."

The Faery Queen again! I recalled the night, back in 1627, when we came upon the elves dancing before their howe, a night of floating sparks and pine boughs and dancing among the stars. Looking back, my recollection of that night was often misty, but three things I remember clearly: Father dancing with Queen Maeve, Mephisto entertaining the High Lords of the Elven Council with juggling and acrobatic tricks after playing his violin for the queen, and myself dancing with Astreus, who laughed at the mockery of his fellows as he swept me off the earth to twirl amidst the starlit sky. I closed my eyes a moment, remembering the fresh windy smell of him and the eerie unearthly way I felt whenever he stood close to me, both that night and, more recently, at Father Christmas's.

But my thoughts were straying from the topic. Schrödinger was speaking of the Elven Queen, not the Lord of the Winds. I recalled the statue Mephisto had carved of Queen Maeve on his great mural. He had certainly captured her beauty, even if he shared it with the demon queen. An odd chill ran down my back as I recalled the "M." in Father's journal. Could that stand for Maeve? Was Father mixed up in Mephisto's madness, too? Oh, I prayed not!

"What is this secret art?" asked Mab.

The ghostly cat replied, "Mephisto knows the art by which the object of one's desire might be summoned and compelled to come. It is the same art Prospero practices, but Prospero draws his power from a Heavenly source. Not so Mephisto."

With a shiver, I recalled the spell Mephisto had spoken of, the very same one we hoped to use tonight to summon Ulysses, the one he claimed Father used to summon my mother.

Aloud, I asked, "So, he summoned up Queen Maeve, and she cursed him for his impudence? No wonder she was annoyed to see him at her table over Christmas!"

"You race ahead. A good cat pauses and lets the knowledge approach, waiting until it has grown close before springing," said the ghostly cat. I received a distinct impression of it washing its hind leg.

"I'm sorry. Please continue," I said.

"The Faery Queen grew terrible with wrath. Cowed, yet still besotted, Mephisto begged to be allowed to do her some boon. The Faery Queen asked if he were truly Mephisto the Beast Tamer, from whom, it was said, no beast could escape. Mephisto acknowledged he was. The Faery Queen then demanded that in return for his transgression, he vow to bring her whatever part she might request of whatever beast she might name, and, furthermore, that should he not do so within seven years, he would forgo his freedom forever, becoming her faithful and adoring slave."

"Tell me he said, 'No!'" prayed Mab.

The ghostly cat continued. "Believing she would request a feather from a phoenix, or perhaps the hoof of a hippogriff, Mephisto agreed and swore the oath upon the River Styx."

"No!" Mab cried, hitting his fists against his head. "Never offer a supernatural creature a boon! Especially an elf! I can see why you might offer a boon to, say, an Angel, but an elf! Was he crazy? No offense, Ma'am but I'm beginning to think your brother was a harebrain even before he lost his wits."

"No use in crying about it now, Mab," I replied. "It happened over three hundred years ago."

"I can see what is coming," Mab continued. "He swears, and she asked him to bring her the blood of the Sun or the heart of the Beast called Fear, or some such feat no man could achieve."

"You, too, have pounced too soon, child of the air," said the ghostly cat. "An ancient law allows for the annulment of oaths that cannot be performed. Only knaves and imbeciles, ignorant of this law, fall prey to such contrivances. No, the Faery Queen's decree was nothing so innocent." The cat paused, and I received the distinct impression of green eyes staring directly at me.

The ghostly cat said softly, "She commanded him to bring her the head of the Unicorn."

"Merciful Mother of God!" I whispered in fifteenth-century Italian.

"By unicorn . . . do you mean a unicorn, or the Unicorn?" Mab asked, his face white as a sheet.

"The Faery Queen demanded the head of Eurynome, the White Lady of Grace."

Shocked, I could make no sense of Schrödinger's story. Then, I remembered Mephisto's wall.

"Queen Maeve is Lilith in disguise! Eurynome's ancient enemy!"

"At last, Prospero's daughter, you have pounced and captured. By this foul request was her true nature revealed, for Queen Maeve is naught but another face of Lilith, the Queen of Air and Darkness. Mephisto believes she slew the true Faery Queen by foul treachery."

"You mean old Titania was murdered?" Mab gasped, as shocked as I had ever seen him. "I thought she retired to go live in Arcadia, or maybe the Elysian Fields! Geesh! Poor Titania!"

"So the poets were right! The Queen of the Elves really is the Queen of Air and Darkness!" I said.

Mab colored. "Sorry, I mocked 'em, Ma'am."

"No wonder he owned a chameleon cloak!" I exclaimed.

Schrödinger nodded. "The Queen of Air and Darkness gave it to him so that he could hunt the Unicorn. At first, Mephistopheles scorned it and would have nothing to do with it. Later, however, he forgot why he had objected so strongly and wore it so that he could slip about unseen. When in public, he hid it beneath a poncho. Still later, he put it down somewhere and could not remember where it might be."

"He pawned it," Mab replied bluntly, "up near Theo's."

"Ah," answered the cat, "Yes. That makes sense."

Slowly, I said, "We know Lilith, the Queen of Demons, has reason to hate Eurynome, whom Lilith feels stole mankind from the demons. She must have been the one who sponsored the Unicorn Hunters to begin with. This explains what the dark angel at Theo's meant by 'Prospero's blood has already condoned our work.' He meant the cloak belonged to Mephisto, who was of Prospero's line, and thus Prospero's authority could not be used to unmake the cloak."

The ghostly cat nodded graciously. "Have you more questions? The daylight tires me."

"Just one," said Mab. "How did the Harebrain become a Prince of Hell?"

Schrödinger licked her paw. "Of that, I am not permitted to speak."

"Was he tithed by the elves? Is that how it happened?"

"Tithed?" the cat asked archly. "No. He was a Hellish lord before he summoned the Elf Queen. Had he not been, he would not have had the authority to cast the summoning spell."

"I have two questions," I said. My mouth seemed dry and the words came haltingly. "Was my father involved with this somehow?"

The cat shook its ghost-head. "To the best of my knowledge, Great Prospero knows no more of this than you did this morning."

That was encouraging. It gave me the courage to ask the next question. "And what of Lord Astreus?" My heart beat unnaturally fast as I spoke the elf lord's name. I awaited the cat's answer with both eagerness and dread. "How does he fit into this?"

"Lord Astreus made a compact with Mephistopheles, the details of which were never made known to me. The Lord of the Winds was present when Mephisto summoned Queen Maeve and when he swore the fateful oath."

"Did Lord Astreus put him up to it?" demanded Mab. "Were he and the Queen working together to trap Mephisto?"

"I know not," the ghostly cat replied. "I know only that Lord Astreus brought Mephisto a decanter of water from the River Lethe, which Mephisto drank in order to forget his oath and, thus, avoid his appointed fate as Lilith's eternal slave. Should Mephisto's memory return, and he remember what he has sworn, he will be compelled to carry out the terms of the oath. Only his forgetfulness protects him now."

"Thank you, Schrödinger," I said. "You have been a great help."

The ghostly cat, its voice growing weak as it faded away, replied, "Of course."

A Toast to Miranda

Mab and I spent the morning in the orchid garden, discussing in hushed voices what we had learned from Schrödinger.

"So, let me get this straight," Mab said, his stubby pencil moving quickly across the pages of his notebook. "Mephisto swore a dire oath to the Elf Queen, who is secretly the Queen of Demons. This oath impelled him to hunt the Holy Unicorn or become the slave of the Queen of Air and Darkness. Lord Astreus gives Mephisto water from the River Lethe, which wipes out Mephisto's memory. This lets him escape the consequences of his oath, but it also drives him mad." Mab scratched his chin and jotted something else down in his notebook.

"No wonder Mephisto's crazy!" I said.

"No wonder he freaked when Lord Astreus offered him a drink!"

"And what is Astreus's part in all this?" I wondered. The memory of our ride through the stars grew more vivid with each passing day, as if the elf lord were becoming more and more of a presence in my thoughts. Until yesterday, it had been easy to dismiss him; for between an inhuman elf and a flesh-and-blood man, the choice was simple. With Ferdinand nonexistent, however, I now had nothing to shield me from the lure of stardew and wonder. Silently cursing the elf for the marvels he had shown me, I wished anew that I had listened to Mab and skipped the Christmas feast.

Meanwhile, Mab was saying, "Good question, Ma'am. Was he trying to help Mephisto? Or was damaging Mephisto's mind part of the Queen's plan, and Lord Astreus just her agent? Did Lord Astreus put Mephisto up to trying to summon the Elf Queen in the first place?"

Remembering something Caurus told me, I asked suddenly, "Mab, is Astreus actually your father?"

Mab stared at me expressionlessly, and then snorted. "Who told you that, Old Northwesty? Caurus is overly poetic, Ma'am—too many sips out of Kvasir's cauldron."

"Ah. Okay. At least, we can now discount your theory about Mephisto having been tithed. That party the Elf Queen threw because Lord Astreus freed the elves from the tithe to Hell for one sevenyear apparently had nothing to do with Mephisto." As I spoke, I recalled the haunted look in Astreus's eyes as he explained that the price of that free sevenyear had been too high. A shiver ran up my spine.

"Don't know, Ma'am, but . . ." Mab frowned, troubled. "I hate to say anything bad about Lord Astreus, after all the good he's done for me and mine, but if he is in with the Queen—if he's hunting the Unicorn, too—perhaps he brought you the *Book of the Sibyl* hoping you would lead him to your Lady."

Learning that Mephisto had been damaged by water from the Lethe, rather than tithed to Hell, had renewed my faith in Astreus. Now, that faith took another tumble. I sighed, closing my eyes, tired of the emotional roller coaster I had been riding lately.

I loved my flute. Then, I feared the effect its demon might be having upon my soul. Now, there was no demon, but I feared my Lady may be angry with me for keeping her consort trapped these many years.

I adored my father. Then, I feared he had harmed Ferdinand. Now, I knew him innocent of that crime, but discovered that he may have lied to me about my mother and perhaps even had me under a spell.

I was overjoyed when Astreus gave me the *Book of the Sibyl.* Then, I feared he had tithed my brother to Hell. Now, I knew he was innocent of that charge but was troubled that he may have even more sinister designs.

This cycle of fears and suspicions was exhausting. And yet, had I been more suspicious of Ferdinand, I might have saved my family a good deal of suffering. What is more, a suspicion like this might go a long way toward keeping the specter of the elf lord from haunting my thoughts.

Except, I recalled how Astreus had stood up to the Elf Queen during the Christmas Feast, ten days ago, when he had insisted upon sitting next to me, and how harshly Queen Maeve had regarded him. What was it he had said?

For no elf, be she maid or queen, would fail to honor the Handmaiden of Divine Eurynome, who is adored by all TRUE *elves.*

Astreus had been mocking Lilith!

Before the entire court, he had called Queen Maeve a false elf and berated her for her enmity against Eurynome, though only he and she must have understood his meaning. Taunting one's queen to her face hardly seemed like the action of a loyal henchman. Good for him, I thought, obscurely pleased by his defiance.

However, my earlier conjecture that the "M." in Father's journal might stand for "Maeve" now took a sinister turn. Schrödinger claimed Father knew nothing of Mephisto's plight. Perhaps so, but that did not rule out the possibility that Father had conspired with the Elf Queen in other matters, such as to bring my uncle Antonio, the King of Naples, and his eminently marriageable son, Prince Ferdinand, to the shores of our island prison so long ago. I searched for another candidate but there were none that made sense. The more I contemplated it, the more certain I became that Father's "fair queen" must be the Elf Queen. But, did Father know that Maeve was Lilith in disguise?

Eventually, Mab and I reached a point where we were merely repeating our previous questions. Realizing that while the sun shone brightly here, it was the wee hours of the morning back home in Oregon, I left Mab to his own devices and retired to my old room to sleep.

I WOKE to the call of storm petrels and realized it was nearly dinnertime. Upon rising, I reached for my cell phone to check in with Prospero, Inc., but of course it was back at Erasmus's and would not have worked here anyway. It troubled me to be out of touch. The turn of the year was a tricky time in the world of spirits; at least one of our Priority Contracts—the bargains between supernatural beings which we enforced and maintained, so that the Earth did not quake, oceans and rivers did not flood, and oil continued to burn evenly in engines—always went awry. As I was stuck here, incommunicado, until we retrieved Ulysses' staff, there was nothing I could do except pray that Mustardseed and my other company officers proved up to any challenges that arose.

I had removed my Worth gown and slept in my linen chemise. Now, I donned the gown again, for I had nothing else to wear. After brushing out my silvery hair and deciding to leave it down, I set off for the dining room.

It was strange to walk down the old store halls again. Everywhere I went, I encountered the ghost of my father. Not a real ghost, of course, but such a clear memory that I constantly felt as if, were I to turn quickly enough, I might catch sight of him.

I pictured him as he had been in my youth: tall, imposing, and kindly, garbed in robes, with salt-and pepper-hair and a full beard. In the corridors, I thought to see him strolling along deep in thought, his brows furrowed, his hands clasped behind his back. As I passed the Astronomy Chamber, he seemed to recline on his specially designed chair as he peered at the stars through the crystal dome (spyglasses not having been invented yet). In the library, I could have sworn that he sat at his desk, turning the pages of some gigantic tome, perhaps researching spells for summoning oreads and gnomes to move the earth and stone for a new wing. In the solarium, I thought I caught sight of him drawing sketches of objects he desired the airy servants to fetch from afar. (There was no way to instruct them to buy as opposed to steal, but he always had them leave more gold than the object he desired was worth.) And I would have sworn I caught a glimpse of him in the parlor, sitting before his chessboard, waiting for me to join him for a game.

Suddenly, I missed him terribly. All my long life, he had been the strong presence to which I turned in times of distress or tribulation, always calm, always wise, always offering a practical answer. I, in return, had been his stalwart helper and companion. Now he was a prisoner under torture, in pain, and I could do nothing to help him. I loved him so dearly and missed him tremendously—despite all my suspicions. Without him for me to stand by, I was not even sure quite who I was.

I sat down on a bench in the solarium, before the wide, sunny window that looked out on the sea far below (another open space enchanted with a protective air cushion) and put my face in my hands, weeping. I wept for my father, whom I loved and for whose life I feared. I wept for the death of Ferdinand, slain by my wicked uncle, whom I had never properly mourned, and I wept for the loss of this more recent Ferdinand and for the false vision of future happiness the infernal incubus had raised in my heart.

Apple Blossom's soft call of "Supper, Milady," brought me back to myself. I sent her for a basin of water and rinsed the tears from my face. After examining myself in the shiny surface of a helmet and deciding I looked presentable, I set out to dinner again.

I CAME upon Theo sitting slumped against a wall with his head in his hands. The sight shocked me, for I thought, for a moment, that it was Father. Seeing my brother, alive and whole, did much to raise my spirits. Stooping beside him, I touched his shoulder and asked, "Are you well?"

He raised his head, and his eyes met mine. There was a fierce intensity to his gaze that I recalled from ages gone by, but which I had not seen in some decades, almost as if the ghost of his younger self were possessing his old man body. I found it eerie and yet encouraging.

"Gregor's not dead," he said. "Never has been."

I nodded.

"I've been such an idiot!" he announced candidly.

I nodded again, smiling.

He reached out a hand, and I helped him to his feet. Instead of releasing my hand, he used it to pull me against his chest and gave me a fierce hug. I returned the embrace, laughing.

"I missed you," he said when he released me.

"I missed you, too," I replied.

He offered me his arm, and together, we went in to dinner.

DINNER consisted of fish from the sea caught by the airy servants, wild edible greens, and wine from Father's cellar. It was served in the great dining hall, which was smaller than I had remembered. But, then I was a mere child when I lived in this house. Many things I recalled from those years had proven false.

When the dishes had been removed and only wineglasses remained, Erasmus sat back in his chair, smiling through his lank black locks. Reaching into his pocket, he held up a tiny, spherical, crystal vial about the size of a plum. Unstopping it, he lifted the stopper to his nose and sniffed it as one might a wine cork. The air about the tables rustled with the sudden motion of Aerie Ones. Mab sniffed, alert. At the opposite side of the table, Cornelius broke off his conversation with Titus and flared his nostrils to catch the marvelous scent as it spread through the dining room.

"It is New Year's Day, you know," Erasmus said, holding the tiny vial up for all to see.

I had forgotten the family practice of taking their yearly drop of Water of Life on New Year's Day. No wonder everyone attended Erasmus's New Year's parties. It offered them a reminder and an opportunity to maintain their immortality together. Having access to the Water whenever I wanted made such rituals less important to me. Yet, this time, I was glad to be among my siblings when they renewed their immortality for another year.

Cornelius felt his pockets. "You will have to drink without me, Brother. I fear I left mine back at your mansion."

"I suspect many of us did," Erasmus replied smoothly. "But, perhaps Miranda would be so kind as to provide for those who have not."

"I would be delighted," I said.

I took my pear-shaped vial from a little reticule made of the same violet cloth as my vintage gown. In it, I had placed belongings from in my pockets: my spare vial, a comb, and the dried bits of moly leaf from my trip to the Wintergarden. I wanted to carry the enchanted, razor-edged fighting fan as well, but the reticule was too small.

Walking around the table, I stopped beside each place to let a single drop of the sweet smelling pearly liquid fall into the dark red wine. Mab shook his head and covered his glass with his hand when I came to his place, muttering, "Can't afford to be tipsy while on the job." Mephisto, after offering his own cup, held up Calvin's, saying, "Daddy gave me a supply for him, but it's not here, so can you do his, too?"

"Father gave you a supply of Water for your Bully Boy!" I asked, taken aback.

The dining room was suddenly very quiet. Erasmus and Titus gazed at Mephisto with particular intensity. Erasmus's face had gone an odd shade of green.

"Yeah . . . so?" Mephisto asked cheerfully. His staff was still handcuffed to his left arm and stuck up beside him, jerking about whenever he gestured or cut his food.

"Why did he give extra Water to you for your manservant, but none to me for my . . . to Titus for his children?" Erasmus asked, pronouncing each word with careful precision.

But I had glanced over at Calvin. Earlier in the meal, he had slouched over his dish and shoveled food into his mouth, until Mephisto had elbowed him. Then, he had straightened up and used proper manners. But there was something about that slouch, the shape of his shoulders, the way he had practically inhaled his food, that seemed to fit in this dining hall. My stomach clenched, and a strange dizziness took hold of me. The room seemed to swim and spin. Calvin saw me watching him and gave me a sweet hopeful smile, like a dog who knew he was about to be whipped, wagging his tail before his master.

I knew that look. The clothes were wrong, and the smooth, clean-shaven skin, but the expression had not changed. I remembered racing the wind along the beaches of this island, the apron of my skirt filled with clams, with my best friend dogging my footsteps, that same expression on his hopeful face—the same "best friend" who later attacked me so vilely.

No, it could not be!

I leaned closer, staring. His five o'clock shadow covered not only his jaw, but his cheeks and his nose and part of his forehead. Thick tuffs of hair protruded from the cuff of his sleeve. If he were to hunch his shoulders . . . if he stopped shaving . . . if he were merely wearing a loincloth . . .

The edges of the world blurred. I wondered abstractly whether I might faint.

"Miranda?" Theo reached up and touched my arm. "Are you all right?"

I pushed Theo's hand away without looking at him. My throat had gone dry. It took me two tries to speak.

"Hello, Caliban." My voice cracked. "It's been a long time."

"Caliban?"

"Caliban!"

My family all began clamoring at once.

"I thought Caliban was some kind of furry monstrosity." Erasmus peered across the table. His voice sounded odd, and his complexion was still a queer green.

"I was, until Master Mephisto civilized me." Caliban beamed at Mephisto. "Now, I shave a lot."

"Fascinating," purred Logistilla, who was seated beside Caliban. She trailed her fingers over his bulging biceps. "So, the beast tamer tamed you, did he? What kind of tricks can you perform?"

Caliban blushed noticeably under Logistilla's scrutiny, but his eyes remained trained on me.

"I'd like to apologize for my behavior toward you back in our youth, Miss Miranda," he said shyly. "I was an ignorant brute."

In the back of my mind, I could hear my own voice speaking, calmly telling myself that it was ungracious not to forgive a man for something he did as a mere youth five hundred years ago. Yet, I had hated Caliban so fiercely and for so long, I was not sure I was capable of forgiving him. After all, he had treated me badly when we were children together, and he tried to rape me and rob me of Eurynome's favor—the most traumatic event of my early youth. A part of me wanted to strike him down instantly. A mere toot on the flute, and a bolt of lightning would cleanse the world of his stain forever.

The man standing in front of me, however, looked more like the fellow who repaired the fireplace in the Lesser Hall last spring than like the cruel, depraved monster I remembered. I imagined Beowulf arriving at a formal tea and discovering one of his fellow guests was Grendel, all decked out in tux and tails; or St. George at a garden party where the dragon was roasting marshmallows for the other guests. I wondered how they would have taken it.

"Yes, you were . . ." I began coldly and would have continued in the same vein, except that, out of the corner of my eye, I caught sight of Erasmus smiling smugly. Color had returned to his face, and he looked expectant, as if he were waiting for my coming tirade. His reaction disturbed me. Was I as cold and callous as he believed? Or as predictable? "However, that was a long time ago. Let us put the matter behind us and not speak of it again. You may consider yourself forgiven."

With a Herculean effort, I forced my arm to rise. My skin crawled as he reached forward to shake my hand. Yet, it felt like any handshake, firm and . . . human. Caliban squeezed my hand kindly, giving me a wide and genuine smile. To my right, Mephisto was grinning and giving Caliban a thumbs-up. Erasmus, however, looked faintly disappointed.

I thought less of him for it.

"Why did Father want Caliban kept alive?" asked Cornelius.

"Good question." Erasmus frowned down at his wineglass.

"Does it have something to do with him being Miranda's brother?" Theo asked.

"Maybe Daddy promised Sycorax to take care of her other kid, back when he was shagging her," Mephisto chirped.

"Mephisto, please!" Theo snapped. "Ladies are present."

"My mistake," Mephisto admitted cheerfully. "When he was 'pooning her." He glanced back at Theo. " 'Pooning's okay in mixed company, isn't it, Theo?"

Theo groaned and rested his head on his hand.

"My sister?" Caliban turned to me for an explanation. "We were close once, like sister and brother, but all that ended when . . ." he hung his head sadly. "After that, the master banished me from the house."

"Miranda is literally your sister," Erasmus stated succinctly. "As in: You share the same mother."

Caliban looked to Mephisto, who nodded happily and slapped him on the back.

"Yep! Welcome to the family, Miranda's half-brother! That makes you and me . . . what?" he looked at the rest of us for help. "Stepbrothers? Cousins twice removed? Applesauce?"

"Which is really the same as not being related," Logistilla purred, sliding her chair closer to Caliban's. She slipped her slim hand around his massive arm. "Only friendlier."

"Beware," growled Titus. "She turns her lovers into bears."

"Not all of them." Logistilla pouted prettily and snuggled closer to Caliban.

"Yeah, some of them she turns into pigs or cheetahs," offered Mephisto.

Caliban gave Logistilla's hand a gentle clumsy pat and swallowed. Logistilla continued to smile up at him and batted her eyelashes. Caliban blushed, not entirely dismayed by the sudden shower of feminine attention, yet alertly aware of proximity of the glowering Titus.

"What are you?" She ran two fingers up his enormous bicep. "A construction worker? A football player? Truck driver?"

"I am a professor at NYU," Caliban replied modestly.

"A professor!" To Logistilla's credit, she recovered her aplomb almost immediately. "Really? What do you teach?"

"Poetry and the classics."

"Oh my!" Logistilla put her hand to her heart. The rest of us murmured in surprise at this news, except for Mephisto, who smiled as proudly as a new father.

"Didn't I do a good job!" Mephisto waved a hand as if presenting Caliban. "They don't call me Mephistopheles the Stepbrother-Cousin-Applesauce Tamer for nothing!"

"I don't get this, Ma'am," Mab spoke up. "I thought your mother was the dame whose portrait hangs over the Wife's Throne."

"So did I." I ran my finger absently over the cut crystal of Water of Life vial. "Erasmus and Mephisto claim Father told them otherwise."

Mab glanced from Caliban to me and back again, frowning. "You make an incongruous pair, Ma'am. While I admit this fellow doesn't look like the ogre's get of Spearshaker fame, he's still . . ." Mab made an expansive gesture. "Well, the word 'enormous' comes to mind. You, on the other hand, are more like a porcelain doll come to life. I don't see the resemblance."

Caliban's brow furrowed and he rubbed his temples, as if trying to remember something. Whatever it was did not come to him. He looked up at me hopefully. Somehow, it was hard to revile him when he looked so puppylike. Steeling myself, I laid my hand on his shoulder for an instant, and then moved on. If he really was family, then I owed a duty to him, even as I did to my father's sons.

I continued around the table, pouring a single drop of Water of Life into each of the remaining goblets, including Caliban's. Finally, I came to Theo. His gaze rested on mine, and a shadow of the old sparkle returned to his eyes.

"Why not!" He thrust forth his glass.

I poured liberally, giving him extra Water. As the shining pearly drops fell into his glass, the entire table broke into applause, though Mab looked sheepish afterward, recalling his disapproval of immortal mortals. Recalling Theo's delicate health, I gave him two extra drops for good measure. Then, I poured some wine and three drops of Water into a silver dish in the middle of the table for the local airy servants to share. Coming back to my own place, I let a drop fall into my own glass. The pearly drops swirled into a golden-white liquid that spread through the darkness of the wine. The scent was glorious. We sat breathing in the fumes for a time before sipping the draught.

"May we flourish and prosper in the year to come," said Cornelius, as he raised his glass to his lips. The others murmured their assent.

My siblings all began talking at once, describing what they wished for in the year to come. I sat listening to their excited chatter and smiling, at peace even with Caliban for the first time in over five hundred years. Cornelius, who was seated to my left, leaned over and asked, "What would you do if you could be or do anything, Sister?"

I laughed. That was easy. "I want to be a Sibyl."

"Ah, of course. Have you ever questioned the current Sibyls about this? What do they say?"

"What current Sibyls?" I asked sadly. "I cannot find a single one. I have not even met another Handmaiden since the 1860s, over a century and a half ago."

"I wonder why they are hiding?" Cornelius mused.

"Hiding?" I asked sadly. "Or dead? Killed by Unicorn Hunters. And you? What would you do, if you could do anything?"

"Retire to the Riviera, or maybe to an island like Father's," Cornelius replied, cutting his fish.

"Retire? You?"

"Is that so very strange?" Cornelius smiled faintly. He leaned back. "Mortals get to retire. Their usefulness comes to an end, and they are rewarded for their toil with a period of leisure. Have you ever had a period of leisure, Sister? I know I haven't. I so envy Father's recent retirement."

"What would you do if you retired?" I asked.

"Sit on the beach, feel the sun on my face, and listen to music. At night, I would hire my own string quartet to play my favorite pieces exactly as I like them."

I blinked. "That . . . would be nice. Can't you try it?"

Returning to cutting his fish, Cornelius snorted. "If I retired, who would run the world?"

Before I could think of an answer, Logistilla's voice drifted dreamily down from the far end of the table. "I have always been of the opinion this must be what the nectar of the gods tastes like."

"You'd be right," said Mab. "That is what nectar tastes like. I should know. Had some once."

"You have tasted divine nectar?" Erasmus asked with interest.

"Got invited to—well, you'd call it a party—once, by Zephyrus. Ganymede showed up and brought his cup. Very pretty boy, Ganymede, too pretty for his own good. Got him in a lot of trouble and Zephyrus, too, for that matter. Or maybe I'm thinking of Hycanthus. Anyway, I got a swig out of the cup. Wonderful stuff, but sent me into a dither like straight proof might to you folks. I was a woozy wind for weeks."

Erasmus chuckled loudly, his laughter echoing, and even Cornelius smiled.

"A toast," Titus cried, holding his glass aloft, "to Miranda, whose unfailing virtue and chastity brings us this gift denied to all other men."

The others raised their glasses, even Erasmus.

"To Miranda," they chanted in unison.

"Thank you. It is my pleasure," I said gravely, and a warmth spread through me fueled by their gratitude, such as I had not felt in many many years.

We sat together, sipping and smiling, as we watched the burning sun sink into the western sea.

AFTER dinner, we spread out and searched the house for anything that might be useful for the spell. Originally, Mephisto, Erasmus, and Cornelius were to make all the preparations. As they discussed the ingredients necessary for the protective wards, however, Theo constantly interrupted them with suggestions and corrections. After a time, my other brothers grew tired of this.

"You are not a magician, as you are so fond of telling us," Cornelius said pointedly. "Perhaps, you should leave this matter to us, hmm?"

"I'm too old for this," Theo replied with a growl. "All right, you've got me! I admit it. I am the best darn magician in the family. Now, get out of my way!"

Erasmus, Cornelius, and Mephisto gave way. Theo squatted down and examined the paraphernalia we had gathered so far, sniffing the alchemical salts and examining the sacred knives. Finally he grunted. "Not sure this stuff is still good. Could use a second opinion here."

"Of course," Erasmus glided forward. "Anything for you, Brother. Why don't you let me—"

"Not you," Theo cut him off with a curt wave of his hand. "Mab."

Erasmus stepped back, eyebrows raised, while Mab lowered the brim of his fedora and stepped forward to squat beside Theo, the ghost of a smirk tugging at the corner of his mouth.

"Sure thing, Mr. Theophrastus. Just pour a bit of it on the ground. If I can pass my hand across it in comfort, it's no good."

I LEFT them arguing over whether salt tin or sea water was better for deterring wandering spirits and set out for a walk. A thousand troubles shouted for my attention, but I pushed them back, determined to spend a few moments peacefully reacquainting myself with my old home.

I walked through the cedars and fig trees, brushing past hibiscus bushes and sweeping tree ferns. The air smelled of evergreen and orchid blossom, with no trace of winter present, and of course, of the ocean, which I could hear crashing against the bluffs in the distance. Near at hand, blackbirds trilled, and a wood pigeon cooed. Farther away, probably on the rocks to the north, a seal barked.

Some of the individual trees I recognized as great old versions of youthful saplings I had known. The rest had sprouted in the centuries since I last ran carefree through these woods. The makeup of the forest itself had changed, I noticed, more oaks and pines, fewer birches.

Walking through the old forests, broken here and there by lawns dotted with fairy slipper orchids, was an eerie experience; rather like shopping in one's favorite chain bookstore in a strange town, where everything looks familiar, yet nothing is where you expect it to be. I wondered what magic Father had performed to keep the orchids blooming in January. I could never get mine to bloom properly in the winter—outside of the enchanted gardens behind Prospero Mansion. Come to think of it, perhaps the same enchantments protected these blossoms as had created that place.

I passed between the cliffs and entered the ravine. Here in the shadow of the high rock walls, the vegetation became less tropical. To my right, I could hear the roaring of the river Father had dubbed the Eridanus. In the deepening twilight, the tiny feylings twinkled and sparkled like unfixed stars. The moss was soft and spongy beneath my feet and filled the air with a loamy scent. I drew nearer the river and felt the cold spray from where the rushing water struck and tumbled over rocks. A rabbit nibbling the long grasses that grew on the bank raised its head but did not run or give alarm. The rabbits here had no predators, save for hawks and other winged creatures. Nothing that walked on legs had ever menaced them.

Cresting a small rise, I came upon a gentle dell. As I walked through its slender beeches, I began to feel an odd sense of familiarity. This section of forest was new and unfamiliar, but here and there something triggered a feeling of déjà vu: the old gnarled stand of lilacs, the rock that reminded me of the back of a beetle. It was not until I came to the semicircular growth of mountain laurels, nearly lost amidst the younger taller trees, that I realized, with a sharp sting of astonishment, where I was. In my childhood, this had been an open glade, with only the lilacs, the laurel bushes, and a stand of hortencias growing here. How different the old place looked overgrown with tall stately trees.

I closed my eyes and pictured the glade as it had once been, taking my bearings from the mountain laurels and Beetle Rock. Stretching out my arm, I opened them again and walked in the direction I pointed, dodging poplars and beeches. Between the trunks of twin white pines, I glimpsed a cascade of mountain grape. Circling the pines, I approached slowly and, reaching out, as if in a dream, pulled aside the vines.

They parted to show granite. Pushing aside more, I stepped forward and found myself standing on a flat rock about four feet square with two hefty pillars of crudely carved granite on either side. I ran my finger over the rough stone, tracing a bas-relief of a horned equine. Once, there had been a spiral carved on the rock beneath my feet as well, though, due to weathering and decayed leaves, I could hardly see it now. The grape vines spilling down either side of the pillars like a leafy-green veil added a sense of sacred seclusion that had not been here in my youth.

"The Shrine of the Unicorn," I whispered aloud, remembering.

I came here for the first time on my fifth birthday, the day Father consecrated me to Eurynome. How fresh and beautiful the glade had looked. It was early May, and the island was still glistening from the spring rains. I remember a profusion of flowers and the wonderful scent of blooming lilacs.

How I had looked forward to that day! When we arrived here, I was aquiver with excitement; so much so that I danced about the glade, spinning until my apron stood straight out before me, while I hummed the song Father had taught me to sing during the ceremony. Even when Father ordered me come stand beside him, I could not stand demurely as was my usual wont, but stood bouncing and humming, too filled up with joy to keep still. Even now, the memory of that moment brought a smile to my lips.

I had not known exactly what was to come, but Father had told me many wonderful stories of the White Lady of Spiral Wisdom and her brother, who so loved the world He incarnated among us so as to save mankind from the Wrath of Heaven. So, I knew whatever was to come would be something overtly good!

Of course, when we returned to Milan, I learned a rather different version of the salvation of man. Later on, in England, I can recall overhearing a lively discussion between my father and that notable churchman, Sir Thomas More, during which Sir Thomas pointed out that the Bible clearly stated Jesus was the only begotten son of God. To which my father replied, "True, but it was silent on the matter of whether God has other sons who have never been begotten, much less upon the matter of daughters."

I myself took a less heretical view than Father. I made no attempt to affix Eurynome's place in the hierarchy of Heaven. It was enough for me to know She was numbered among the Forces of Light.

Father had placed me on the altar stone and departed, so that I was alone in the grove. For a time, all was quiet and still, then I heard a sound in the distance so beautiful that I thought I would die from the beauty of it. In retrospect, I now realized it must have been Father playing to summon a storm, but at the time I had never heard my flute's music and did not know what it could be.

A storm rose. Black clouds warred overhead, and thunder rolled through the ravine like cannon fire. Rain came down in sheets, drenching me where I stood in my pretty little dress. My hair stuck to me like a slick black shawl. But I was used to the rain, and it was not cold, so I did not mind. Dutifully, I sang the song my father had painstakingly taught me.

Then, lightning struck.

The searing white-hot bolt fell from the heavens, striking the imprint of a deerlike hoof in the center of the spiral carved into the altar stone beneath my feet. Sparks of blue-white fire leapt everywhere, crawling over my body like a shocking caress. I screamed, both in fear and joy, for although I could not move my limbs, I felt no pain.

The electricity snaked about, curling and leaping. Gathering together before me, it formed a figure of white living fire, a slim deerlike horse with eyes the color of lilac petals and a curling horn of lightning upon Her brow. She tilted Her head, regarding me. I spread my arms and sang Her song as loudly as my little lungs could bear.

And then She stepped into me.

I can think of no other way of explaining what happened. First, I saw Her standing before me, then She came toward me, and then She was gone. For an instant, however, between when She stepped toward me and when She vanished, She and I became one being, and I knew all there was to know about love, the universe, and God. Then, I was myself again. The great wisdom was gone, save for a few traces. Yet She had stayed with me, a soft comforting presence, deep within. As I stood in the vine-covered shrine today, over fifty-three decades later, I could still feel her presence.

Later, after the storm ended, Father came to collect me. As we walked home that day, I recalled expressing gratitude that we had been so lucky as to land on this island where Eurynome had once stepped. Striding beside me, his long legs slowing for my benefit, Father smiled mysteriously and murmured, "Luck had nothing to do with it."

Back in the present, my blood ran cold. How had we come to live on an island sacred to Eurynome? Might it have been because my Father's patron, Queen Maeve of Fairyland, wafted us here? Could my consecration have been part of her plan to destroy Eurynome all along? But if so, why wait so long? Why had she not acted back when I was a child? Of course, Father might not know Maeve was Lilith. Perhaps, he was useful to her in other ways—he was after all a dread and powerful magician—and the Elf Queen bided her time so as not to alienate him.

I leaned against one of the granite pillars, frowning. The rock was damp beneath my head and smelled of wet lichen. Father duped by the Queen of Demons? I found that difficult to believe. Father seldom remained anyone's fool for long, much less for centuries. The very concept of someone duping Father struck me as far-fetched.

Of course, if my realization on Erasmus's roof was correct, and my judgment was suspect, then my faith in my father's cunning told me nothing.

A murmur of voices alerted me that I was no longer alone. Not wishing to speak to anyone, I searched for a place to hide. Just behind the shrine, the mountain grape had smothered some laurel bushes. I ducked under the vines and tucked myself out of sight between two of the nearly dead bushes.

Around the corner came the unlikely pair of Erasmus and Caliban. I could not see their faces, but I recognized Erasmus by his green velvet pants and Caliban because he was the only one on the island wearing jeans. Instantly, a feeling of rage welled up within me. Erasmus had no doubt brought Caliban out here to pump him for tidbits he could use later to abuse me!

Forcibly reminding myself that there was no point in wasting anger on the inevitable, I leaned forward to hear what they were saying to each other.

"Interesting. Sounds like a busy schedule. Must have been quite a shock after all those years of solitary existence." Erasmus paused. "What was life like, here on the island, before Father came?"

"Don't know." Caliban kicked a stone with the side of his foot, as one might kick a soccer ball. It flew across the leaves and bounced off the bole of a dead oak. "I don't remember life before the master and Miranda. I suppose I lived here, but I have no memories of that period. 'Lost to the mists of time,' as the master would say."

"And you have no idea . . . Hallo, what's this?" Erasmus's feet stopped before the granite pillar I had uncovered when I first arrived.

"The Shrine of the Unicorn," Caliban replied reverently.

"Ah, the place where Father sacrificed his infant daughter to the lightning bolt."

"I beg your pardon?" Caliban growled darkly.

"Nothing, just a little family joke." The vines rustled as Erasmus drew them back. He knelt down and brushed some of the leaves and debris from the altar stone. "Interesting. Did you and your mother build this?"

"No, my dam kept it up, though. She used to wash and polish it, fancying herself the priestess."

"How did you come to be living here? Were you shipwrecked like my father?"

"My dam came seeking the White Lady." Caliban knelt and pushed the dirt and debris away from the center of the altar stone, until he had uncovered the slim cloven hoofprint. It was all there. "She told me this footprint is the first place on Earth the Unicorn ever stepped."

"What did Sycorax want from Eurynome?"

"Her lost beauty. She had great beauty once, but it faded when her former master cast her aside. She hoped the Unicorn could return it to her."

"I gather not everything went as planned."

Caliban shook his head and stood, so that I could only see his calves and feet again. "My dam did not understand the Unicorn. When She did not come to her, my dam tried to capture the Serpent of the Winds, hoping to use him as a hostage. Only all she managed to capture was the South East wind."

"Ariel?" asked Erasmus.

"Ariel."

"Which explains why she shut him up in that pine," Erasmus said. "Apparently, he was very happy to get out. Happy enough to vow a thousand years of service to our family."

"My dam was not very nice to him." Caliban paused. "She was not nice to anyone."

"Rather like our dear sister Miranda," snickered Erasmus.

Here it comes, I thought.

"Miranda? I could not think of any two creatures less alike," Caliban objected. Then, he chuckled. "To quote the words the Bard wrote for my mouth: Miranda 'as far surpasses Sycorax as greatest does least.'"

"What was our dear sister like?" asked Erasmus. "And apparently she is 'our' sister. A cross we must bear in common."

"Miranda," Caliban breathed my name as if it were a prayer. "What a creature she was! Guileless and considerate of all living things. I remember her standing in a field of orchids in a green gown, her dark hair blowing in the wind like a banner, her face shining as she sung to a broken orchid, hoping her song would help its stem heal. She was so innocent, so pure—like an angel walking upon the earth." He paused. "I've gotten around quite a bit in the years since Mephisto tamed me and gave me the . . . and took me off the island. I have seen many women. I have known many women. I've watched children growing and young women laughing with their friends. And none of them . . . none come close to my Miranda. If she can truly forgive me, if she can see me as more than a monster, then this old carcass is worth something yet."

Touched, I pressed the back of my hand against my mouth. How beautiful Caliban's memories of me were. How unkind I had been to remember only his crudity and not his good heart. Had I sung to an orchid, hoping to make it grow? I tried to recall what I had been like before Ferdinand failed to show up for our wedding, before those cold lonely days in Milan. I had been different, that much I knew, but had I really been . . . sweet?

It was hard to believe. And yet, being here, inhaling the island air caused a vague stirring, deep within me, as if something that slumbered turned in its sleep, yawning.

A tremor of fear shot through me. What if the Miranda Caliban remembered—the one whom I just recalled as being so docile even before Father brought me to be consecrated—was the result of Father's magic, like the ever-blooming orchids, and the original me, the one that was waking, were more like Sycorax?

Over by the shrine, Erasmus replied to Caliban. His voice sounded muffled and strained. I expect this was caused by the effort he was making not to laugh. "Not exactly what I would have said, but nice to know you feel that way."

"You don't like her," Caliban leaned against one of the stone pillars and crossed his feet. So, he had noticed. This new Caliban was definitely more perceptive than the old one.

"Not even a smidgeon," Erasmus replied mildly. "She took something from me once, something terribly precious."

I was so surprised that I nearly stood up and objected. What precious thing could I possibly have taken from Erasmus? Most likely, he was inventing this story on the spot to gain sympathy from Caliban. But he did not sound as if he were making it up. He sounded . . . melancholy.

"I am sorry," replied Caliban.

"Tell me, Stepbrother," Erasmus spoke lightly, but there was an intensity in his voice, a tension that betrayed a heightened emotion. "Do you have any idea why Father instructed Mephisto to give you a portion of Water of Life?"

"Um-Um," grunted Caliban.

"You see, the finer points of who is allowed Water and who is not is a bit of a sore spot in our family. As you might have guessed, having heard what Titus said about his children. Miranda is extraordinarily tightfisted. She won't even give it to us to share with our w-wi . . ." He stuttered, paused, and then took a deep breath, continuing more calmly. "Our wives and children. I've never heard of Father going behind her back before. But, go behind her back, he must have, because we all knew how she hated you—no offense."

Me? Tightfisted? But I only ever did as Father asked. Erasmus must know that. Why would he tell Caliban such lies about me?

"None taken," Caliban replied.

"So, do you have any notion why Father did it? Why you?"

"As Master Mephisto suggested, the master may have made some promise to my dam."

"That could be, I suppose. If so, she must have had some extraordinary hold over him. Wish I knew what it was."

"It grows dark." Caliban stepped away from the pillar. "Won't the others be starting the spell soon?"

"Good point. Always a bad idea to be caught without a light at night in unknown territory." Erasmus turned and began walking back toward the mouth of the ravine.

Caliban followed him, laughing. "No fear there. We would only need to call the feylings together until they formed a ball big enough to light our path. Besides, I know this island so well, I could crisscross it with my eyes shut. It's not unknown territory to me. No, sir!"

As they disappeared into the forest, Erasmus's voice drifted back, amused. "So, you quote Shakespeare, do you, Stepbrother? Have you read 'Caliban upon Setebos'?"

Caliban's voice was louder than Erasmus's and carried better, as did his chuckle. "Robert Browning was a friend of Master Mephisto's. We had many a chat. He held that I must curse the parents who named me after such ungainly a character. I was not yet called Calvin then."

CHAPTER
SEVENTEEN

Gregor

The circle of trees known as the Grove of Books grew near the top of the bluffs that faced northeast, back toward the Continent. The night was clear. A three-quarter moon hung low in the sky amidst a field of a thousand thousand stars. The stars were mirrored below, both by the calm black reflective ocean waters, and by the twinkling of a myriad of feylings, whose tiny lights danced among the dark silhouettes of the surrounding forest. If one tilted one's head just right, it appeared as if the stars were everywhere: overhead, amidst the forest, and below in the dark velvety waters.

Just beyond the grove, the bluff fell away to the ocean, whose waves could be heard crashing against the rocks below like some Cyclops's relentless hammer. The breakers sent a spray high into the air. Mingling with the perfume of the orchids it formed a scent both salty and sweet.

We stood midst this faeriescape in our rumpled party clothes, watching Mephisto put the final touches on the preparations for the upcoming spell. By unspoken agreement, we had each gravitated to the tree from which our own staff had been cut.

I sat at the north end of the grove on the stump of the split pine that had once served as a prison for Ariel, the pine from which my flute, the *Staff of Winds,* had been made. To my right, Cornelius waited beneath the boughs of a gnarled apple, said to be a scion of the tree of the knowledge of good and evil. His cane was wrapped in black cloth, and a black ribbon circled the trunk of the apple tree. Apparently, this was some kind of ward meant to keep the demon in his staff, the *Staff of Persuasion,* from interfering with our efforts.

To the west, Theo rested against the trunk of the great oak whose wood formed the core of the *Staff of Devastation.* Oak, the tree most often struck by lightning, was sacred to Zeus, and thus a good choice to house a weapon of such power. After him, Titus, still weak from his wounds, relaxed beneath the feathery branches of a cedar, whose wood warded off spirits the same way it repelled moths. Titus had asked the airy servants to bring him a chair. Now he reclined, garbed in one of Father's scarlet velvet smoking jackets, reading, by the light of a flashlight he had found in the pantry, a six-month-old paper he had discovered in Father's study.

Due south, Erasmus half sat against the ash—the tree of death, from which spears used to be fashioned—that had supplied the core of the *Staff of Decay*. He had pulled his straight black hair back into a short queue. This had been his regular hairstyle during the eighteenth century. Apparently, I was not the only one for whom fashions changed too quickly.

The next tree was an ebony, the darkest of woods. It had supplied the *Staff of Darkness,* which was currently carried by Seir of the Shadows. Caliban stood there, arms crossed, in the place that should have been Gregor's.

The eastern tree was a great weeping willow. I did not know the significance of willow and could not speculate as to why Father had picked it for the *Staff of Transmogrification.* Logistilla peered disgruntledly through the drooping branches, unable to decide if she should stand by the trunk or in front of the veil of leaves. Her gown of spun night had not been designed to hold up for twenty-four hours of wear. She had discarded it in favor of the only blue garment she could find, a pair of Father's silk pajamas.

The next tree was the tall teak from which the *Staff of Transportation* had been fashioned, the staff Ulysses now carried. Father associated teak with traveling. For years, he had stored his books in a teak chest that he had lugged with him wherever we went.

The final tree, which stood quite close to me, had so many different varieties of branches grafted on to the same trunk that I could not say what kind of tree it had once been. This arboreal chimera had engendered Mephisto's staff, the *Staff of Summoning.* Mab stood before it now to fill out the circle, since Mephisto was officiating the ritual.

I glanced speculatively around the Grove of Books. Teak did not ordinarily grow this far north, nor could any natural process have produced Mephisto's tree, with species as diverse as birch and cherry and mahogany all growing together. Father must maintain this grove with the same magic that kept the orchids always in bloom.

Not trusting the alchemical salts Father had on hand, Theo and Mab eventually decided to construct the wards in the Atlantean manner. Thin channels had been cut into the earth, lined with metal roof flashing, which Titus found in the cellar, and filled with dragon's blood, a barrel of which Erasmus had discovered in Father's *sanctum arcanum*.

When they were done, three tiers of wards guarded us from wandering or malicious spirits. The outermost circle encompassed the entire grove. The middle one separated the trees from the center area, and the inner one circled the pentagram at the very center, which had been drawn with its top pointed at the teak tree. Within the inner circle, four triangles had been arranged about the central pentagram, one in each of the four cardinal directions. Individual wards had also been inscribed about each tree, protecting us individually. Short straight channels connected all these wards, so that the flaming dragon's blood could flow freely throughout the entire design.

In the center of the grove, facing the pentagram, stood Mephisto. Unlike the rest of us, he wore a fresh suit of clothes, no doubt fetched for him by one of the entities upon his staff: a voluminous-sleeved shirt of purest indigo silk with a black satin waistcoat and matching indigo pantaloons that spilled over the top of wide-brimmed black boots. The outfit resembled many he had worn during the 1600s. It had been made for him by Logistilla and was an enchanted garment as durable as my tea gown—which I really regretted having left at Erasmus's. The indigo silk perfectly matched the blue panache atop the hat Father Christmas had given him, which he carried in his right hand. In his other hand, he held his six-foot totem pole of carven figurines, the *Staff of Summoning*. I saw no evidence of the handcuffs he had been using to secure his staff to his arm. He must have removed them for this august occasion.

Mephisto stood in his own small circle. To his north, south, east, and west, framing the pentagram, were the invocation triangles. Father's best guardian talismans had been placed in their appropriate triangles. The eastern triangle held a wide goblet of blue crystal. Upon the bowl of the cup, dolphins leapt surrounded by spray. To the south, a pentacle of beaten gold was set with precious and semiprecious stones. To the west lay a parchment scroll wrapped about a sandalwood rod, while the northern triangle held a golden-handled sacred knife, silver runes shimmering like liquid moonlight along its black blade. In the last triangle of the pentagram itself stood a fifth talisman, a slim winged slipper of silver cloth. At Mephisto's insistence, I put a drop of the Water of Life on each talisman.

Theo bent and lit the wards. With a flash, fire spread along the dragon's blood until the entire pattern was burning. In addition to its other properties, dragon's blood had the virtue that it ignited quickly but was consumed slowly.

Mephisto stood amidst the glowing wards, his face lit by the steady ruby light of the burning blood. He raised both his hands and chanted.

"Holy guardians of the four directions, I conjure thee and call thee to your posts. Guard us from all who mean us harm. Raphael, guardian of the east, healer, warden of the Water of Life, come, drink of this cup and protect us. Michael, guardian of the south, Warrior of God, whose strength is greater even than the titan Atlas, come, stand upon this precious Earth and protect us. Uriel, guardian of the west, Regent of the Sun, whose wings are hotter than the fiery inferno, come, consume this holy fuel and protect us. Gabriel, guardian of the north, Trumpeter of Heaven, whose breath will usher in the Last Days, come, take up this blade and protect us."

A silence fell across the grove, and though I saw nothing, I knew the angels had come. Their presence was unmistakable, like the soft touch of a feather against one's cheek.

Mephisto now gestured at the winged silver slipper, calling. "Psychopomp, lord of messengers, he who conveys the souls of the dead, I call you by your secret name. Hermes Tristmegistes, hear my command. Seek out the *Staff of Transportation,* whose essence is contained within this teak tree, and bear it to me upon this spot. Bring it unharmed and harming none. For your efforts, ye may drink of the nectar within this homage to your fleet-footedness. Go now. I compel ye, according to my authority as a Prince of the Sixth Circle. Recognize me and obey."

Merciful Mother of God! So, this was why only Mephisto could perform the spell. He was calling upon his authority as a Prince of Hell! No ordinary magician could compel the gods. No wonder Mab was nervous!

We waited. The rosy light from the burning wards illuminated the faces of my relatives, revealing expressions of intense concentration. Seconds crawled into minutes. Then, just as Erasmus stepped to the edge of his ward, about to call off the effort, there was a flash of blinding white light. Curving about, the light formed a surprised-looking Ulysses clutching his teak staff for dear life.

Ulysses took one look at our gathered company and in a second burst of white light, teleported away.

GROANING, Mephisto cast the spell a second time, though he seemed less confident. Beside me, in front of the orange tree, Mab stirred in agitation. I understood the cause of their distress. The guardians of the four directions were still present; however, fleet-footed Hermes would have to be summoned again. Only, Mephisto could not reach the slipper to renew the supply of Water of Life without breaking the sanctity of the wards. Resanctifying the wards would require snuffing out the whole design and beginning again, and Theo had already used nearly all of Father's supply of dragon's blood. So, what was Mephisto to offer the psychopomp in return for his services? On principle, it was not a good idea to shortchange the god of thieves.

On the other hand, a drop of Water of Life was more than even the gods were usually paid for a task as simple as this one. Perhaps, the Swift One would be willing to perform a second task for that same price. Ever optimistic, Mephisto charged ahead with the spell, repeating his previous words exactly.

This time, the blinding flash came almost immediately. Risking all, Theo, Erasmus, and Titus charged forward, leaping across the burning wards with no thought for the consequences. Erasmus grabbed Ulysses and laid his staff across his throat, while Theo and Titus seized Ulysses's staff and wrestled it from his grasp. Ulysses, with the *Staff of Decay* at his throat, looked as terrified as I had ever seen him. Ironically, in his fear, he did not notice the staff was not humming. Having crossed the burning wards without invitation, Erasmus's staff slept. It would remain inert until Theo and Mab revoked their wards and quenched the flames.

A wind blew in from the ocean. The flames of the ward-lines my three brothers had leapt sputtered and died. We all readied our staffs. Theo, Erasmus, and Titus's staffs, all of which had crossed the wards, did not respond. Beside me, Mab opened his mouth, then shut it, cringing. He could revoke his wards with a word, which would return life to the sleeping staffs; however, it would also extinguish the remaining wards, including the one protecting me.

"Do it, Mab!" I whispered, readying my flute.

"Shhh!" hissed Mab.

A mist was rising off the sea. It moved silently over the bluff and began drifting toward the Grove of Books. My brothers had only crossed the inner lines, so the outermost ward still held. The mist circled the grove, pushing at the wards. The ruby flames hissed in places, but they continued to burn steadily.

Out of the darkness came a voice, cold and inhuman, such as a glacier might have, or a rock slide. This was not the voice of the honey-tongued psychopomp. Something else had approached us.

"*Heirs of Prospero, hear your fate. Doom do I foretell for the race of Men. At midnight on Twelfth Night, once-great Prospero shall die. Within a century of his death, all his great works will be undone. Foolish Prospero! Had the legacy of Solomon been passed to one heir, this doom might have been avoided. One heir might have preserved it and kept us at bay. Instead, in his pride, he split Solomon's secrets among his quarreling offspring, who have not the wherewithal to put aside their grievances and take up their Father's work.*

"*Denizens of the night, rejoice. Prospero shall fail, and Hell unmake Solomon's efforts. The spirits shall rebel. Mankind shall be undone. Chaos shall reign, and all shall return to the sweet darkness of Old Night.*"

"It's Abaddon!" screamed a petrified Logistilla.

Abaddon? A shiver of pure dread traveled across my body. Abaddon was no mere demon. He was the Angel of the Bottomless Pit, one of the Seven Rulers of Hell!

"*One within has named me. I accept the invitation and enter,*" said the voice.

The outer ward went dark. Fingers of mist began drifting toward the center of the grove where Theo, Titus, Erasmus, and Ulysses stood unprotected. Tiny flaming circles still protected Cornelius, Caliban, Mephisto, Mab, and me. Logistilla's ward flickered into nothingness, however, and a tendril of mist reached toward her.

As soon as Logistilla spoke the demon's name, Ulysses began to scream. He lunged for his staff, apparently more frightened of Abaddon than of Erasmus. Despite his flailing, however, he was unable to pull free of Titus's grip. He kicked Erasmus and Theo repeatedly, until Caliban leapt his ward and grabbed my brother's legs. Even Ulysses's hysteria-induced strength was not enough to wrench him free of Caliban's viselike hold.

The rest of us stood petrified. Then, above Logistilla's shrieks and Ulysses's screaming, came Theo's voice, calm and commanding:

"As you love your lives, pray!"

Some of my siblings began reciting the Lord's Prayer aloud. I prayed to my Lady, asking for her protection for myself and for the others present, and felt her answering warmth about me. I could see Cornelius's lips moving, and could hear Titus's strong voice join Theo's in a recitation of "Onward Christian Soldiers." Logistilla was still shrieking, and Ulysses was weeping. Caliban and Erasmus joined the hymn, and even Mab began to sing. Mephisto, however, stood very still with an odd look on his face, staring at his staff and his hat. I suspected he was debating whether to fight fire with fire and assume his demonic stature or to call upon his sanity and join in the singing. Christian piety won. Mephisto joined in the song, though without the hat. Perhaps, Prince of the Sixth Circle was not of high enough rank to face down one of Hell's Great Seven.

Within the western triangle, the sandalwood rod ignited, bathing the parchment scroll in pure white-gold flame. To the north and east, the sacred knife and the blue crystal goblet rose suddenly into the air. In the south, the gems set into the pentacle began to glow, as if lit from within.

Four pure angelic voices joined the hymn: one as deep as the Earth's heart, one as gentle as morning rain, one as fierce as the burning sun, and one like a trumpet, loud and triumphant. Their voices sang out for only a single stanza. Yet in that time, it was as if the whole world had been remade, and we stood in a newly created grove, clean and fresh and free from all stain.

The mist recoiled. The wards all burnt steadily again. We stood motionless, without making a sound, for perhaps twenty minutes. Then, Mephisto ended the spell, banishing the psychopomp, any lurking spirits and, finally, the guardians. Once that was done, Mab and Theo revoked the wards.

"Pheew, it's over!" breathed Mephisto, wiping his brow.

"That went . . . surprisingly well," observed Mab.

"You call that 'well'?" Erasmus asked, bemused.

"All things considered? Yeah, I call that 'well,'" Mab replied. "No one was carried off into the night sky by their ear, no one was flayed alive, and none of your sisters are presently married to loathsome beasts."

Erasmus gave him a wan smile. "If you put it that way . . ."

There was a brief argument about who was to go to Mars, during which it was pointed out that Theo was an old man with a heart condition, Titus was wounded, Cornelius was blind, Ulysses was currently bound up with some of Father's rope, Logistilla was an accomplice in this matter, and Mephisto was mad. For whatever reason, Mab, Caliban, and I were not considered. Erasmus, as the only whole and hale son, finally said he was going and would choose who went with him. He chose Mephisto. After a few words of instructions from Ulysses, the *Staff of Transportation* flashed its brilliant white light, and they were gone.

We waited.

They returned about ten minutes later holding Gregor between them, or at least I assumed it was Gregor. They supported a tall gaunt figure half Gregor's customary bulk, whose black beard curled to his navel and whose hair hung down his back. He wore a burgundy nightshirt that left his calves and feet bare. I wondered if this was all Ulysses had provided in the way of dress, or if Gregor had merely been roused from his bed.

Gregor was rushed inside to bathe and rest, with Logistilla cooing over her twin, and Titus dragging the captive Ulysses behind them. Theo and Mab stayed to gather any remaining dragon's blood, and clean up the grove. Caliban wished me a good night before offering to carry the nearly empty barrel of dragon's blood back to the house. Eventually, I found myself standing alone, accompanied by feylings, a few Aerie Ones, the roar of the surf, and the night.

I WALKED along the bluff—the same where Father had sat with me so often, telling me tales of my mother and their great love. Hugging my elbows, I stared down at the white spray visible atop black breakers. Mab was right. The day had gone better than expected, all things considered. The family was back together. Theo had put aside his plan to die. Gregor, so long thought dead, was alive. Father was in deadly peril, but according to the demon, he still lived, and we had five days in which to save him. Perhaps, we could cast this spell again using the dogwood in the Wintergarden and bring him home.

The peace brought by the angelic song still lingered. The air smelled fresh and new. As I breathed it, hope buoyed my heart, and I felt certain Father could be saved. I now knew what the doom was that awaited us upon Twelfth Night—Father's death by the hands of his captors. I asked my Lady for her help, and felt the telltale warmth her guidance brought. She knew how to save my father. She would show me the way. I had merely to be patient until the time was right.

Standing atop the rocky bluffs, listening to the rhythm of the sea, I surveyed my flute thoughtfully. Perhaps Mab's people could be freed. If not today or tomorrow, at least sooner than I had expected. If they could learn to obey me without the flute, as Boreas had in the eyrie, if they could be brought to swear lesser oaths before we released them, then perhaps, I could let them go, release Ophion, and join the ranks of the Sibyls, as I so desperately desired.

Once I was a Sibyl, I would have the power to absolve oaths . . . Mephisto could be freed from his promise to the demon queen. Perhaps, his sanity could even be regained. I recalled hearing somewhere of a river called the Eunoe whose waters were said to wash away the amnesia of the Lethe.

I gazed down at the black waves. I could do it right now. I could break the flute and fling its worthless pieces into the sea.

For one mad second, I considered it, but I knew this was not the way it should be done. While I had reason to believe Eurynome would accept me should I release the Aerie Ones from bondage, I also felt reasonably sure she would be less than kindly disposed to me if I needlessly caused a great many mortals to be killed in the process. No, if I were to free the Aerie Ones, it would need to be done properly, in a step-by-step fashion: lesser oaths would need to be sworn, replacements found for those who wished to leave, and many other such details dealt with in a calm and rational manner.

Departing the bluffs, I walked, contemplating all that we had learned. After a time, I found myself standing before Caliban's old cave, the very spot where, centuries before, he had attempted to ravage me. Once a place of horrors, this oft-hated spot now brought a faint smile to my lips. Even Caliban was no longer to be loathed and feared. Instead, he had become a member of my family, despite my reluctance to acknowledge my new mother. With Baelor dead and Caliban a friend, it was as if all my enemies had been defeated.

A rustling within the forest caught my attention. Turning, I spotted a figure standing motionless among the trees, a silhouette framed by the twinkle of feylings. I did not need more than a silhouette to recognize this stranger. The fashionable cut of his garments betrayed his identity.

My stomach knotted oddly, uncomfortably. Annoyed by this inappropriate display of girlish jitters, I called out pleasantly.

"Hello, Ferdinand . . . or should I say Seir! I was surprised you didn't show up for the fight at Erasmus's."

I waited as he came toward me. There was no real point in fleeing from a teleporter, besides I was reasonably sure he would not harm me. After all, he had not attacked during our entire time together at Prospero's Mansion when he had been pretending to be Ferdinand. However, I kept my flute close and made a gesture behind my back indicating that one of the attending Aerie Ones, whom I knew to be following me, should summon my brothers. Charming as Seir may be, he was still an incubus and after our staffs. If they could capture him . . . well, that would be yet another enemy who would not trouble us again.

He stepped out into the moonlight, some five feet away from me. Even in the dimness of the night, I could see there was something wrong with the color of his eyes.

It was Osae the Red.

He lunged. He was too close for me to begin a song, as he would reach me before I could play out any instructions. Hoping to outsmart him, I threw my flute into the air, calling to Apple Blossom to catch it and hold it out of his reach. It was a risk, giving the flute to an Aerie One, but it was better than letting it fall to Osae. As soon as he took upon himself some flying form so that he could pursue it, I would ask her to return it to me and summon a whirlwind to cast him from the island.

Only he did not go after the flute.

I tried to flee, racing through the night in my flimsy dancing shoes. I might as well have tried to outrun a cheetah or a freight train. He caught me just before the opening of the cave and threw me down in the very spot where Caliban had overpowered me long ago. Last time, my father saved me. This time, my father was in Hell.

Foxglove had already departed to summon my brothers. I screamed, hoping they would hurry. With a gesture, I commanded Apple Blossom to bring my flute to my outstretched hand. A tiny penknife was hidden in its haft, enough to wound him or poke out an eye. All I had to do was keep him at bay long enough for Theo or Mephisto to get here.

And I probably could have, if I had been wearing my impenetrable enchanted gown. Instead, I was clad in a concoction of violet silk created over a hundred years ago by the foremost designer of a bygone age. Lovely to behold, it offered as much protection as wet tissue paper.

"Why follow the flute when the prize is nigh?" Osae's breath came in heavy pants as he ripped my gown. His voice was his own, though his form was still Ferdinand's. "What care I for lost staffs? If I recover them, I must return to the pit. Better to stay here and enjoy myself."

The delicate silk of my Worth original parted as easily as soft rose petals, exposing my bare flesh to the moonlit night.

Summoning the whole of my supernatural strength, I fought him—wrestling, twisting, jabbing, kneeing, even biting. My desperate efforts would have made a wildcat proud. Yet, without a weapon, I was no more of a threat to the denizen of Hell than a kitten was to a pit bull. Against his demonic bulk and might, my supernatural strength availed me nothing.

In the end, he was a monster . . . while I was merely a woman.

CHAPTER EIGHTEEN

Alone in Dreams of Sorrow

I will not linger on what came next, except to say: there was pain and more pain. The demon reverted to his stockier "Osae" shape, for which I was grateful, as I did not wish to have my memory of Ferdinand sullied. His ghoulish hair spikes stank of dried blood, and his breath stank of worse things. The stench so overpowered me I feared I would be sick.

Nearby, out of the corner of my eye, I spotted my little violet reticule laying among the dirt and leaves, where it had fallen during the struggle. My wrists were pinned to the ground, but by stretching my fingers to their utmost, I managed to reach it, open it one-handed, and find within the dried remnants of the moly leaf I had plucked in the Wintergarden. While Osae was distracted, I stuffed the moly into his shirt cuff, which I knew to be actually a part of his substance.

It was not much, but it was all I could do.

Of all my brothers, Caliban reached me first. He came loping through the forest, his footsteps thundering against the ground. Bellowing like an angry bull, he seized Osae the Red about the waist, lifted him, and smashed him against the bole of a large oak.

Osae snarled, twisting in his grasp. Had he been able to turn into a bird, or a mammoth, or a serpent, he might have escaped or done Caliban harm. However, the moly leaf lodged in his cuff hindered him, much as that herb had protected Odysseus from Circe's magic long ago. His attempts to alter his shape availed him nothing.

While his man-form had been strong enough to overpower me, it was no match for my giant gorilla of a half-brother. Osae's howl of terror was cut short, after his third violent encounter with the oak sent him into unconsciousness.

Erasmus came pelting through the forest, sliding to a stop as he reached the opening in the trees. His staff hummed in his pitted Urim gauntlet. His eyes traveled from my torn dress and bloodstained body to Caliban and the unconscious cacodemon. As I sat there beneath his scrutiny, my arms and the remaining shreds of silk insufficient to cover my exposed flesh, I wished Osae had killed me.

Only Erasmus did not sneer. Instead, a cold black anger such as I had never seen took hold of him. Without speaking, he strode to where Caliban was still slamming the unconscious demon against the oak and struck Osae with the full force of the *Staff of Decay*. The shapeshifter's body collapsed upon itself, expelling a cloud of dust. When the dust cleared, Osae's mortal seeming was gone. Some part of the demon was immune to the ravages of time. Only a black slimy something remained, twitching feebly upon the dried leaves.

I had managed to sit up, but was still half exposed, with blood and dried leaves stuck to my skin—which gleamed under the moonlight with unnatural, almost frightening paleness—when Theophrastus came running out of the forest, his staff humming on his shoulder. He stopped, panting heavily, and looked down at me. As comprehension dawned in his eyes, I realized there were worse things than being found thus by Erasmus.

"I'll finish off the abomination, Erasmus. You take her back," Theo commanded, when he found his voice. Then, he stalked forward, unlimbering the *Staff of Devastation* as he went.

"That abomination is Osae the Red," said Erasmus as he returned to my side. "Watch out for starfish."

He took off his velvet jacket and helped me slip into it. Then, he lifted me up like a child and carried me back through the dark woods. I heard him give orders to Apple Blossom to follow with my flute and saw the brilliant flash as Theo's staff illuminated the forest, but I was aware of little else during that midnight walk. I remember being placed in a soft bed, feeling an odd vibration against my head, and hearing the concerned voices of Mab and Logistilla coming from far away. I fell asleep to the improbable fantasy of Logistilla clucking over me as she had cooed over Titus and Gregor.

WHEN I awoke, bright sunlight streamed through my floor-length window, revealing large yellow and orange orchid blooms on the balcony beyond. The windows were open, and the sweet scent of the orchids mingled with a whiff of sea air filled my bedchamber.

Groaning, I took stock of my aches and injuries. My arms and back muscles were sore from the struggle. Other parts of my body felt even worse. I closed my eyes and turned to my Lady for solace.

She was gone.

Shaken and panicked, I sat up. My Lady, the fount of peace and wisdom whom I followed and obeyed with total faith; She upon whom I had depended since I was a child of five; She who led me through obstacles and over hurdles; She who protected me from harm; She who was to lead me through Hell to rescue my father . . . She was not there.

She had abandoned me. The place within me where Her peace and warmth had dwelt was empty. A great gaping chasm had been ripped in my soul.

I was alone.

For the space of a breath, or maybe a thousand breaths, everything stopped. I lay absolutely still, unable to move or even think. The horror, the abject starkness of my new reality, was too much to bear.

No nightmare had ever been this bad.

As my thoughts thawed and sluggishly began to move again, recriminations rained down like hail. If only I had recalled Mab's warnings about the Summoning spell attracting bad spirits! I would not have been so stupid as to wander off alone. I could picture Mab perfectly, his face screwed up as he scratched his five o'clock stubble, "I hate to say it, Ma'am, but I told you so."

If only I had raised my flute immediately instead of walking toward the demon. I even knew it was a demon, a demon from Hell! But I walked *toward* it. Why? Because I thought it was Seir, who had beguiled me once before? I heard Erasmus's icy laughter so clearly in my thoughts, that I wondered if he was out there right now, mocking me before the others. I pictured him, seated in the music room, in one of the green plush armchairs, with one leg crossed over the other, smugly telling the others, "Who would have thought it, our ice princess of a sister, swept off her feet like a schoolgirl . . . by whom? A prince? A wise man? Hardly, an incubus!"

If only I had thought to inquire of my Lady when I first saw Ferdinand. She could have warned me and protected me, and it would never have come to this. In fact, I realized with a lurch of dismay, she had warned me. I remembered the horrible roiling feeling in my stomach. I had ignored her, mistaking her guidance for girlish folly. Instead, I had thought I could finesse the demon. Why? Was I such a fool as to believe his protestations? Did I think the demon, rather than the part he played, had affection for me? That he would pause in his demonic purpose for my sake?

How could I have been so naïve?

If only I had remembered Osae's previous attacks. If only I had not discarded my enchanted dress for some flimsy ballgown . . . if only . . . if only . . . if only. . . .

MUCH later, I finally stirred upon my bed and sat up. I must have slept longer than I had realized, for the sun shone stubbornly into my chamber. It annoyed me that the glaring orb had not even had the decency to cover its face with dark clouds in mourning for sympathy for my loss.

It amazed me that life could go on. Yet, it did. Outside, orchids bloomed, and birds brazenly sang their songs. The storm petrels cried, and the breakers crashed against the bluffs. Somewhere in the mansion, Mephisto's sweet tenor rang out, accompanied by the sounds of a mandolin. He was still singing "Onward Christian Soldiers," but the words had mutated under his ministrations:

Onward Christian Soldiers
Marching as to war
With a slice of pizza
Going on before.

His cheerful irreverence seemed horribly at odds with my sorrow. I covered my head with my pillow and wept.

SEVERAL times, someone had knocked on my door. I had ignored them. The most recent would-be visitor knocked longer and more fiercely than the rest. I did not answer the summons, but once the visitor withdrew, I rose, slowly and painfully, and hobbled across the wide chamber to the mahogany dresser upon which my violet reticule now lay.

I opened the reticule, thinking to ease my aches with a drop of Water of Life. I had actually taken out the crystal vial and was starting to draw out the stopper, when the horrible truth struck me.

We were mortal again. We were, all of us, going to die.

Horrified, I let the vial drop unopened back into the reticule and quickly put the little bag back on the dresser with unsteady hands. Our immortality required Water of Life. Only a Handmaiden of Eurynome could reach the Well at the World's End where the Living Waters flowed. I was no longer a

Handmaiden. As soon as the small supply I kept in the chapel ran out, we would begin to age.

I did a quick calculation in my head. There was enough Water to keep us immortal, including Father and Caliban, for about fifty years, maybe less. Erasmus's staff could keep us young, but it could not heal our wounds, make us strong, or protect us from disease. Erasmus had performed many experiments along these lines. Humans kept young by the *Staff of Decay* alone, without Water of Life, died from accident and illness even more often than ordinary mortals. His magic might help extend our lives a few years. Alone, it was not enough to preserve us.

A shiver ran up my spine. The prediction of the Angel of the Bottomless Pit was coming to pass. Within a hundred years, whether Father died on Twelfth Night or not, the Family Prospero would perish from the Earth, and our great works would be undone.

A doom had fallen upon the Family Prospero by Twelfth Night after all.

How strange to come to this realization in this room, the room of my childhood, almost as if I had come full circle, returning to die in the place of my birth. It was much as I had left it the day we sailed for Milan, so many years ago: the lacy canopy bed (recently refurbished by Father), the mahogany dresser, the wide window leading to the orchid-strewn balcony. A green velvet armchair, a more recent addition, sat beside the hearth. Next to it stood a small end table fashioned to look like a chessboard. Upon it, dusty pieces still stood in a half-completed game—the last game my maiden self had played with Ferdinand, the real Ferdinand, over five hundred years ago.

On the mantelpiece stood a tall oval mirror with a gold-speckled frame that Father must have added recently, along with armchair, for I could not recall anything like it from my youth. Flanking the mirror were my favorite childhood playmates, two smooth, featureless wooden dolls Father had carved for me. One was winged; the other had gentle curves indicating a woman.

Seeing them brought a faint smile to my lips. I recalled many happy days playing on the bluff. Sometimes, the woman was my mother and the winged doll was an angel who watched over her in Heaven. Other times, I pretended the woman was me, riding the Unicorn, commanding the lightning bolt, and doing other great things I intended some day to do, while the angel, my mother who was now with Our Lord, watched over me from her place in Heaven. Seeing them again brought me a meager bit of comfort.

I started toward the mirror, then hesitated. I did not want to look at myself this morning and see myself, unchanged. Oh, my face might be temporarily marred by a cut or a few bruises, but fundamentally, I would see the same self I had seen yesterday, and last year, and last century . . . when She had been with me. This struck me as wrong, as if I were beholding a lie.

I glanced at the mirror anyway.

A stranger regarded me, a pale young woman with large eyes as green as emeralds and hair as black as the feathers of a raven's wing. I thought I must have mistaken a portrait for a mirror, until her lips parted in sync with mine.

Erasmus!

He had returned the color to my hair. That vibration I had felt must have been him running his staff over my head when he placed me in the bed. Most likely, he had meant this as a peace offering, or a sign of his compassion during my hour of woe. Only, I wished bitterly that he had not done it.

Coming so quickly on the heels of my Lady's desertion, this new youthful me was more disconcerting than the familiar silver-haired reflection I had dreaded beholding only moments ago. I turned away, dismayed.

On top of the mahogany dresser, in a neatly folded pile, lay the belongings I had left at Erasmus's house: my white winter cloak, half a dozen other items I had brought with me, such as the silver circlet inset with horn Father Christmas had given me, a second pair of shoes, and my emerald tea dress. Apparently, someone had made use of Ulysses's staff to retrieve our things.

Slowly, I reached out and touched the shimmering green satin of my tea gown. The cloth felt cool and smooth beneath my bruised fingers. Reaching into the pocket of my cloak, I drew out the silver fan and laid it across the enchanted dress.

How differently last night—and the rest of my life—might have been, if I had just had these two things with me.

Seeing the circlet caused yet another pang of pain. While I had been telling myself that I would never see Astreus again, in my heart I had believed otherwise. I had secretly hoped that if I merely waited long enough, we would chance to meet again: perhaps during another Christmas feast, or when his tasks in the Void were finally complete and he was again left to his own devices.

But, that was when I had imagined I would be around two hundred, three hundred, even a thousand years. With only a scant century left, my chance of running into the elf lord again shrank to naught.

As I pushed the circlet back under my cloak, where its glittering silver would not mock me, something about it caught my eye. I paused and peered at it more closely. It was made of alternating lengths of horn and silver. Only, what I had previously taken for horn looked exactly like the substance that lined Mephisto's hat—horse's hoof, according to Mab.

For an instant, I wondered why Astreus had worn this at the Christmas feast instead of his customary crown of stars and what had prompted Father Christmas to give it to me. Then my misery smothered any curiosity, and I put the circlet away.

Beside the pile of garments lay my flute. Picking it up, I lay its cool polished wood against my cheek. Thank goodness, I had not given in to my foolish whim and thrown it into the sea. Without my Lady to calm me and Father to guide me, its music was the only solace that remained.

I COULD not hide from the world forever. The next time someone knocked at the door, I answered softly, hoping whoever it was would not hear me and go away.

"Who is it?"

"Gregor."

Gregor! He was alive again! How could have I forgotten! Rushing forward, I threw open the door.

My long-thought-dead brother stood in the doorway garbed in one of Father's black scholar's robes. He had been washed and groomed since last I had seen him. His hair now fell to his broad shoulders in a soft black wave, and his black beard had been trimmed close, like Theo's, emphasizing the strength of his chin. His skin was still swarthier than mine, despite his many years of indoor confinement in the underground bunker Ulysses had apparently imprisoned him in, but his once bulky stature had been replaced by a lithe lean build. While his eyes still retained their old ferocity, the intensity had been muted by a new reflective introspection. All this gave him the appearance of a sixteenth-century priest, or perhaps, a Spanish poet.

Gregor came into my room and spoke. His voice had not changed. It was still the same hoarse near-whisper I recalled from ages passed.

"Miranda, I have come to express my gratitude," he said. "I have been given to understand I have you to thank for my liberation."

"Me?" I squeaked, astonished.

"I have been speaking with one called Mab. He tells me you orchestrated the search that led to my release."

I nearly demurred, explaining that he owed his rescue to Mab's good detective work, but it occurred to me he was right. Mab had originally been against my investigating the whereabouts of my brothers. He had wanted to concentrate on the disappearance of Father. Only my insistence had led to the investigation, which eventually revealed Gregor's whereabouts.

"You are welcome," I said, as graciously as I could, and then, tears welling up in my eyes, I burst out, "Gregor, Eurynome has deserted me! W-we are all going to die!"

Gregor stepped forward and took my hands in his. His hands were large and warm. "God works in mysterious ways, Miranda. If it is His will our family linger upon the Earth doing His works, then we shall remain. If not, we shall depart for a better place."

"But, She was . . . What will I do without Her?" I wept.

"Pray, and your answer will come. The answers God in Heaven gives us may not be as easy to hear as the will of your pagan goddess, but His kingdom is greater, and His blessings more certain."

"How can you believe that?" I asked, pulling one hand free to wipe my eyes. "You were imprisoned for nearly a century! Do you think your God intended you to suffer like that? Didn't you lose hope?"

"No," Gregor's eyes glittered with stern conviction. "There were dark days, but I knew God would not desert me, whether I made my bed in Hell or on Mars. He would not have allowed me to remain in such a situation unless there was something for me to learn. So, I strove to learn all that I could during my imprisonment."

"And this comforted you?"

Gregor nodded. "I spend much of the time meditating on the differences between the Catholic and Protestant doctrines and trying to reconcile them in my mind. I believe I have come to some kind of conclusion."

"But decades in prison! Why would you put up with a god who treats you in such a manner?"

Gregor hesitated, as if listening. A twinkle of amusement appeared in his dark eyes. "If your Lady, as you called her, asked you to spend a century in seclusion for some purpose of her own, would you have hesitated?"

"No," I admitted, "not even for an instant."

"We are not so different, you and I. We just serve different powers. My God, however, never abandons those who serve Him."

I pulled away, ashamed. Reaching forward, he took my hands again and squeezed them. "He is a generous God, Miranda. He turns no one away, not even those who previously defied him. Turn to Him now, and He will comfort you. You think your present sorrow is solid, like a sphere of diamond encasing your soul. But, the nature of sorrow is closer to that of ice. Ice melts when warmth is applied. Seek Him, and He will lift your sorrow, freeing you as the spring sun frees the land from winter's ice."

I had never thought of myself as "defying the Christian god." In fact, I considered myself a good Protestant; however, Gregor, the ex-pope, did not see things as I did.

I murmured, "I met another Handmaiden once who told me Eurynome was a Holy Spirit that God had granted to some race of creatures from an earlier cycle of creation, a race that has since been entirely saved. She said Eurynome had been offered a place in Heaven, but had chosen to remain behind, helping others."

"Pagans often make up stories in an attempt to lend the majesty of our God to their deities," Gregor replied, nodding. "It shows how much they wish to be objects of His regard."

I was too heart-sore to argue theology. "You must be very angry with Ulysses. Can God free you from that, too?"

"He already has. I was tremendously angry with Ulysses for, oh, the first decade or so. But then I began listening to God. He told me I had better things to do. For myself, I have forgiven Ulysses. I leave the matter of his punishment to the rest of you."

"You are a better man than I." I shook my head and smiled wanly. "I could never do that."

"Is that so? Caliban tells it otherwise," Gregor replied gruffly, a faint twinkle in his eye.

He had me there. A feather's breath of warmth brushed against my soul, like a single green sprout peeking up amidst a field of snow.

Then, I remembered our current plight and my weariness returned. "You didn't seem surprised by my news—that we were mortal again."

"It's all the others have talked about since your attack," Gregor snorted in disgust, looking more like his old more volatile self.

"All? What about rescuing Father? We only have a little over four days left. Haven't they been putting together a plan?"

"Four days until what?" asked Gregor, frowning. "Erasmus explained Father is a prisoner in Hell, but no one mentioned a rescue attempt."

"But the Angel of the Bottomless Pit said they were going to kill him on Twelfth Night! And today is January Second; that gives us just under five days!"

Gregor's frown darkened. "No one spoke a word of this. Apparently, concern for their own eventual demise has erased all more immediate concerns from their minds."

"I thought they would be planning an excursion to Father's mansion in Oregon—so we could use the dogwood in the Wintergarden to summon Father's staff, the same way we used the mahogany to summon Ulysses . . ."

Only as the words left my mouth did I realize that I had not had a chance to tell anyone my idea before I met Osae. No one else even knew about the dogwood.

I picked up my enchanted tea gown. "I had better come out. Just give me a minute to get dressed."

WHEN I finally emerged from my room, Mab was standing guard beside my door. I balked, suddenly awkward and uncomfortable, fearing he would say: "I told you so."

"Ma'am?" Mab stood against the wall, his hands stuck in the pockets of his trench coat. "I'm . . . It sucks, Ma'am. Should never have happened."

I tried to maintain my composure but failed. Tears spilled down my cheeks. Pulling a handkerchief from his pocket, Mab patted it against my face with uncharacteristic tenderness.

"Don't cry, Ma'am. Breaks my heart."

Smiling through my tears, my voice faint and breaking, I echoed the words he had spoken to me way back in Chicago. "Didn't know you had one."

CHAPTER NINETEEN

Our Darkest Hour

My family had gathered in the music room again. The roar of the waterfall was still muted, but the flues in the wall were open, and a lilting windy symphony filled the chamber. Cornelius sat in the corner near the lever, his head cocked as he listened to the music of wind and stone. Near him, Ulysses and Logistilla sat at a small table playing cards with a set of antique *tarocco* trumps from Father's library. A length of chain had been passed through one of the fluting holes in the stone wall. One side of it led to a metal ring clamped about Ulysses's ankle. The other side led to a ring on Logistilla's leg. Neither of their staffs was in evidence.

Erasmus lay stretched out on the divan, his hands crossed behind his head, a half-empty bottle of wine beside him, and two more empty bottles on the floor. Theo was sitting in one of the plush green armchairs, sipping from a long-stemmed glass and frowning. Gregor had joined them in the second armchair. He appeared to be drinking coffee.

In the opposite corner from Cornelius, Titus smiled with paternal pride at two boys, the same two that Father Christmas's scrying pool had shown in the library that held the dollhouse version of Prospero's Mansion— apparently someone had used Ulysses's staff to fetch them from Georgia. The elder, a slender nervous boy, wore glasses. He sat upon a stool reading a book. The younger, who was rounder of face and more athletic build, had taken one of the antique mandolins off the wall and was running in circles making a *zoom-zoom* noise, pretending it was an airplane.

Caliban sat near the fireplace, just beside the grand piano. He had taken apart one of the trombones and was tapping out a dent in the brass with tools from Father's workroom. Mephisto sat near him on the piano bench, singing softly and accompanying himself on one of Father's lutes.

As I approached, Mephisto was still singing his rendition of "Onward Christian Soldiers."

Like a mighty army
Moves the Church of God
Brothers we are treading
On some gooey sod.

"Please, Mephisto," Cornelius called from where he sat trying to hear the fluting of the winds. "I beg of you! Can't you play somewhere else?"

"Miranda!" said Theo, coming to his feet. He looked both frightened and relieved to see me.

Everybody else looked up and stared.

They gawked at me. My brothers and sister stared as if my shame were visible to the eye. I would have been too ashamed to move, or even breathe, but was rescued by my mounting indignation. How dare they! They did not deserve the effort I had gone to upon their behalf! Oh, if only I had listened to Mab and stayed home.

Glancing across the room, I noticed that Erasmus looked faintly amused, as if he had expected this.

Oh. Of course, it was not the loss of my virtue that caused this unexpected scrutiny, but the return of my jet black locks.

Mumbling something about Erasmus, I collected the scraps of my dignity and greeted Titus's sons, whom he immediately brought over to meet me. The elder one, the bookworm with the glasses, was Teleron. The younger one, the nine-year-old, was Typhon. As they returned to their corner, it struck me that I would always be just another brunette aunt to these nephews. They would never know the calm, level-headed woman with silvery hair whom I saw in my mind's eye. Nor could I ask Erasmus to put it back. Erasmus's staff could only age my hair, making it colorless and fragile. In order to achieve my former lustrous silver-white color, I would have to bathe that aged hair in Water of Life—a luxury I would never again be able to afford.

Only then did I realize: We were all together! All of us, except for Father, were in one room. It had been nearly a century since that happened and that had not included Typhon and Teleron, of course. I wondered if it would ever happen again.

"So, you've come to join us in our misery," mocked Erasmus, without getting up. I heard the slur of his words, but still my mind balked, hesitating to come to the conclusion that he might be drunk. I could not recall the last time I had seen Erasmus drunk. Mephisto? Yes. Ulysses and Titus? Certainly. Even Theo. But, Erasmus? He had been drunk as often as I, which was to say, hardly ever. Usually, he preferred keeping his wits about him.

No wonder no one was organizing a rescue for Father. When I had thought "someone would be doing something," I now realized that what I had really meant was I thought Erasmus would be doing something. Much as I hated him, I had to admit, he was by far the most organized and self-motivated of my siblings.

"What are you doing?" I cried, perhaps more stridently than was necessary.

"Awaiting the bitter end." Erasmus waved a hand at the bottle. "Care to join us? I would get you a glass, but you know where they are, and I don't. Come, Sister, drink and be merry, for on the morrow, we all shall be dead.

"Well, maybe not on the morrow," he continued. "But, soon enough. Ironic paradox we're in. If we conserve Water and take it less often, we grow weaker and slower. On the other hand, if we don't conserve it, it will soon be gone. Then we follow in the footsteps of good Theo, here, becoming prey to no end of maladies. Either way, we're screwed."

Raising his glass, he recited:

I that in health was and gladness
Am troublit now with great sickness
And feblit with informity:
Timor mortis conturbat me

Our pleasance here is all vainglory,
This false world is but transitory,
The flesh is bruckle, the fiend is slee:
Timor mortis conturbat me

The state of man does change and vary,
Now sound, now sick, now blithe, now sary,
Now dans and merry, now like to die,
Timor mortis conturbat me

"Enough. We have years to discuss this matter," I snapped. "We need to make plans to rescue Father."

Erasmus scowled, "What do you want us to do? Go spit upon the fires of Hell and hope our saliva puts out the flames? I suppose we could sit back and watch the hands of the clock move until the hour of his predicted death. We could use my antique grandfather clock. Oh, wait, no—destroyed by bears."

I crossed to the middle of the room, closer to Erasmus and Theo. "Father recently made himself a staff. It has a tree, just like the trees in the Grove of Books. Couldn't we use that to summon him back, the way we summoned Ulysses?"

"Ah, and the demons have conveniently left Father's staff in his hands, just so we can use it to retrieve him. Good thinking, Miranda. That's brilliant. Any other bright ideas? Perhaps, if we asked the demons nicely, they'd let us buy our father back. Maybe we could offer to install modern air-conditioning. I hear it's hot down where they are."

"You shouldn't be so hard on her," Theo began sternly. Then his voice faltered, his face going red, as he was called upon to put into words exactly why Erasmus should go easy on me.

Erasmus sneered and raised his glass, paraphrasing *The Tempest*. "O, for those idyllic days, Miranda, when *"more to know did never meddle with thy thoughts."*

From his seat by the piano, Caliban replied. "She came to learn that the magician Prospero was more than *the master of a full poor cell and her no greater father.*"

"O bravo!" Logistilla threw Caliban a come-hither look. "He can even duel in Shakespeare!"

Titus gave Caliban a long, dark look.

I stood there at a loss, staring at my siblings. What had happened to the Family Prospero? Once, nothing had been able to withstand us. Now, we could not even organize the rescue of our own father.

I had been so certain that, if we ever got back together, we would again be able to overcome any obstacle. Was it just Father who had held us together? Were we worthless without him, mere dogs without a master? Puppets with no string to guide them?

Were we fated to fade away, as Abaddon had predicted?

"Look, I admit it's a long shot," I said, "but what if Father does have his staff, and we don't even try?"

"No good," called Mephisto, from where he sat near the hearth. "It's the nature of the *Staff of Transportation* to travel. Most staffs would be much harder to summon. What's Daddy's staff do?"

"It's called the *Staff of Eternity*. He wanted to use it to resurrect—" I began.

" 'Nuff said," interrupted Mephisto. "Let's try it!"

When everyone else just stared at him, Mephisto continued, "That's what we're trying to do, isn't it, get someone out of Hell? It resurrected that Eli Thompson guy. Why not Daddy?"

"He's not dead," murmured Ulysses, discarding a card.

"So? He's in Hell, almost the same thing," Mephisto responded. "Only, I better warn you. It's going to take more than a wee drop of Water to convince Mr. Swift-Guy-Psychopomp to go to Hell and back. And there'll be no chance of a two-for-one this time! You all ready to spend the wet?"

"We have to spend it whether he finds Father or not, don't we?" asked Erasmus. He sighed. "I don't see we have a choice . . . unless someone is going to suggest we abandon Father in order to keep the Water to ourselves? Anyone? Do I see any hands for being the ingrate who suggests we abandon our *Pater Familias?*"

The chamber was silent except for the fluting of the wind and the *whirrr* noise of Titus's son, the human airplane.

"No? Good. "Then, we are all in." Erasmus again raised his glass. "At least, we've established we are all overly dutiful children willing to die, and thus endanger all of mankind, rather than let our old Daddykins down. That out of the way, what do we need to do, Mephisto?"

"Same as last time. Wait for dark. Do the spell. Where is this tree?" asked Mephisto.

"In the Wintergarden," I said.

"You mean in the one at Daddy's house? Right next to the Faery Glade? Ouch!" exclaimed Mephisto. Then, he shrugged cheerfully. "Could be worse. It could be *outside* the Wintergarden, in the Glade! Let's gather our stuff, teleport there, and check it out."

"No need," Mab came walking into the music room. He pulled a baggy containing sawdust and wood chips from one of the many pockets of his trench coat. "This is from the dogwood in the Wintergarden. Sent one of my men down there after you mentioned it, Ma'am. One of the perquisites of us spirit types, easier for us to move through that house than you humans. I think there's enough here to cast the spell. What do you think, Mr. Theo?"

Mab tossed the evidence bag to Theo, who hefted it on his palm and nodded.

"This should do," he said.

"Then, it's decided," Mephisto declared cheerfully. "We do the spell here, tonight."

"Might as well linger at the scene of the crime, letting everyone know where we are," muttered Erasmus. "Maybe demons can rape my other sister this time."

A silence followed, interrupted only by the rise and fall of a hundred windy flutes.

"That was uncalled for," Cornelius remonstrated gently. He turned to the rest of us. "Perhaps there is a seed of truth to the taunts of the Angel of the Bottomless Pit. If all the remaining Water of Life were given to one of us, that one could live another five hundred years. By then, Father's work might be complete and might be able to continue without our guiding hand."

"Ah, but which one, Good Brother?" slurred Erasmus. "Which one? Funny isn't it, Miranda? After your recent protestation about how it was Father who decided who lived and who died, the decision is now in your hands, after all. You have the Water, and if Father is gone, you will have to decide who gets it."

The irony of his comments only made the truth more painful. How could I make any decision now, with neither Father nor Eurynome to guide me?

Theo spoke, his voice gruff and low. "I am willing to forgo my share. I have been expecting to die for some time now. And while I would embrace life again, if the situation warranted, I am ready to let it go, if that is the more noble course."

"Theo!" I whispered. "No!"

Cornelius spoke softly, his face turned half away from us. "I as well. Over the years, I have grown accustomed to the darkness, and perhaps, fear its coming less than the rest of you. I will not run from its cold embrace."

His sentiments shocked me. I had expected him to fight greedily for his share to the end. Apparently, they surprised Erasmus as well; when he spoke, he sounded as shaken as I had felt when Theo made his offer.

"Cornelius! How extraordinarily noble of you," Erasmus said. "I fear I lack your aplomb. I want to live!"

"It's in God's hands now," Gregor said quietly. "Let us leave it there. If He wants us here, we shall remain. Otherwise, we shall depart."

Ulysses looked up, a brace of diamonds in his hand. "Say, here, I have an idea. The Elven Royal Court occasionally offers Water of Life as a reward for daring quests."

"Use our staves to try to beat the Elven knights errant to their quarry?" said Theo speculatively. "Interesting idea. We may be able to accomplish feats elves could not normally perform."

"Perhaps," Ulysses shrugged, "but, why go to the flowers when you can go to the bees, I always say? Let's steal the Water directly from the Royal Court. They must have buckets of the stuff, or they couldn't offer it to their knights."

"Don't mess with elves!" Mephisto warned. "They're bad juju."

"Isn't that the kind of thinking that got you into this mess?" asked Logistilla, without looking up from her cards.

"Not at all," replied Ulysses blithely. "Curiosity is what did me in. I asked my staff to take me to the first place it had ever been, and I found myself in Hell."

"Just that. You arrived in Hell, and they jumped you?" asked Erasmus.

"Isn't that enough? Well, I guess it would have helped if I hadn't stopped to nick that—"

"You stole something from a Lord of Hell?" croaked Theo.

"I admit now it was a mistake," Ulysses said, fanning his cards.

"Geez, didn't you learn anything from that experience?" asked Mephisto, of all people.

"Sure," said Ulysses. " I learned not to steal from Lords of Hell."

"When you hear 'elves' think 'Lords of Hell,' " Mab said glumly.

"What about you, Mephisto?" asked Erasmus. "What's your stance on 'family water use'?"

Mephsito shrugged and went on strumming the lute.

"Don't you have an opinion?"

Mephisto shook his head. "Nope, doesn't matter to me. I came to grips with this immortality thing long ago. We can't save everyone. That's just the way it is. It took Miranda a year and a day to get the Water of Life. Even if she had turned around and gone back immediately, with no rest after that grueling trip, she couldn't have gotten enough water to save everybody on earth. So, I learned to stop mourning those who could not be saved. Besides, if we all lived on Earth forever, who would go to Heaven?"

"What about the current issue? Don't you want a say in who in the family gets the Water from this day forth?" pushed Erasmus.

"Whatever happens, happens." Mephisto put down the lute and leaned his cheek on his right hand. He smiled at Erasmus and gestured lightly with his other hand. "Look at it from my point of view, Brother. I'm a madman with half a mind. Most of the time I can't remember where I left my wallet, or where I slept last night. What kind of a life would I have if I worried about the future? Besides, it's a moot point. The decision is Miranda's."

"Not entirely," said Cornelius. "Miranda may decide to keep doling the Water out equally. This does not keep the rest of us from agreeing to redistribute it among ourselves."

Titus had left his sons and come to join us. Now, he lowered himself into the black leather recliner next to Gregor. "I am willing to give up my share of Water of Life," he said, his voice low, "but only if it is given to my sons. Give them my share and Logistilla's as well. Let them have their day. We've lived long enough."

"I beg your pardon!" snapped Logistilla. "I most certainly do not agree!"

"Woman, you disgust me!" growled Titus. "Even among brutish beasts, females are willing to give their life for their young."

"Children! What do men know of children?" Logistilla scowled.

"A great deal more than you do, you unnatural witch," said Erasmus, rising to one elbow. His eyes glittered dangerously.

Logistilla stared stony-faced at her cards.

"We have more regard for our children in our little pinkies, Titus," Erasmus continued, "than our dear sister has in her whole body."

Logistilla's face contorted with anger. She glared at Erasmus. "You know nothing! Have you carried an unborn babe, housing it in your very body, for the better part of a year? Have you borne it in pain and fed it with your own bosom? No? Men! You men think of children as some kind of trophy, a prize for which you should be rewarded. A man's life is his own, to do with as he pleases. A woman, her life is her children. You men! You know nothing of children!"

"And you know more? You, who have hardly even spoken to your sons since they arrived?" spat Erasmus. "I've talked to them more since they arrived here today than you have."

Logistilla rose and lunged at Erasmus. The chain on her leg rang loudly as it clanged against her chair. It kept her from crossing to where Erasmus lay, but she made it as far as Theo. In a low harsh whisper that would not carry to where the two boys played, she said, "I have borne over fifty children in my time, birthed them and raised them with my own blood, sweat, and tears. All of them, save these two, are now cradled six feet beneath the heartless earth. You have no idea what that does to a mother!

"The first time one of my sons died, I thought I, too, would die. Surely, no one had ever suffered so, I thought, for such pain could not be borne. Sea level rose that year, so great was the volume of my tears. I feared the sheer magnitude of my pain might cause time itself to end.

"But then another one died, and another, and another: some in infancy, some as soldiers upon the battlefield, some growing old and rotten and forgetful before they fell into the grave. And worst of all, some bitterly resentful of the youth and beauty of their own mother, the woman who bore them. And all the while, cool Miranda held back the Life that could have saved them." She spared a glance for me. Her black eyes glittered with hate.

"All my early children were sons," Logistilla continued. "When I finally had a daughter, I determined things would be different. My Marisa was the most precious thing that ever breathed air, a sweet-natured creature, inquisitive and joyful. Even as she grew, she did not lose her innocent charm. She was my heart, the very purpose of my life.

"I resolved to move Heaven and Earth to keep her alive. I had such plans for us. She was to be my lifelong companion, my bosom friend. We would spend years together studying magic and raising beasts. She loved all animals, my little Marisa." Logistilla's eyes shone with unshed tears. A single teardrop began running down her high-boned cheek. "I started squirreling away Water of Life. Taking my share only every second or third year, so that I would have enough for her, so that we could be young together, forever. . . ."

Silent tears now streamed down Logistilla's cheeks. She wiped at them absentmindedly with the back of her hand.

"What happened?" Erasmus asked, leaning forward. He was drawn into her story in spite of himself.

Logistilla's voice sounded as if it came from a great distance. "When she was still a young woman, as mortals count years, a mother herself, with two tiny infants of her own, she was raped and killed by street thugs one night in Edinburgh. Just like that—the most precious thing in my life—snuffed out as one might snuff a candle."

Logistilla paused, unable to continue. Gregor stood and crossed to where she stood and put his arms around his twin. She put her head against his chest and wept. The rest of us remained silent. Eventually, Logistilla, still leaning against her twin, began to speak again, her voice low and heavy with sorrow.

"When we buried her, I stayed behind after the mourners had left. Upon her grave, I swore I would never put my hope in my children again. That I would never love them, as I had loved her and her older brothers. A piece of my soul lies buried with each of those early ones. What soul I have left is cold and tough, like a stringy old chicken. It lacks the breadth of courage necessary to love children properly. You men. You know nothing of children."

She pushed Gregor away, and without another word, returned to her seat. Dabbing at her tears with a white handkerchief and sniffing, she picked up her cards and continued to play her hand.

Erasmus reached for the wine bottle on the table, then slapped it angrily, sending the bottle flying across the room toward the fireplace. Mephisto, who had resumed playing his lute, reached up, caught it out of the air, took a swig, and placed it on the floor beside him.

Rising to his feet, Erasmus said, "I think I've drunk quite enough for one day. Today we've learned that I make a maudlin drunk. Isn't that dandy." Without another word, he left the room, leaving the rest of us to our private thoughts.

LUNCH was a subdued affair. We gathered in the dining hall, some of us dressing for dinner, some not. People came and went without much interaction. Erasmus did not put in an appearance, to no one's surprise. I sat in my old seat, poking at my fish and keeping my own council. My simmering resentment of Erasmus's new weakness of character, this dereliction of family duty in our time of need, was the only thing keeping me from the gaping jaws of dark depression. Yet, it sickened me that I had come to such a state where the only thing keeping me going was hatred, especially as I feared my antipathy might be fueled by envy.

When we first arrived, Erasmus had spoken to Cornelius about the "great project." He must know what Father was attempting to achieve with the Aerie Ones. And Erasmus was the one who had Father's arcane journals and for whom the phoenix fire message had been intended. All these years, I had been under the impression I was the one with whom Father shared his most intimate secrets. Why had he told my brothers these great secrets, but not me?

I was deep in the midst of a mental diatribe against Erasmus and his insensitive wickedness, when Cornelius's voice broke the spell of my reverie.

"I fear I can no longer restrain my curiosity. Miranda, where is the Ark?"

"A-ark? What ark?" I asked, taken aback by this strange non-sequitur. "The Ark of the Covenant? You have it, don't you?"

"There is little point in playing dumb, Sister. We know your people stole it. What I wish to know is why. I believe you, at least, owe me an explanation."

"I have no idea what you're talking about!"

"You disappoint me, Sister," my blind brother sighed. "I had at least expected you to be honest when cornered."

From the other side of the table came a low groan of exasperation. Mab slammed his wine cup down with a bang and pushed up the rim of his hat.

"Begging your pardon, Mr. Cornelius," his voice was a low growl, "but all this dumping on Miss Miranda stops right now! When the demons framed your people for having blown up our warehouse, Miss Miranda wasn't fooled, not even for an instant. The evidence pointed right at you, but she laughed at it and insisted, 'My brother Cornelius would never do that!'

"So, I ask you—whatever stupid, badly placed clues you found aside—who do you *think* stole your Ark of the Covenant? The Handmaiden of the Unicorn, guardian of the family fortune? Or the family klepto, who was being chased by demons?"

"Hey, I resemble that remark!" objected Mephisto. He looked rapidly back and forth down the table. "Oh! You mean Ulysses! Phew! Off the hook!"

"What warehouse?" asked Cornelius.

Mab told him briefly about the accidents that had befallen the company in this last month, since Baelor of the Baleful Eye glimpsed some of our company secrets in my thoughts back in Chicago, and of finding the burnt body of the man Mephisto called Mr. Mustache in the damaged warehouse.

"Edwardo." Cornelius lowered his head, observing a moment of silence for the dead man. "He was one of Erasmus's people. I feared the worst when he did not return. I thought perhaps Miranda had killed him," Cornelius continued sadly. "He called me from the Caribbean to say she was being shadowed by three demons. He insisted on trying to warn her. That was the last I heard of him."

Unexpectedly, tears came to my eyes.

"I did kill him," I said softly. "Or, rather, I might as well have. He tried to chase me through rock-strewn waters in the dark. His boat crashed. I-I thought he was a servant of the demons."

There was an awkward silence as we each dealt with our private sorrows. Yet another pebble in my jar of self-recriminations. Had it not been for the séance and the spirit that disrupted it, I might have stopped to talk before running, and an innocent man would not have been killed. Mab was right. Magic was too dangerous for mortals. And that was what now we were: mortals.

Mab broke the silence. "The demons must have gotten ahold of his body. Because, as I explained, it showed up in the damaged warehouse. But Miss Miranda was not fooled, not for a minute. Even before I told her forensics had discovered the body was a plant, she was defending you. She knew what you would do and what you wouldn't do. Apparently, she knows her family better than you do, Mr. Cornelius. You and Mr. Erasmus keep accusing Miss Miranda of all sorts of nonsense she'd never participate in."

"Enough, Spiritling. It is unwise to criticize your betters," said Cornelius.

Mab laughed out loud. "You? A blind man who manipulates his own people and interferes with their economy? My better? Ha!"

Cornelius's calm expression never faltered. He lifted his staff. The amber stone twinkled. Mab's eyes narrowed. Grabbing the salt shaker, he stood and spun in a circle. Salt sprayed everywhere.

"Kneel," said Cornelius.

Mab, surrounded by a scattering of salt, gritted his teeth, resisting. His body jerked several times, but whether it was the salt or pure willpower, he managed to remain standing. As there was no point in glaring at the blind man, Mab turned his angry glare toward me. The time had come to put an end to this.

"Enough, Cornelius!" I commanded.

"Are you giving me orders now, Sister?"

"If you trifle with my people, you shall live to regret it!"

"Is that so? What can you do?"

"You want Father's work finished? You need my help. Cross me, and no one gets the Water. I'll throw it in the sea. Worse, I'll give it to Mab, and only those he favors will live."

"You would risk Father's great work for this spiritling?" Cornelius asked.

"This spiritling, as you call him, *is* Father's great work!" I blurted. "He and his kind will remain upon the Earth far, far after you and I have perished and turned to dust. If they are going to be the keepers of mankind's destiny, we had better start appealing to their better nature, don't you think?"

"Do they have a better nature?" asked Cornelius.

"Ask Mab," I replied.

"Do you?" asked Cornelius.

I am not the judge of voices Cornelius claims to be, but I thought his question sounded sincere.

"'Course I do," replied Mab. "All God's creatures have better natures. Some just don't listen to 'em . . . or do you think there are things between Heaven and Earth that were made by some power other than God?"

"Good point," Cornelius said quietly. "There is much Father knew about, which the rest of us can only guess at. He received his information from some supernatural source. We only received our instructions from him. If Father believes spirits should walk as men, who am I to disagree?"

"Great," said Mab. "So? Who's for going down to the Music Room and pummeling the truth out of Ulysses?"

"SPILL the beans, perp, or it won't go so easy for you." Mab smacked his trusty lead pipe across his palm, as he glared down at where my brother Ulysses sat playing cards with Logistilla.

"Sorry, chap, can't," was Ulysses's glib reply.

"I'll 'can't' you, you good-for-nothing . . ." Mab began. I touched his arm lightly and he reluctantly stepped back, still slapping the lead pipe against his hand.

I said, "Can you tell us about the Ark of the Covenant?"

"Found out about that, did you?" he asked cheerfully.

"Then it was you!" Cornelius accused.

"Indeed! Indeed!"

"Why?" asked Cornelius and Mab together.

"Sorry, can't oblige," Ulysses responded again.

Cornelius lifted his staff. "Can't or won't?"

Ulysses lowered his cards, facedown, and stared speculatively at the winking amber on Cornelius's staff.

"Look, chaps, I'd love to tell you everything, but I can't. Literally, can't. Not won't. You can try your staff though. Maybe that will get around my geas."

"We shall see," said Cornelius. "Now, you want to answer Mab's questions, right?"

The amber stone twinkled. Ulysses's mouth opened obediently.

"It's like . . ." He began to choke. His face turned white, then red, then purple blue. He grabbed at his throat, coughing and hacking. Writhing like a man under torture, he fell out of his chair and began to fret and froth upon the ground. His blue-gray eyes sought mine imploringly.

"Enough, Cornelius. He can't obey you!" I cried.

"Stop," commanded Cornelius.

With a whining hack, Ulysses began drawing in breath again. He lay panting on the Music Room floor, his hands massaging his throat. In a hoarse croak, he whispered, "Would love to oblige you, but . . . can't."

"Perhaps I can help," said Titus, stepping up behind Cornelius and me. "Miranda, send all the Aerie Ones away. The spirit ones, I mean." Turning to Mab, he said, "Detective. Write down your questions."

I nodded and sent the airy servants from the room. Mab brought out his notebook and stubby pencil and quickly wrote five questions.

1. *Why did you steal the Ark?*
2. *Why did you steal the Ring of Solomon?*
3. *Why did you arrange Gregor's supposed death?*
4. *Did you steal the Water of Life from Miranda's chapel?*
5. *Why did you tell Theo to get Cornelius to enforce his oath?*

Titus leaned over and took the notebook and pencil from Mab and shoved them at Ulysses. Then, he lifted up his hand. A thick, solid, length of cedar wood with a "Y" at the top rose up from where it had been resting beside the fireplace and flew across the music room into his waiting grasp.

"Write!" he ordered Ulysses.

Titus struck his staff against the table and then held it aloft, as if it were a tuning fork. Only no natural tuning fork resonates silence. The rushing of the water, the fluting of the wind, the noise of clothes rustling and lungs breathing and the soft taps of cards in play; all fell suddenly and unnaturally quiet. In the silence, the mustiness grew stronger, and I could smell the metal filings from the work Caliban had been doing.

Deprived of his dominant sense, Cornelius threw up his hands. His lips moved rapidly, but no voice issued forth. Frantic now, he skidded backward, bumping into chairs and sending instruments flying as he went. Eventually, he must have reached a place where the effect of the *Staff of Silence* tapered off, for he slowed his flight and stood, his chest heaving, his skin parchment white. Watching his awkward odyssey, it occurred to me that he probably had not known Titus was about to use his staff. To Cornelius, it must have seemed as if the world suddenly ended, without warning.

Ulysses spared only a brief glance for Cornelius's plight and then started to write. He wrote hesitantly at first, as if he expected the demon geas to interfere again. When nothing impeded him, he began to write more rapidly, scrawling his answers as quickly as he could move his hand. He wrote:

Help me!!! Had to promise all manner of unwholesome things in order to escape Hell. Oath forces me not to ask for help or to warn anyone. I stole the A. of C. and the R. of S. to try and ward off demon. Worked somewhat, but I don't know how use! Advice to Theo and death of Gregor part of demon's plan. Faking death of Gregor, my own idea, of course. Stolen W. of L. was for Gregor. Thought Theo would overcome C. staff. Dingbat. Demon's goals: snuff family members who were greatest threat to demons. Any ideas?

Mab wrote:

What's Logistilla's part?

Ulysses replied:

Logi. envied Mir. her goddess. When a supernatural deity offered her a sibylship, she jumped. Turned out cute fuzzy goddess Abaddon in disguise. Ouch! Since both of us obliged to the same demon, Abdn, he let us help each other. Logi's part not so bad, merely consigned to silence.

Titus loomed over the table, placing a note of his own next to Ulysses's. He had written,

When I put down the Silence, do not speak of my staff. Wiser heads will ponder and get back to you. That my staff can interfere with demon magic is closely-guarded secret. Never understood why Father kept secret. Understand now. Had it been known, I would have been

on demons' death list, along with Gregor and Theo. Secret may have saved my life. If you blab, I will consider it a murder attempt and will defend myself as I see fit. COMPRENDO?

Ulysses nodded fervently. Titus looked around at the rest of us. I nodded. So did Mab. Cornelius had withdrawn to the corner, where he sat huddled near the fluting pipes. Logistilla, though craning her neck, was too far away to read the message.

Theo leaned across the table from the far side and took the pencil from Ulysses's fingers. He tugged on Gregor's sleeve and then wrote:

The name of the monster who stole our lives: Abaddon.

Looking up again, he met Gregor's eyes. Something passed between them, some unspoken promise to which the rest of us were not privy.

With a start, I realized Theo was right.

Father was trapped in Hell because he had ripped open a hole to the Inferno. He did this to resurrect Gregor—whom he thought was dead. Really, Gregor had been taken prisoner by Ulysses, who was obeying the orders of Abaddon.

Theo had taken his vow because of his false belief that Gregor's reward for his many years of service was to burn in Hell. In fact, I believed that part of Father's motives for rescuing Gregor was that he hoped seeing his brother alive might rouse Theo from his vow-induced folly. But actually, Theo's trouble was caused by the fact that he swore his oath upon Cornelius's staff—the staff that Baelor's Great One woke up so that it worked its magic upon him, despite Cornelius's best efforts. And this idea—swearing upon the *Staff of Persuasion*—had been suggested by Ulysses, at the request of Abaddon.

Abaddon was responsible for all the harm my family had suffered in the last century. Logistilla, too, had been tricked by him. His actions had deprived Prospero, Inc. of Gregor and Theo, resulting in difficulty binding new spirits and enforcing our Priority Contracts, which, in turn, led to natural disasters and the death of mortals.

I had a pretty good idea who Baelor's "Great One" must be.

Finally, we had an enemy, a target against whom we could direct our wrath at the ill treatment of our brothers—assuming we could figure out how to descend into Hell and challenge one of the seven devils who ran the place to personal combat. I could tell from the look in their eyes that Theo and Gregor had in mind something exactly like that.

When they took on Abaddon, I wanted to be with them. I wanted to be there when the creature that nearly destroyed my family fell.

The only injury we could not pin on the Angel of the Bottomless Pit was Mephisto's madness. That was apparently the Queen of Air and Darkness's doing. She would have her comeuppance as well.

The demons were right to fear us. No one could smite the Family Prospero and escape unscathed—not when we worked together. Only apart could we be defeated.

Titus touched the butt of his staff to the floor, and the world rushed in upon our ears again.

"Ah! That was . . . disconcerting," Mab said, covering and uncovering his ears. He tore out the pages upon which Ulysses and Titus had written and handed them to Titus, before pocketing his notebook. "Here, I think that's all the weirdness I can take at the moment. I'm going down to the kitchens for a cup of coffee. Anyone care to join me?"

To my great surprise, Cornelius stood. "I'll come with you, Spiritling, if you are willing to endure my company."

Mab's eyebrows shot up. He glanced at me. I shrugged. He said, "Sure, no problem. Be warned, though, I reserve the right to spill coffee on you if you get all high and mighty with me."

"It is a chance I shall have to take," Cornelius replied, rising and carefully falling in step with Mab, his white cane tapping the way before him.

Still holding the torn notebook page, Titus said, "I shall show all this to Erasmus when he wakes. We can then discuss how to proceed."

"Lot of good Erasmus will do you," I muttered, turning away.

I LEFT the room and came upon Caliban, returning the instrument he had repaired. He paused and said in a low voice, "Miranda, you are too hard on Erasmus. He blames himself."

"Blames himself for what?" I snapped. Caliban just looked at me with dark eyes as deep as mountain pools. Realization came slowly and painfully. "Y-you mean . . . for the attack . . . on me?"

He nodded. "He feels if he had taken proper precautions, you would not have been harmed."

"And he would still have his precious Water of Life," I muttered.

"Do you really think so badly of him?"

"He hates me! What makes you think his motives are more noble?"

"I was there when he found you last night. I saw his face," said Caliban, adding, "You may not be his favorite sister, but you *are* his sister."

Robbed even of my righteous indignation toward Erasmus, I walked dejectedly back to my room.

It had been a dark day for the Family Prospero.

CHAPTER TWENTY

Crowns and Figurines

The heavens opened and the earth shook. Thunderclouds, dark as pitch, rolled across the sky, raining sleet and hailstones the size of roc's eggs down upon the island. Gale-force winds tore branches from trees and tossed sea birds about like so much flotsam. The tower creaked, groaning under the onslaught of the winds.

Standing upon the balcony outside my bedroom, I orchestrated the storm. The skies wept at my command, winds and rain dancing to the strains of my flute. The music gave voice to the anguish in my heart, and the elements obeyed the music, raging and storming in time with my torment.

For over an hour I played thus. The tempest shaking the island was kin to the one my father summoned to shipwreck Ferdinand—the real Ferdinand—and his father so many years ago. Eventually, however, I grew weary and withdrew. As I lay down upon my bed, the fervor of the winds abated some, and the noise of the driving sleet changed to the soft patter of rain.

How long I lay, I cannot say. My thoughts chased each other like gray ghosts, each blaming the other for its demise.

If only . . . if only . . . if only . . .

Worn and weary I turned for comfort to . . . an empty gash in the fabric of my soul. My Lady was gone.

All day, this had happened to me; yet, no amount of empty repetition of the sad and dreary fact that She was gone helped it to sink in. I would only just finish reminding myself, when, torn by sorrow, I would again seek comfort by turning to that inner place, now a vast empty abyss, where once Her gentle and comforting presence had dwelt. Habits are hard to break, especially habits born of over five hundred years of dutiful obedience.

"Grieving," men called this horrible pain: the pain of a lost limb, the pain of a lost loved one, the pain of losing one's guiding star.

Seeking a distraction, I rose and paced the room. My path took me by the mirror, where, from its silvery depths, my new reflection mocked me. How young and vulnerable my raven locks made me look—I, who felt as aged as an ancient mountain. "Black as obsidian," Ferdinand had said. Or had that been Astreus?

Thinking of the elf lord reminded me that I had never returned Astreus's figurine to my father's mantel. I crossed the room and reached into the pocket of my white cashmere cloak. Sure enough, the statuette Mephisto had made for me was still there, where I had stuck it when I went to help Zephyrus. I drew it forth.

It was a good likeness of the laughing elf lord with his dancing eyes, evoking within my breast both longing and dread. Astreus's presence worked upon me like a strong wine, and part of me, the part that could still think of the *Book of the Sibyl* without weeping, longed to thank him in person.

"What is your part in all this, Elf? " I demanded of the little statue, with its twinkling sapphire eyes. It did not answer, of course, but as I regarded the figurine, it struck me that this looked remarkably like a piece of Mephisto's staff. I examined the figurine more closely, stroking the smooth polished wood and peered into the gems that made its eyes. It was the same general size as Mephisto's aborted carving of Mab. Mab had claimed that carving was magical. Could this figurine be magical, too?

Impulsively, I tapped it on the mantel, the way Mephisto would tap his staff to call his creatures. Only afterward did the sheer folly of my action strike me. What if it worked? Elves were tricky, and I hardly wished to entertain one in my boudoir! I glanced around nervously, but nothing occurred. Feeling foolish, I put the figurine on the mantel and returned to sit on the foot of my bed.

As I sat there, without hope, my glance fell upon the stone wall of the balcony. I considered what it might be like to seek oblivion by launching myself from that stony height. I imagined plummeting toward the valley, arms outstretched, but dismissed the thought with a shake of my head. Not only would my pride not allow me to take such a coward's way out, but also this was my father's island. His airy servants would, likely as not, catch me before I hit the ground, and I would be left very much alive, having to explain my foolishness to a mocking Erasmus.

The rain was still falling, and night was coming. It would soon be time to attempt the summoning of Father. Only, why did I think night was coming?

Outside, the sky was no darker, in fact, as the rain lessened, it grew lighter. Yet, my room was dark and gloomy. The darkness seemed to be emanating from the corner near the fireplace. My heart skipped a beat.

Seir of the Shadows!

Determined not to be caught unarmed again, I lunged for my fan, which lay on the mahogany dresser. My hand closed around its cool handle. Only then did I realize that, in my hurry to arm myself, I had left my flute resting against the wall, a mere yard from where darkness was solidifying into the form of the handsome sable incubus.

The pounding of my heart echoed in my ears louder than any thunder. The flute. I could not lose the flute, too!

Seir stepped from the shadows, blood-red eyes glancing about my room. Darkness poured from Gregor's staff, causing the incubus's black opera cape to billow. In the semidarkness, his perfect face looked so beautiful, as if a statue carved from black marble by one of the masters of old had come to life. My heart nearly stopped. He turned his head at the sigh of my breath.

Seir's scarlet eyes met mine, and he gazed at me in fascination, drinking in my features as might a long-parted lover. I kept my eyes trained on him, willing myself not to glance at the flute.

"Sweet Miranda," he murmured. His lips parted in delight, and he leaned Gregor's staff against the wall. "All alone."

An alarming tingle traveled through my body. Just looking at his beauty produced an unpleasantly heady sensation, like honeyed wine laced with poison. Thankfully, I need not endure this. I turned to my Lady for protection.

Only, She was not there . . . oh, Lord!

Trembling, I brandished my fan. Its silvery slats gleamed like the moon in the gloom. Without taking his eyes off my face, he raised his hands, as if to show he was harmless. Glowering, I stood my ground.

"Depart," I warned, "or you shall follow your companions back to Hell!"

"Your brothers dispatched my companions, did they?" he asked. "I cannot say I am dismayed. Vile creatures, both. They are back in the Inferno, and no longer 'shadowed,' so I am, at long last, free from the burden of concerning myself with them. Baelor writhes in the torture pits of the Malbolge, where the Torturers debate with him upon the topic of his recent failures. While Osae sits at Queen Lilith's feet, basking in her twisted affection and drinking from her cup—his reward for some evil deed he accomplished before his demise. Did he take one of your brothers with him?"

"No" I whispered hoarsely.

"Ah. A pity."

The thought of Osae being petted and coddled as a reward for assaulting me filled my throat with bile. The idea so disturbed me that I nearly missed Seir's other piece of information.

"Lilith! The Three Shadowed Ones work for the Queen of Air and Darkness?"

"Did you not know that our original duty was to retrieve the Spear of Longinus?" Seir replied.

"Of course! The Spear of Joseph of Arimathea!" I cried, recalling that after the Vatican raid, Father built the spear into the *Staff of Devastation*. "That's why you three started hunting Theo, wasn't it?"

"Exactly. It was Her Majesty, the Queen of Air and Darkness, who provided that spear to the Roman centurion, Longinus." He tilted his head, his scarlet eyes regarding me unblinkingly. "Surely, you do not think just any spear could have killed the Son of God?"

"Oh my!" I breathed, stunned.

His words made a sickening kind of sense. Just as Lilith had given the Unicorn Hunters enchanted weapons, she must also have supplied the spear that stabbed Christ on the Cross. She would hate the Savior for reasons similar to those that caused her to hate Eurynome.

This hatred of hers was destroying my family.

First, it had led to Mephisto's madness. Now, Osae had given Lilith yet another victory against my Lady, robbing Her of one of Her loyal Handmaidens—and it had been centuries since I had come upon another one. No wonder Osae supped from Lilith's own cup!

Lilith and Abaddon. Between them, the Family Prospero was nearly a memory.

Seir cocked his head and glided closer. "How beautiful you are! Like a white rose on a misty day. Pristine and beautiful and untouched."

He reached out and touched my cheek, and I let him, mesmerized. Despite my desire to recoil or to slash off his head, my hand would not rise to stop him. Where his sable fingers touched my skin, pleasant tremors raced through my body. My thoughts swam, and I found myself able to think of nothing except how nice it would be to lie down.

Closing my eyes and drawing a ragged breath, I slid the tip of my finger along the edge of my fan. The pain woke me. I stuck the finger in my mouth, licking the blood. The incubus watched in rapt wonder, as if he were as spell-bound as I had been moments before.

I swung the fan, slashing at him. He vanished, appearing three feet away.

"Sweet, my love! You need not carry on so. Come to my arms, and I shall show you such wonders as will transport you beyond mere mortal plea-sure. Your body shall sing like a harp, and your heart will match mine in its enduring love."

"You? Enduring love?" I laughed.

Would my brothers hear me if I screamed? Unlikely, the walls were thick, but perhaps Mab waited by the door.

Seir tilted his head. His inhuman eyes trained on my lips. "Do you think we incubi do not love? You do women an unkindness! Women are not such fickle creatures. A few can be fooled with sweet words and gentle ca-resses, but only the unusually naïve. To truly lead a virtuous woman astray, we must offer her genuine love, or she would see through us as easily as one sees through a transparent window. So, of course, I love you. How could I look at you, so brave and fair, a thing alone and unappreciated in such a cruel, callous world, and not adore you?"

"You admit you are trying to lead me astray!"

"I am an incubus. You would hardly believe me if I said otherwise."

"You are too late," I muttered, turning away.

Seir turned, too. I heard the sharp intake of his breath and the soft words, "So, that is why I am here!"

Fearing he must have seen my flute, I spun around. He was staring not at my instrument, but at the mantel. I followed the direction of his gaze. The oval mirror above the mantelpiece reflected both the sable incubus and the little wooden figurine with its sapphire eyes. A chill ran up my spine. What I was seeing made no sense.

Then, suddenly, it did.

I crept backward until my back was to the mahogany dresser. Resting against it, I reached behind me and felt around until my fingers closed upon the object I desired.

"Seir? Come to me," I called softly. When he came, I whispered, "Close your eyes."

To my amazement, he did. His red eyes closed, and he leaned toward me, as if to meet my kiss. Seeing the incubus, who knew I was still carrying the war fan, close his eyes in trust made me feel obscurely less foolish about having walked toward the Ferdinand I thought to be him on the bluff. With his neck so exposed, it was a pity I no longer wanted to kill him.

I placed the circlet of silver and horn upon his head. In my mind, Father Christmas's deep voice echoed: *"When the time comes to use it, Child, you will know."*

"What becomes of tithed elves?" I whispered softly.

A puff of black snow surrounded Seir, and my heart skipped. I recognized that ebony snow. It was the same stuff that had surrounded Astreus when he walked into Father Christmas's feast hall on Christmas. The dark, sooty cloud that had made me start with fear and regret having left my flute in my room—because I feared that it contained Seir.

Apparently, it had.

The incubus grew taller and more slender. The dark cloud cleared, and Lord Astreus of the High Council of the elves stood before me. Seir's black opera cloak fell from his shoulders like sable wings. His presence illuminated the room, lending a dreamlike quality to the dappled, rain-filtered light and transforming the drab chamber into a place of wonder.

My lips parted to speak, but the joy of seeing him so unexpectedly, after I had just feared we would not meet again, was too great. No words came.

"We tithed elves join the ranks of the demons of Hell," Astreus answered, his changeable eyes a storm-tossed gray. He adjusted the crown upon his head, running a finger over an insert of horse hoof. His gaze searched my face keenly, lingering on my smooth brow where the Sibyl's mark was not in evidence. "How goes my gift?"

He did not know. My heart felt as if it had turned to ash and was slowly blowing away. How could I put such a thing into words? I stammered several beginnings, only to be unable to continue. Finally, the words came haltingly from my lips.

"A gracious gift, my lord, but I fear I can make no use of it."

"How so?" he frowned, his gray eyes growing still more tempestuous.

"I . . . I am . . . Eurynome no longer . . . Osae . . . he came . . ." My mouth went dry, and my voice fell silent. However much I tried, I could not say, "He came in the disguise you used to deceive me and win my trust."

"He defiled you?" The elf's voice was as soft as rose petals.

I nodded. Tears spilled over my lashes and burned their way down my cheeks. Yes, that was the word: "defiled," as in "no longer a holy vessel worthy of my Lady."

"Then, all is lost," said the elf matter-of-factly.

"For me . . . it is." I wiped my eyes.

Astreus watched the falling rain, his golden profile a study of motionless grace. I ached to reach out and touch him. Almost as if hearing my thoughts, he moved forward until he loomed over me, his breath warm upon my face. I gazed back at him and found I was trembling. Though fully awake, I dreamt a flock of doves took flight all around us. I could hear the sound of their wings beating against the air.

"Did my gift mean anything to you? Did you cherish it before your loss?" he asked, his words barely audible above the noise of wings.

"It meant a great deal." I gave my head a hard shake and took a deep breath. The dream of doves vanished. "I have been wanting to thank you."

"Then grant me one last boon."

"I make no promises!" I countered quickly. Pleased as I was, I had not taken leave of my senses. Was he mad? He was an elf and an incubus! So far, he had blown up part of my father's house, destroyed the statue of Theo, finagled his way, disguised as Ferdinand, into my house, my dreams, and—as long as I was being brutally honest—my heart, and betrayed the location of the family New Year's party to the Three Shadowed Ones, resulting in Titus getting shot.

I would be wiser to grab a lightning bolt with my bare hands than to offer him a boon.

Astreus dropped to one knee. My heart began to beat oddly, joyfully. I felt faint and leaned against the dresser for support. Human men only knelt like this for one reason. Surely, he was not about to . . .

"Slay me!" He gestured at the Japanese forge god's fighting fan, which lay atop the bureau. "Slit my throat with your enchanted blade and grant me the gift of Oblivion."

"Ex-excuse me?"

He did not stir but knelt watching me. His eyes had gone as red as rubies.

"Is th-this some kind of trick?"

"No trick. You were my last hope. If I return to being Seir now, I will be lost."

"But . . ." I sputtered, "you cannot expect me to cut you down in cold blood, without any explanation!"

"You are right. You deserve to hear the tale," He rose lightly to his feet.

"I will tell you all, and you may choose whether to honor my request or no. Come, let us to the balcony and speak beneath the open sky. Whatever your decision, this is likely to be the last time I shall ever see it."

I LET him walk before me, holding my breath when he paused beside the hearth. He glanced at the chessboard and moved a black knight, before continuing over the threshold to the balcony. The moment his foot touched the stone, I sprinted across the chamber and grabbed my flute, hugging it to me. With the instrument held tightly in my hand, I joined him outside among the orchids.

Once upon the balcony, he leaned against the stone railing and stared out at the rushing sky, the rain pelting his head and shoulders. The storm was lighter now, the clouds a billowing collage of pearl, charcoal, and dove gray. The winds, though slower, still whistled and moaned through the towers of the mansion.

"Ah, old friends! How I have missed you!" he laughed, and I was reminded of the joy with which the false Ferdinand had greeted Ariel and the other Aerie Ones at Prospero's Mansion. At the time, it had puzzled me, because Ferdinand had hardly known of Ariel, but now it made sense. It was Astreus, not Ferdinand or Seir, who had been so happy to see the Aerie Ones—his people, if Caurus was to be believed: his children.

As I approached the balcony, a trick of the light made him appear to be merely a tall handsome Chinaman with a burnished tan. Then, he turned, and I was struck anew by the unearthly beauty of his elvin features. Something of this must have showed in my eyes, for he raised his hand as if to touch my cheek, though his fingers curled around a lock of my hair instead.

"Your quarrel has been mended."

"Perhaps," I muttered. "You were going to explain?"

"Was I?" His lips caught a smile the way a lake catches the reflection of midnight stars. "It is a sad tale. Perhaps, you would prefer to hear another? Something cheerier, so my last moments might be filled with laughter instead of tears. Would you hear how I traveled East of the Sun to woo the Rainbow's Daughter? Or how once I surprised a bevy of nymphs in the midst of their water dances and what came of it? Or perhaps a tale of the beautiful Sylvie and the three quests I once undertook to garner her favor?"

I crossed my arms, frowning. I had no desire to hear tales of his dalliances with other women. "It won't be your last moment, if you don't convince me to kill you."

"I have reached my end, willy-nilly. Only the manner of my demise remains undecided. But such things are not pleasant and are hardly fitting upon so lovely a day. Shall I tell you tales of my travels instead? Would you hear tell of the City of Night with its great pyramids and ziggurats and perfumed night gardens? Or shall I tell you of the Star Forge, where the great smiths fashion new ornaments for the dome of the heavens? Or perhaps of Bright Aldur, a fresh world, newly made? Or of Dread Avernus, where the Wayfarers plot their strange connivances? Or maybe you would prefer tales of the Silver Meadows, where it is always twilight and the Unicorn can be glimpsed walking through the argent fields, flowers springing up behind Her with each footstep?"

His words stirred a longing in my heart to hear more of these distant marvels. Fields where my Lady walks? Stars forged? Astreus could, most likely, tell me of places of which even Erasmus, with all his arcane learning, had never heard. But my longing for places wondrous and far away was nothing compared to the burning curiosity as to how Astreus would explain his death wish.

"Much as I would like to hear such tales, I would prefer to hear about the matter at hand," I replied.

He did not speak for a time, but continued to gaze out at the storm, oblivious to the rain on his face. I leaned against the inner wall of the balcony, waiting. Cool orchid petals, bright orange with tiny yellow speckles, brushed softly against my cheek and eyelashes, their sweet scent wafting into my nostrils. How lovely it was here, nestled among the flowers in the rain. If only I could stay right here forever, and never face the cruel world again.

Astreus stirred and, hardly moving a muscle, leapt lightly to the top of the balcony railing, a move no human could perform. He gazed out at the sky, heedless of the narrow rim or tremendous drop beneath his feet, as if it had never occurred to him that balance was a thing that could be lost.

Seeing him, standing atop the balcony rail as casually as a cat, I was reminded of Mephistopheles—not the current zany Mephisto, but my brother back when he was clever, witty, and sane. He loved walking about on high narrow places, causing even Father to fear for his safety. The two of them were strangely alike, Astreus and my brother. I could imagine them striding about on a narrow rail together, Astreus gliding with the ease of a swan, while Mephisto casually spread his arms to steady himself. They would have made fine companions.

Finally, Astreus began to speak.

"Hell is not the cheery and amusing place your poet Dante described," he said. "Nor could he have put into words its true horrors. The creatures who dwell in the Pits are prey to sins and hungers no material being could comprehend. To this mockery of life, I have been consigned, my memory and wits stolen from me. Without them, I cease to be; we elves have not that sacred gift given to the race of Man—the Soul. No part of us safeguards our true selves when our memories are robbed.

"Elves who take the Last Walk become demons; their very nature transforms. The beautiful and fey thing we once were is no more. Instead, a creature of hideous evil is born. Their elvish self, all that makes them unique from others, is lost, gone forever, never to be seen again, even unto the end of time.

"The nature of a tithed elf is transformed; his strengths and abilities remain and are used by the nether powers for nefarious ends. For, without a Soul, he has no capacity to resist evil. Usually, those who are chosen to Walk are the feeblest of us: weaklings, petty criminals, beings of little consequence in Faery and of as little in their service to Hell.

"I, however, am no bogey or feyling—whose addition to the forces of Hell is like unto a drop of rain in the ocean. I am one of the Lords of the High Council, a creature of power and prestige, a lord of wind, and rain, of stars and sky. If I am destroyed, and a demon comes to be in my stead—woe to all whom I once ruled and loved."

Astreus fell silent and gazed up at the sky. When he continued, there was a different quality to his voice, something I could not place.

"Yet, even my position as a Lord of the High Council is of little consequence, when compared to my true estate."

He turned his head. His irises burned with a golden fire.

"Once, I was an angel." Might and majesty whipped about him like a cloak. It was as if he had suddenly grown in stature, filling the entire sky.

I stood, awed. I should have expected something like this. While we waited for our host back at Father Christmas's, Mab and I had visited the mansion's enormous sauna. Three other members of the elven High Council had come in, and I had glimpsed the long teardrop-shaped scars that marred their shoulder blades.

Yet, it was one thing to know that their wings had been shorn and another entirely to see Heaven's fire burning in Astreus's eyes. Even in the eyes of elves, I had seen nothing like it.

"No mere messenger was I," Astreus's voice was stern and majestic, "but a member of the Choir of Cherubim, the second highest order of angels. If

I am destroyed, and a demon is born in my place . . . it shall be a dark day for all who love the Light."

My jaw sagged open in astonishment. He had been of the Choir of the Cherubim? Only one level below Heaven's highest? I felt suddenly unworthy to stand in his presence. Even Muriel Sophia, the angel whose visit had so filled me with awe had only been a virtue, two whole steps below Cherubim.

To have known Heaven's warmth and lost it . . . I thought of my own recent loss and suspected I had an inkling of what that might be like.

"And, if you should die . . ." I asked.

"All that I am shall be extinguished like the flame on a candle, and Hell shall be robbed of its victory."

"I'm confused . . ." I tried to sort it all out, but my mind whirled. "You've been Seir for some time, right? And yet, right now, you are Astreus."

He touched the circlet upon his head. "I am only Astreus while I wear this crown. The horse hoof set into it protects me from the effects of the Lethe. While I am wearing it, I recall all the things its waters have caused me to forget."

I remembered the first time I saw the circlet, resting on a pedestal at Father Christmas's beside the barred and locked Uttermost Door.

"Father Christmas knew you were coming?" I asked. "He put the crown out for you?"

Astreus nodded. "He called me from the depths of Hell, so that I could present you with the gift you had requested." A gentle smile curled the corners of Astreus's lips. "Bromigos certainly takes his gift-giving seriously."

I nodded, recalling that Bromigos was the elvish name for Father Christmas. "So you have been Seir all this time, since 1634, except for this Christmas and now?"

"There have been one or two other moments of clarity, but . . . yes."

"But . . . if you are going to entirely turn into Seir and lose Astreus forever, wouldn't this transformation have happened already? Why is today different from yesterday?"

"I had hope."

"What changed?"

The heavenly light faded until his eyes became a dull lusterless black. When he answered, his gaze was focused far away, as if he saw some remote place or time, his voice distant and flat.

"For over three hundred years, I have endured horrors and hungers too terrible to name. Yet, I have escaped total annihilation because I did not quaff the entire cup of Lethe water, but held some in my mouth and spat it out upon the black sand when none were looking—a trick taught to me by Mephisto. Because of this, I have been able to hold on to a tiny vestige of myself, hidden beneath the darkness of my incubus mind.

"Each moment I dwell in the Pit," he continued, "this true part of me suffers unspeakably. If I were to succumb and forget myself, even for an instant, what little is left of me would be shredded into pieces and dispersed into the darkness, never to be reunited. Astreus Stormwind would be no longer.

"I have been able to resist this onslaught of torments because the hope burning in my breast was greater than any sorrow. Each time pain threatened to engulf me, I endured because I believed that someday I would be saved."

"How?"

"By you, Miranda, daughter of Prospero."

"By me?" I cried. "Saved how?"

"I would away, whither I will, even now—spirit myself to some secret glade or hidden grove and never return to the ravages of the Pit—except I cannot. My oath to Hell binds me."

"A Sibyl." My voice barely broke a whisper. "You needed a Sibyl to absolve you of your oath."

No wonder he had copied Diaphobe's book with his own hand!

"It had been my cherished hope that you would one day reach that high estate," he replied. "Able to free men from unwise oaths. First, you would free your brother. Once Mephisto was able to remember the truth, he would recall what I had done for him, and how he had created an enchanted figurine in my image. Then, in gratitude for my efforts upon his behalf, he would summon me up and ask you to free me from my imprisonment. For three centuries, this hope kept me afloat amidst a sea of darkness and torment. A hope Osae has dashed, even as he stole from you your heart's desire."

Tears welled up and slid down my cheeks. I turned away, hiding my face in the orchids. He stepped lightly to the balcony floor, his footsteps echoing softly against the stone as he drew closer. He came up directly behind me, so close that, while we did not touch, I could feel the warmth of his body against my back.

Suddenly, I soared through the tempest-torn sky, storm winds for my wings, Father's island far beneath me. My chamber, the balcony, my body, all had fallen away and I could not find them. Panic rose, though I had no body in which to feel it. I strained vigorously to shake myself free, to awake, but this dream gripped me like a madness and would not relinquish its hold.

From somewhere, far away, I still heard Astreus's words falling as softly as morning dew. Listening to them I was able to follow the sound back to myself, but the dream of the storm remained around me, joyous now instead of frightening. I wished I could dream this dream forever.

"I blame myself," Astreus spoke calmly. "If I had been more vigilant, this tragedy would not have occurred. I knew of Osae's scheme and had been shadowing him. When he came to you in the guise of Mab, I was present to protect you. Though I was not needed, due to the timely arrival of the Demonslayer. But, alas, this time I was recovering from grievous wounds— dealt me by the spear *Gungnir* and Prince Mephistopheles, whom I encountered outside the mansion of your brother Erasmus—and could not be there at your side."

I recalled watching Mephistopheles launch himself from Erasmus's roof, having scented one of the Three Shadowed Ones. Apparently, he found Seir and fought him before the incubus could enter Erasmus's house. That explained why neither Ferdinand nor Seir ever showed up at the party.

My back still to him, I asked softly, "Astreus, what happened to Mephisto?"

"That fateful night when first you and I met, your brother Mephisto and I recognized in each other something of our own nature. We fell in together and swore an oath of eternal brotherhood. In return for his promise to me, I vowed to help him win the heart of the Faery Queen.

"Unbeknownst to me, Mephisto knew dark arts. Foolishly, he employed these arts to bind the queen. Only Queen Maeve had darker secrets of her own. She tricked him into swearing by the Styx, a terrible oath, too terrible to speak of."

"To slay Eurynome," my voice quivered.

"You know?"

"I also know that Maeve is Lilith. Were you . . . were you in league with her?"

He uttered a short harsh laugh, drawing back. The dream of storm and wings of wind vanished, and I stood upon my own two feet again, blinking and unsteady.

It was a frightening thing to lose touch with one's senses. Mab's admonitions against mortals trafficking with elves took on new meaning, and I wished again that I had taken him more seriously. As I drew back, farther from the elf lord, I wondered if this was how Mephisto felt in his madness.

"Would that I was!" Astreus lowered his head. "No. I was merely a hapless bystander, constrained by my oath of fellowship to aid Mephisto. I brought him water from the Lethe, so that, in drinking it, he could forget his oath and escape. In revenge, the quee . . ." He doubled over coughing, as he had once before upon my hearth in the guise of Ferdinand. I stepped toward him, but as I did so, the earth fell away again, and I soared among the stars, which revolved around me like burning diamonds. I could not have reached him to help him had his life depended on it. With a great effort, I wrenched my thoughts back to my body. Backing away from him, I found myself in my father's house again, my feet again firm upon the stone of the balcony.

Recovering from his coughing bout, he said hoarsely, "I beg your pardon, Miranda. Part of my heinous oath forbids me from revealing the truth about she whose true nature you already know. For my part in helping your brother, I was sentenced to take the Last Walk—to drink of the Lethe myself and fulfill that sevenyear's obligation to Hell."

"And then she held a celebration in your honor." I nodded.

"A cruel ruse. The queen could hardly tell the court she intended to tithe a Lord of the High Council!"

"Why did you not ask the Elf King for help?"

"She had bound me to secrecy with dark oaths, then compelled me join in the merriment and smile as she mocked me."

"But how could you be Seir? The demon Seir was already hunting Theo when we first met you, back in 1627.

"The Demonslayer destroyed the previous Seir, back in 1635. This was soon after I reached the pit. Before his demise was published, I donned his robes and took his name. True demons, such as Baelor and Osae, return to Hell when they are slain. But demons who had once been elves die the True Death when they are killed. The previous Seir had been a tithed elf, too." He scowled. "Apparently, we elves make good incubi."

For some unaccountable reasons, I blushed. "I can't imagine why."

Raising my head, I blurted out a question that had been haunting me. "Do you remember the things you said and did as Seir and as Ferdinand?"

He tilted his head back and narrowed his eyes. My cheeks grew even warmer as I recalled some of the things he had done.

"Much of it. Some is hazy. I remember my time as Ferdinand better than as Seir, but this might be because so many things Ferdinand encountered—

you, Ariel, Mephisto's figurine—were familiar to me as Astreus." His mir-ror gaze gave nothing away. I had no notion which parts he remembered and which were hazy.

Of course! That had been his own figurine he picked up by the fireplace, the one he was counting upon to save him! No wonder he had questioned me about it so intently. And to think I had thought he was jealous.

"Why did you, as Ferdinand, claim my father had sent him to Hell?"

"It is the calling of demons to breed mistrust and discord."

"That makes sense," I replied, especially considering the distress these claims had stirred in my heart. "Mab kept warning us about that."

"Mab is wise in the ways of spirits. He knows much."

I found myself gazing up into his eyes, which had turned a brilliant blue. "You did all this for my brother's sake?"

"For him, and for the hope his friendship brought me. The hope that, with my help, his sister might one day become a Sibyl and free me from the oath that binds all elves to Hell."

Astreus stepped closer. His eyes were now as green as emeralds, the same shade as mine. He placed a hand on my shoulder and lowered his head. His breath came warm upon my face. Heart hammering, I hoped he might kiss me.

Perhaps he did, but if so, I was no longer present to enjoy it.

CHAPTER TWENTY-ONE

Pride of Angels

I dreamt of a tower of thorns rising from mist the color of a dead man's face. These barbs were so terrible that my eyes burned, and blood ran down my cheeks, just from looking at them. Then, I was within the tower, bound by spiny vines to a bed of thorns. Their spiky tips gouged my flesh, sending shooting pains throughout my limbs. Beneath me, needlelike points pushed into my spinal cord. I feared I would soon be paralyzed.

My thoughts chased each other endlessly. I could not understand where I was, or how I had left the safety of my father's home. Perhaps Astreus had betrayed me. Perhaps he had been Seir all along.

Oh, why had I not listened to Mab?

Robed figures carrying mist-gray sickles glided into the chamber where I lay. They opened their mouths and spoke pain instead of words. As I writhed, spasms of agony racking my body with each utterance, I understood them to be asking me to denounce Heaven and swear an oath of obedience to Hell.

I cried out to my Lady, but she did not heed me. Terrified, I struggled, striving against the vines that immobilized me. The bindings held fast, and my efforts only increased the agony. Pain exploded in my mind, washing out thought the way a brilliant light washes out vision. Yet pain is merely sensation and can be resisted. It was the wrongness that undid me.

As I lay, writhing in agony, I became aware of strange unnatural impulses that grew more powerful by the moment, until they ruled me like a burning lust. Much the way a lover longs for the caress of his beloved, I longed to rip open my stomach and play with my innards, running the intestines lovingly through my hand. I wanted to impale my eyeballs upon the thorns—so vividly could I picture the exquisite moment when the sharp point would pierce the soft gelatinous globes and they would go splat. I desired to strive against the vines so as to force the cruel barbs to plunge repeatedly into my tender flesh. Hunger gnawed at me, but it was a hunger to consume fire and to drink bile, to eat refuse and lick grime. Most of all, I wanted, thirsted for, *needed* the pleasure that comes from violating innocence and sullying goodness. Without that, surely I would die, my very body consumed by the heat of my desires. Yet, even that thought caused a blush of eager excitement.

Anything! I would do anything to end this nightmare . . . if it was even a nightmare.

Swear, whispered a voice in my mind, *swear the oath and be free of this anguish. What is Heaven to thee?*

THEN, the tower was gone. In its place, a glade of feathery ferns beneath towering ancient pines. I knelt there, curled against Astreus's chest, his arms encircling me. My body quaked with fear. The elf lord held me tightly, caressing my hair and whispering soothing words.

"Hush, Sweet Miranda, all is right with the world. The nightmare is banished."

"Where are we? What happened to me?" I whispered, my voice shaky.

"We have become intertwined, you and I, our fates linked, ever since that fateful midsummer's day when first we breathed the same air. Now, you even dream my dreams, for which you have my deepest regrets. We elves often walk among one another's dreams. But humans cannot, so I took no steps to guard you."

"If men cannot . . . how did it happen? Unless . . ." I blinked back tears. Astreus regarded me silently, waiting. "My brothers claim that my m-mother was . . . some kind of ogress."

"That would explain much," the elf replied gravely. "I offer you my condolences."

"How so?"

"Sheep huddle in flocks and wolves run in packs, but we elves are of no congregation. We belong neither to the Company of Men, nor to the Choir of Angels. A gathering of elves is like unto a clowder of cats. While scholars may have put a name to a collection of felines, no one has ever witnessed a clowder. Upon occasion, cats are seen perched near each other, but there is never a community among them.

"So it is with us. Nor can we find pity in our heart for those unlike ourselves, any more than pack pities flock, or swarm pities gaggle. Thus, we find our days solitary and cold. Is it so with you? Do you find yourself separate from all around you, like the offspring of a sheep and a horse, neither of flock nor of herd?"

"Something like that," I murmured tremulously, resentful to learn yet another thing that supported Erasmus's theory regarding my mother. In my heart of hearts, I felt certain Erasmus was wrong, and yet there was so much evidence suggesting otherwise.

Almost as if reading my thoughts, Astreus reached forward and tilted my chin, regarding my face. "You have none of the brutishness common in ogre-get. Perhaps, your mother was some more celestial spirit: a fairy, perhaps, or a sylph."

I did not answer but thought glumly to myself, Or perhaps my father consecrated me to Eurynome to cure me of that very brutishness.

I trembled in his arms, amidst the fragrant ferns and silent pine trees. He bent his head and kissed the center of my forehead. A warmth spread through me, and some of the fear began to drain away.

"What . . . was that I just . . . You dream about pain and torture?"

"A memory only," Astreus said soothingly. "Dredged up by our words."

"That was your memory?" I was shocked to think of him as suffering such torment. "No wonder you swore the oath!"

Astreus's eyes went the color of dried blood. "After the war between Heaven and Hell, the gates of Paradise were closed against us. Of those left outside, most descended below, becoming demons. Those who were left remained in the places in between, becoming elves. The Great Seven of Hell then made war upon the elves. When the battle finally ended, the terms called for the elves to pay a tithe to Hell. The members of the High Council were called upon to swear an oath promising to uphold this new order.

"I was the last elf to swear the oath to Hell," he said. "I would not swear, for so long as I did not acknowledge the demons as my master, I was still free to reenter Heaven should the gates open."

"But weren't you cast from Heaven for rebelling?" I asked.

"I, rebel?" Astreus drew himself up, his eyes suddenly tempestuous. "Never!"

"Then how did you come to be trapped outside the gate?" I asked.

"In the days before the fall, I was—for lack of a more apt term—an explorer angel. My task was to fly into the Void and bring the light of Heaven to places where it had not previously shone. When the trumpet call came to return and join the battle against Lucifer and his rebels . . ." A great sadness came over Astreus's face. "I tarried."

"And by the time you got back, the gates were shut?" I asked, placing my hand gently upon his arm.

He nodded and lowered his head, ashamed.

Raising his head, he continued. "In an effort to persuade me to swear, the demons kept me imprisoned in the Tower of Pain for well past a thousand years, the thorns of which are so painful that even glancing upon them causes harm."

"I saw them." I trembled again. Reaching up, I touched my cheek. My fingers came away stained with blood. I cried out, terrified, and Astreus drew me more tightly against his chest.

"Hush. 'Tis only a dream," he promised reassuringly.

So, this was a dream, too? That made sense. It explained why I was not back at my father's house. My senses told me I was seated amidst sweet-smelling pines and soft feathery ferns. If I concentrated, however, I could feel the hard stone of the balcony under my feet. I looked down at my hands, still dripping red with my blood, and shivered.

"But for you . . . it was real."

His eyes turned pale as bone. "Each day, I was tortured thus, yet still I would not yield to Hell, for that meant forgoing all hope of returning to Heaven."

"You withstood *that*? F-for centuries? For a millennium?" I cringed, embarrassed at my own weakness. "I had hardly lasted ten seconds."

"I would have resisted forever, except the other elves began tithing my people, and I could not conscience that. So, I relented and swore. These events took place long, long ago—before the birth of your planet, probably before the birth of your sun—yet still they weigh heavily upon me." He paused. "It was because of this same oath to Hell that I was constrained to obey when Queen Maeve ordered me to take the Last Walk, after she discovered how I had helped your brother Mephisto to escape her trap."

"But I thought your people were of the air. Surely, there was not air before the birth of our sun?"

Astreus laughed. "Do you think your world is the only one with air? Nay, Mab's race is far older than that."

"A thousand years!" I repeated, looking at him with newfound respect. "I could not have held out an hour!"

"You do not know what it is like to have known Heaven's glory and lost it."

Astreus turned away and gazed off into the dream forest. I was left looking at his profile, which was beautiful and filled me with longing. Eventually, he began speaking again.

"Imagine you went to live in a house that looked a great deal like your father's mansion, only nothing was ever quite right. The doors would not close properly. The well did not work. The servants were rude. The walls were moldy. The halls smelled of rotting fruit, and no matter how many logs you put on the fire, you were always cold.

"Nor can you ever grow used to this new house, precisely because it reminds you so much of your old home. You cannot see the blighted rose without recalling the beauty of your old gardens. You cannot walk the corridors without its layout bringing to mind the house you loved. You cannot look through the dingy windows at the overcast sky without remembering the glorious skies above the mansion of your youth. Everything you see makes you heartsick for the original, of which this current place is but a dark reflection. That is what it is like to remember Heaven and dwell on Earth."

ABRUPTLY I was back on the balcony, as Astreus—the real, waking Astreus—drew away. I was not sitting, but standing exactly where I had been when he leaned toward me and I thought he might kiss me.

I felt a pang of regret.

Nervously, I put my hands to my face, feeling my eyes and cheeks. They were damp, but my fingers came away wet with tears alone.

The elves had been tithing his people, Astreus said. The Aerie Ones were his people. Mab's voice echoed in my thoughts: *Lord Astreus did my people a great good once.* Was this what Mab had meant? No wonder they loved him!

The elf lord had walked over to the railing where he gazed silently into the storm. A full five minutes went by. I waited patiently, stray raindrops dampening my hair. When he finally spoke, his voice was low, as if coming from a great distance.

"One day, many eons ago, Carbonel Lightfoot told me of a fabulous beast, the White Hart, whom he claimed could free men and elves from sorrow, even from the very clutches of Hell. I followed her for a year and a day, and when I finally came upon her she looked not like a hart, but like a white kirin with a single horn rising from the center of her head. I knelt before her and asked her to free me from my oath to Hell, that I might try to find my way back to Heaven. She told me that one day a maiden would come, a Sibyl bearing her mark, who would free not only myself, but all the elves. I thought . . . you might be she."

"All the elves . . . !" I gasped.

Oh, how I would have loved to have been the Sibyl who freed the elves from Hell! Much of the evil elves do was done to placate their dark masters. What might they be like if they were free? They may still be freed someday, of course, but I would not be the one to do it. It was someone else's story now.

"Unaware of her duplicitous nature," Astreus ran his finger along an orchid pedal, "I foolishly told all I had learned to Queen Maeve, for I assumed the Elf Queen would be as delighted as I to learn that Fairyland might one day throw off the yoke of Hell. She aped interest, of course, plying me with questions. Only much later did I realize her dark intent. Since that day, she has done all she could to oppose me, and it was to keep me from pursuing this matter that she tithed me. My theft of the water of the Lethe on Mephisto's behalf was but an excuse.

"Even at Father Christmas's, she sent Sylvie—whom she knew I had once desired above all others—to me in hopes of keeping me from withdrawing with you, a Handmaiden of the Unicorn. Had she known what gift I held for you, I am certain she would have made a much greater effort to keep us apart. Alas, for us, she found a simpler and crueler way to kill both of our dreams."

"I am so sorry," I whispered. "But why did you wait so long to begin with? Why didn't you ask another Sibyl?"

"I have not been able to find one," he replied. " 'Twas a time when Sibyls were often seen in Fairyland, but these last handful of centuries, there has been nary a one. Even Handmaidens are hard to come by these days. You were my last hope."

Astreus returned to watching the rain, which had died down to a light pleasant drizzle.

"This is the last time I will ever see the sky, yet the storm fails. Does it not know the agony in my heart?" he whispered, his voice ragged. Turning to me, he eyed my flute and asked, "Will you play for me, Miranda?"

Wordlessly, I raised the flute and began to play. The winds rose. The rain danced. Dark thunderheads raced like black galleons across the gray heavens. The tempest howled, shaking rocks free of the mountainside to bounce and crash into the valley below. Astreus watched this as might a caged and bedraggled eagle that stared through the bars of its prison at the wide freedom of the sky.

He turned his head, and our eyes met. The pounding of the rain sang to us, and I saw reflected in his stormy eyes the same love of wind, storm, and weather that beat so fiercely in my breast. While he spoke not a word, I felt as if I could hear his voice in my heart, whispering.

"*It is as if we were made to be together, Miranda. The storm calls to us, and our hearts cannot help dancing. We are the same, you and I. You know it to be true.*"

I lowered my flute and closed my eyes, just listening to the storm. I could not kill Astreus, I realized, not matter how he beseeched me. Surely, there was another way. Surely, my Lady could . . . Only I no longer had a Lady. Tears spilled over my lashes and mingled with the rain.

Astreus leaned over me and wiped away my tears with his fingers. As his fingers brushed my cheek, the modern world fell away, and we were dancing, he and I, amidst the May Day revel where we first met. Fairy lights glittered in the pine boughs overhead, and elvish music played from the open door in the hill. Farther away, slightly blurred, I could see the others— Erasmus, Father, Cornelius, Logistilla. A sane Mephistopheles danced with the Elf Queen, and Theophrastus, young and hale, partnered a lovely elf maid.

We danced together, gliding over the grass. His eyes mirrored the night sky, and his laughter rang about us like song. Leaning toward me, he brushed his lips against mine. His mouth tasted of wind and honeysuckle. I moaned softly, and he drew me tightly against him. Our kiss deepened, my arms snaked about his neck . . . and encountered empty air.

I stood back on the balcony. Astreus stood a little ways away, his expression unreadable. I blushed and turned away, uncertain whose dream I had just been dreaming.

"Ah, the glories of what might have been . . ." he murmured as we stared into the storm.

"I could not have become a Sibyl in any case," I murmured sadly, as I watched the rain plunge into the depths of the ravine. "To do so, I would have had to free the Aerie Ones, and I could not. My father's plan requires that they be bound a while longer . . . for mankind's sake."

Gone was my noble companion. Where he had been stood some fey and wild thing. The winds whipped about him until his sable opera cape billowed and his storm-dark hair rippled about his head. His eyes burned like black coals, blazing with barely controlled fury.

I drew back, frightened.

"Fool!" Astreus cried. "Had you but freed me from my oath, I could have curbed the Aerie Ones upon your behalf! They are my people! Commanding them not to harm your precious mortals would have been the least of prices to pay. Had you but freed them—I could have been free! Mephisto could have been saved, and you would have been a Sibyl. Everything you and I desire could have been ours!"

"I-I didn't realize . . ." I whispered, heartsick.

"Slaver and daughter of a thief!" he spat, drawing splendor about him like a cloak. "You and your family have been the undoing of me. You have done me irreparable harm, while I have done nothing to warrant this terrible fate which befalls me. Every fond thought I have held of you has become a burning coal in my heart. The hope you represented was nothing. You are a lie!"

"That's hardly fair. I never promised you anything!" I cried. "It was not even me you wanted, but a Sibyl. I have never been and never will be a Sibyl!"

"Obviously not! You are unworthy of the station!"

I recoiled, eyes stinging.

"Enough, I return to Hell. I would not allow one such as you to kill me! You are contemptible! Perhaps I can leave enough of myself in Seir to force him to seek death at Theophrastus's hands."

Astreus stormed away, yanking the circlet of silver and horn from his head. Darkness began gathering about him.

Frightened, I stuck my flute behind my back and grabbed my fan. I started to move forward, but he raised a hand to stop me. I halted.

"Stand over there," he pointed to the balcony railing.

I could not tell if this was Astreus or Seir talking. Dubious, I backed up until I was pressed against the stone railing, facing him, my hand curled around the haft of my fan, which was hidden behind my back. For a moment, he stood regarding me; my dark hair and pale features framed by the violence of the storm.

"Why over here?" I asked hoarsely.

As Seir's dark shape faded slowly away, Astreus's voice hung in the air: "Because I would have my last memory be of the two things I most loved."

I SANK to my knees and knelt, cradling my head in my arms.

Oh, if only I had listened to Mab when he told me to leave well enough alone! Perhaps, if I had turned my back on the message in Father's journals, my pleasant orderly life would never have come unraveled. Instead, I had lost my innocence. My Lady had abandoned me. The lovely mother I had always idolized had turned out to be a myth. The holy love between my father and his wife, which I had believed in since my childhood, might be a lie. I had learned my father, whom I had always adored, had secretly enslaved me so I would not take after my birth mother, an ugly twisted witch. My dreams had been dashed; my immortal brothers and sisters made mortal. The only glimmer of love I had found after an eternity of solitude was now lost forever. I had lost Astreus. I had lost Ferdinand. I had lost my Lady. I had lost everything.

How long I wept, I cannot say, but the sky was growing dark when I finally wiped my eyes. So black was my despair that I could not go on or move without some kind of help or guidance. If my Lady would not answer me, I would have to go elsewhere. I thought of Gregor and, for the second time in my long life, I prayed to God.

"Please," I prayed. "Help me. Give me hope."

The setting sun coming through the leaves cast a deep golden light over the balcony, and the freshly washed air smelled of water lilies and of some heavenly scent I could not place. A calm seemed to settle over the ravine, soothing my ragged spirits. Only, I was facing south, so how could I be bathed in the light of the sunset?

Something hovered above me shining with a golden glow. My fan and the flute were both out of reach, scattered across the balcony where I had dropped them in my misery. Yet, even as I began to panic, a sense of peace came upon me that was so pervasive as to utterly banish fear.

An angel stood upon the air, shining with a golden light. Delicate silver slippers shod her feet. Pearls the color of a new moon glowed at the waist, sleeves, and neck of her gown of purest green. Five sets of wings—white with a touch of black, like the wings of sea gulls—spread out from her shoulders and back, and five halos, each a perfect circle, rose above her head: one of white light, one of ocean spray, one of water lilies sprinkled with perfect water drops, one of white river foam, and the last of golden light, like a shining wedding ring.

"Rejoice!"

The sound of her heavenly voice was so lovely as to bring tears of joy to my eyes, as if I heard the speech that divine thing of which a flute was merely a material approximation.

"Who are you?" I breathed.

"I am she who brings the wisdom that shatters illusions, the draught that is sweet upon the lips but bitter in the stomach. At the Will of the Most High, I once brought such a draught to a boy called Solomon. Do you not know me, my Child?"

"I know you," I whispered.

Muriel Sophia! The angel who first visited me long ago, after the death—I knew now—of Ferdinand! When she had appeared to me, I had been wandering, ghostlike, down the red corridors of *Castello Sforzesco,* aimless and hopeless. I had been lost to grief, and her visit had saved me.

"You ask me to rejoice." My voice cracked from sorrow and awe. "How can I, when everything worth rejoicing about has been taken from me?"

"Sorrow does not become thee, Child. Rejoice and fear not, for it is the Father's good pleasure to give you the Kingdom."

"What Kingdom? Heaven?"

"Earth."

"The Earth?" I rocked back and rose to my feet. "What do you mean?"

"Into the hands of Solomon, the Most High placed rulership of the Earth," replied the Virtue. *"Prospero and his children are Solomon's heirs. Yours is the duty to guard the mortal world from the forces of Hell."*

"Will Solomon's dream die with us?"

"Throughout the ages, I have watched over the ORBIS SULEIMANI, *sheltering them beneath my wings; inspiring them to remain true to their purpose; shepherding them when they have strayed. This charge shall I continue until the end of the world."*

"The *Orbis Suleimani!*" I cried. "Of course!"

I had not considered their role in all this. As we grew old and feeble, we could place our staffs back into the hands of the organization Solomon set up as jailers for these very demons. With an angel guiding them, perhaps they could hold out against the mechanizations of Baelor and his ilk. After all, they had held out for centuries before Father came along.

This was not just any angel, I realized abruptly. This was the guardian angel of mankind; the angel who was charged with the task of protecting the human race from the ravages of the supernatural; the angel for which the *Orbis Suleimani*—and therefore my family—worked! A feeling of awe and wonder flowed through me so all-consuming that for a time, I could not speak.

"Is there no hope for my family?" I asked finally. "Will we perish as the Angel of the Bottomless Pit predicted?"

"Hope is eternal, as certain of your poets have said."

"How? What can we do?"

"Each member of your family carries a secret flaw, a private sin. You must overcome these vices and act together, if you wish to complete your task."

"You mean the sin that carrying a demon-infested staff has engendered?" I asked.

The glorious woman placed her palm upon my head. I saw a vision of my family: Erasmus sitting with his head lowered in despair; Theo raising his fist, his face red with wrath; Mephisto lying in a bed with three barmaids; Cornelius placing pins sporting the symbol of the *Orbis Suleimani* on a map of the world, his calmness belying his ambition; Titus lazing on a couch, too slothful to rise; old stocky Gregor, his eyes dark with hatred; Logistilla gnawing on her fingers as she stared enviously; Ulysses greedily slipping someone else's jewels into his vest pocket.

Muriel Sophia spoke in her heavenly voice. *"Only Gregor comes close to mastering of his passions and conquering his sin, and only of late, since his seeming death."*

I nodded, but my thoughts were elsewhere. Erasmus, despair? Malice I would have understood, or pride, but when had cool casual Erasmus become a victim of despair? Was this a recent thing, since Osae's attack? I thought of asking, but decided the angel might not take kindly to being doubted.

I had seen nothing of myself. For a moment, I congratulated myself on being the one perfect child among my father's flawed offspring. Yet, I knew better.

"And what of my sin, Angel?"

"Pride, my child, the sin of Lucifer." The angel lifted my chin with her shining hand. *"You carry in your heart the Pride of Angels. It is your great glory and your great sorrow."*

It was not to my credit that her words pleased me. "Pride of Angels"— it sounded glorious. And yet, at the same time, I knew despair, for I recognized her pronouncement as true. My pride was like a great crown, stiff and unwieldy, keeping me from bending even when bending would serve me.

"What should I do?"

"Prospero is yet needed on the Earth. He must not be allowed to perish before his time. Recalling him with the Staff of Eternity *will fail. Waste no time upon it. Go to him and bring him bodily from Hell. Between you and your siblings, you have all that is needed to succeed."*

I had expected more platitudes. This practical advice startled and cheered me. Could Father be saved? For the first time since Osae's attack, hope rekindled in my heart.

"Is there anything we should know?"

"Only that no man is asked to give more than he is able," the beautiful Virtue replied. *"Yet oft' men underestimate what it is within them to give. Give what is required, and your reward shall be greater than you can now imagine."*

Her words struck me as ominous, and yet, here in her presence, I could not recall exactly what fear felt like. I recalled that I often had a nervous feeling in my stomach and a tension in my shoulders, and that sometimes my heart beat rapidly . . . but I could not recall the exact sensation, or why it troubled me so much.

Once, I walked across a battlefield strewn with dead French soldiers in their handsome blue and white uniforms. I recalled stepping respectfully over their bodies, a handkerchief perfumed with lavender pressed against my nose to keep out the stink of rotting corpses. Everywhere was war and desolation, burnt cottages, ruined crops, the horrible, buglelike bellow of wounded horses.

Rounding around a broken supply cart, I came upon a stone church. The door hung open. I called out to the priest and entered. I do not remember what I was looking for—directions, perhaps, or clean water. I do not remember if I found it, or even if there was a priest present after all. What I do remember was the cloister.

After passing down the aisle through the dark pews, I stepped out the back door and into the walled garden that stood between the sanctuary and the rectory. A mosaic pebble path ran between two ponds upon which lotuses floated. Lily-of-the-valley grew around the ponds. A little wagtail wet its wings in a bird bath. The moss-covered walls rose to either side of me, blocking out all but the canapé of a tall birch.

I let my handkerchief fall to the pebbly path and breathed in the fresh earthy scent. Above, the sky was a pure and cloudless blue. I could hear no sound from outside the thick walls—no soldiers moaning; no weeping of wives, too recently widowed to have yet donned their black weeds; no beasts in pain—only the splashy flutter of a single blue-headed wagtail.

Standing there, amidst that island of serenity, I found I could no longer remember the war outside the wall. The beauty and tranquility here were so incongruous with the horror outside, that they could not both exist in the same universe. I could recall it, as if from a dream, but I could not really believe in it.

Once I stepped outside again and inhaled the smoke of burning flesh, it all came rushing back. So much so that the cloister was now the dream. And yet, it was a dream that would not fade, a dream that reminded me that even in the midst of devastation, peace still bloomed.

Speaking to the angel was like stepping again into that cloister and breathing once more the fragrant air within the shelter of its tall mossy walls.

"I will," I vowed. "Whatever is required, I will accomplish."

"One last thing, Child. Obedience is a virtue, and yet so is discernment. Angels have no free will for they partake of the Divine Word directly, but the children of men must learn to listen to the whisper of Divine Will within their hearts, that which men call wisdom. You were not meant to lean on your Father, or even Eurynome, forever."

The fifth halo grew brighter, its golden glow warming me like sunlight. The more I basked in it—letting it spill into and illuminate the dark spaces in my mind—the more real it became to me, until the gold light seemed substantial, and the world around me faded like a dream. The stone of the balcony, the orchid-covered wall, and my room beyond all grew misty and indistinct, insubstantial. Glancing down, I experienced an instant of panicked vertigo, for the rock beneath my feet was fading, and I could see the sheer drop of the ravine beneath me. The instant passed, however, for I could not truly fear while I abided in the secret place of the angel's radiance.

"I have stayed too long and must depart," the angel said. *"Your material world is too fragile to long sustain one of my high estate. It will fade like a dream should I stay longer. I must away before it vanishes altogether, as I wish no harm to those dwelling here within."*

The golden light of the fifth halo grew so bright I could hardly see anything else, and yet no matter how bright it became, it did not hurt my eyes. As the lovely form of the Virtue faded into pure gold, I heard her beautiful voice ring out one last time.

"Fear not, Child, for I am with thee always."

EVEN after the heavenly glow was gone, I remained where I was, silently basking in the peace that remained in the wake of the angel's visit. My heart felt so calm and filled with hope. The sorrow that had gripped me only minutes before seemed something of a forgotten age.

I knew it would return, that the peace brought by the angel would fade, and the agony would come again—the terrible loss of my Lady's presence, the sorrow over Astreus's fate, and the pain caused by our less-than-amicable parting. At the moment, however, all was peaceful, and the causes of my distress seemed as far away as the moon.

Returning inside, I glanced at the chessboard beside the hearth to see that the black knight now threatened the white king. Peering closer revealed the check to be mate. My chuckle died in my throat, however, as, upon glancing up, I discovered the gift that had been granted my family.

Next to my fireplace, against the wall, rested a length of black wood marked with blood red runes. Whether by accident or design, Seir of the Shadows had left me Gregor's staff.

CHAPTER TWENTY-TWO

Abandon All Hope, Ye . . .

"This has got to be the most cockamamie thing I've ever let you talk me into, Ma'am," grumbled Mab.

"You didn't have to come," I reminded him.

"What, and let you all stomp off to face demons without a cautious voice among you?" Mab scoffed. "Might as well kill you myself, Ma'am. Besides, someone has to keep an eye on that accursed flute and make sure it doesn't fall into the hands of the enemy after you Prosperos all perish horribly."

We were, all of us, crawling on our hands and knees down a lightless, dusty passage. The tunnel began in the crate Mab, Mephisto, and I had found in the Maryland warehouse—the crate containing the gate through which Father had originally fallen into Hell. Mephisto and Mab had fetched it using Ulysses's staff, and Theo had warded it in such a way as to keep ghouls and barghests from pouring out of it onto Father's Island.

We had started out with flashlights and headlamps, but they failed after only a hundred feet or so. Gregor managed to suck up the palpable darkness into his staff, but we were still stuck crawling through darkness of the regular sort.

But none of this mattered to me. Finally, we were underway, all together. Nothing could stop us now.

"Please, Miranda," came Ulysses's voice from somewhere behind me. "It's bad enough we are willfully crawling into Hell on your say-so. Can't you keep your man from talking about our imminent demise?"

"Mab, please don't frighten the masses," I requested.

"As you wish, Ma'am," came his grunted reply.

Erasmus's voice floated back from the blackness ahead of us. "Tell me, again, why I am crawling through this dismal tunnel? Because some demon put on a pretty face, called itself an angel, and told Big Sister Miranda the quickest way to damn us all? Aren't we supposed to be keeping our staffs out of Hell? If so, this hardly seems the wisest course."

"It was a true vision," Cornelius's voice replied. "I do not trust our elder sister, but I trust what I hear. When she spoke of her vision, Miranda's voice held joy. Demons come in many guises and bring many passions—among them glee, excitement, and false hope—but they never bring joy. What Miranda saw was an angel."

"But our angel? It makes no sense! Miranda was never initiated into the *Orbis Suleimani*. Why would our angel come to Miranda? Why would she not appear to those of us who serve her?" asked Erasmus.

"God moves in mysterious ways," replied Gregor's husky near-whisper, "and fills what vessels are available to him. Perhaps Miranda made herself available when the rest of us did not."

"Oooph! Oh, this is ghastly," Logistilla complained as she bumped into Titus. "Ulysses's staff has been to Hell before. Why can't we just teleport there?"

"Because I can only go the one place my staff has been," Ulysses replied. "Believe me, you would not want to go *there!*"

"I don't want to go at all!" whined Logistilla. "What evidence do we have that any other place in Hell will be any better?"

"Light!" cried Mephisto, from up front. From the start, he had abandoned his hands and knees in favor of the hip-stomach-and-elbow wriggle of a soldier's crawl. "I see light! I think we're coming to the end. Yippee!"

"Only Mephisto would cheer our successfully crawling into the Inferno." Logistilla's voice floated up from behind me. "Oh, do hurry! I have a most horrible cramp in my leg!"

I EMERGED from the tunnel through a hole in a clay embankment and adjusted my shoulder bag. Outside, the world was a swirl of featureless mist. Mephisto, Erasmus, Cornelius, and Theo were already standing when I reached the mouth of the tunnel. I climbed to my feet and waited for Mab, Logistilla, Titus, Gregor, Ulysses, and Caliban to join us.

Erasmus and Cornelius had objected to bringing Caliban, so Mephisto had sent him away. Then, once we were in the tunnel, Mephisto had tapped his staff, and Caliban had reappeared, making the point moot. Now he crawled along with the rest of us, toting a heavy club. Titus's children were not with us. They had been deposited back in their home in the Okefenokee, where they were being looked after by their own au pair, along with trusted Aerie Ones, who had been sent by Mustardseed, whom I had managed to speak with briefly.

As I had feared, two of the Priority Contracts had gone awry over the holiday. Mustardseed had handled the first one readily, but the second had resulted in an earthquake in Guatemala I could have prevented had I been in the office. With a heavy heart, I gave Mustardseed orders to carry him through the next few weeks. If I was not back by then, he would have to contact the *Orbis Suleimani* for instructions.

Now, standing in the mists of Limbo, I examined our surroundings. The ambient light issued from the mist itself, which offered a dim glow hardly bright enough to let us see our own hands in front of our faces, much less each other. This swirling mist was all that I could see in any direction, except straight ahead, where, some distance away, two enormous half-moons shone, the points of their crescents facing each other. I recognized it from the sketches in Father's journal. This was the Gate of False Dreams.

Faint manlike shapes, long and drawn, moved through the mist about us, seeking and fleeing each other in some eternal chase. One of these phantom inhabitants passed through Ulysses, who shrieked. His face went utterly pale, and his eyes nearly bulged out of his head. A second tried to pass through me but was turned aside by my enchanted tea gown.

As my gown deflected the shade, an emerald glow, reminiscent of sunlight seen through the canopy of a tall forest, flared. In its bright gleam, I could see my brothers and sister staring at me. I gave them a puzzled glance, and Mephisto pointed over my shoulders.

Behind me stretched wings of emerald light that seemed to originate from the shoulders of my enchanted tea gown. They were not like the wings of birds, but rather an impressionistic indication of the top of a wing; as if painted with thick brushstrokes but unfinished. They were beautiful.

"Whatever bumped into me must have woken some defense in my gown," I said, awed. "Logistilla, you made my dress. Do you know what caused this?"

"No," she frowned enviously.

My sister deliberately stepped in front of a passing shade, who was repulsed by the enchanted fabric of her deep blue robes, which she had retrieved while dropping off the children, but no wings of light appeared.

"Must be some enchantment Father added later," she pouted. "Apparently, he didn't bother to share it with me."

"He must have had his reasons," Theo growled, shifting his pack. He had shaved his beard and donned his Toledo steel sword and his shining armor with its Urim breastplate. It clattered awkwardly against his old body as he walked. Frowning down at himself, he added, "Erasmus, come here and help me secure this armor."

"What, me?" Erasmus looked right and left, as if expecting to see someone else of the same name. His face bore an incredulous expression that reminded me of my familiar, Tybalt, Prince of Cats. Erasmus, too, was wearing the enchanted garments Logistilla had made for him, justacorps and breeches of deep forest green. All those of us who had enchanted garments had retrieved them before gathering at the crate and plunging into Hell. Titus wore his kilt, Gregor his red cardinal robes. Only Ulysses was dressed in perfectly ordinary cloth. Logistilla had never gotten around to making him a set.

"You were my squire, right?"

"When I was six!" Erasmus objected heatedly.

"Nonsense, you were at least ten," Theo replied good-naturedly as he donned his helmet over his goggles. It was winged and had once belonged to an angel.

Sighing, Erasmus trudged over to aid him, while the rest of us began walking through the mists of Limbo toward the Gate of False Dreams.

WE made our way across the spirit-haunted plain. Before us, a great black wall stretched upward and in either direction, as far as the eye could see. Cut into it was a fifty-foot archway, through which we caught a glimpse of more swirling mist beyond. This arching gate was flanked by giant tusks, nine times the size of a man, which shone with an ivory light. While the enormous tusks made us feel insignificant, they themselves were minuscule when compared to the vastness of the wall, which dwarfed everything else. We stood craning our necks and gazing up at this magnificent edifice.

Above the archway, blood-red letters had been carved into the wall. In Latin, it read:

Through me the entrance unto Doom
Through me the gateway to the Lost
Through me the entrance to Everlasting Pain.
Beyond me, Divine power stops, Wisdom fails, and Love ceases.
Justice has weighed: the doom is clear:
ALL HOPE RENOUNCE, YE LOST, WHO ENTER HERE.

"We're planning to walk through there *on purpose?*" Mab asked, gaping at the gate. "You've got to be kidding!"

"This is the Gate of False Dreams . . . meaning that those sucked in by false dreams end up on the far side," Mephisto announced cheerfully. He had attached a string to his magic hat and currently wore it pushed back onto his shoulders. "It marks the boundary between the World of Men and the Nether Realms. Beyond this gate only evil reigns, and that's where we're going."

"Not quite Dante's wording," Caliban stared up in reverent awe. "Though very close."

"Dante had gone all the way through the Inferno into Purgatory and then up through Paradise before he got home to write it down," Mephisto replied cheerfully. "Can we blame the guy for getting a few words in the wrong place?" Turning to the rest of us, he asked, "How are we planning to find out where Daddy is?"

"What a shame we never recovered John Dee's crystal ball," Cornelius said sadly.

Mab hit his forehead with his fist. "Keep forgetting to tell you, Ma'am! That ball can't be destroyed by throwing it! Sure, it explodes when it hits the ground, but it's supposed to do that—a defense built in to protect its owner. After it explodes, it reforms again. It's a famous crystal ball, Ma'am. Merlin used it before John Dee, and Solomon before him. Some people claim it originally belonged to the first magician of all, Seth, son of Adam. It's unlikely Mephisto actually destroyed it. The Catholics must still have it."

Throughout Mab's speech, Mephisto had been shifting uncomfortably. When Mab finished, I calmly held out my hand. "The ball, Mephisto."

The others stared at me.

"Mephisto doesn't have . . ." Titus began, then his voice drifted off, as an abashed Mephisto tapped his staff.

The mist shifted, and I could have sworn a kangaroo jumped upon the plains of Limbo. Then, there really was a kangaroo! The startled creature hopped twice, twitching its long ears nervously. Mephisto gave the beast a playful punch, reached into its pouch, and pulled out a round ball of perfect crystal. The kangaroo nuzzled Mephisto, who tapped his staff again, and it vanished away as quickly as it had come.

"I say!" exclaimed Ulysses, leaning in for a better look at the shiny gleaming crystal ball. "Why didn't you tell us?"

"I, too, would like to hear the answer to that question, Mephistopheles," mused Cornelius, leaning on his staff. The light from my wings dyed the bandages wrapped across his eyes an emerald green.

"Heck if I know." Mephisto shrugged. "Don't remember."

"How convenient," murmured Erasmus.

Mab regarded Mephisto coolly. "And all this time you've been using that ball to learn secrets and spy on people? Humph! Explains a lot."

The rest of us might have had more to say on the matter, but Logistilla began looking fervently about behind us. "Oh, my god! The tunnel! Did anyone think to mark the tunnel? How are we going to find our way home?"

"Mark it how?" asked Erasmus, raising a finger. "Make a note of the nearby currents in the mist? Oh, wait . . . mist moves."

"Don't worry, old thing." Ulysses patted our sister's arm. "We don't need to find our way back to that wretched hidey-hole. The moment we find Father, *banf!* I can teleport us home."

"I knew there was a reason why we agreed to let these two come," muttered Erasmus. "Well, my loving clan, shall we go through together?"

"Any chance Harebrain here could put his over-sized marble to work and find Mr. Prospero, so we know where to go once we're on the other side?" asked Mab.

"I'm getting there, I'm getting there." Mephisto leaned over the crystal sphere and rubbed it once. The white mist within it began to swirl. "I've found . . . Arghhhhhhh!"

Mephisto screamed, clutched his eyes, and dropped the crystal ball. Because Mab had just informed us that it would explode if it broke, we all leapt for it. Ulysses tried the hardest. He threw himself headlong between the orb and the ground, clutching it to his chest as he slammed into the hard-packed earth.

"Some kind of rugby move?" asked Erasmus, standing over him.

"Just so," gasped Ulysses. "Right. Help me up."

"Oh yeah, everyone run to help the guy who deliberately jumped on his head," Mephisto muttered, still holding his eyes. "Never mind the guy who just looked at the Thorns of Pain."

A frisson of terror shot through me. Surely, Father was not in the Tower, that horrible, painful place of wrongness where Astreus had been held! But was that not what the Ouija board had told me, back on *The Happy Gambit,* that Father was the prisoner of the Torturers of the Tower of Pain?

"The Thorns of Pain!" Logistilla was exclaiming. "That sounds unpleasant . . . are you all right, Mephisto?"

"Why does it always have to be the Thorns of Pain?" Ulysses murmured more to himself than to us. "Why is it never the Feathers of Happiness or the Teaspoons of Tranquility?"

Mephisto took his hands away from his eyes and blinked a few times. He patted his cheeks experimentally. "Any blood? No? Then, I guess I'm okay. I found Daddy. He's in a cage in the thickets outside the Tower of Pain. That's . . . that's pretty deep in, guys. It's a long way."

"How do you know all this, Mephisto?" asked Cornelius. "I have never heard of the Tower of Pain."

"I've heard of it," I whispered shakily, memories of crippling pain and horror haunting me. "It is a place of torture, and it is very old. Older than our Sun."

Theo reached up and clicked the side of his goggles, cycling through its lenses: green, blue, gold, silver, red.

"Try these!" He pulled them off without removing his helmet, slipping the band over the top of his head, and handed them to Mephisto. "The red lenses don't let the pain through! "

Mephisto took them and looked cautiously at the ball. When no pain ensued, he studied it carefully.

"He's alive." Mephisto reported finally, handing the goggles back to Theo, who stepped away to remove his helmet to replace them properly. "But it looks bad. We should hurry!"

The lighthearted mood among us died. My siblings and I stood numbly in the cold mist, listening to the slithering whispers of ghostly voices, a constant chatter that always seemed to be on the verge of resolving into understandable syllables, but never did.

"You realize chances are some of us won't be coming back?" Ulysses asked matter-of-factly.

"No point in loitering here." Erasmus gave one of his oily smiles and took a step forward. Glancing to the right, he exclaimed, "Oh my!"

I followed his gaze. Behind us, far away in the midst of the luminescent swirling spirits, two black thrones stood upon a raised dais. They appeared empty, except when I glanced at the throne on the left, a cold, eerie sensation traveled up my spine. The wings stretching from my tea gown flared, showering us in verdant sparks. Curious, I would have approached, but Erasmus put a restraining hand on my shoulder.

"Not our battle," he said simply, and he plunged through the ivory gate.

The rest of us stood as if petrified as we watched Erasmus, of his own will, walk through the gate into Hell. As if the mists had devoured him, he vanished from our sight. We grabbed each other and stared after him. For all that I hated him, I felt an empty feeling in the pit of my stomach when he disappeared.

A figure became visible in the middle of the gate, and Erasmus walked back toward us . . . or at least something that looked like Erasmus. His face was radiant.

"It's beautiful!" he exclaimed, in astonishment. "I've never seen such a lovely landscape! Flowering trees, floating stars, rivulets running across picturesque rocks, knights in armor, ladies dressed in fine gowns, fringed like Spanish shawls. It's . . . why is it beautiful?"

"That's just the way it is," said Mephisto with a shrug. "Come on."

"What if the demons try to take over our staffs, as Baelor did during the party?" Logistilla balked.

Titus gave a grim smile and held the *Staff of Silence* aloft. "Silence is golden. Demons can't command our staves if the staves cannot hear them. Shall we go?"

Logistilla, Titus, Caliban, and Ulysses followed Erasmus and Mephisto through the gate, disappearing into the mist.

"This bodes ill," Gregor said huskily, "to find in Hell a garden of Earthly delights. It is a testament to my great love for our Pater that I walk through this gate. God in Heaven, forgive me." And he passed into the mist as well.

"I don't like it, Ma'am, not one bit," said Mab.

Beside him, Cornelius stretched out his hand. "Spiritling, guide me. I have no eyes to lead my way."

Mab took his arm. "Sure thing, Mr. Cornelius. Just follow me."

Theo and I were now alone in the swirling mist, his face shaded by the glorious Urim of his helmet. He looked up at the words on the gate and sighed.

"How ironic," he said. Despite his regret, his voice sounded younger and hardier than it had in years. "Over the last fifty years, I have suffered such agony, solely to avoid entering this very gate. And now, I choose to walk in with my own two feet. Are we doing the wrong thing, Miranda? Are there some paths one should not take, even for one's family?"

I thought about this, remembering, for once, not to turn to my Lady for wisdom. The angel had counseled me to rescue Father. Surely, she would not ask me to damn my immortal soul?

Finally, I said slowly, "I think this gate is a trick, Theo, a deception.

True Hell is not a place we can walk into, it is something in our hearts. Why should we fear any words written on something called the 'Gate of False Dreams'?"

Theo chuckled and offered me his arm. Together, we walked through the gate into the land of Living Nightmares.

I CANNOT say what I had been expecting. Perhaps, after hearing Erasmus's praise, I thought to see a garden or a pleasant forested way. Upon stepping through the gate, however, I was immediately assailed by the most putrid and rotten of stenches, as rank as any battlefield. Corpses, swollen and half disjointed, floated all around me upon the surface of a dismal swamp. Only these bodies were not dead. Their eyes swiveled to focus on me, and they babbled and moaned, unable to make themselves understood with their broken mouths.

Farther away, on what seemed to be an island, a great black demon stood over five emaciated men who bowed and cowered before him, licking his legs and nether parts with their withered purple tongues. I threw my hand before my face, shying away from this lurid scene, only to have my sight fall upon seven naked women tied into a circle. Throbbing, black sinews violated their bodies, passing in and out of each orifice, even their nostrils and ears. The women, bloated and deathly pale, shivered and trembled as if in the grip of ecstatic pleasure or perhaps suffering some terrible torture.

And I was sinking.

The small hillock upon which I stood sank into the vile swamp. Already, I could feel the fatty slime slithering against the skin of my legs and then my stomach. I flailed about until my feet found purchase, only to discover I was perched upon the corpse of a half-dead whale. Beneath the waters, within its disemboweled belly, an orgy took place. The rotting mangled corpses uttered inarticulate exclamations that might have been pleasure or pain. As I drew back in dismay, I lost my footing and fell into the stinking muck.

Emerging again, I gagged and spat, but the slime was everywhere. A smell like rotting corpses and feces stewed in rancid lard filled my nostrils and mouth. Horrified, I vomited. My vomit hung before me, sinking slowly through the gook and adding to the stink.

It was too much. I screamed, thrashing about until I managed to throw myself through the gate back to Limbo.

* * *

"MIRANDA! What's wrong?"

Theo came crashing through the gate and ran to where I knelt among the swirling mists, retching out my innards. The others followed him, and soon the whole family was gathered about me. I felt unsteady and weak, ashamed to lift my head or look at them.

"It's horrible!" I cried, when I was able to speak. Tears ran down my cheeks. "What was that . . . stuff we were swimming in? How could you call that place beautiful or mistake it for a garden?"

"Slowly now, Sister." Erasmus squatted down beside me. "Tell us what you saw."

I described the bare bones of it, skimming over the obscenities. My brethren listened silently. Ulysses's face gained a pale green tinge, and Mephisto gagged.

"But it was so beautiful," cried Logistilla. "Why should we believe that she is seeing the truth?"

"Don't be such a dope, Logistilla," Mephisto replied weakly, waving a hand. "When you're in Hell, and someone tells you the pretty stuff is a deception, believe them!"

"I shoulda known something was wrong when I couldn't smell the stink of corruption," Mab said.

"It makes perfect sense," Erasmus said. "Of course, Hell could not be a pleasure garden. But why is Big Sister Miranda the only one not taken in?"

"Maybe all her years as Eurynome's handmaiden are protecting her," said Cornelius. When he spoke Eurynome's name, there was a distant crash of thunder. A blue-white light flickered through the swirling mists. For just an instant, in the far distance, I thought I could make out a black armored figure seated on the left-hand throne.

"Maybe it's because her mother was a witch," sneered Erasmus.

Caliban shook his head. "If that were the case, I would see it, too, seeing as we share a mother. Perhaps the angel whom she spoke with gave her a blessing."

"Could be Ophion," said Mab. "Miranda's staff carries my—well, you'd call him an ancestor—the Serpent of the Wind. Maybe, he's protecting her . . . or maybe the rest of you have been seeped in demon magic from your own staffs for so long that Hell has some kind of power over you."

"Maybe a million things," snapped Logistilla. "I fail to see how this speculation gets us any closer to Father!"

Mab turned to Mephisto who was peering into the crystal ball. "So, how ya coming with the oversized paperweight? Can you instruct it to lead us by the safest path? I hear that thing's near omniscient."

"You mean like sneak through the crevices instead of marching up to the front gates of Dis, like that dopey Ferdinand?" asked Mephisto.

"Mephisto, there is no Ferdinand," I said impatiently. "Seir made that story up."

"Oh. Yeah." He shrugged. "Sure, I'll do it. Ball, show us the best path from the Gate of False Dreams to Father . . . Eeeeewwwwww!" Mephisto nearly threw the ball away from himself. "It's disgusting!"

The others peered into the crystal ball. It showed my version of the far side of the gate. Mab and Theo turned away disgusted, but Mephisto, Ulysses, Logistilla, Erasmus, and Caliban all stared in horrified fascination. Gregor, though disgusted, also kept his eyes fixed on the ball, as if determined to view the truth, however unpleasant. Titus kept watch, peering suspiciously into the swirling mists.

Merely seeing it again made me queasy. The memory of that horrible taste filled my mouth. I spat, hoping to rid myself of it, and was sick again, though there was little left to bring up. Theo patted my back supportively.

I could not go back there, not even if I wished to. I could not force my limbs to move toward the gate, knowing what was on the other side. I was too sick and too terrified of returning to the Tower of Pain. The family would have to rescue Father without me.

"Look, a path. If we go this way, we can get through the Swamps of Lust to the Bridge across the River Styx." Mephisto was showing the others something in the ball. "Beyond that is the Wall of Flame, the Burning Plain, the Mountains of Misery, some glaciers, and then the Tower of Pain. All we have to do is follow this path, blast any demons that get in our way, and avoid the Hellwinds."

"What are Hellwinds?" asked Cornelius.

"Black winds that howl," explained Mephisto. "They blow stray souls back to their proper place of punishment."

"What happens if we get caught in them?" asked Erasmus. "Do we get sent back beyond the Gate of False Dreams to the land of the living?"

"No such luck," Mephisto shook his head sagely. "It's straight to punishment. Do not pass Go. Do not collect two hundred dollars. Whatever part of your soul is heaviest, that's where you'll be dropped."

"Remind me to avoid the Hellwinds," Erasmus shuddered. Then, he frowned down at the crystal ball again. "How are we going to follow this path when the landscape looks completely different from what we saw?"

"Miranda, you're going to have to lead us," said Gregor. "The rest of us cannot see the truth."

I cried, "I-I can't!"

"Would you prefer that Father die?" Theo growled sternly.

As I knelt there, a pathetic wreck, Theo's words touched something deep within me. What was the point of bearing the Pride of Angels, if it did not sustain one when pride was called for? Staggering to my feet, I silently swore that nothing would deter me. I would do what it took to save Father—even if it meant my last breath would be of putrid undead gook.

"Very well. Follow me."

IT was worse, even, than I had anticipated. The others walked easily over the swamp, as if they trod on a petal-strewn footpath, but I, who could see the truth, had to frog paddle through the gelatinous slime. Mournful cries and moans of anguished ecstasy came from all sides. By looking only directly before me, I could avoid most of the lurid sights, but the putrid stenches were impossible to ignore. More than once, I stopped to retch out my empty innards. Yet, somehow, I went forward.

"You look really weird, Miranda," Mephisto chimed happily as he strolled alongside me. "Like you're lying on your stomach on the path pretending to be a fish, only you're actually moving forward. And there are all these flower petals all over you. There's one on your nose," He pointed to where a bit of slime clung to my face. "I think you look cute that way."

"I think she looks ridiculous," murmured Erasmus.

"It's hardly sporting to mock her if there's nothing she can do about it, especially as she's the one having a hard time," Ulysses joined in. "We're taking a stroll in a park where girls in bikinis are sunbathing." His eyes tracked a particularly hideous spider-creature admiringly. "While she's swimming through sewage. Hardly fair, really."

Mephisto's orb directed us as to where to go. I tried to avoid the worst of the corpses and rotting fleshy parts, but even this was difficult. Once, I turned quickly to avoid a black-winged demon and found I had swum into an eddy filled with meaty bits and bodily fluids. The stink of rotten flesh and the taste of bile and mucus assaulted upon my senses. I flailed, trying to push the contaminants away from me. My brothers came to my rescue, dragging me backward, but Logistilla and Mephisto, who were watching my progress through the crystal ball, both became ill. The odor of their vomit contributed to the general vileness.

Worst of all was that, in the midst of this horror, I kept, out of habit, turning to my Lady for guidance, only to find an empty area that seemed to ache and throb, like a recently pulled tooth. Eager for distraction, my mind wandered back to my last conversation with Astreus, replaying it at least a hundred times, recalling how we quarreled and how he was now lost to me. I regretted his loss, regretted bringing up the subject of Aerie Ones but, most of all, I regretted—to my shame—that he had passed into darkness without ever having truly kissed me.

The bowels of Hell, amidst victims of the sins of lust, was hardly the most appropriate place to come face-to-face with the realization that I had become seriously enamored of an elf.

A great, bloated monster—half-demon and half-spider—provided a momentary distraction. It shot black webs at us, hoping to ensnare us and pull us into its pulsing womb, where other victims moaned and writhed. I shouted and pointed, and all my brothers leapt forward to parry the webs, waving their staffs blindly. The spider's webs stuck to Mephisto's sword, and one nearly robbed him of it. They parted instantly, however, when even in the vicinity of the *Staff of Decay*.

After that, Erasmus took the lead. Smiling grimly, he walked beside me as I swam.

CHAPTER TWENTY-THREE

The Doves of Oblivion

At last, my foot struck solid ground!

Soon, the muck was waist-high, then calf-high. Finally, a thin strip of solid earth emerged covered with a dull brownish bracken, and I was free of the sludge. The heavy fetid stink of the swamp still clogged my nostrils, but it was not clear whether it came from the environment or from my slime-covered body. As I stood there, dripping, feeling this horrible glop slide down my face and skin, I was at last able to look around.

The orgies and violent grotesqueries had fallen behind now; only a few lone couples—or were they rapists and victims?—remained. I shivered and looked away.

In the distance, a great arched bridge spanned a wide river of black rushing water. Beyond the far side, in the distance, I could see an enormous wall of fire.

"The Bridge over the River Styx," Mephisto cried happily. Apparently, nothing daunted him. Or maybe he was still seeing beautiful gardens, though from the expressions on my other brethren's faces and the way Logistilla was holding her nose, I gathered their illusion was wearing thin. "Didn't they make a movie about that, starring Obi-Wan Kenobi?"

"Who?" asked Gregor.

"No one, Brother Dear. Mephisto is babbling," Logistilla patted Gregor's arm. "Is this really the Styx? I thought it separated the living from the dead."

"It does," replied Mephisto, "but it also winds through Hell itself separating some of the Circles from each other. There's even an Ocean Styx, if you follow it in the other direction."

"I suppose that makes sense." She pointed ahead, beyond the bridge. "Is this the way we are to go? How do we get around that wall of fire? It seems to stretch on infinitely."

"The Wall of Flame? We don't. Go around, that is," Mephisto chirped back. "We go through."

"Just walk through the towering Wall of Flame?" asked Ulysses. When Mephisto nodded, he muttered, "Ducky!"

"What is this wall?" asked Cornelius, reaching a hand out, as if he could somehow feel the flames from here.

Mephisto said, "A towering inferno of burning passions. That's what all the fire is down here, you know. Passions. Even that lurid stuff that floats in the sky. And that gunk Miranda is dripping with? That's made from all the wanton desires of people on Earth, the really dirty thoughts. They condense and drip down here, forming this place, the Swamp of Uncleanness."

That was what had been in my mouth? I bent and vomited again.

"And how do we go through this great wall of burning lusts? Or is it anger? By being stoical?" asked Erasmus.

Mephisto shrugged. "You just have to will it not to bother you." He snickered. "The dweebs on the other side maintain the wall to keep the good spirits out . . . as if any good spirit would be bothered by their silly wall. They're such dopes." He turned to us in all seriousness. "Nobody in Hell is very bright. Otherwise, they wouldn't be down here, would they?" He looked up at the steely gray lights floating above us like luminescent clouds amidst the inky-black smoke that otherwise obscured the heavens, perhaps literally. "Oh, except for the guys who are really bright, but evil. I forgot about them. All that gray light in the sky? It comes from them. It's the light of misguided reason." He tapped both his temples to indicate mental prowess. "But they're dopey, too, in their own way."

"That was clear as mud," murmured Erasmus. "How do you know all this, anyway?" When Mephisto did not answer, he continued, "So, what do we do? What if not all of us can make it through?"

"We grit our teeth and try really hard," offered Mephisto.

"We use my staff," Titus stated evenly.

"Ah, yes! That will do it," smiled Erasmus.

TO reach the bridge, we had to pass through a mangrove swamp. We entered warily, unnerved by the eerie vegetation. Mangrove roots looped above the swamp, upon which floated a thick, dingy foam, such as gathers along the banks of polluted rivers. The roots stuck out above the surface like petrified skeletal elbows, knobby and angular. Fat bulging lizards blinked at us from the fingerlike roots, and reptilian bats, like dinosaur birds but with the faces of men, swooped and screamed overhead, terrifying Logistilla. Above us, dead branches dripped with dull gray Spanish moss, so that the trees stood like shrouded wraiths.

The illusion of the lovely garden had faded, and my siblings now saw what I saw. They gave me wide berth, for they could smell the stinking residue that stuck to my skin and hair. The enchantments woven into my tea dress proved equal to even this terrible environment. Its shimmering emerald cloth soon repelled the slime and filth, and my garments were fresh and clean again. I felt so grateful I even brought myself to thank Logistilla. She merely pinched her nose fastidiously and moved away from me, pausing only to inform me that my hair still smelled atrocious.

Wisps of mist began rising from the swamp. Long pale tendrils of fog wove between us, rapidly growing thicker. Soon, we could no longer see one another. I reached out for Mab and Theo, who had been walking nearby, but my hands encountered only clamminess and a slimy tree trunk.

To have my family so close and yet not be able to find them was unnerving. Nor was I the only one who was disturbed. Around me, I could hear the others calling.

"Titus?"

"Logistilla!"

• "Miss Miranda? Are you there?"

"Brothers? Brothers? Don't leave me!" The last from Cornelius.

"I'm here, Cornelius!" Theo responded. "Keep speaking and I'll find . . . Ahh!"

Theo's cry was accompanied by a splash. I rushed in his direction, but something snaked about my foot. Stumbling, I fell across a twist of roots and plunged face down into the foul-smelling froth. Its awful spongy consistency, like shaving cream blended with medical wastes, brought on yet another wave of revulsion. Flailing about, I managed to grab an arching mangrove root and pull myself from the mire. The slippery foam clung to my face and hands. As I flung it away from me, I heard Cornelius's voice rise plaintively.

"Brother? Are you well?"

"I'm all right," Theo barked hoarsely, "just a bit damp."

"Now, we all know how Miranda feels," Caliban offered cheerfully amidst splashing.

An unnatural, grating sound reminiscent of laughter, as if an avalanche were mocking us, disturbed the landscape, sending ripples through the swampy waters. Logistilla screamed, and the familiar white flare of the *Staff of Transportation* illuminated the mist to my right. No doubt, Ulysses was fleeing at the first sign of danger, leaving the rest of us stranded.

"What's wrong?" Erasmus's voice called. "I see nothing."

"Abaddon!" cried Logistilla. "He's here! He's found us!"

"I don't see . . ." Titus began.

A noise like a thousand wings beating in unison agitated the air. The mist blew away, revealing the mouth of a dark tunnel, like a horizontal tornado, that spun through the air as it approached us. I thought of raising my flute to disband it, but it seemed to be made of a solid, physical substance rather than wind. The breeze coming from it thinned the fog, and we caught glimpses of each other, dark shapes, like trees, walking amidst swirls of gray.

"What's this?" Gregor leaned on his staff, his robes billowing about him. "Is this the Hellwind?"

"No. They're black and thick, like the stuff that comes from your staff." Mephisto's voice floated to us through the fog. "As to what this is"—one of the tree-like shapes spread his arms and shrugged—"I don't know!"

"Looks like the tunnel from Bosch's *Ascent of the Blessed*," murmured Caliban, who was revealed squatting atop a tangle of gnarled roots.

"Maybe it's a way out?" Erasmus took a cautious step forward and peered into the funnel of darkness.

"Fools! Abaddon is near! We are doomed!" Logistilla cried. "Whatever this is, it will be the death of us!"

Abruptly, the tunnel unraveled. Like an Escher drawing come to life, the front edge flew toward us, resolving into black doves. As if in a dream, we watched the dark flock spread outward, flying through the mangroves on wings as black as pitch. So strange and contrary to normal expectation was the thought of danger from such a gentle bird that only Mephisto raised his arm to ward them off.

"Watch out!" he called. "These are Lord Shax's minions. He's one of Abbadon's cohorts, a Marquis of the Third . . ."

Soft as a thistledown, a dark wing brushed my face. There was no scratch or peck, just a cool flick of silky feathers.

Immediately, my forehead and cheeks went numb.

The rest of Mephisto's words failed to reach my ears. Other sounds fled as well: the low rumble, the rustle of Gregor's robes, the squelch of my footstep. Last to flee was the sound of my own breath, which faded so completely that I feared breath itself had failed.

The thought that Titus's staff stopped demons as well as sound comforted me—until I remembered the *Staff of Silence* acted instantly—which meant this silence was not of my brother's doing.

Unnerved, I tried to call out to my brothers, but it was too late. My mouth and jaw were numb, and would not obey me. Worse, darkness was encroaching from the corner of my vision. It spread until all sight had fled. Then, my thoughts began to seep away as well.

Why was I standing here in the darkness?

What had I been meaning to do?

Barely clinging to consciousness, I prayed to my Lady, but that sorrow only drew the darkness more quickly.

Then, even that sorrow was gone.

What balm, oblivion—greater than any Gilead had to offer. No sorrow. No regrets for Ladies lost or elves betrayed. What a gracious gift this demon had given me, when he stole away all sense, suffering, and sadness.

No!

This peace was false. Even in the midst of oblivion, I, who had felt my Lady's breath and spoken face-to-face with angels, could not be fooled by counterfeits. This dullness, this abandonment of care, was not a gift.

It was Hell itself.

DAMNATION: that from which there was no escape. That knowledge had been pounded from the pulpits ever since my return to Milan, over five hundred years ago. I had not heeded it, thinking—in my arrogance—that my Lady would protect me. Now, it was too late. I had strayed from the straight and narrow. I had wandered too far down the primrose path and passed the point of no return.

I had abandoned hope. Or rather, Hope had abandoned me.

There was nothing left but vast eternal emptiness. I might now declare, with Milton's Lucifer: *Which way I fly is Hell; myself am Hell.*

As my thoughts tumbled, slowly growing dim, I remembered kneeling on the hard stone of the chapel at the *Castello Sforzesco* as Father Ignatius lectured me about sin. The chapel was always cold, a chilly draft blew against the back of my neck, but if I squirmed or asked for a shawl, my penance would be increased—penance assigned to me for being beautiful and uncivilized, for surely those things were sins. It was never for actions I had performed, because in the six years that he was my personal father confessor, I had never spoken a word to the man. I had not recognized his authority over my soul.

This had been in the days after Ferdinand's disappearance. My stepmother, who had brought Father Ignatius with her when she came to the
castello, had insisted I attend the chapel and perform his penances. In my
sorrow, it had not occurred to me to object.

So I would kneel in silence, my neck frozen and my knees aching, as
Father Ignatius paced back and forth, describing in painstaking detail vivid
scenes of Hell and damnation, of torment and suffering: how women who
had abortions had their breasts devoured by the offspring they had scorned,
or how those who played the harlot would hang for eternity by their hair
above boiling mire.

"For eternity," he would lean forward and breathe on me with his stinking breath. "With no hope of redemption. That is the fate that awaits you,
Heathen Girl."

How sad that time had proven that wretched man right.

I recalled that I did speak up once. For six years, I heard to him preach
damnation, but I never really listened. Then, one day, the error of his words
penetrated my thoughts. Rising, I rebuked him. "Your theology must be
faulty, Father; damnation cannot be eternal. My Lady has vowed not to rest
until every soul has been redeemed, and surely Love Herself cannot fail."

What the priest thought of my rebellion, I never learned, I walked out.
The next time my stepmother complained that I had not visited him recently.
I went to my father, who excused me from further private instruction.

Back in oblivion, I recalled words from the *Book of the Sibyl*: *"She will
not pause while even one of these remains in darkness."*

Did that include me? Would She save even one whom She had abandoned? Perhaps I should not yield so meekly to oblivion.

Deep in the dark of nothingness, I cast about for some hope, some
weapon against the false balm of unconsciousness, and brought to mind an
image of a single sprout amidst a field of snow. I recalled Gregor's words in
my room: *You think your present sorrow is solid, like a sphere of diamond encasing your soul. But, the nature of sorrow is closer to that of ice. Ice melts when
warmth is applied.*

If this were true, then all sorrow was a sham, even the sorrow caused by
blindness, deafness, and stupidity.

For the time it takes one spark to live, burn, and extinguish in the dark,
I understood the truth of this.

Like a soap bubble popping, the emptiness was gone. I awoke to find
myself standing amidst swirls of waist-high fog. Around me, dark doves still

swooped at my brothers and sister, who stood like dreary statues. Even Caliban and Mab stood motionless, and Ulysses, who had apparently returned to see if the coast was clear. Amidst those I could see clearly and those who were merely silhouettes, I counted only ten, including myself. One of us was missing.

"Woke up, did you, sleepyhead?" came the voice of my brother Mephisto. "Lion, protect my sister!"

Mephisto swooped out of the sky on the back of a winged lion, a life-size version of the figurine that served as the top piece of his staff. It was a magnificent creature with a creamy mane and tail puff glowing with an aura of golden light that made the infernal swamp look tawdry and false. Its eyes glittered like newly beaten gold. Downy wings sprouted from its shoulders. When it beat them, doves were thrown about like oak leaves in winter's storm.

"Come on, you dopes!" my brother shouted, as the winged lion flew over the swamp. "Back to the Island of Misfit Imps!"

I could not tell if he was talking to us or to the doves.

Gregor stirred and slapped a dove with Solomon's Ring. It withered into dust. He reached over and pressed the ring against Titus's cheek. My great bear of a brother stirred and tapped his staff.

The world became silent again, only this time sight and thought remained. The doves caught within his effect exploded like sable milkweed pods. The smell of brimstone, accompanying each dying bird, assailed my nostrils.

Then, Titus released his effect and sound rushed in.

"That was . . . disturbing," Erasmus sat in the swamp, surrounded by looping roots with only his head showing above the low clinging mist.

"You are disturbing!" Logistilla snapped back. "Stand up. Your floating head is giving me the willies!"

"Certainly, O Sister, I live to serv . . ." With a soft *plop,* Erasmus's head disappeared beneath the foamy surface.

"Brother?" Cornelius stretched out a hand tentatively. "Are you . . . Something has grabbed my leg!"

"Let's hope it's Mr. Erasmus," Mab muttered.

Cornelius shouted and sank out of sight, his arms flailing.

"Oh no," Mab muttered. "This can't be good."

We nervously glanced around, unable to see anything below the frothy surface. Caliban poked among the dark, crooked roots with his club. Uncurling like the fingers of a mummified giant, the roots seized his weapon and began dragging him forward. Another root snaked around his neck, pulling him under.

Something hard that had been poking into my ankle gave way. As I glanced down, a dark root encircled my legs. I had time only to grab my fan before it dragged my feet out from under me. My arms flailing, I managed to slice the root constricting me cleanly in half without cutting my leg. That root recoiled, quivering, but another began slithering up my calf.

Lunging, I grabbed onto the lion, who still hovered beside me, protecting me as Mephisto had instructed. Hanging from the creature's neck, my nose stuck in its perfumed mane, I cried, "Mephisto! Get us off the ground!"

The lion rose up, so I was now dangling some ten feet above the groping feelers of the mangrove roots, several of which were reaching high out of the water in their search for me. Mephisto held up his staff and tapped the bottom against his boot.

"*Staff of Summoning* to the rescue!" he shouted. "Everyone reach up!"

I began to imagine a flurry of great flying beasts. Then, the air above the mangroves was filled with wing beats as a gryphon, a harpy, and the magnificent roc appeared beside the winged lion. The gryphon dove down and grabbed a screaming Logistilla in its front claws. The roc hooked a talon through the collars of Titus, Caliban, and Theo, so that all three men dangled from its right foot. Leaping across the writhing roots, Mab made a running jump onto the roc's other foot, wrapping his arms tightly about its scaly leg as the great bird rose higher.

Screeching with delight, the harpy swooped down and grabbed the waist of the one remaining person standing among the mangroves, my brother Gregor. As she raised him skyward, she pressed her pendulous breasts against his red-robed back and cooed lovingly in his ear. Grimacing in disgust, my priestly brother raised his staff to swat at her. Glancing down—and, presumably, seeing the long drop to the swamp—he thought better of it. He remained stony-faced, stoically enduring her caresses as she rubbed her ugly cheek against his silky, shoulder-length hair.

The misty surface beneath us trembled and coughed up Cornelius, who sputtered and flailed, swinging his staff wildly, as if to hold off approaching assailants. The magnificent roc dropped like a stone, caught him up by his collar, and lifted him away from the murk. Mab, who stood atop the talon that now held Cornelius, knelt down to shout words of comfort to my disoriented blind brother.

"Okay, Erasmus!" Mephisto called down, leaning over the winged lion at a precarious angle. "All's clear. Do your stuff!"

There was no response from below, except that a few more roots swayed seeking their prey. Then, they settled down, again becoming crooked, bark-covered fingers, and the water was once more placid and calm. We all gazed down, craning our necks in our attempts to catch some sign of Erasmus beneath the froth-covered water.

"Erasmus!" Titus bellowed, the power of his voice causing the dead branches to shiver. "All clear!"

The mangrove trees withered. The dark branches stiffened and curled and turned to dust, which floated down to settle upon the ubiquitous foam. Erasmus's head popped up through the newly fallen lay of dust, followed by his foam-covered body.

"That was truly vile." He looked to the left and right. "Where is everyone?"

Dangling above him, with my arms wrapped about the lion's neck, I felt an odd sense of *déjà vu*. Had it been only a week ago that I had clung similarly to the neck of Pegasus for dear life?

The lion was harder to keep hold of than the flying horse. It had no middle ridge along the top to grab, and its mane was closer to its head. Nor did it seem happy when I stuck my fingers into the thick hair with its heavenly fragrance and held on. I tried to keep my arms wrapped about its neck, but my sweaty palms kept slipping on the slick fur.

Hoping for a firmer purchase, I took the risk of momentarily loosening my grip. My gamble failed. The slick feline pelt slid through my fingers. I plummeted the ten feet to splash down beside Erasmus, spraying him in murk and froth.

"Oh, very good, Miranda," Erasmus intoned. "Leap out of the sky and break my neck. Pity you missed, eh?"

Slightly stunned, I found myself up to my chest in muck and foam. "For Heaven's sake, Erasmus!" I replied bitterly. "We are in Hell, surrounded by deadly enemies, and all you can do is think of ways to annoy me? I'm glad I didn't land on you and break your neck, because we need every one of us. But it is a pity I couldn't have caused you to bite your tongue!"

"Now, now, Children, let's not fight among ourselves!" Mephisto leaned down from the winged lion at a precarious angle. "Baddies coming! Luckily, the evil twisty things are gone—all withered, thanks to Erasmus, here—so you don't need to be grabbed from above."

I began to imagine a glorious white stallion, with feathered wings up-lifted, rearing in the swamp beside me. Then, Pegasus stood in the murk, snorting at the foam into which his hind legs disappeared. When he brought his forelegs down, Erasmus and I clamored onto his back. Then we were air-borne.

Erasmus pushed in front, where he could hold the horse's neck. When I reached around to grab him or the horse's mane, he pushed my arm away. Left with nothing to hold on to, I clasped the steed's sides tightly with my legs.

It was one of the few times in my life I wished I were Logistilla. Her bareback riding skills were far superior to mine.

We soared through the air. Below, a wide misty area was followed by more mangroves and then a tract of firmer earth that rose to meet the stone bridge. The bridge spanned an expanse of black water some four hun-dred yards wide. Beyond lay a boggy bank, a dismal plain, and the Wall of Flame.

"Can we move on?" Gregor called dourly from where he hung. The ec-static harpy was rubbing her feathered belly against his back and trying to embrace him with her wings, causing the two of them to plummet errati-cally. He endured her attentions grimly.

"Can we fly to the Wall of Fire?" called Erasmus.

"Whatever we are going to do, do it quickly," shrieked Logistilla. "This beast is going to drop me any moment now."

"What baddies?" asked Titus, who still dangled awkwardly from the tip of the roc's talon. "Where?"

"There!" cried Mephisto. "Twelve o'clock. Straight ahead. Right between us and the bridge."

At first, it looked like a flock of red birds flew toward us. As they drew closer, I could make out a swarm of red, horned imps, each carrying a long pitchfork.

"Oh, look. Traditional denizens of Hell," mused Erasmus. "How cozy."

A swirl of light below heralded the return of Ulysses, who glanced about frantically, searching for us.

"Roc, swoop down and get my other brother, will you?" called Mephisto. The great bird quickly obeyed. Jarred by the rapid descent, Theo, who had been reaching over his shoulder to unlimber his staff, which he carried on his back separated into two parts, nearly dropped the lower portion. He shouted as it fell through his fingers but managed to grab it before it entirely escaped him. Startled, Ulysses glanced up. He began to raise his staff but stopped to chuckle at the bemused expressions of his brothers as they hung helplessly from the roc's claws. His grin continued, even after the roc soared upward with him hanging beside Cornelius.

"You!" Logistilla screeched, as the gigantic roc passed the gryphon. She swung her staff wildly, as if wishing to bonk him on the head. "How dare you leave us like that!"

"Sorry, old chaps. Didn't want the bugger to catch me. Is he gone?"

The air shook as if the universe itself were grinding each atom against the next. *"On the contrary, Ulysses Reginald Prospero. I still abide. Focalor, attend!"*

CHAPTER TWENTY-FOUR

Bridge over the River Styx

Ulysses screamed and raised his staff. Before he could vanish again, however, Mab leaned over from the top of the talon and snatched the *Staff of Transportation* from his hands. Blind with panic, Ulysses twisted about and clung to the claw above him, clutching it for dear life, as if he could hide beneath it and escape notice.

"Focalor? I know that name," murmured Erasmus.

I replied, "He has power over wind and water."

"The demon who sank the *Titanic*?"

"Exactly," I said. "I've fought him twice, at sea, where his storm imps dance and stir up cyclones."

Both times I had been the victor, but only after a drawn-out battle that had left me exhausted. I grasped my flute nervously. What would come if I played my flute? Not Mab's kind, that was for certain. The Aerie Ores did not venture down here. It would do no good for me to play, if my songs summoned the likes of Focalor! Was that all the flute could summon down here? Or could I call up something more wholesome?

From my left came the familiar whirr of the *Staff of Devastation* powering up. As soon as the noise became a steady hum, Theo raised the silver-white length and pointed it at the approaching flock of imps. A beam of pure white fire came from the staff and sizzled across the sky, causing the very air it passed through to burst into flame, until a corona of red-orange flame surrounded the white-hot beam.

It struck the flock. Imps exploded into tiny white stars. They scattered, causing much of the force of Theo's beam to be wasted, dissipated upon the air or lost as it continued unimpeded over the horizon. About a third of those approaching evaporated or dropped from the sky, burnt.

The rest regrouped.

The force of the beam threw Theo backward, pulling the roc with him. The great bird tumbled beak over talons, sending my brothers flying. Luckily, Theo had the presence of mind to stop firing as soon as he started to spin; otherwise the magnificent roc, and possibly some of my brothers, would have met a white-hot death. The roc righted itself and stooped after those whom it had dropped, catching everyone except for Theo himself, who smashed to the ground below. Diving, the roc snatched Theo up in its huge curved beak. It was impossible to make out whether Theo was injured.

Then the surviving imps were among us, stabbing our flying beasts with their long, pointy pitchforks.

"Fly for the far side!" cried Ulysses.

"No! We mustn't risk the chance that one of us might be dropped into the Styx," cried Gregor. "Make for the solid land this side of the bridge."

The roc reached solid land without dropping anyone except for Caliban, who rolled and came quickly to his feet, club ready. Gregor raised his staff. He and the harpy disappeared inside a ball of darkness. No imps approached his hovering ball of Hellshadow as it floated down to the ground beside the roc. The winged lion landed as well. It had a glow of holiness about it that kept the imps from coming too close, and when they tried to stab it with their tridents, Mephisto parried with the *Staff of Summoning*, wielding the length of carved wood as if it were a sword.

The rest of us were not so lucky. A mob of imps forced the gryphon down in the midst of the last mangrove, Logistilla disappearing beneath the trees in a glow of pale greenish light. Not waiting for the roc to release him, Titus leapt forward—breaking off the sharp, curved tip of the roc's talon when the collar of his enchanted garment would not give way. He charged toward Logistilla's position, shouting the war cry of his mother's Scottish clan: *"Creag an Tuiric."*

"Blimey," murmured Ulysses. "He's determined! The poor roc. Doesn't seem to be in pain, though. Hopefully, it was like ripping a fingernail."

As for Erasmus and me, the first few imps that came near shriveled, withered, and evaporated, all except for a dark bit of writhing wormlike thing, apparently impervious to the ravages of time, that dropped to *pitter-pat* against the ground below. After that, the imps stayed back and tried to poke at us with the cruel barbs of their tridents. These I parried or sliced in two with my war fan. Only without my Lady to guide my blows, I felt slow and awkward, unsure when and where to swing. One trident slipped past me and jabbed Pegasus in the haunches. The flying horse reared. Erasmus held on to the mane, but I, who was not holding anything, tumbled off.

As I fell, I managed to catch the winged steed's tail and cling to it with both hands. This kept me from falling, but the horse did not like it and kicked. My enchanted gown protected me from the sharpness of the hoof but not from its impact. The air was knocked from my lungs. I hung, gasping, my mouth moving like a fish's. When the land beneath grew close enough I let go, curling into a ball to avoid another kick. I landed and rolled, then sat, battered and sore, until I regained my breath.

Titus came running toward us, Logistilla clinging to his back. Mephisto tapped his staff, and the magical beasts—the roc, the flying horse, the winged lion, and the harpy—vanished like a dream, the harpy still blowing kisses to a weary Gregor.

"Fall in!" Theo barked in his best "Major Prospero" voice.

Nine of us formed a circle back to back—our staves in our left hands and any weapon we carried in our right. Caliban and Mab, who had never fought with us before, stood to one side. Mab caught on and quickly muscled in beside me, but Caliban stood uncertainly until Mephisto grabbed his arm and pulled him into the ring.

We stood shoulder to shoulder, facing the enemy. The green streaks of light hovering like wings behind my shoulder glittered. Beside me, Theo looked spectacular in his silvery titanium armor, which he wore over the enchanted gambeson Logistilla had quilted for him along ago. His breastplate of shining Urim gleamed so brightly in the gloom of Hell that it was hard to look at him. Some of the imps veered away, mistaking him for a warrior angel. Erasmus had done such an excellent job of fitting the armor to him that Theo now looked like his splendid self of old. No wonder he had asked for his old squire!

Since the others, except for Ulysses, wore their enchanted garments—all fashioned by Logistilla in centuries past—we resembled living versions of our statues in the Great Hall. Titus wore his MacLaren tartan kilt. Gregor's dark, wavy hair brushed against the red half-cape that fell from the shoulders of his crimson cardinal's robes. Logistilla, in her dark blue split-skirt garment with its enormous collar, looked every inch the fairy-tale villainess. Mephisto, garbed in his voluminous-sleeved shirt and matching pantaloons of indigo with his black vest and wide-brimmed boots, resembled a pirate or perhaps a circus ringmaster. Beside him, Erasmus wore the garments of a gentleman of the eighteenth century, dark green justacorps and even darker waistcoat, with matching breeches and a silver garter beneath each knee, while Cornelius wore his purple *Orbis Suleimani* robes, an eye emblazoned in a triangle upon his chest. A matching purple blindfold covered his eyes.

Ulysses, leaning upon his staff and playing with his slight mustache, wore a gray domino mask and tuxedo. Mab and Caliban also lacked the protection of enchanted garments. Mab slouched beside me in his trench coat and fedora, and Caliban was clad in ordinary jeans and a flannel shirt.

We looked glorious.

The imps dropped out of the sky—some directly atop us, others gathering in hordes before charging. Wherever they stabbed the ground, large potbellied demons with stinger tails and pitchforks as long as lances appeared out of nowhere. These new demons opened their mouths and blew icy cold winds, strong enough to lift a grown man off his feet. These were Focalor's servants, not the dancing storm imps I knew from our sea battles, but servants of his, nonetheless.

Theo stabbed three of the imps that landed close at hand, followed by a pot-bellied demon. I slashed one of the latter across the chest, though it vanished again before I did it much harm, and Mab knocked two imps out of the air, bashing their wings with his lead pipe. Titus swung his thick length of cedar like a golf club, sending imps and demons spinning head over heels, and Erasmus withered all who came near him. Ulysses fired at the enemy with matching dueling pistols. They must have been enchanted, for he fired and fired, never once stopping to reload. His accuracy was astonishing, every shot piercing the brainpan of an imp or a demon. To his left, Caliban screamed like Tarzan and bashed skulls and leathery wings beneath his club, while Mephisto ducked behind him shouting instructions and encouragement.

The demons struck back, slingshotting their long flexible tails over our heads, their shiny stingers curling to strike our backs. Theo, Cornelius, Gregor, and I would all have been stung had it not been for the protection of our enchanted garments. The pitchforks, too, were turned aside by the magical cloth, but a barbed tine caught Erasmus's unprotected hand, and another stabbed Caliban in the thigh, before he broke its shaft with a blow from his club.

Gregor pushed Cornelius into the middle of our ring, for with his staff out of commission he was useless in a fight. Once our blind brother was safe, Gregor stood poised, the Seal of Solomon glittering upon his finger, ready to slap any denizen of Hell who ventured too close. Those he touched shriveled up until they were the size of a pea. Some he managed to capture in glass vials he carried under his robes. Others fell beneath our feet and were lost.

Then, an imp managed to evade our blows and strike the ground with its weapon inside our circle. Immediately, three pot-bellied demons appeared behind us, blowing us from our feet and freezing us with their icy breath. Our circle was broken. Mab, Theo, and I were thrown headlong.

Theo and I rose and stood back to back, while Mab turned angrily toward Focalor's servants.

"Damn if any puny puff is going to blow me around!" Mab cried. "Don't you know who I am, you pathetic gutless gusts? If it weren't for me, there wouldn't be such a thing as an icy wind!"

He opened his mouth, and the air grew colder. An icy gale-strength wind threw the demons from their feet, coating them instantly with rime. The startled demons flew through the air, flailing their limbs and trying to stab their stingers into anything that might give them purchase. A few had the presence of mind to wink out, appearing elsewhere. The rest either did not think of this or could not.

Mab's wind whipped about, catching imps and demons in its blast. Then, it swung out over the river, carrying them with it and dropping them into the black waters. Icy rime coated the path it had followed. Some demons reappeared, and some imps had escaped the Northeasterly rage, but many of those it had captured fled, dripping with icicles. They refused to return, and enemies' numbers began to dwindle.

Mab's body flopped over. I ran to him. Remembering Caurus in the Vault, I did not panic when he showed no sign of life. Instead, I held the body upright, mouth open, while Theo guarded my back. Sure enough, there was a second blast of cold, and Mab's eyes opened. He straightened, then twitched and jerked awkwardly as he situated himself within the fleshly body again.

"Sorry about that, Ma'am," he muttered embarrassed. "I shouldn't let them get my goat." Then a grin broke out across his stony features. "Sure felt good to see them scurry, the poseurs!"

A little distance away, Logistilla held up her staff. Long streamers of pale greenish light spilled from the globe at the top striking our opposition. Red-skinned imps trembled and shivered and collapsed into toads, who sank beneath the murk, while the larger pot-bellied demons turned into equally pot-bellied pigs. A moment or two later, however, imps began popping up again, as they used their own magic to transform back.

"Bother! That's no good," she cried. "Titus!"

Again streamers of verdant light spread from her staff, striking our enemies. This time, both imps and demons were transformed into swine. Then, Titus raised his staff, and everything went silent. My enormous brother strode forward, making no noise as he moved through the misty waters. He began striking pigs on the head with the *Staff of Silence,* caving in their skulls. Caliban quickly joined him, killing swine with a single blow of his stout club.

Mephisto ran backward, dodging demons or doing backflips over their heads, until he was beyond the range of Titus's staff, the effect of which inhibited the operation of the rest of our staffs. As soon as he was able, he began tapping his staff, summoning his friends.

The winged lion swooped out of the sky and landed on a sow. The gryphon followed suit, and the magnificent roc carried off six fat hogs. A three-headed hound, a cockatrice, and four giant, green, fairy dogs loped across the ground chasing swine. The *Cu Sith* could not enter the area of the silence, but they moved together as a pack and tackled the first animal to break free of Titus's effect, howling their eerie fey howls. Farther away, the mammoth silently stomped on a nest of toads, and the hamadryad dripped its long sinuous body out of one of the remaining mangroves and swallowed a squealing pig whole.

All of this happened silently, as if we were all part of a well-choreographed film to which the sound track had been lost.

I slit the throat of three hogs with my fan. As I looked around for a fourth, gnarled arms grabbed me from behind, squeezing me painfully. More demons were among us now, and Logistilla could not transform them while Titus's deadening silence remained. Twisting my wrist like a fan dancer, I cut the hand holding me and turned, kneeing my assailant. Alas, there was no vulnerable spot where my leg connected, just a hard ruby carapace that bruised my kneecap.

The large demon leered and poked at me with his trident as I hopped with pain. His blow slid harmlessly off my enchanted gown. As he struck again, I waited until the tines touched my dress and brought my moon-silver war fan down, cleaving the trident's haft. He looked down in consternation at his broken weapon, an almost comical expression upon his ugly face. I wasted no time but lunged forward, despite the sting in my knee, and slit his throat. His chin flopped back, black ichor spurting like a fountain. My blow had not cut all the way through his neck, however, so his lolling head hung helplessly above his windmilling arms. A second strike separated the head from the body, which I then pushed over with my foot.

Sound came rushing back: breathing, wheezing, screams, and thuds. Caliban was still uttering his ululating yell, and Mephisto was riding a big squinty-eyed pig, whooping like a cowboy.

"Brother, come, be my guide," Gregor's voice spoke nearby. Turning, I saw Gregor grab Cornelius's shoulder and hold up the *Staff of Darkness*. Shadows poured out, surrounding the both of them. As the black cloud about them spread, demons and imps disappeared within its growing radius. None emerged again. Turning to parry another stinger tail, I smiled at the irony of Cornelius, who was familiar with pitch darkness, acting as a guide for his seeing brother.

Somewhere nearby, a great voice cried: *"Strike not Focalor! His armor corrodes all that touches it."*

I spun around but was too late to see who had spoken. Overhead, a figure descended from the sky, borne upon tawny wings shaped like those of Mephisto's gryphon. His body was clad in rusted armor, pitted and ruddy. The surface had a wicked sheen reminiscent of acid or poison. The figure carried a shield, the device of which was too corroded to be distinguished.

So this was Focalor, whose minions had so often harried us at sea. He did not look so imposing—until he landed and revealed himself to be well over seven feet tall, with a wingspan of over twenty-five feet. His great wings closed with a loud *whoosh,* and his armor clanked as he moved, shedding reddish metallic dust. Even the air near him was damaged by his passage, for it hurt my nose and throat to breathe it.

The demon regarded us contemptuously and spoke: "Despair, Children of the Dread Prospero, and kneel to me! For I am your doom!"

"Not likely!" murmured Ulysses. He raised his pistols and fired both barrels at the newcomer. The bullets disintegrated to nothing. Ulysses's cocky grin faded to a frown. "That doesn't even make sense! Lead doesn't rust!"

"But it does age," murmured Erasmus, studying the rusty armor carefully.

Focalor ignored Ulysses and cried out, "Long ago, I was one of the Great Seven who ruled Hell. When the unaccursed Solomon crept among us, binding and kidnapping, I was wrongly held accountable for his treachery—a charge that should have fallen to Asmodeus—and robbed of my throne. The throne that had once been mine was granted to Abaddon, the Angel of the Gateway, when he changed sides and joined our infernal forces. It has been promised that after I defeat the Family Prospero and retrieve the stolen demons, my rightful place shall be restored to me."

"Oh, and you believe them?" Logistilla gave him a look of disdainful sympathy. "Take it from me. Devils lie."

Focalor ignored her as well. "Compose yourselves to remain here, in Hell, for all eternity. Who will die first?"

Theo stepped forward, his expression hidden by his faceplate. "I challenge you to single combat."

"Then, you may die first."

"Theo, wait!" Erasmus unbuckled a sword that hung at his side and held it out to Theo. "Take this. Your sword will never survive the fight."

"What is it?"

"*Durandel*, the unbreakable sword of Orlando. I borrowed it from the Vault, thinking it might be useful."

"*Durandel!*" Theo drew the sword from the sheath. It seemed brighter and more substantial than its surroundings. He saluted the demon with it. The demon eyed the sword with distaste but drew his own blade—which had been partially eaten away by rust—and returned the salute.

The battle began. Theo fought hard, but his enemy was faster, stronger, and had reach on him. Theo parried many of the incoming blows but failed to strike his foe more than once or twice, at which time *Durandel* skidded harmlessly off the demon's armor, his rusty plates clanging loudly.

The sword *Durandel* held its own against the corrosive blade of the enemy, but Theo's normally untarnishable titanium grew black and dull wherever the rusted blade struck it. Only the Urim breastplate and helmet remained unharmed. When struck, they chimed like leaded crystal, evoking memories of Easter and the ringing of church bells. Around us, the imps and lesser demons held their heads at the sound.

I watched, my heart pounding, as my beloved brother pitted his life against the demon Focalor. It seemed impossible that he, old and weary, in armor made for a much younger man, might hold his own against this great duke of the Inferno. Yet, amazingly, Theo did not falter. After five or ten exchanges, the imps began to mutter and dance about impatiently, amazed anyone could last so long against their master. Apparently, Focalor was considered an expert swordsman, even among the denizens of Hell.

My brethren were similarly impressed.

"Theo's rather good for an old man," murmured Titus.

"Good? He's astounding!" Logistilla replied, wringing her hands with concern. "Oh! I do hope he's careful!"

Only Mephisto remained unconvinced by Theo's performance. He leapt upon the winged lion again and soared up above the match shouting advice. "Go left. No, down! No, it's a feint! Duck!"

Theo, who could not respond in time, was thrown back when Focalor reversed his feint and swung his great sword at Theo's head. He managed to successfully block the blow to his face, but the corrupting blade struck the upper part of his sword arm, leaving a black, sullied spot on his shiny titanium armor, deeper and larger than the previous marks. The place sizzled as if the metal itself were being consumed by some virulent, sinister acid.

Before Theo could rise again, the winged lion swept down upon him and his opponent. With a single fluid motion, Mephisto leapt from the creature's back, did a double backflip that knocked the cavalier's hat he wore over his shoulders onto his head. He grabbed the sword out of Theo's surprised fingers, knocked Focalor's blade to one side, moved the tip of his own weapon around his opponent's rusted breastplate, and stabbed him in the armpit, driving his blow home to the demon's heart.

"*Touché!*" called Mephistopheles. The indigo panache atop his hat bobbed jauntily.

"Good work, Meph!" Erasmus cried, unconsciously calling him by a nickname from an earlier age.

"Excellent, Master Mephistopheles!" cheered Caliban.

"Wow!" murmured Mab. "That was . . . wow."

The demon Focalor fell backward, crashing to the ground. As the lesser demons drew back, murmuring in awe, Mephisto swept the hat off his head and bowed.

Immediately, Focalor's servants either fled—the imps flying away, and the demons disappearing in a dark puff—or ran forward and leapt upon their master's body, poking and stabbing him in a frenzy of malicious vengeance. We backed away, putting distance between ourselves and our erstwhile attackers.

All around us, dead imps, demons, and swine lay scattered; some were being munched upon by Mephisto's friends. Hatless again, Mephisto returned *Durandel* to Erasmus. He ran his hand up and down his staff, tapping it repeatedly, until all his friends had vanished, returning to more wholesome stomping grounds.

We began jogging, covering the remaining eighth of a mile between us and the bridge. Beside us bobbed an enormous dark mass of Hellshadow, as Gregor had left the *Staff of Darkness* running. The sooty stuff that issued from it now stretched across the countryside, winding its way along the river bank like a dense, charcoal fog. Mab kept a wary eye on it, fearing that some nasty thing might pop out, but the locals seemed afraid of it. Those few individuals who could be seen walking near the Styx moved quickly away from the drifting darkness.

Without warning, the muddy ground beneath us shook and parted, throwing many of us from our feet. A chasm opened in the earth, stretching for nearly a mile along the upstream riverbank. The noise was deafening, and the putrid odor of hot brimstone escaped from the crevasse. Nearly half a mile down the bank, an angel, if such a thing could still be called by so holy a name, rose from the pit.

The creature was monstrously huge, towering over us like a mountain. Its armor was black as pitch. Its seven pairs of sooty wings were patchy, molting. The great pinions had been clipped. One wing looked as if it had broken and healed at an awkward angle. The face, once beautiful beyond bearing, was now partially rotted. Only, the angel seemed unaware of this gaping wound and carried itself as if it were still as beautiful as in days of yore. The creature was both glorious and horrible, like a dark, twisted mockery of some precious thing. Around its neck, a large golden key hung on a thick iron chain.

"Abaddon! He's come for me!" cried Ulysses, leaping behind Titus and curling up into a ball. I wondered briefly why he did not just run, but he did not even try. "Save me! Theo, shoot him!"

Theo raised his staff and then lowered it again, shaking his head. "He's too far away. He must know what my range is."

I gazed up at the monstrosity. This *thing*, this twisted angel, was Ulysses's dark master, the cause of all our recent suffering and agony. It was he who had compelled my youngest brother to bring about the ruin of Gregor and Theo.

I had wished there were an enemy we could unite against. I had thought that Abaddon, who had caused our family so much harm, would be an ideal target. As I gazed up at the enormous fallen angel with its terrifying, damaged beauty, I wondered if, in the future—assuming I was lucky enough to be granted a future—I should be more careful what I wished for.

The Angel of the Bottomless Pit opened its mouth. What sounded forth was a grating noise like unto an avalanche. We had heard this before, near the bluff, the night we rescued Gregor. Nor did it seem in any way diminished, though the speaker was over a mile away.

"Imprudent Prosperos. Do you revel in your fleeting victory? It is of no sig-

nificance. We of Hell need do nothing. There is a traitor amongst you who will do our work for us."

Beside me, Theo met Gregor's gaze. Gregor nodded grimly, his eyes gleaming with steely purpose. Taking Cornelius's arm, he gestured to Theo, and the three of them stepped into the darkness still issuing from Gregor's staff. As they disappeared into the ever-lengthening ribbon of gloom, Theo muttered under his breath: "Keep him talking!"

I reached out to call Theo back, but the Hellshadow had enveloped him. My heart ached in my chest. I feared suddenly that I would never see him again.

Mephisto took up Theo's request with zeal.

"Oh yeah?" he bellowed back toward the gigantic angel. "Then, why did you try to attack us? Hmm? Hmm?" He brandished his staff. "That's right, flee before our superior might."

"Now, Mephisto," purred Logistilla, who had not heard Theo, "let's not taunt the devil. I think he's letting us go."

"Your sister speaks truly. I shall make no effort to hold you. My work is already done."

"Done, in what way?" Mephisto called back. "Or, perhaps I should say, in what respect? By exactly what definition of the word 'done' is your work done?" He gestured cheerfully toward the rest of us with the hand to which his staff was again handcuffed. "I ask, only because most of us seem to be here, alive and kicking, which goes against this idea of"—he made quote marks in the air—" 'doneness.' "

Coming up beside me, Mab whispered softly, "Remind me, if we ever need somebody to stall for time, that the Harebrain is definitely our man."

The horrible fallen angel spoke. Again his voice grated like an avalanche, but now the sound was so immediate that it felt if the stones were grinding against one another within the cells of my body. The sensation was painful. Around me, I heard moans of agony from my siblings.

"Lowly worm. Show obeisance to me!"

"Er . . . why should I do that again?" Mephisto cupped his ear and leaned toward the gigantic demon. "Because you're so . . . What? Goofy? Dorky-looking? Tall? Being tall is important. Many people are worth worshipping because they are tall."

The Angel of the Bottomless Pit turned toward my brother, and the weight of his infernal gaze fell upon him—literally. Mephisto stumbled and dropped to his knees, as if pressed down by a terrible heaviness. Logistilla ran to help him, but she, too, was borne down, until she collapsed face first against the ground, unable to rise.

Titus ran to her, throwing himself between her and the gigantic demon. He tottered and slowly dropped to his knees, but so long as Logistilla kept the bulk of his body between her and Abaddon, she was able to rise a little.

Ulysses, who had been hiding behind Titus, let out a loud bleating sound and dived behind Caliban. I now saw why he had not teleported away. Erasmus had a firm grip on the *Staff of Transportation*. Caliban, however, was striding forward to stand between Mephisto and Abaddon. So, Ulysses was left exposed again. He scrambled behind Erasmus and begged for his staff, weeping with fear.

I could not blame him. He was the one Abaddon had a hold over, the one who would suffer when the demon learned how Ulysses had deceived him.

Abaddon's gaze now fell upon the rest of us. A tremendous weight oppressed me. I felt as if I were trying to keep a semi-trailer from tumbling sideways by supporting it with my shoulder. Beside me, I heard Mab grunt with exertion. His legs gave out just after mine did, and we both collapsed to the ground.

I tried to get up, but the ground seemed stuck to me. My chest would not rise to allow in air. I opened my mouth, gasping for air. The tremendous weight continued to press upon me, forcing me downward, compacting me. If my back grew any closer to my front, something was going to break.

From the corner of my eye, I could see my siblings struggling. Logistilla had curled up behind Titus and, like Ulysses, lay crying, but Titus, Caliban, and Mephisto struggled against the demon's gaze, trying to rise, trying to resist the incapacitating gaze. One then another rose, only to fall down again, as the weight of the infernal gaze grew greater. I saw Titus reaching for his staff, which presumably could have stopped this attack, but it had rolled from his fingers, and he could not stretch his arm long enough to reach it. Caliban succumbed last; not even his legendary strength was enough to save him.

Great. He had been planning to let us go, and, at Theo's request, Mephisto had antagonized him. Now, we were all going to die.

We were going to die, and it was my fault. If I had not gathered us together, if I had left well-enough alone, we would not be here, facedown in the filth of Hell, being crushed to death by the demon who had wrecked our family. We would have been spread out in our separate haunts, safe and secure.

Except for Father, of course, who would still be trapped in Hell, but our dying here on the banks of the Styx was hardly going to help him.

On the other hand, I thought as lights began to dance before my eyes—whether from the pressure or the lack of oxygen, I did not know—if the Demon of Envy was going to destroy the Family Prospero anyway, it was a comfort to be with my siblings when the end came, rather than alone dying somewhere of old age. The Angel of the Bottomless Pit spoke again, his words reverberating like rolling boulders within my body: *"Gregor the Witchhunter is dead. Theophrastus the Demonslayer is old and decrepit and will soon follow. And the Dread Magician Prospero is the prisoner of Fair Queen Lilith, she who raised me to my high estate, so that I now rule as one of the Seven of Hell. It is only a matter of time before the rest of you Prosperos join the sad fate of your fellows and perish. . . ."*

"All very well, Destroyer," Theo's voice called out from somewhere ahead of us, "except that you have made three mistakes!"

The demon turned his head, and his gaze lifted. Air rushed back into my lungs. Nearby, my siblings flopped around on the ground, gasping for air.

Some distance ahead, Theo stepped from the billowing darkness that had drifted upstream from Gregor's staff and stood squarely before Abaddon, a tiny figure looking up at the splendid, horrible, gigantic angel. He looked resplendent, despite the tarnished spots on his otherwise shiny titanium. His breastplate of Urim glowed like a candle in the gloom.

How handsome he looked—as brave and fierce as I recalled him from old—as he faced the monster responsible for robbing over fifty years of his life.

"How so?" grated the dark twisted angel. His gaze fell on Theo now, but while my brother looked as if he were struggling against a fierce wind, he did not drop. Perhaps the darkness that issued from Gregor's staff, which was still present where he stood, dampened the effect.

"One, Gregor is not dead!" Theo gestured grandly.

The darkness swirled again, and Gregor stepped forward. His long hair and the skirt and half cape of his crimson cardinal's robes billowed about him. Gregor inclined his head gravely, bowing. The avalanchelike voice hissed.

"Two," Theo reached up and pulled off his helmet, "I am not old!"

My heart leapt out of my chest and straight up into the heavens. The old man with the grizzled white beard, whom I had once mistaken for my father, was gone. In his place stood my brother Theophrastus. He was young and hale, as I remembered him, as Mephisto had immortalized him in the statue that Seir of the Shadows had destroyed in his first attack upon Prospero's Mansion, back in early December. Glancing back at us, Theo winked, and Erasmus chuckled.

No wonder he had insisted that the brother with the *Staff of Decay* act as his squire.

O glory be! I had done it! Theo was saved! (Now, if he could only survive the next five minutes.)

Abaddon, the Angel of the Bottomless Pit, the Demon of Envy, one of the Seven Rulers of Hell, yowled in outrage, shaking the landscape, causing trees to tumble and an enormous black wave to splash over the banks of the Styx. *"Ulysses! You have drawn your last breath. Prepare to pay for your failure!"* Turning to Theo again, his voice grated, *"And my supposed third mistake?"*

"You are in my range."

Theo fired the *Staff of Devastation.*

A beam of sizzling white death blasted from his staff, burning the air through which it passed. Abaddon sneered disdainfully, his beautiful yet damaged face replete with disbelief—until the weapon caught him full in the chest. White-hot fire consumed his torso, igniting three pairs of his wings into huge, white, flaming brands.

Horror dawned upon his face. Then, with a terrible, deafening, earth-grinding howl, he exploded into a colossal pillar of incandescent fire. It illuminated the landscape, sending shadows scurrying in all directions and outshining the distant Wall of Flame.

Theo had not had time to brace himself. The force of the blast threw him backward and slammed him against the ground. Along his upper arm, his armor crumpled where it had been weakened by Focalor, twisting his arm at an unnatural angle.

Erasmus, our family doctor, winced. "Oh, that doesn't look good." Or at least, that was what I thought he said, for my ears were still ringing from the scream of Angel of the Pit.

The pillar burned out, leaving a small crater filled with smoldering ash and a glint of gold. Theo ran forward and, kneeling beside the smoking crater that, even as we watched, was filling with black water from the Styx, grabbed the glitter of gold and stuck it inside his breastplate. Then, he strode back to us, his face shining with courage and victory.

We all ran to Theo. His youthful features looked so strange and yet so utterly normal. His hair was dark again, except for the forelock above his goggles, where the blasts of his staff had bleached it to palest blond.

Gregor came up beside Theo and grabbed his forearm. "Brother, we are free! Free at last!"

"Indeed!" Theo laughed aloud. "Free and alive!" He threw his arms around Gregor, who returned the embrace joyfully.

We all began hugging one another. Gregor embraced Cornelius and then Ulysses, who trembled weak with relief and gratitude. Titus gave Logistilla a bear hug, which made her giggle. I hugged Theo, who picked me up and swung me around, laughing, and Mephisto embraced everyone.

"Is he dead?" Logistilla cried, clutching Theo's good arm. "Is he finally gone? Are we finally free of Abaddon forever?"

Such hope shone upon her face that my heart went out to her. I had forgotten she, too, had been hoodwinked by Abaddon, sucked in by her envy of my Lady.

Theo shook his head. "He is immortal. However, my staff contains the spear of Longinus. It was designed to send its victim to the icy fields in the Ninth level of Hell. Even demons do not have an easy time escaping from there. Satan, in his misery, loves company."

I gave out the smallest drop of the Water of Life to Erasmus and Caliban, in case the tridents that had stabbed them had been poisoned. I offered one to Theo for his broken arm, but he just smiled and shook his head.

"So close upon our drop at New Year's, I'm sure this will heal quickly," he said chivalrously. "Let's save the Water, for we do not know what horrors are still to come. Now!" He raised his good arm triumphantly. "On to rescue Father and then home!"

"so, who exactly is this traitor in our midst?" Erasmus asked as we walked toward the bridge. He addressed us all, but his eyes rested upon me.

"Oh, no, Professor Prospero," Mab warned, "don't go there! Don't let that devils lead you down their thorny path! You can't trust 'em! You can't believe them! They only say what they say to cause harm and spite."

"What if it's true?" Logistilla looked quite shaken. "Abaddon's earlier prediction about our family being destroyed seems to be coming true."

"Nonsense!" Theo laughed cheerfully, despite having his arm in a sling. "We're as strong as we ever were!"

"But even if we rescue Father," she insisted, "we will still all die as soon as Miranda's Water of Life runs out."

"Oh. Yes." Theo frowned. "That."

"Look," Mab said. "Some of what the demon said might be true. It's often the case, in fact. Demons love throwing in a sliver or two of truth in to muddy the waters. But, it's not the kind of truth you can use. Trust me in this. You start banking on infernal predictions, and the next thing you know you've brought it about through just the suspicion the prediction caused. Or, you find out the 'family traitor' is a cousin three times removed, someone you never would have trusted anyway. Now, I'm not saying it isn't wise to keep your eyes open, and maybe keep a sharp eye on the Perp, er, I mean Mr. Ulysses, who's already proven himself capable of mischief, but I beg you—all of you—don't let the demon get to you."

"Don't blame me! I didn't want to do all these things! Abaddon made me!" Ulysses cried. "Damn fine shooting there, Theo!"

"He wouldn't have been able to make you if you hadn't been acting foolishly to begin with," Theo chided him. Then, unexpectedly, he threw his good arm around his younger brother and gave him a hug. "But, I forgive you."

Ulysses grinned, delighted. "Bloody good of you! Thanks!"

THE bridge across the River Styx was a long arch made of gray stone with a low railing. It reminded me of a thousand footbridges I had crossed in my day, only it was much longer, spanning what looked to be nearly a quarter mile over the wide black waters of the River Styx.

Mephisto took the lead, launching into another chorus of his personal version of "Onward Christian Soldiers." Behind him came Logistilla and Ulysses, who linked arms with Cornelius and led him along the way. The rest of us followed, with Theo and Caliban making up the rear guard. Mephisto's cheerful singing seemed an apt celebration of our recent victory. One by one, we joined in, until, by the second time through, the whole family was singing:

> *Crowns and thrones may perish,*
> *kingdoms rise and wane,*
> *but the Family Prospero*
> *constant will remain.*

> *Gates of Hell can never*
> *Against Prosperos prevail;*
> *we have Theophrastus,*
> *and that cannot fail.*

And we did have Theophrastus! Young Theophrastus; healthy, hearty, and strong Theophrastus.

We had done it. We were back together! Nothing could prevail against us now!

I laughed with joy, as if some great weight had been lifted from me. I wanted to celebrate, to do something more than just sing along. What we needed was music!

The wide river to either side stretched away from us, calm and serene. This seemed like a good place to find out what kind of infernal gust—if anything—my flute called here. Since its power depended on the bound Winds and their servants, most likely, it would do nothing at all. Nudging Mab to put in his earplugs, I lifted my instrument and began playing the melody to "Onward Christian Soldiers."

We were halfway across the bridge, having just finished a third rendition, when we heard it. A terrible roaring that reminded me of the sound a hurricane makes when its hundred-foot waves are sweeping down upon one's sailboat on the unprotected sea. Black and roiling, it came pouring down the river bed, along the course of the river, toward the bridge.

"The Hellwinds!" Mephisto screamed in terror.

"God in heaven, Miranda," Erasmus cried. "You *called* them, didn't you?"

I stared at my flute in horror. "Not on purpose!"

"Don't argue!" Mephisto bellowed. "Run!"

We bolted, scattering. Half of my family ran forward, half ran back. Mab and I, close to the center, gripped each other, uncertain which way to flee.

"Prosperos, to me!" shouted Gregor, and he lifted his staff. Billowing blackness rolled from its rune-carven length, surrounding those of us who were with him. Near us the Hellwinds formed a small twister as it was sucked into Gregor's staff. The smell was not as bad as the slimy bog, but was hot and dry and came with gritty particles that stung our eyes and made breathing difficult.

In the darkness I could make out at least one of my siblings heading back toward Gregor. Mab hunkered down behind Gregor and grabbed onto my skirts. Pulling the pins from my head, I wrapped my hair across my mouth like a veil, to filter out the grit. With my other hand I reached into the winds, urging my siblings to come to us.

The swirling ebony gusts picked up Mephisto and Logistilla as they ran, tossing them about like rag dolls. I could not see most of the others, but Ulysses was thrown backward as he raised his arm to use his staff. The winds slammed him headfirst into the stone banister along the bridge. His body went limp, and he was carried up, over the edge, and away into the darkness.

Theo's armor gave him some ballast against the raging gale. He strode toward me, resisting the winds that threatened to push him backward. Cheering, I reached out for him, and our hands touched, his fingers warm against mine.

Relief rushed through me. To lose him again, now, when he was finally young and whole again . . . that would have been too much.

Then, he winced, his face crumpling in pain. In his urgency, he had reached out with his right arm, the sling being too flimsy to restrain him. His wounded arm was not strong enough to hold against the wind. His fingertips slid through mine and away.

Screaming, I watched his pale face until the winds carried him into the whirling darkness.

I still had my flute. I lifted to my lips and tried to control the Hellwinds, to deflect them or disperse them, but their terrible roar, like five squadrons of fighter jets, drowned out any attempt at music. Eventually, Mab pulled me down, and I huddled close to Gregor, my fingers gripping his crimson robes. Closing my eyes, I prayed into the empty chasm within me where once my Lady had been, begging for their safety and deliverance.

Then, the Hellwinds swept past us, and their roar became muted, like distant thunder. The shores were devoid of life, as far as my eye could see, and on the bridge there remained only four of us.

Except for Gregor, Mab, myself, and Erasmus, my family was lost.

Here ends Part Two

To be continued in Part Three:

PROSPERO REGAINED

*In which we finally meet the Dread Magician Prospero,
and Miranda learns the truth about many things.*

ACKNOWLEDGMENTS

Thank you to Mark Whipple, Dave Eckstein, and Catherine Rockwood, without whose encouragement, this novel would have been abandoned in its infancy.

To Von Long, Diana Hardy, Erin Furby, Kirsten Edwards, Bill Burns, Dave Coffman, Jeff Lyman, Jessie Harris, Donna Royston, Robin Buehler, and especially Don Schank, for their support and advice, and to Danielle Ackley-McPhail and the Yesterday's Dreamers, for all their useful ideas concerning the craft of writing itself.

To James Hyder, without whom this book would contain two copies of Chapter Seven and none of Chapter Eight.

To my wise editor, Jim Frenkel, and my noble agent, Richard Curtis.

To Lisa at Mama Lisa's World (www.mamalisa.com/world), for her wonderful collection of Italian Lullabies, and to Ernestine Shargool, for her beautiful translations.

To George Bernard Shaw, whose title *Don Juan in Hell*, this one echoes.

And, most important, to my mother, Jane Lamplighter, without whose selfless devotion to her grandchildren this book literally could not have been written.

ABOUT THE AUTHOR

L. Jagi Lamplighter lives with her husband and children in northern Virginia, where she's working on *Prospero Regained,* book three of Prospero's Daughter. For more information, visit her Web site at www.ljagilamplighter.com.